IMAGE
of the
INVISIBLE

a novel

RACHEL FAHRENBACH

979-8-9989988-0-5 (eBook)
979-8-9989988-1-2 (Paperback)
979-8-9989988-2-9 (Hardcover: case laminate)
979-8-9989988-3-6 (Hardcover: dust jacket)

First Edition: July 2025

Library of Congress Control Number: 2025910682

This book is a work of fiction. Names, characters, places, and incidents either are products of the author's imagination or are used fictitiously. Any resemblance to actual persons, living or dead, events, or locales is entirely coincidental.

Scripture quotations marked CSB have been taken from the Christian Standard Bible®, Copyright © 2017 by Holman Bible Publishers. Used by permission. Christian Standard Bible® and CSB® are federally registered trademarks of Holman Bible Publishers.

Cover design by EAH Creative
Interior design by Rachel Fahrenbach

Visit the author's website: rachelfahrenbach.com

Printed in the U.S.A.

Contents

PRAISE FOR IMAGE OF THE INVISIBLE

"Suspense and soul collide in this sharp, page-turning novel about how faith quietly yet powerfully shapes our everyday decisions." Erin Greneaux, award-winning author of the *Gold Feather Gardeners* series

"A fast-paced, compelling story of young professionals navigating public pressure and private moral dilemmas—this novel had me cheering each character on to the end." Sarah L. Frantz, award-winning author of *The Quickening*

"A powerful invitation to see the sacred in the unseen. This novel brings beauty and insight that will grip your heart and open your eyes." Daisy Dronen, spiritual essayist and poet

Steve,

I may have started this novel before you were in my life, but I couldn't have finished it without knowing you.

People wonder why the novel is the most popular form of literature; people wonder why it is read more than books of science or books of metaphysics. The reason is very simple; it is merely that the novel is more true than they [books of science or of metaphysics] are.

— G.K. Chesterton

Image Dismissed

Do you see him? It's asked in the hush of my heart. *Look up.*

It's gone then—the earthly reality of Chicagoans en route on their morning commute, dodging tourists planted like trees in the middle of the sidewalk, gaping at skyscrapers—replaced with something different, yet just as true.

First, the vibration: a pounding deep within my chest.

Then, the sound: hooves against a dirt road.

Finally, an image: the white legs of a horse urgently extending and retracting with grace and grit. The horse carries a man along a path toward me.

A man I know well. Too well, actually, and for too many reasons to name.

Andrew.

Determination outlines his face, and his gaze is locked on an unseen destination behind me on the horizon. So much baggage sits in that unwavering focus.

Urged on by Andrew's vocal cues and the whip, the animal increases the speed of its rhythmic movements, past its feelings of exhaustion. With the increased intensity of hooves digging in and pushing against the dirt road, the pounding in my chest increases speed. I press my hand to my chest and feel my heart fall into a rapid, frantic beat. A vice grip around my heart and lungs replaces the pounding, causing me to stumble forward a step. Concrete sidewalk meets my knees as they give out, but dirt meets my eyes.

It's always jarring to the senses—this juxtaposition of earthly and spiritual realities.

I'm really too old for this, Lord.

Do you see him? Look up.

Andrew is getting closer. Soon, he'll pass me.

I have to stop him.

This path is a lie lined with false promises.

I have to stop him.

This pursuit will only end in loss.

I have to stop him.

I manage a breath deep enough to shout Andrew's name as horse and rider pass me.

He doesn't even look my way.

I'm invisible to him.

But she isn't.

She stands right in his way, the bottom of her dress mingling with the dirt of the road he travels. The gap between them closes quickly with each pressured stride taken by his horse.

Andrew sees her—I know he does, but he looks right through her, past her, to his destination behind her.

She is not invisible, but she is ignored.

She calls out his name, a pleading wrapped around each word, and the sound of it emits from her lips in a wind made up of memories, promises, and expectations. Just like the horse did moments ago, the wind picks up speed in a swirl of urgency.

Andrew's gaze breaks from the horizon and falls on her. Noticing the whirlwind forming around them, he leans back and pulls up on the reins, bringing the horse to a stop just a few feet from the woman. Reins in one hand and the other raised to protect his eyes from the gathering storm, he drops from the saddle to the ground.

"Andrew." The voice drips with femininity and strength. "Look at me, please."

He obeys, dropping the hand he is using as a shield and letting it hang listlessly at his side.

Neither of them move.

The swirling wind settles.

The pounding in my chest lessens. Maybe she'll be able to stop him.

But something in Andrew's peripheral vision distracts him, pulling his attention from her back to that destination on the horizon.

The woman's lips part, and the wind stirs back into a swirl that encircles the couple and cuts them off from the surrounding landscape. It picks up speed, faster and faster, and with it, the memories, the promises, and the expectations play in front of Andrew's eyes, reminding him of what he doesn't want to be reminded.

He looks away and yells, "Stop!"

Grief collects in the wells of her bright blue eyes and overspills as tears. "Do you really mean that? Is that what you really want?" she asks over the noise of the wind.

Her question compels him to focus back on her.

His eyes betray his answer: No. No, he doesn't want this storm.

He doesn't want to keep going down this path.

Not without her.

She smiles at revealed truth. She smiles at birthed hope.

A rumbling underfoot begins.

Terror rips the smile from her lips and replaces it with a panicked: "Andrew!"

Her panic commands the whirlwind from the circle's edge into a single thread of powerful energy that propels across the gap from her to him. Andrew instinctively raises his arms to protect himself, but just as the thick thread threatens impact, an invisible force stops its advance and fractures the whirl of memories, promises, and expectations into shards.

The shards hang in the space between Andrew and the woman like thousands of broken mirrors, taunting them with what once was and what will likely never be again.

"We don't know that," the woman says, rejecting the unspoken prediction felt by all but voiced by none.

"He does though. Don't you, Andrew?"

The question brings with it that infamous sound of nails on a chalkboard, prompting both me and the woman to cover our ears. But it draws Andrew in like a fly to a bug zapper.

The rumbling underground increases in intensity, dirt particles reverberating and clinging midair to an unseen being as if magnetized. They first create an outline and then gather at a quick pace to fill in where flesh should be.

Or rather, where scales should be.

Because this is, after all, not a man but The Dragon.

I can recognize the stench of his slander anywhere and in any shape. That's what happens when you've been rescued from the suffocating grip of his presence.

I hurry to stand—something that is getting difficult to do these days—and as I do, the vision before me glitches in and out of earthly and spiritual realities.

Clearly I can see The Dragon materializing in the space between man and woman, and, just as clearly, I see The Investor stepping out of the Mercedes-Benz onto the street's curb.

The Dragon cracks his neck.

The Investor buttons his suit jacket.

One image overlaying the other.

"Andrew!" I call out.

"Stay out of it." The Dragon aims the warning my way. For the first time since the start of this vision, I am acknowledged.

I resolve to ignore him; Andrew's need is bigger than my fear ... or my pride. I will my legs to hurry toward the younger man.

Wait! It's not time yet.

Just as The Dragon's voice brought pain upon my ears moments before, this command—heard only by myself and The Dragon—produces the same effect on the beast. He winces, then shakes himself, much like a dog drying its fur, as if to rid himself of the remnants of the voice.

But for me, the command spills warmth over my anxiety, and I draw up short, responding to the only voice here that has authority over me. Noticing my obedience, The Dragon rolls his eyes and turns from me to the woman who weaves in and around the shards, making her way toward Andrew. She grabs a nearby shard, looks at it, then holds it out to him. She speaks softly to him, asking him to look at her and to remember.

"Let's not." The Dragon waves a hand the woman's way, freezing her body and words into place. He checks his handiwork and, finding it satisfactory, dusts off his hands and sets his focus on Andrew.

With a casual confidence, The Dragon saunters over to him, swiping the shard from the woman's hands and studying it along the way.

Andrew doesn't break his gaze away from the woman until The Dragon holds the shard out to him. He recoils, but The Dragon jabs it his direction until Andrew relents and takes it from him. He holds it up to eye level.

I can see an image play inside it like a movie. In it, Andrew puts his arm around the bare shoulders of the woman. They sit together at a round table set for a special event. Her dark, shoulder-length hair pinned back on one side, revealing a diamond dangling from her ear. She turns to him with a smile and raises her eyebrows teasingly. He returns the smile and lets his gaze fall to her lips. He leans in and kisses her. When he pulls away, her grin tells him she approves.

As someone new takes the stage, they both turn with eager anticipation. The man at the podium pulls a card out of an envelope and reads from it.

The woman's face registers surprise, and she looks at Andrew ecstatically. He beams at her with pride. She throws her arms around him and kisses him. Pausing for a moment to search his face, her eyes convey gratitude before she makes her way to the stage.

"You remember that night, don't you?" The Dragon asks Andrew while inspecting a scale on his arm. He doesn't wait for Andrew to answer. "It was what? Four years ago? She was so excited, wasn't she?" He looks up at Andrew. "So excited to rub her success in your face."

Andrew looks over at the frozen woman. For a second, I think he is going to disagree. He just watched the same image I did—it's obviously a lie. But, The Dragon reaches out and puts a claw on Andrew's shoulder and catches Andrew's gaze.

"She never really appreciated your genius."

Andrew blinks.

"Just pretended to support you."

Andrew blinks again.

"When the time came, she stepped from your side and took the limelight for herself."

Andrew closes his eyes tight. A resistance of sorts.

The Dragon smirks at the attempt. He hisses out a warm breath in Andrew's face. "She despises your success because it threatens her own."

Andrew winces at the rancid smell filling his nostrils.

The Dragon balls his free claw into a fist, raises it above Andrew's head, and brings it down hard.

Everything goes black.

When I open my eyes, the woman from my vision stands before me in jeans and a T-shirt, laptop bag swung over her shoulder, a baseball cap pulled down over her short black hair, and a coffee thermos in hand. "Sir," she says softly, "are you okay?"

She's talking to me.

I shake my head. "Oh yeah. I'm good." I look around, but The Dragon and Andrew are nowhere to be seen. Her blue eyes tell me she doesn't believe me. "You didn't look so good a second ago," she says.

I reposition the shoulder straps of the violin case on my back. "Yeah, just got a bit dizzy there." She's not buying it, so I add, "Old age ... and I'm diabetic. Didn't eat enough for breakfast."

"Oh! My grandma had diabetes, so I know how that can be. Can I help you? Here." She opens up her purse. "I have a granola bar." She fishes it out of the purse and hands it to me.

"Nah, no need. I'm good. Thanks though."

She puts the bar back in her purse. "No problem." She picks the headphones dangling around her neck and places them back in her ears. "Have a good day."

"God bless you." I respond with a slight wave.

She turns from me, her thumb moving over her phone's face to resume whatever she was listening to before she checked on me. She walks away from me toward the building that houses Andrew's office.

It's not yet time. I am reminded.

If not now, then why give me these visions, Lord? I ask.

To ready you.

Well then. That's that.

I head in the opposite direction from the woman, crossing the intersection of Michigan Avenue and Wacker and navigating north across the Chicago River.

Day One

STANDING OUTSIDE THE REVOLVING door of his office building, Andrew Salvatore debated if he should have agreed to meet Katie. He probably should have told her he had a meeting. It wasn't a lie—he had just welcomed Larson Carr and sent him upstairs, where he promised to meet him in a moment. But her text harkened back to a time not too long ago when life felt full of promise and not regret and, for whatever reason, he wanted a bit of that this morning.

At least he did, until Carr asked him, "How's that little wife of yours doing these days?"

Andrew knew that was actually code for, "Have you started with that divorce we talked about last time?"

Andrew stretched his arm out and glanced at his watch, a fluid and smooth motion to shift fabric and bring visibility to the timekeeper on his wrist. The watch was one his father gave him when he graduated college and started his first job almost fifteen years ago.

He shook his sleeve back down over the watch. She was late. He couldn't keep Carr waiting. Andrew turned and pushed through the revolving door.

"Andrew!" Katie's voice cut through the chaotic noise of the city.

He let go of the door, but the momentum he had triggered with the push brought the door smack dab against his back and ushered him into the building.

His cell rang. "Answer," he said. The Bluetooth in his ear beeped into action. "Hello?"

"Hey Andrew, Carr is asking where you are."

"Tell him I'll be right there." Andrew reached up and pushed the button on his Bluetooth to end the call. He watched as the doors spun to deliver Katie to him. She was wearing a wider leg jean than her usual skinny ones, and a T-shirt that fell loose on her petite frame, also a deviation. Until a few years ago, Katie had styled herself in dress pants and blouses that screamed professional and carried name-brand logos. Not that she had gone cheap or frumpy—her last shopping spree put a dent in their checking account—but she seemed to have reinvented herself from boss babe to chic casual.

Just another way things had changed so much since ...

He shook his head to get rid of the thought.

Though the baseball cap was a nice touch, he had to admit.

Katie smiled when she saw him waiting there for her. "I thought you didn't hear me."

Words that would have landed softly on his heart three years ago cut this morning like an accusation. Defense was his response: "I couldn't keep waiting for you. I have a meeting."

Her smile dropped. "Oh." She extended the coffee thermos she held in her hand. "Here, you left this at home."

He eyed the offering. "Is that why you wanted to meet?"

"Well," she adjusted the laptop bag on her shoulder, "not really. I was headed over to the park to work on some of the marketing pieces the publisher wants ..." her voice faded.

Andrew knew his face was to blame; he could never hide his emotions from her. She knew him. And he hated it.

He motioned toward the elevators. "I really have to go, so if you don't need anything else."

Her eyes widened. "Oh, I just—sorry. I didn't mean to ... there was this man who looked like he needed help, so I stopped ... I'm sorry, I shouldn't have stopped."

"It's fine. I just have to go. I'll see you at home later." Without waiting for her response, Andrew retrieved his badge and proceeded toward the turnstiles that granted entrance to the elevators.

"I leave tonight, remember?"

The words hit the back of Andrew like hundreds of tiny pinpricks. Where he had previously inserted interpretation, now each word truly dripped with deep hurt, shielded in a protective coat of accusation. He closed his eyes against the confrontation, willing himself to respond with anything other than defensiveness. He knew this was just one more mark in his column on the scorecard of offense in their marriage. Still, a small part of him wanted to dismiss his mistake with, "I have a lot on my mind right now." If only she could put herself in his shoes, she'd get it finally. She might even forgive him.

You know she'll never forgive you.

A chill ran from his head down to his toes.

Do you honestly even care if she does?

Did he?

He whirled back to Katie "Sorry—"

The sight of her wiping away tears with the back of her hand kindled the protector instinct within, and an overwhelming desire to gather her into his arm as he battled her enemy lit every nerve in his body.

But the enemy wasn't out there, was it? It was here within him—the monster that didn't care enough to remember Katie was leaving for two days. Shame stirred in his battle-ready mind until he remembered why she was leaving. The warrior within braced again. "When's your flight?" he asked, simply.

Unapologetically.

"The car comes for me at 4:30 p.m."

"How long will you be gone?"

It was Katie's turn to bristle. "I'll be back in time. I know it's important to you."

"That's not what I meant."

"Yes, it is. We both know it is." She turned her back on him and aggressively tossed a "bye" over her shoulder before pushing the revolving door to exit the building.

He should just let her go, right?

Or should he go after her?

His cell rang once again, pulling his attention away from his leaving wife.

Leaving or escaping?

The thought was so quick in its sting, but its burn lingered in Andrew's mind for the remainder of the day.

Katie didn't look back as she walked briskly south down Michigan Avenue, away from Andrew and toward her favorite writing spot. She was determined to not let Andrew kill her joy—especially not today. Today was reserved for making progress on her dream. There was no room for fixing her crumbling marriage. And there was definitely no room to contemplate the little question that popped up so innocently last night as she crawled into a big, empty bed: did she even want to stop the crumbling?

The question flitted around her mind like an annoying gnat she wanted to swat away. It was so small, barely noticeable, until it flew right into her face and forced her to reckon with it. She had been swatting it away all morning, but the interaction with Andrew just now brought it front and center.

He obviously doesn't care about me anymore. Why am I still fighting it?

She took the stairs up to Millennium Park, fixing her bag back up onto her shoulder, and shook her head to reset herself. If she had been in the suburbs instead of the city, someone might have noticed the distraught shake, but here, everyone was in their own little world. Those who lived in the city were too busy living their lives to notice, and the visiting tourists too absorbed in their own vacation to care.

At the top of the stairs, she turned to her right. She was a woman on a mission. Her favorite table was first in a row lining the ledge overlooking the park's principal attraction: a steel structure shaped like a bean. Tourists weaved around and under the center, looking up at their reflection and snapping pictures. Katie smirked. It was such a stupid-looking piece of art, but it brought smiles to the faces of everyone who visited it. She supposed it did its job.

Unfortunately, an elderly couple occupied her favorite table with their coffee cups and unfolded newspapers. Glancing around for another option, Katie noticed that the next best was located a little too close to the garbage can. *It'll be fine.* She reassured herself as she walked over to it.

As she set her items down on the table, she realized she was still holding the thermos of coffee she brought for Andrew. He had never taken it from her, and she hadn't noticed in the heat of the moment. She unfurled her hands from around it, balancing the thermos playfully on her palm, the red container a stark contrast against her pale skin.

Katie's brain connected the dots, as creative minds often do, to a moment not too distant in the past. Within seconds, she was back in her kitchen, cradling an avocado in one hand while slicing it with a paring knife in the other, the summer breeze finding its way inside through the open balcony door.

Andrew was home that day and in a good mood, an occurrence that had become a rarity in the past year, and had offered to help her make dinner. He was browning hamburger for tacos when she had yelped in pain. He dropped the spatula and wrapped his arm around her shoulders, leading her over to the sink. Gently, he cupped her hand with his own and tended to her wound. With the shock of the cut wearing off, Katie realized it was the first time her husband had touched her in weeks.

Her eyes traveled up his tanned and toned arm to his firm jawline, freshly shaven that morning. She noted a little gray at his temples. That was new, but not surprising. Even though they were only in their late 30s, Andrew had been under a lot of stress during the past few years.

Her eyes flitted down to his lips. A sudden urge to kiss him overwhelmed her, but she had resolved not to initiate anything until Andrew seemed to take an interest in her again. She wouldn't chase his affection.

Katie was grateful Andrew's light brown eyes still narrowed in on the cut so he didn't notice the tears, ones that sprang from a different pain, one deeper than the cut on her hand. She turned away from him and quickly wiped them away with her free hand.

Now, here in the park, that pain she had been trying to outrun for months caught up to her. She felt it slam into her chest and spread up into her throat, balling up into a knot. It repeated the question for her, louder so she could hear it with her heart as well as her mind: *Would it be so bad to have it all crumble?*

If it all crumbled, she would finally be free ...

The time's coming to tell the truth ... to tell them who he really is.

A baby's cry interrupted the thought and brought her back to the park. She watched as its mother rescued the baby from the stroller, holding it up to her shoulder and patting its back as she bounced.

Katie glanced down to the thermos.

Two steps, and she was at the garbage can.

One toss, and the thermos was gone.

———— • ————

Andrew hesitated a few feet from the conference room. He knew what would happen once he went inside. Larson Carr would look up from his phone, annoyance etched into the lines of his sun-weathered face, and say something to the effect of, "Andrew, this isn't my only meeting today." Then he'd instruct Andrew to just give him the high-level points so they could "get on with things."

He knew, too, that his high-level points would cause the annoyance on Carr's face to morph into disapproval. Andrew needed a moment to adjust from his fight with Katie to get ready for the next one waiting for him in the conference room.

"I'd say he won't bite, but we both know that's a lie," a soft voice teased in his ear.

He sighed.

"What? No witty come back?"

Andrew turned and shrugged his shoulders. "I don't have it in me today, Summer."

She eyed him for a second. "Hold still," she commanded as she put a hand on his shoulder. She used him to balance as she took her left foot out of the high heel. She rotated her foot and then flexed it. "You know what would have been great, Andrew? If you had a passion for women's footwear. You would have made millions of women so happy with that brain of yours." She put her foot back in her shoe, then smoothed out the shoulder of his suit. "But that's not what we're doing here, is it?" Her hand dropped from his shoulder, and she looked at him pointedly.

Andrew studied her face for a moment, noting how the years he had known Summer had grown her from a shy girl to a woman who walked confidently in her own skin.

He smirked at her. "I know what you are trying to do."

"I don't know what you are talking about," she protested with mock indignation.

After a beat, Andrew asked her, "What nightmare are you headed to?"

"Um, if you remember, I'm living the dream." She motioned to the office space around her. "This world is my kingdom."

Andrew rolled his eyes. "That's because you're in denial. And, technically, it's my kingdom."

It was Summer's turn to roll her eyes. "You keep telling yourself that."

"Um, I'm the one headed into the meeting with Carr, aren't I?"

"Just because the queen has a prime minister to do the dirty work doesn't mean she's not still the queen."

The dirty work.

She couldn't possibly mean something with that phrase, could she? Did she suspect something? Andrew dismissed the panic. He could trust Summer. And besides, there was no way she knew. At least, he didn't think there was.

Maybe it's time she did.

Summer pulled her phone out of the pocket of her dress slacks and checked a notification, completely missing the momentary panic in Andrew's eyes. "It's the weekly marketing department meeting," she explained.

"That's right." Andrew glanced toward the conference room and the dirty work that awaited him. He really shouldn't keep Carr waiting any longer. He needed to summon that battle-ready spirit he had felt just moments before. The people who worked for him, and the work they were accomplishing together, depended on him entering that conference room fully ready to do what he needed to do to protect and defend. He just wished it didn't all depend on his shoulders.

It doesn't have to.

"Hey." He turned back to Summer. "Can you and Derek come by after your meeting? I need to talk to you both about something."

She hesitated, but then said, "Sure," before turning to leave.

Andrew reached out to stop her. "Hey, you okay?"

The seriousness on her face alarmed him. As if sensing that, Summer flashed a smile to dismiss his concern. "Yeah, I'm good. Just late."

———— . ————

Summer couldn't get away from Andrew fast enough—though she walked at a steady pace until she rounded the corner and was certain he could no longer see her.

Then she ran.

She barely made it into the restroom stall and slammed the door closed behind her before the contents of her stomach heaved out of her and into the clean toilet. Normally, she would have done everything in her power to avoid touching the walls of the stall, but right now, she used them to steady herself.

When she straightened up, she realized that there was vomit in her long brown hair. The sight brought up more contents from her stomach. This time, she held her hair back as she retched.

When her body stopped convulsing, she hurried to the sink, mumbling, "So gross, so gross," as she rinsed the chunks of regurgitated food out of her hair. "Could this day get any worse?" She slammed the hand-dryer into action.

It helped dry her hair, but the damage was already done; one side of her head held beautifully crafted beach waves and the other side dangled flat against her cheek.

Her pockets yielded only a bobby-pin. It would have to do; she was significantly late, and as the chief operating officer, this meeting was really for her. They wouldn't start without her, but she didn't like wasting people's time. Summer adjusted her part from the center of her head to the side and pinned back the flattened side section.

She eyed her reflection for a moment, making sure there was nothing on her blouse, then tucked and smoothed her clothing back into perfection.

Summer sighed. "Time to run the kingdom."

Scanning the room for an empty chair, Sadie noted with both excitement and dread that there was an empty one across the table from Derek Salvatore. She hesitated in the doorway. Would anyone notice if she sat in that chair? There were others open around the table, so it might look suspect if she plopped down across from the sharped-dressed, perfectly chiseled man that had caught her attention on day one of her internship.

Not that she would plop. God no. That would be so embarrassing. She would be as gracious as her tall and slender frame would allow her. Actually, now thinking about it, everyone would definitely notice if she sat there. She wasn't exactly someone who blended in. So if she sat there, they'd figure out why.

And he'd probably notice her.

Which she wanted.

But, actually, she didn't.

It was a conflict that made for both butterflies in her stomach and scorpions stinging in her mind. She knew she shouldn't be so enamored with him ... that he wasn't someone she should be ogling—him being the director of marketing and all. Gosh, she really shouldn't be ogling anybody, but goodness, if he wasn't so ridiculously handsome, it would be easier. She couldn't help thinking about him and wishing things she shouldn't be wishing. The crush was instantaneous, even though she had never said a single word to him, and he had never said a word to her.

Sadie first noticed Derek when she was being led to her cubicle. Her supervisor, Cynthia, who appeared barely older than herself, pointed out the break room, but Sadie's attention was fixed on Derek. He stood just down the hallway, arms crossed, examining a banner with another employee. The posture tightened his white dress shirt around his toned shoulders.

As they continued the tour, they walked right by Derek, and Cynthia greeted him. He looked up, smiled, and said hi. That's when Sadie saw his hazel-green eyes and fell smitten.

The same hazel-green eyes that just now caught her staring his way. He offered a friendly smile before turning his attention to the coworker on his left. Sadie felt the heat jump to her cheeks. There was no way in hell she was going to sit across from him now. She took the chair closest to the doorway, which was on the same side of the table as Derek, but about six people removed from him. He wouldn't be able to see her—especially once Summer arrived, and all attention turned to her seat at the other end of the table.

Sadie flipped open her notebook and wrote *Marketing Dept. Meeting* across the top of her page and dated the page. It was a habit formed from the past three years of note-taking in college. She wondered if she would ever outgrow it. She glanced around the room and noted that a few others had done the same. Maybe this was just a good note-taking habit then and not a sign of immaturity.

She heard someone ask: "Derek, do you know where Summer is?" He responded he didn't, but had texted her a few minutes ago.

"I'm sure she'll be here soon," Cynthia said. "If Summer's late, she has a good reason."

The woman to Sadie's left leaned over and whispered, "Late for Summer is five minutes early for the rest of us."

Sadie turned to her and offered an "Oh." She didn't know what else to say. Having only been at the internship for less than a week, she still was getting the lay of the land. However, she had caught on pretty quickly that, as the COO, Summer had the ultimate respect from her staff, and it was pretty obvious why. She was a visionary, smart, organized, composed, firm but kind, and treated her staff with the same respect she expected from them. Sadie was completely enamored with Derek, but she was completely impressed with Summer.

"I want to be like her when I grow up," she told her friend Adriana the other day.

"How about you just be like yourself?" Adriana had responded.

Sadie's coworker leaned in so Sadie could hear her over the hum of conversation in the room and asked, "You're a new intern, right?" She held out her hand. "I'm Blair Dolton."

Sadie took her hand in her own, casually glancing at the paws of a tattooed tiger clawing out from under the cuff of Blair's shirt sleeve. "Sadie Albright."

"Well, Sadie, what college sent you our way?"

"St. Vincent's University."

"Ah, my niece just graduated from there. Her name is Christine Stewart. Did you know her?" Blair gently shook her head a bit to move her hair out of her eyes. It was cut short on the sides, leaving the top long and parted off to the left. It struck Sadie that while Blair had made bold choices in her appearance, her overall presence was unassuming.

"Oh, yeah! I had a class with her last semester."

"What a small world. How long will you be with us?"

"My internship ends the first week of December."

"That's right, we only get you guys for one semester. Then they send a new batch in. Hey, do you want an unsolicited piece of advice about your short time here?"

Sadie wasn't certain she did, but out of politeness, she answered, "Sure."

"Be smart about the relationships you make. Some people actually want to help you grow while you're here, and others will see you as just a dispensable intern. They will use you and then toss you aside when your time here is up. Just be smart."

"Good morning, everyone. So sorry I'm late." Summer breezed into the room.

Blair sat back in her chair as she repeated, "Just be smart."

Caught off guard by Blair's warning, Sadie was grateful the start of the meeting negated any need to respond to the woman. She poised her pen above her notebook, ready to capture ... whatever it was she needed to capture during this meeting.

The meeting was a pretty straightforward update regarding the status of various marketing campaigns and projects ongoing for the department. Sadie took copious notes just in case she needed to know the information in the future, but most of the words and phrases she had no idea what to do with. It might be the beginning of her internship, but she was walking into everything mid-conversation.

She supposed it really didn't matter much; her role here was to do what she was told. That, and learn how things take place in the real world.

"Okay, last agenda item," Summer announced as she took a sip of her water. "What's going on with the items for the conference?"

Cynthia looked up from her note-taking and gave Summer a detailed rundown of the marketing pieces they produced for their booth in the expo hall, as well as the materials they had produced for the attendee swag bags.

"Pretty much everything has been packed up. We have a few last-minute boxes to finish up today, but we'll be ready to drive them over to the conference hall tomorrow."

"Who's on the team?" Summer asked Derek.

As Derek answered Summer, Sadie nearly melted into her chair at the sound of his voice—as crisp and dreamy as his eyes. She barely registered his explanation that top sales reps, social media coordinators, and a few videographers made up the team. Derek turned Sadie's direction, and a lump jumped to her throat. Was he about to address her? What would he ask her? What could she add to the meeting?

"Blair has a team of her scientists that will be at the booth as well to answer any more technical questions."

Sadie felt the heat jump to her cheeks. Of course, he wasn't looking at her but her coworker at her side. That made more sense. She didn't take any notes, but Sadie kept her focus on her notebook and prayed no one would notice her now flushed skin.

"What about our marketing interns?" Summer asked.

Derek shrugged. "We haven't talked about them."

"Cynthia, can you work out to have the interns there in the booth, too?"

They wanted the interns to attend the conference. Sadie could barely contain her excitement, and she was pretty sure anyone looking at her could see it plastered on her face. She wasn't worried, though; everyone's attention focused on Summer and Cynthia as they hashed out details for intern supervision since Cynthia wasn't planning on attending.

"Can't they take care of themselves? They are adults." Summer laughed, then quickly picked up her glass of water and took another sip.

"Yes, of course—I just mean they'll need marching orders from someone since they probably have never been to one of these things. We don't want them just wandering around and not being useful."

"Um ..." Summer wiped the condensation off her glass as she thought about it. She smiled. Tilting her gaze to Derek, she said, "You'll be there." It was a statement, not a question.

"Yes." He smirked.

"And you really have nothing to do ..." Summer remarked, her tone light.

"You know that's a lie." There was no fight in the response.

"Okay, that's settled. You interns will report to Derek each day of the conference. He'll figure out a schedule for you. Two will be in the booth while two walk the vendor floor and attend sessions. Of course, you all should attend Andrew's keynote." She turned her attention back to Cynthia. "Anything else they should do?"

"What about Thursday's party?" Cynthia asked.

Summer swiveled her chair back toward Derek. "Thoughts?"

Derek leaned sideways, placing his elbow on the table, bringing the back of his head into Sadie's line-of-sight once more. His fingers curled slightly as he rested his chin in his hand, his index finger tapped his cheek as he answered, "They should go. It'll be a good learning experience for them." His posture was relaxed, and Sadie imagined there was a playful glint in his eyes, maybe even a subtle smile playing on his lips, giving him a casually coy demeanor.

Summer rolled her eyes. "I'm sure it will be. Cynthia, can you make sure they have badges for the conference?" She glanced at the wall above Sadie's head. "Okay, we're out of time for today. If there was something we didn't get to, shoot me an email. Thanks, everyone."

The quiet room sprang to life as chairs pushed away from the table, notebooks and pens gathered into hands and bags, and lunch suggestions became plans. Sadie stayed seated while others moved out of her way. She didn't mind the wait; her exit was blocked, but her view of Derek was not.

Derek and Summer exchanged a quiet conversation before rising from their chairs with a fluid synchronicity that spoke to a long work history together. Derek gently placed his hand on the small of Summer's back to guide her out of the room, a gesture that hinted at a deeper intimacy between them.

Sadie clicked the top of her pen to retract it and shoved it into her notebook's wire spiral.

She didn't want to grow up to be like Summer.

She wanted to *be* Summer.

———— · ————

Andrew never noticed the artwork in the conference room before. But today, as he tried to avoid Carr's searing gaze, the abstract paintings on each of the conference room's walls across from him captured his attention. Blues, purples, yellows, and pinks (or was that technically red?) dived in and out, swirling, slashing, and dotting the canvas in a dynamic dance of color.

Behind Andrew sat a wall of windows offering a southern view of Millennium Park and Lake Michigan. His family had moved to Chicago from Houston when he was a kid, but the sight of the sun playing on the lake's surface still filled him with wonder, just as it did when he first saw it at ten years old. The view from this room was a favorite of his.

"Don't act like you have a moral compass all of a sudden, Salvatore." Carr leveled at him. "You made your bed, and now I'm asking you to lie in it."

Moral compass, huh? He hadn't thought about his moral compass in years. His parents had certainly tried to instill one in him, making sure to bring up God as often as they could in conversations, embodying the good southerners they would forever be, despite now calling the north home. Whatever moral compass Andrew had once possessed had weakened over the years, starting in college when a science professor gave him enough evidence to question the need for God.

He shifted his gaze from the artwork to Carr. The investor leaned back in his chair with his hands folded across his stomach. He had perfected a commanding air of confidence that came from rubbing shoulders with influence and accomplishment. They were supposed to be peers, Carr was only a few years Andrew's senior, but right now he looked more like a disapproving father than a friend.

Andrew shifted in his seat. "What you're asking me to do ... come on, man, you know it's crossing a line."

Carr brushed a piece of lint off his pant leg and casually said, "You never did answer my question about how Katie is doing."

"She's fine," Andrew answered abruptly.

Carr pursed his lips together and nodded. "Her book releases tomorrow, right?"

"Yes."

"And she has interviews tomorrow and Wednesday?"

Andrew wondered how Carr had Katie's interview schedule, but knew it was a waste of time to ask the question. Carr had a way of getting the information he needed to get what he wanted. And what he wanted was for InnovGene's newest product to make him a large return on his investment in the company.

For Carr, Katie was a threat to that ROI, though Andrew could never pin down exactly why Carr felt threatened by her.

Andrew glanced back at the artwork and said, "I'm not sure what Katie has to do with this meeting."

Carr smirked and shrugged. "Just trying to make friendly conversation. Taking an interest in a colleague's life, that's all."

"Katie is not your colleague."

"But she's your wife ... still."

There it was.

Carr had been cajoling Andrew to divorce Katie for years, arguing that she didn't really have Andrew's back. That they wanted different things. That she didn't respect him.

"You're unhappy, Andrew. I can see that. Surely, you can see that. After all these years, I'd like to think that you and I are friends, and friends don't let friends stay married to women who make them feel small."

Silence fell in the room.

Carr stood from his chair and walked over to the windows, forcing Andrew to decide if he should turn and watch him or hold his ground. He locked his gaze on one of the abstract paintings to fortify his resolve to not give into Carr's manipulative tricks.

"Here's what's going to happen, Andrew. And, let's be honest, we both know this is necessary."

This particular painting was heavy on the pinks and purples swirls. A combination that felt way too artsy for a business conference room. The others focused more on the blues and yellows. Andrew would have to talk to Gloria about replacing the artsy one later.

"Katie is going to go on her podcast and TV interviews. If directly asked about Katie's book, you will play the supportive husband. But we need to get ahead of this before Katie's book release sparks any unnecessary controversy. We need to control the narrative and reassure our stakeholders. Your PR team is going to draft a statement to the effect that the events depicted in the book are purely fictional and bear no relation to any events or practices at Innov-Gene Solutions. Have them make it sparkle, of course."

"Already done."

"What? Why didn't you say that then?" Carr asked jovially.

Enough was enough. Andrew had told Summer that this was his kingdom, and he meant it. No one—not even Carr, the man who held the threat of withdrawing funding—could take his authority unless he gave it.

Andrew stood from his chair slowly and walked over to Carr, buttoning his jacket. "The last time I checked, this is my company. I hold majority ownership, and I don't answer to you." He shrugged. "I don't answer to you about how we respond to press inquiries, and we sure as hell don't bribe a committee to get a license for a product. So, I suggest you take your suggestions out of my office."

Pride spread from Carr's eyes down to the corners of his lips, tugging them into a wide smile that sent a shiver down Andrew's back. It was not the response he was expecting from Carr and, as such, it was unnerving. Andrew took a step back, slipping his hands into his pockets as Carr walked to the table and picked up his briefcase, silently chuckling to himself. He moved toward the door but paused, as if about to say something. Instead, he clasped one hand over the other, holding the briefcase in front of him. Carr took a long breath, eyes fixed on Andrew.

A desire to escape sent Andrew's nerves into hyperdrive. It took everything to keep his composure, though he wondered if Carr could sense his unease.

"About damn time you took the lead." Carr said, turning to leave once more.

Finding his confidence again, Andrew stopped him. "I'm serious about the bribe. We're not doing that. There's no hurry."

Carr shook his head. "See, that's where you're wrong, my friend."

"What do you mean?"

"Andrew, do you think I'd suggest bribing the committee to license us this week if there wasn't a threat?"

Understanding caught up with Andrew. "GenTech." He mumbled.

Carr nodded. "Yep. They are submitting for a license review this week. Making an announcement at the conference."

"Which means they could go to market just months after us."

Carr glanced at his watch. "I've got to go. You have until Wednesday night to decide if you want me to move forward with my part in things."

Andrew shook his head and said, "I'm not changing my mind on this," but the conviction wasn't there like it was moments before.

The conference was the largest one in their industry. Everyone who mattered, on both the scientific and corporate side, would be there. If they announced this week that RegenX—a gene therapy designed to accelerate healing by stimulating the body's stem cells—was heading to market, InnovGene would solidify its reputation as the leader in groundbreaking biotechnology. Any future moves by Gen-Tech would be seen as second-rate, merely following in their footsteps. With the announcement, significant deals could be struck this week. Deals that would position him to buy out Carr and ensure he would never have to deal with the investor ever again.

"Tell you what, why don't you talk things over with Summer and Derek? I'm sure they'd want to know. They could help you make a wise decision." Carr emphasized the word wise. He paused as he walked out the door, putting a hand on the door frame and looked thoughtful. "If they don't help, maybe you could reach out to Katie. Or, if you want me to, I could reach out to her. Explain everything. Get her feedback."

"Don't you dare."

"Then do your job, boss, and get me an answer by Wednesday at 5 p.m. I don't like to take work home with me, you know."

Andrew followed Carr out of the conference room, making sure he made his way directly to the elevators. Then he made a beeline for Gloria's office.

The office manager was writing notes on her large wall calendar. "I want the artwork in the conference room changed." Andrew announced in her doorway.

Gloria paused, marker in hand, hovering over the box for Monday of the following week. "Good morning to you too, Andrew."

"Sorry, I just ... I just got out of a meeting in the conference room. I'm heading to another meeting, and I just wanted to make sure I told you before I forgot."

"Couldn't you have just sent an email?"

He normally appreciated the pushback from Gloria. As office manager, she kept things in check with it, but today it was irking his already frayed nerves. "No. I needed to tell you now because it needs to be changed now."

"Oh?" Gloria capped the marker. "Well, do you want me to send those pieces to your condo?"

"Why would you do that?" Andrew asked, confused.

"Because Katie painted them." Gloria answered matter-of-factly, as if to jog his memory.

Andrew facepalmed and groaned as he suddenly remembered their early days when money was tight and decorating the office required creative effort. Katie brought in the paintings and hung them proudly. He assumed she had found them at a thrift store. He never thought to ask her.

"Never mind," he said, his voice low and tired. "Just leave them for now." He rubbed the back of his neck as he retreated into his office a few feet away.

———————·———————

Andrew looked up from his desk at the sound of a knock to see Derek standing in the doorway of his office. He sighed as he rubbed a hand across his face. "Oh, right. Where's Summer?"

"She'll be here in a second. Had to use the bathroom first."

Andrew waved to a chair. "Why don't you close the door and sit down? This might take a bit." He watched as his brother smoothly unbuttoned his jacket and took the seat. "Remember when Dad taught us how to do that?" He asked, motioning to Derek's jacket.

"It's important you not only look the part, you act the part too." Derek quoted, impersonating their father's southern drawl.

The brothers chuckled at the memory. The lesson had served both of them well over the past decade, though neither of them had followed their dad into the world of corporate law.

"It's bad timing with his surgery."

Andrew sighed. "Yeah. The doctors said no traveling for six more weeks."

"I'm sure he wishes he could be here for your keynote."

"Yeah, he told me that. I told him it's no big deal."

The levity dropped from Derek's face, and he leaned forward. "What's going on, Andrew?"

Andrew eyed his brother and sighed again. He had been carrying the weight of his secrets alone for so long; he wasn't sure if he was ready to let anyone else in on it.

But Carr had been very clear that he had to tell Summer and Derek or else he would tell Katie everything, including things Andrew didn't want Katie to know if their marriage was to have a fighting chance. Summer and Derek would understand. Katie wouldn't forgive him.

Do you even care? The question picked at the scab covering the interaction between Andrew and Katie that morning.

Summer knocked briefly before entering the office. "You wanted to see me too, right?"

Andrew nodded and motioned to the chair next to Derek. Summer shot Derek a questioning glance as she sat.

Derek shrugged.

Andrew closed his laptop and put both hands on the top of it. He studied it for a moment. "I don't know how to tell you what I'm about to tell you." He said without looking up. The confession dug its heels in at the back of his lips.

"I think I know what this is about," Summer said matter-of-factly. Andrew looked up from the laptop and saw that she knew. How she knew, he wasn't sure, but that was part of what made Summer, Summer.

"Larson Carr." She said simply.

"What the hell does that asshole want?" Derek asked.

"He wants us to make the announcement this Friday."

"During your keynote?" Summer asked.

"Yep."

Derek leaned back in his seat. "I don't understand. We already sent out the press release announcing that we are seeking licensing and hope to have it secured by the end of the year. Everyone in the industry already knows."

Andrew shook his head. "No, he wants us to announce that we're ready for market."

"What? But, I thought you said ..."

"Apparently Carr has heard that GenTech has their own product they want to announce at the conference."

"There's no way they are ready for market."

"No, but they will announce that they submitted for licensing as well. And since we announced first, Carr wants us to be a clear winner."

"Kinda is out of our control." Derek glanced at Summer, looking for back-up. "We can't announce going to market when we don't have a license."

Summer didn't look at Derek, but kept her gaze on Andrew. "Larson Carr offered to bribe someone on the committee to have the license by Friday, didn't he?"

Andrew noticed her voice held steady. His own, however, croaked as he managed a "yes."

"Shit!" Derek exclaimed, jumping up from his chair. He ran his hands through his hair. "You've got to be kidding me." His hands rested on his hips as he paced. "That's ... that's ..." Derek leaned on Andrew's desk and eyed him. "You told him no, right? Please tell me you told him no."

"I told him no. He told me I had until Wednesday night to reconsider."

"You aren't reconsidering, right?"

Andrew didn't answer.

Derek slammed his hands on the desk, muttering another expletive under his breath. He turned to Summer. "Can you believe this?"

She didn't acknowledge Derek, keeping her gaze leveled on Andrew. "What's different about this time?"

Andrew's hands dropped from his laptop. How did she know about the other time? How did she know and had not asked him about it? He didn't know if he was more impressed that she had figured it out or mad that she hadn't called him out on it.

"This time?" Derek looked from Summer to Andrew. "What does she mean?"

Andrew ignored Derek's question and focused instead on answering Summer. "Katie. Her novel releases tomorrow.

She drew inspiration from our lives and didn't realize just how close to the truth she was hitting with the storyline. Carr thinks it is going to blow up in our faces when it releases. He wants me ready with a statement."

"We already have that."

"Right. He's going to tell Katie everything if the three of us don't decide to move forward with the bribe."

Derek sat back down in his seat. "What do you mean, everything? What aren't you telling me?"

Summer placed a hand on Derek's arm. "Give him a second. He's about to tell us."

———— · ————

"Hey, intern, you want to join us for lunch?"

Sadie looked up from her desk to see Blair and Cynthia standing in front of her. "Um, yes, please!" She answered, grabbing her purse from under the desk.

Blair looked at Cynthia. "Told you she would be game."

Cynthia rolled her eyes. "Ignore her. I totally thought you would join us."

"Where are we going?" Sadie asked as they made their way to the elevators.

"There's this little cafe just down the street. Best sandwiches and soups."

"Sounds yummy."

Blair pointed to Cynthia as if suddenly remembering something. "Did you ask Summer if she wanted to come?" she asked.

"I did, but she said that she had a meeting with Andrew and Derek."

The elevator doors opened.

"Bummer, but Katie said she'd join us." Blair pushed the button for the ground floor.

"Really? Fun."

"Who is Katie?" Sadie asked as the doors closed.

Sadie caught the quick smirk exchanged between the women. "A friend of ours. She was working nearby," Blair said, obviously leaving out a detail. Sadie wondered if she should push for the info, but realizing how unique the lunch invitation was, considering she was just one of a handful of new interns at the company, she decided not to push her luck. She wanted these people to like her, after all.

As they made their way to the cafe, Sadie asked Blair what she did at InnovGene.

"Chief Scientific Officer. That's my official title."

"Sounds fancy." Sadie joked.

"It sounds fancier than it is. It just means I oversee the research and development team. And then I have the joy of telling our stakeholders that we're on schedule ... or not."

Sadie walked around a group of tourists. "Sounds stressful."

Cynthia let out a bemused chuckle. "You'll learn, Sadie." she said, slipping into her mentor tone. "Pretty much any job in the corporate world is stressful."

Blair nodded. "Exactly. Everything is due yesterday, and the only thing that matters to anyone is the bottom line."

"Because you're trying to do good, right?" Sadie asked, knowing the answer as soon as she posed the question.

Cynthia turned to her. "Don't get me wrong—yeah, people want to do good. I mean, here at InnovGene, we're genuinely trying to help people's health. But if I'm being honest? Everyone's got their own stuff going on and, at the end of the day, most of them are just trying to hang on to their jobs."

The jaded response was unexpected, and Sadie felt the optimist within her soul fight against it. She didn't want to believe that all she had to look forward to after college was a life full of work stress.

Cynthia stopped in front of the cafe. "Here it is."

Blair, noticing the distress on Sadie's face, reached out and placed her hand on Sadie's shoulder. "Hey, kid. Take a breath. It's really not that bad."

"It really is that bad," Cynthia tossed casually over her shoulder as she opened the door to the cafe. "But that's why God created wine, men, and the weekend."

Now it was Blair who rolled her eyes and said, "Ignore her."

The distress moved from Sadie's face to her heart. Even though she knew drinking and sleeping around was part of the "real world," she wasn't quite ready for it to be mentioned so casually. As a freshman, she got plugged in with the on-campus Christian organizations and surrounded herself with others who held similar values to her own. That's how she had met Adriana. Even though the party scene at the school was alive and well, Sadie had avoided it for the past three years and planned to do the same for her senior year. She hadn't even tried alcohol yet, despite turning twenty-one a few months ago. It hadn't dawned on her that she would have to face the Chicago nightlife during this time as an intern. To be honest, Sadie didn't even feel like she was missing out. She and her friends at school managed to have just as much fun as the other students—even if sex and alcohol weren't in the mix.

You sure about that?

The question hit like an electric shock to her nervous system, waking a dormant emotion she couldn't identify. An image of a certain pair of crisp hazel eyes played unsolicited in Sadie's mind.

Cynthia's laugh interrupted Sadie's daydreaming. With a twinkle in her eye, she held the door open to the cafe. "Seriously, though, you'll see at the party on Thursday night. Conference week is stressful for everyone, but Thursday night makes up for it."

Derek will be at the party.

The thought of the possibility of pushing boundaries that had always kept her in check was both exhilarating and terrifying. Needing to switch her mind away from the thought, Sadie asked Cynthia, "You'll be at the party but not the conference?"

Cynthia entered the queue to order as she answered, "Yeah, all upper management will be there, since Innov-Gene sponsors the event."

"This is probably a dumb question, but why?"

Cynthia fluidly switched back into her mentoring role as she answered the question, explaining that the event gave attendees both a chance for fun after long days of educational sessions and a chance to network. She explained InnovGene encouraged those in lead positions to make connections that could help the company move forward.

The twinkle returned to Cynthia's eyes. "It's also Andrew's way of thanking us for our hard work," she added.

"How so?"

Cynthia counted the list on her fingers. "Good food, dancing, and an open bar. Need I say more?"

A cafe employee asked Sadie for her order, allowing Sadie to save face with Cynthia. She took a step up to the counter and placed her order. As she handed her credit card over to the employee, she heard Blair say, "Oh, shoot."

Sadie turned around to see Blair reading a text.

"What's up?" Cynthia asked.

"Katie can't make it after all."

"Shame. I was looking forward to seeing her."

"Yeah."

Cynthia looked thoughtful. "I haven't seen her in, like ..." She paused, counting on her fingers. "Five or six months."

"You could always come on Wednesday nights, you know." Blair waved her phone pointedly in Cynthia's direction.

"Um, I love Wednesday nights for you." Cynthia waved in Blair's direction, then gestured toward herself. "But not for me. Sadie, your receipt."

Sadie whipped around to see the employee's out-stretched hand holding her receipt and table number. She collected both and sheepishly moved from her coworkers to the pickup counter.

———— . ————

The suitcase stood ready at her side. Her laptop bag leaned against it, ready as well.

Her purse in her lap held her plane ticket.

Her hand held her phone.

A blank screen.

No call.

No text.

A noise made her look up at the condo door, but no one came through it.

Her eyes found the clock. 4:25 p.m.

Five minutes left.

Her phone screen lit up.

She quickly swiped the lock-screen away. A text:

your ride is here.

She opened her email and refreshed the screen.

Nothing.

She refreshed her texts.

Nothing.

She opened the dial pad.

She hesitated.

One swipe took the temptation away from her fingertips.

Even as she made her way to the rideshare, Katie's heart held out hope.

Even as she opened the door to the hallway …
Even as the elevator doors opened to the lobby …
Even as the doorman wished her a good night …
Even as she walked down the building steps …
Still, Andrew didn't show.

"Oh, it's you."

Katie's eyes snapped up from the sidewalk at the sound of the vaguely familiar voice. The older man she had tried to help that morning stood in front of her. Earlier in the day, she was worried about his far-off look and the sweat collecting on his forehead, but now on the quiet street outside her condo, Katie got to take in the full picture. Her earlier concern for his well-being blinded her to how sharply dressed he was. His suit, though impeccably maintained, was clearly an older one. She recognized the care with which he had put his outfit together because it was the same care Andrew gave to his own appearance. She had also not given any attention to the violin case he carried on his back. Now, she noticed it, and it brought to mind a picture she had seen in an illustrated version of *Pilgrim's Progress*, with Christian and the burden he carried on his back as he journeyed to the Celestial City.

The man in front of her removed his hat and ran a hand over his short, tightly coiled black hair peppered with gray. "I'm sorry, you probably don't remember me," he said, tugging his hat back down firmly.

"I do," she said kindly, noticing how the dark skin of his hands was smooth and well-moisturized, a sign of the same meticulous care he put into his dress. "Glad to see you're doing okay."

"Thank you again for trying to help me." He motioned toward her luggage. "Headed out on a trip?"

"Yeah, New York."

"Oh, the Big Apple." As he adjusted the straps of the violin case over his shoulders, a certain look filled the creases of his face. Katie recognized it immediately: longing.

"I always wanted to visit," he confirmed.

"Me too." She tilted her head questioningly. "Do you play the violin?"

He brought his gaze back to her face, a little surprise crossing his features. "Yes, ma'am. I do."

"Where do you play?"

He smiled and spread his arms wide. "I go where the people are," he declared loudly, circling to emphasize the empty sidewalk.

The laugh that escaped Katie's lips hadn't reached her ears in such a long time that it surprised her. She covered her mouth with both hands. "Oh, I'm sorry! I don't mean to be rude. I'm not sure why exactly I did that."

He waved away her apology. "I'm too old for all that nonsense." He leaned toward her, as if sharing an important secret. "I'm a street musician."

"Ah."

"Yeah, I go where the people are. And, of course, where God tells me to go."

"Where is he telling you to go now?"

The man pointed down the block to the intersection of the street they stood on now and a busier road lined with restaurants and boutiques. "I'll be playing there for the dinner crowd."

"Well, good luck."

"Luck has nothing to do with it. My provision comes from above," he answered her.

She smiled. "Amen. Good night, sir."

"Good night." He tipped his hat toward her.

She had barely taken a step past him when he called, "Wait! Please!"

Katie bristled. *He's going to ask for money.* She thought about ignoring him, pretending not to hear him, but then he said, "I know what it feels like. What it feels like to be lonely."

She froze.

"It feels like," he continued, "standing on a street corner, playing a violin. Having the ability to command the attention of strangers, but knowing that attention isn't the same as really being seen. You end your song and dismiss them so they can shift their attention to the next thing.

"Then you go home to those you care about. To people who command your attention. To people who can really *see* you. But something or someone else commands their attention, so they never do. Instead, they tell you your song is done, and they dismiss you."

He slipped his hands into his pockets, the motion tightening the straps of his violin case over his shoulders. "But—"

Katie followed his gaze up.

"Feeling lonely and being alone are two different things. I am not alone. And you are not alone, no matter how lonely you feel."

He spared her the need to respond by resuming his journey down the sidewalk to his post for the evening.

"Miss, do you need help with your bags?"

The driver's question returned the breath to Katie's lungs and her focus to the car waiting to take her to O'hare airport.

———·———

Derek leaned back on his stool at Barrel & Brine's bar, savoring the bold, hoppy notes of his IPA. The craft beer's bitterness was a perfect match for his mood this evening. He would have invited Summer to join him, but he knew where she would be tonight, and he didn't want to deal with her lying to his face. Not tonight.

Recently opened, Barrel & Brine was a trendy spot in the Chicago neighborhood where Derek lived. With a rustic yet modern interior featuring reclaimed wood, exposed brick, and eclectic decor, it was a local favorite for those looking to enjoy unique brews and creative takes on classic pub fare.

Another bitter swig and another bitter thought: *Andrew doesn't deserve his life.*

He was right to be afraid of what Katie would think of him. Derek was his brother, and the revelation Andrew had laid out in his office earlier in the day had gutted him. He could only guess what it would do to Katie, to Andrew's *wife*, once she found out.

Andrew had everything anyone ever could hope for: money, notoriety, success, and love. He was one of the youngest scientists to give a keynote at one of the most prestigious conferences in this industry. Andrew had the keys to the kingdom and a beautiful queen to sit at his side and yet ...

It wasn't enough.

His brother just kept pushing for more. More money. More prestige. More success. At what cost? Derek could see that Andrew was losing Katie a little bit each day—hell, anyone could see that. And after what Derek heard today, apparently, he was losing his sense of integrity—or rather, he had already lost a chunk of it.

He had so much. Why couldn't he just be content? If Derek could just have one of those things. Just one.

He took another swig. The glass was empty.

Like my life.

He pulled his wallet out of his pocket, fished out enough bills to cover his tab and a generous tip, then stood from his stool. The room shifted a bit, and he grabbed the counter to stabilize himself. He noticed a pretty blonde watching him. He smiled at her.

She smiled back.

Maybe tonight wouldn't be a waste.

Katie checked her phone one last time before putting it on airplane mode. By now, she didn't expect him to text—but a persistent, and annoying, hope still lingered in her heart that Andrew might have a come-to-his-senses moment and realize he should say goodbye.

They would be apart for a couple of days, a first in their five years of marriage. That had to count for something, right? Though, Katie supposed, if you counted the number of days they physically occupied the same space but didn't say more than a few words to each other, her being gone to New York for a few days wasn't that unique.

And if you added up the number of nights she'd slept alone in her bed while Andrew stayed out until God-awful hours with God-knows-who, it painted a pretty pathetic picture. In the past few months, Katie woke to find Andrew on the couch, still in his clothes, more times than she cared to count. At least he tried to be considerate and not wake her by crawling into their bed.

The violin man's words echoed in Katie's mind: *their attention is commanded by something or someone else ...*

Katie could feel the heat leap to her cheeks. Andrew swore up and down that he had just gotten caught up at work and slept at his office, but the denial was almost worse than if he had just told her the truth. She refused to contemplate who it might be.

"Good evening." The captain's voice spoke over the speaker. "We'll be taking off here in a moment. At this time, please switch all mobile devices to airplane mode."

It's time to tell the truth. Time to make it all crumble.

In a decisive move, Katie sent Andrew a text before turning on airplane mode. She shoved the phone into her bag in another decisive move and opened the novel she had carefully selected for the plane ride, settling in for a reprieve from her troubles.

———•———

An empty apartment greeted Andrew when he arrived home, reminding him of his fight earlier with Katie. Reminding him she was gone. Reminding him she had left him.

Not that she had left him, *left* him. She would be back in a few days. Back in time for his keynote on Friday. She would be back in time. Katie knew it was important to him. She would come back to him, and she would come back in time.

You keep telling yourself that.

He glanced at his watch. Her flight was supposed to land in New York an hour ago. He should probably try calling her to check that she had gotten all settled at the hotel, but first, he needed to get something to eat. He grabbed the menu from their favorite Thai place on the corner.

As he pulled his phone out of his pocket to call in an order, he noticed a text from Katie. After the confrontation with her in the lobby, he had silenced his phone, using his meeting with Carr as justification. He had never taken it off silent mode and ended up missing the text from her.

He opened it up and read:

> Getting on the plane. With me doing interviews and you at the conference, we probably shouldn't expect to talk to each other the next couple of days.

Andrew could read the message behind the message: You didn't come after me.

You didn't call me to say goodbye.
You didn't call to check that I was okay.
You cared more about work than about me.
I don't want to be forgotten.
I don't want to be hurt.

Andrew dropped into a nearby armchair and stared at the message.

I'm sorry

He deleted the words and tried again:

I think that's for the best

He pushed the backspace until all the words disappeared. Then typed:

If that's what you want. See you Thursday. Love you.

She'll be back, but she's not coming back to you.
She says you don't care, but neither does she.
She doesn't understand what you're building here.
She doesn't respect your genius; she just wants what she wants.

Andrew read the message out loud, deleted "love you," then hit send.

The empty apartment mocked him with its eerie silence. He shoved his phone into his pocket, realizing Thai food delivery to the condo was now out of the question—he didn't want to be alone tonight. On second thought, he pulled his phone from his pocket again.

Usual place?

He hit send.

He didn't have to wait more than a few seconds for the phone notification to ping.

Sure thing. Be there in 10.

As Andrew stood on the street curb waiting for his Uber, a melodic song carried by the evening's cool breeze, one that hinted at the pending arrival of autumn, reached his ear. He recognized the notes of a violin and glanced down the sidewalk toward the figure of a man on the corner playing. Though too far to make out the man's face, Andrew could hear his sincerity in the notes.

The song ended just as Andrew's ride pulled up. Before getting into the car, he could hear the beginning notes of "It Is Well with My Soul."

Andrew hesitated, an unrest suddenly gripping his body deep down into his bones. He hadn't heard his mom's favorite hymn in years.

Not since May 21, 2015.

The day Katie attended church for the first time and he for his last.

Yellow roses filled the stage.

He closed the black sedan door firmly on the song and the memory.

Image Distressed

As I DRAW MY bow over the strings, coaxing notes from the instrument and sending them over sound waves and into the ears of those gathered around me, I notice her among the crowd.

This is not the first time she has stopped to listen to me play, and each time I see her, I wonder if she recognizes me. If she does, she doesn't give the slightest hint that she does. Instead, she stands there poised—calm and collected, watching my fingers create notes with the same precision that I use to move them. Her long white trench coat, no wrinkle in sight, skims her frame, hinting at soft curves while not hugging them too tightly. The coat's pockets protect her hands from the chill of the morning and its upturned collar protects her neck. Today, gray slacks and bright red heels peek out below the hem of her coat, the shoes' lift making her seem taller than she actually is. Her long brown hair, curled with perfection into loose waves, falls forward over her shoulders as she tilts her head ever so slightly, as if to open a path between my violin and her ear to better catch the melody.

And, just like every other time she has stopped to listen to me play, she closes her eyes, the muscles of her face relax, and she exhales.

And with that exhale, it begins.

First, the vibration: the resonance of string against my fingertips.

Then, the sound: birds trilling their song.

Finally, an image: a blanket of grass unfolding end over end from my feet to hers. Then, past hers until lush green swallows the gray of concrete. Chicago is completely gone, except me, her, and my violin.

Unlike every time before, however, a lifeless man lies in the empty space between us. His skin is ashen, a sharp contrast to the brown dust settling around him. He *needs help.*

Except, I can't move.

I am being restrained.

I am being calmed.

I am being instructed: *Watch, don't miss it.*

So, I watch.

And I see movement: vibrations on the air.

The vibrations collect into a small whirlwind.

It gathers speed.

In the image of God, He created him...

The whirlwind divides into two, then dives into the man's nostrils with a propulsion that ignites synapses.

He gasps for breath.

With that breath, his chest expands and contracts. I hear—and feel—the beat of a heart jumping into rhythm. Brown replaces the ash in a pixelated pattern, starting under his heart and spreading out toward his fingertips. The pixelated pieces merge and smooth into skin.

He flexes his fingers wide. Dragging the tips back in, he grabs fistfuls of grass and releases them.

Again and again.

He opens his eyes.

The vibrations hovering on the space around the man play a song of their own: *It is good.*

I fall to my knees. What else can I do? I'm not worthy to stand in the presence of something so sacred. In the presence of such a holy moment.

In the presence of new life.

I want to share this feeling of joy and awe with someone.

I turn back to the woman, ready to celebrate with her. But she stands tense, the pockets of her coat bunched from the inside where her fingers grip tight, her wide eyes locked onto something behind me. I follow her gaze.

A lone oak tree stretches its lush branches toward the bright blue sky. Twisted tightly around one branch is a snake—its head poised, its gaze locked on the woman.

She missed the beauty of the moment because of fear.

Suddenly, the greenery falls away from me, like I'm zooming out on Google Earth. First, I see the ground beneath me, then a large parcel of land, then the tops of mountains, then clouds, sky, then the entire earth.

I am suspended in space, watching the globe make its rotation around the sun. Time speeds up and I see the surface of the earth change as years pass. It spins faster and faster. Then it all zooms in: sky, clouds, mountains, earth, concrete.

Back to Chicago.

Back to her.

Summer.

The stiffness has left her stance, but her gaze now locks on something new—and it's not my fingers moving across the violin strings.

It's on the man standing off to my left: Derek.

The other Salvatore brother.

I know he remembers me; he lets me know by putting five twenty-dollar bills, folded over to hide their quantity, in the open case at my feet at least once a week.

As I finish the song, Derek leans over, dropping in his monetary gift of acknowledgement, not realizing that Summer is nearby watching him intensely. He hesitates, then adds two more twenties than normal. His eyes meet mine. Something is different today. He gives me a curt nod before weaving around the gathered audience and heads toward InnovGene.

I begin my next song and Summer's attention pulls from Derek's exit back to me.

Our eyes meet.

There in her almond-shaped, deep-brown ones swims the question: do I really know him?

No, she doesn't.

How could she? He doesn't even know himself.

Exactly.

But she needs him.

They need each other.

Reaching into her purse, Summer retrieves a pair of sunglasses and slides them on, masking both her eyes and the unspoken questions within them. Without waiting for the song to end, she follows Derek's path down Michigan Avenue.

Day Two

Tuesday, September 11, 2018

Exiting the elevator, Derek turned left toward his office in the marketing department but allowed himself a casual glance down the hallway to the right, where the executive offices were located. As he guessed, Andrew was already seated at his desk, peering at his computer screen.

For a moment, Derek thought about diverting his path and saying good morning to his brother, but he was still reeling from the bomb of information Andrew had dropped in their meeting yesterday. He just wanted to get to his own office and start working.

A few years ago, they redesigned the space and Andrew had tried to give him an office in the executive wing. But Derek had requested for an office near his teams. He wanted to be close to the action. Creating marketing campaigns and hitting sales targets were like a game to Derek's mind, and he thrived off of the high-energy production that was generated in the departments that flanked either side of his office.

He also didn't want to be reminded that he wasn't in the position he truly wanted.

"Derek."

The sound of his name stopped Derek in his steps. For a split second, he thought it was Summer calling after him—he had seen her entering the building as the doors of the elevator closed—but he quickly realized that it was Blair trying to get his attention. "Hey. What's up?"

He watched her cover the distance between them, the pissed look on her face signaling an imminent barrage of words. Blair was usually calm and collected, so whatever had riled her up must be serious. Only one thing came to mind that could provoke such rage in her.

"What the hell?" she hissed, her voice hushed, but each word laced with fury.

Derek played it cool. "How can I help you, Blair?"

Her eyes narrowed as she searched his face. "I know you know."

"We've got a lot going on here. You're gonna have to give me some context."

"I won't just let this fly. You have to stop him."

Derek glanced around and then ushered Blair into the empty conference room, closing the door behind them. He shifted the bag on his shoulder. "Seriously, Blair, what are you talking about?"

She crossed her arms. "Andrew telling me to update the conference team's talking points to say that we have our license and are going into production for Re-genX." She jabbed her finger toward Andrew's office, each thrust punctuating her words with sharp, angry emphasis. "There's no way he got us a license without doing something unethical."

Derek raised a hand to calm her, his brow furrowing in worry. "Hold on, did he actually say he got the license, or did he just tell you to update the notes?"

The rage sharply diminished as Blair contemplated the question. Derek could see her mentally replaying the conversation. She looked up at him, her anger replaced by uncertainty. "No, he just asked me to update the notes."

Derek placed his hands on Blair's shoulders and crouched down a bit to catch her gaze. "Okay. Trust me. That means he hasn't actually done anything yet. He's just getting ready. I'll talk to him."

She sighed. "Derek, please don't let Carr mess things up for us. We're doing something good here."

Derek dropped his hands from her shoulders. "What ... what do you ... why do you think Carr has something to do with this?"

Her look said it all. Derek sighed as he ran a hand over his face. "Of course ... Katie."

"She's mentioned in the past that she thinks he's ..." She paused to select her words. "Kinda shady." Blair searched Derek's face. "She's right, isn't she?"

"You know I'm not going to answer that question, Blair. But, I give you my word: I'll do my best to make sure nothing unethical happens here."

Blair nodded. "Okay." She wrung her hands. "I need you to know how important this is. We have something here that will change people's lives. We can't risk it by doing shady shit. Seriously, Derek. We've managed to do the near impossible. He could wreck all of that, and for what?"

Derek sighed exasperatedly. "I get it. Blair, I know." He calmed his voice. "I'll do my best."

"Even if it means going against your brother and Summer?"

Derek recoiled. "What's Summer got to do with this?"

"Derek, please act like you know who runs this place." Blair turned to go but stopped suddenly, her shoulders slumping as she turned around. "Oh, there's one more thing I need to talk to you about. Totally off topic."

"Yeah?"

"The new intern."

"Which one?"

"Her name is Sadie. She's in the marketing department. Straight, shoulder-length brown hair. Tall."

He tried to place the name with a face but came up short. He shrugged. "Don't know her."

She chuckled. "You may not know her, but she knows you."

"Yeah?"

"She's a little enamored with you."

Derek felt his body relax and a smirk tug at his lips. "Not surprising."

"See!" Blair exclaimed. "This is why I wanted to mention it. You might not know her now, but over the next couple of days, you're going to get to know her because she's working the conference with us. And she's all googly-eyed over—" She took a step back and motioned in a circular gesture toward Derek. "All of this."

"What do you expect me to do about that?" Derek asked through a laugh.

Blair's expression sobered him, though, as she said, "I want you to be careful not to do something stupid. We have enough going on with Carr possibly wrecking things—we don't need HR drama on top of all of it."

Derek felt a surge of defensiveness, even though he knew he deserved the criticism. He had never been one to turn down a good time, and after eight years of knowing him, Blair was well aware of that fact. Trying to dismiss her concern, he scoffed and said, "We're all consenting adults, right?"

"She's practically a baby."

"Our interns are always college seniors."

"So?"

"That makes her at least twenty-one."

"Are you serious right now?"

Derek smiled, "Are you?"

"Dude, have you not watched any of the HR trainings? Just keep it in your pants, okay? She's young and impressionable and you're a freaking VP. Imbalance. Of. Power." Blair framed each word with her hands before folding her arms across her chest.

Derek held up both hands in a defensive posture. "Okay, okay. Jeez, Blair. I was just kidding around. If you are that worried about it, I'll be extra careful around her."

Blair eyed him distrustfully but finally accepted his answer. "Good," she said.

Derek opened the door of the conference room for her and said, "After you."

"Are you going to go talk to Andrew about Carr?" She asked, not moving a muscle.

He motioned to the bag on his shoulder. "After I put all my stuff down in my office."

"Promise?"

"Blair, come on," he smirked, "I may not be one to say no to a good time, but I am a man of my word. You know that."

She rolled her eyes. "True to both things." Her face sobered. "Thank you, Derek."

"No problem."

Derek watched Blair stride out of the conference room, her figure disappearing down the hallway toward the research wing. His gaze shifted between his office and the executive wing. He hesitated, knowing he should just go talk to Andrew now.

"First, coffee." He said to no one in particular as he turned toward his office.

———— • ————

So Blair knew about Carr's offer.

Summer contemplated this as she slowly unbuttoned her coat and hung it up on the door hook. She pulled her laptop out of the briefcase and plugged it into her docking station on her desk before sitting down.

Seeing the panicked look on Derek's face as he pulled Blair into the conference room, Summer hung nearby and out of sight instead of making her way to her office. The closed door muffled their conversation, but when Derek opened it, Summer heard Blair ask Derek if he was going to talk to Andrew about Carr. She had also heard him reassure Blair that he would. That he was a "man of his word."

Summer also watched Blair walk away and Derek contemplate confronting his brother. For a moment, she wondered if the man she had watched put a roll of twenties into a street musician's case that morning would be the leader she knew he could be.

But, just as she had come over the years to know him to do, Derek avoided the hard and sought comfort instead of facing the giant.

"First, coffee." He had said. He might as well have said, "First, I'm going to hide until someone else fights the battle."

That someone else being Summer, of course.

Summer hit the enter key to launch her computer screen a little more aggressively than necessary. She was getting a little tired of fighting the Salvatore brothers' battles. As much as she joked about this place being her kingdom, and as good at her job as she was, the truth was she owned what was essentially a miniscule piece of equity in the company. She was an employee—appointed by one prince to do the work he couldn't do, and the work the other prince wouldn't.

A wave of nausea rolled up from Summer's toes to the back of her throat. She closed her eyes and took a steadying breath.

Those men better start acting like they actually owned the place; Summer had her own battles to fight.

———·———

The set of the morning show was surprisingly a lot smaller than Katie had imagined it, but it was still intimidating.

Soon, her face would air across the nation, and she would have the chance to tell thousands (she refused to think in millions) of viewers about a book she had written. But she wondered if the one person she wanted to watch this morning would even remember to tune in.

This was it. This level of success was what every novelist wished to attain but knew was a rarity. For every bestselling author, there were millions (here it was okay to acknowledge) of fiction writers who never got their moment in the sun. It was not lost on Katie how unique a privilege it was to be here on the morning of her book launch.

As soon as she sat down in the makeup chair, Katie rehearsed her talking points over and over. The more she practiced them, the dumber they sounded. Would she be able to pull this off? Would she be able to make the most of her five minutes of fame? Would it be enough to make it all worth it? All the hours spent alone with her computer? All the fights she had endured with Andrew?

Her publicist had instructed her to stick to the five bullet points she'd given Katie to repeat throughout the day. "Every interviewer will come at it a little differently, but they will all cover essentially those same five points," Laura explained. "Your goal is that anyone watching or listening walks away knowing that they want to buy your novel."

Easier said than done.

How do you sum up 350 pages of story, characters whose depth you've carefully cultivated, and a plotline you've agonized over for thousands of hours—in a single persuasive soundbite? How do you convince someone they should spend hours of their life reading it ... that it won't be just a big waste of time? A complete letdown? She wasn't one of those authors who believed her novel was going to change the world; she just wanted people to enjoy the story, and maybe to feel a bit seen as they did.

For months, she had let one pivotal scene ruminate in her mind—a scene inspired by an interaction she had accidentally witnessed between Larson Carr and Andrew. She treated it like a coach reviewing game footage, rewinding and replaying it. When that didn't work, she treated it like a cameraman, moving around in the scene from various angles. In her mind's eye, she shifted from narrator to first person. She embodied the characters and looked around the scene from their perspective. Explored. Analyzed. Played.

Finally, she gave space to it. Upon putting fingers to keyboard, the permission she needed to go searching for the rest of the story was given, and *The Lies that Became Us* formed quickly into a manuscript. What didn't happen quickly was publication. That process felt like it took a lifetime, though it was only three years.

As Katie folded up the talking points, a memory of her mother-in-law surfaced, bringing a smile to her face. It was from one of their weekly family dinners. Brenda had encouraged her to attend a writer's conference to pitch her novel. A vase of yellow roses in the center of the table partially hid Brenda's face, but nothing could hide the excitement in her eyes.

"Do it, Sugar!" she said. Brenda called everyone *dear*, but she reserved *Sugar* for her loved ones. "It's good," she added with conviction. Katie burst out laughing and protested, "You haven't even read it!"

Tears welled up in Katie's eyes, blurring the talking points on the paper in her lap. "Gosh, I'm a mess," she mumbled, dabbing a finger beneath each eye, careful not to smear the work her makeup artist had just finished minutes earlier. (She'd hired one for the day to make sure she looked okay during each of her interviews.) "How am I going to make it through this?" she asked no one in particular.

You're not alone.

"I know, Lord," she whispered.

No, she was not alone. Not anymore. The day she said goodbye to Brenda was the day she said hello to a relationship with Jesus, and she hadn't been alone since.

"Hey, Katie, you're up next."

Katie looked up into the face of a young woman with a clipboard. "Oh! Okay."

"You can follow me."

As they made their way to the set, Katie tried to take a few calming breaths. This was the first interview of the day, a segment on a national morning show. Later, she would record a radio spot and some podcast interviews. Her publicist had explained that podcasts were gaining in popularity and could expand their reach to a warm audience ready to buy. Tonight's book launch party was the capstone of a long day.

Katie waited in the wings for her introduction, going over her talking points once more. Upon hearing her name, she forced her body into action, even though every fiber of her being wanted to flee the studio as fast as she could. On the outside, she was the picture of calm and confidence as she walked over to the hosts, Craig and Linda, and shook their hands. Like a pro, she waved to the cameras, then took a seat on the chair waiting for her. It was bar-height and Katie mentally patted herself on the back for choosing pants over a dress. She crossed one leg over the other, hooking her heel on the chair rung to help stabilize herself.

Linda took the lead. "We're so excited to have you here, Katie! I actually just finished your novel the other day. I couldn't put it down!"

Katie smiled. "I'm so glad you enjoyed it."

"Even though it just released today—congrats, by the way."

"Thanks."

"It's garnered great reviews from both critics and early readers. Even well-respected book critic Matt Ziegle said it should be—*and I quote*—'on everyone's must-read list this fall.' High praise, indeed. So, tell us a bit about the premise of the novel for those watching at home."

Bullet point number one. *Here we go.* Katie launched into the two lines she and her publicist had crafted. "It's about a couple entangled in a web of lies. It starts innocently, with each trying to protect the other, but the lies eventually take over their lives. They're trapped in a world of corporate deceit and devious dealings, unsure how to escape."

"Ooh, sounds intriguing. How did you come up with the idea?"

Bullet point number three. "I was watching a couple interact on a bus in Chicago"—a half-truth, as the couple was actually Andrew and herself—"and you could just tell that they loved each other very much. But then the woman asked the guy how his meeting had gone. He said 'good' but then his eyes darted away, and I remember thinking, he's hiding something. That made me think about all the little lies that we sometimes can excuse away in the name of loving the other person. Little white lies, you know? And how sometimes, little white lies add up to the same damage that a big lie can. The question then plagued me: what was he hiding? They got off at the next stop and took their answer with them. So, I made up one."

The hosts chuckled.

"You are a journalist by trade, right?" Craig asked.

Bullet point two. "I was for a long time, but I left that field about three years ago."

"Writing fiction must have felt like such a deviation after years of writing facts."

Craig set up the conversation, and Katie followed him into it. "It was a little tough, but my background in journalism helped me research the story and craft it in a way that felt truthful and realistic. At least, I hope it comes across that way."

"Oh, it really does! In fact, one might even wonder if more than a bus ride inspired this tale?"

This was not a bullet point. Where was this going?

Craig leaned forward, as if trying to entice a secret from Katie. "Your husband is a businessman, isn't he?"

A hollowness carved a space in Katie's stomach. "Um, actually, he's a scientist."

"But he owns InnovGene, correct?"

"Yes, he does."

Craig glanced down at his notes quickly and then looked back up at Katie. "I can only imagine that there might be fodder for your book within a company that is in a race to create innovative technology."

Katie blinked. They were supposed to stick to the bullet points, not dive deep into her life. "Excuse me?"

"Just wondering if maybe there's more fact than fiction in this book?" Craig smiled through the question.

Linda playfully slapped Craig's shoulder with her note cards. "Oh, stop trying to dig up drama, Craig! There's enough in Katie's novel to satisfy your need for sensationalism." She turned to Katie. "You and your husband are so sweet. I saw the press release his company sent out this morning stating his support and love for you. Really, the entire company's love and support of you." She covered her heart with her hands, notecards and all. "That's just so touching."

What press release? What is she talking about?

"Thank you," Katie managed.

"Now, would you like to read us an excerpt from your novel?"

Forget about the press release, focus on now. Katie forced a smile and nodded her head. "Sure." She opened her book to the page she had tabbed, cleared her throat gently, and read:

> The day I left him at the train station with a kiss goodbye and an understanding we would never see each other again, that was the first lie. That was the first lie that became us.
>
> He dropped me off at my request. I wasn't sure I'd make it to the train without crying. I told him it was because I wouldn't make the 7:50 train if I took the bus. That was a truth. But another truth was that I wasn't ready to let go of him yet. So we got into his gas-guzzling truck, and he navigated the streets of Chicago at a quick pace. Quick enough that when he pulled up to Union Station, I had time to kiss him one last time. Time to tell him goodbye. Time to wish him luck on his new job. Time to look into his eyes and make a wish that we'd see each other again.
>
> I wonder now what he was thinking when I said all those things? When I kissed him so deeply? He made it seem as if the breakup was a mutual agreement. That our relationship was too new to weather long distance. That we both needed to pursue our lives—separately.

Katie heard the nerves in her voice and reminded herself to slow down.

> When I emailed two months later to touch base, I told myself it was just friendly interest.

That was the second lie. And when he responded with "Great news, I've actually been transferred back to Chicago," that was the third one.

Three strikes and you're out.

We were out ... out of our damn minds. I don't
know how we didn't think that the little white
lies would catch up with us. I've lost track of
the count over the years. Now he stands with
one hand on a Bible, swearing to tell the truth,
the whole truth, and nothing but the truth. The
irony isn't lost on me and a chuckle escapes
my lips in the quiet courtroom. Aaron's mother
turns to me with a shush. I want to respond,
"He's not your good little boy anymore, Karen."
But I stay quiet. The rest of the courtroom
glances my way, but they collectively decide
to ignore the pregnant lady and listen to the
testimony of the witness on the stand.

Don't believe a word he says, people. He's a liar.

It takes one to know one.

———— • ————

12:42 p.m.
   Summer needed to make the call ... get it on the books.
Especially with the demands of the job this quarter com-
mandeering every last free minute in her schedule. The
conference had pulled the normal busy into a peak of
stress-wrapped meetings and execution.

Emma had waved her magical assistant's wand and re-arranged the puzzle that was Summer's calendar in order to open up a spot for the appointment.

Of course, she didn't know what the appointment was for, which added a layer of awkwardness to the situation. Emma came over to InnovGene with Summer and knew the ins and outs of Summer's life—including the parts no one else knew—almost better than Summer did.

But this, this wasn't something Summer wanted to share with anyone.

He deserves to know.

Summer shook her head to rid herself of the thought and picked up the bowl of soup on the desk to toss it in the garbage. On a second thought, she set it back down.

The soup had cooled off a while ago, but she had promised herself she would make the phone call by the end of lunch. She knew if she stood up before making the call, she would never do it. Plus, she had a one o'clock meeting to get to.

Do what you need to do.

With quick and decisive actions, Summer dialed the number, then raised the phone to her ear. Using the speaker phone wouldn't do, even if she was in her own office with the door closed.

It only rang once before the receptionist greeted Summer and led her through a series of questions. Then came the most important one: "When do you want to come in?"

"Do you have anything Thursday morning?" Summer asked. She picked up the spoon and dragged it through the soup, making a swirling pattern as she did.

"I actually have a spot right when we open at 9 a.m."

"That works perfectly." She let the spoon rest against the bowl's edge once more.

"Great, you're all set. Just so you know, even though it's just a consultation, some patients find it helpful to have someone come along for support. Even if that person just sits in the waiting room."

You should ask him.

A tightness formed in Summer's throat. "Oh, okay," she managed.

"We'll see you Thursday."

"Thanks. Bye." Summer ended the call and placed the phone face down on the table next to the soup.

Ask him.

Her fingers wrapped around the phone once more.

"The soup is cold," she said to no one. "I should throw it away."

Phone in one hand, bowl of soup in the other, she made her way over to the trashcan near her office door. She tossed the bowl into the abyss, then checked her phone.

12:54 p.m.

Good. Enough time to get to the conference room for her next meeting.

As Summer stepped out of her office, her gaze landed on Andrew, seated at his desk and staring out the window, lost in the view of Lake Michigan.

He doesn't know how small he looks when he does that. Summer thought as she swiped the texting app open on her phone.

Summer had seen that pensive look on more than one occasion over the years as they built this kingdom. Andrew's zone of genius was his scientific mind. His role as business owner was his weak spot. Once meant to be a boost to his pride, the business had become a self-made prison of anxiety—with Carr holding the keys.

If only they could be rid of that man in their lives, they would all be the better for it.

She hit send on her text:

I won't be at the meeting. Fill me in later.

The prince needed his counsel, even if half of it refused to do the job.

She knocked on the open door.

Andrew turned in his chair and, seeing it was Summer, waved her in.

It's time to storm the castle.

Summer closed the door behind her.

———————·———————

Lunch was a welcomed break from the packing and hauling of the morning for Sadie and the other interns. Even if it was just a hamburger from one of the hotel's restaurants adjoining the conference center. Though, at the price point for said hamburger, Sadie figured it better be the best hamburger she had ever eaten. Her bank account was taking a beating with this unpaid internship.

Cynthia sent the pack of interns off to the restaurant with a "Leave me be. I need a break from your questions." Having ordered last, Sadie stood waiting for her food at the counter. She glanced over at the group just in time to see Chloe laugh at something Noah said.

Are they laughing at me?

Sadie shook her head to rid herself of the random thought. Where it had come from in that exact moment was unknown to her, but it was a familiar worry for Sadie.

They are just enjoying the break. Knock it off.

The conference team was in full go-mode when Sadie arrived to work that morning. She barely put her stuff down when one of the other interns, Priya, found her and instructed her to go to conference room D to help pack up materials for the booth.

They worked all morning, following Cynthia's instructions as the woman plowed through the list on her clipboard. By 11 a.m., they had loaded up employees' vehicles with boxes, then jumped in and headed to the event hall to begin unpacking.

"If the conference wasn't being held down the road, we would have shipped these boxes ahead of time and the event staff would have taken them to our booth," Cynthia explained on the drive over. "But, since we are literally up the road, Summer decided we could save the money and do it ourselves."

Sadie noted a bit of bitterness in Cynthia's tone. She was about to ask her about it when Noah, another intern, jumped in and said, "Isn't that a waste of employee time? Wouldn't it be more efficient to pay a little extra so employees aren't doing this kind of work instead of focusing on their actual tasks?"

Cynthia eyed him, the slight smirk on her lips betraying the fact that she agreed with him. However, she answered, "What would we have you interns do then?"

"Touché." Noah responded.

"Listen," Cynthia's tone turned teacher-y. "In business, it's always a give and take. Sometimes, those in leadership positions make good decisions with the information they have, and sometimes they don't. Your job at this level is to do your best work, regardless if you agree or not. Because, one day, you'll be the leader trying to make the decisions and you'll make some good decisions, and you'll make not so great ones. But you better hope your team has your back, for the sake of all of your jobs."

Unconvinced, Noah pushed back, "If a leader isn't doing the right thing, isn't it important we speak out about that so that, ultimately, our jobs don't become jeopardized?"

"Depends." Cynthia answered as she turned into the parking garage. "The question that you have to ask yourself is this: 'is this unethical or just different from how I would do it?' If unethical, yes, speak up, speak out. If it's just different from what you think is right or helpful, or even most efficient, shut up and do your job to the best of your ability."

Sadie couldn't make heads or tails out of Cynthia. One moment she seemed so nonchalant about things, then the next, she's dropping wisdom like some battle-worn soldier. She figured that's probably why they put her in charge of the interns.

"Order 53."

The call out interrupted Sadie's contemplation. She gathered her food and made her way over to the table.

"So, this party on Thursday … everything's free, right?" Priya swept her long, wavy black hair away from her oval face into a hair tie. Once done, she popped a fry into her mouth. "Because my college ass is broke."

Noah nodded. "InnovGene sponsored the party, which means they paid for everything. It's like advertising and networking all rolled up into one."

"Whew. This must be costing them thousands!" Chloe scooted her chair over to give Sadie more room at the table.

"Well, I'm just glad we get to enjoy it. I'll take free food and booze any day." Priya took a sip of her soda.

"Exactly. You don't have to twist my arm."

Sadie unwrapped her burger and poured out her fries on the paper wrapper next to it. "Can anyone come?"

Noah nodded. "If they are a conference attendee."

"Oh good. My friends are going to the conference. I'll see if they are planning to go to the party."

"Friends from college?" Noah asked.

"Yep. They are taking a class about how science advancements impact society and the ethical stuff that comes along with it. Attending the conference is part of the course."

"Dang, that's cool."

"Are they science majors?"

"Mackenzie is. She wants to go into the whole gene-therapy thing. Adriana is a business major like us. She's actually trying to get this internship for next semester. Anyone want this pickle?"

"I'll take it." Noah snatched the pickle off Sadie's plate and took a bite out of it.

"Did you guys see the schedule Cynthia emailed us?" asked Chloe.

Phones emerged from pockets and email inboxes swiped open.

"I thought Derek was making a schedule for us?" Sadie willed her voice to sound as natural as possible as she said Derek's name.

"He probably delegated it to Cynthia." Priya offered.

"It looks like she's got Sadie and me helping in the booth to start while you two attend the sessions. Then at lunch, we swap." Chloe explained as the others skimmed the email.

Noah ran a hand through his crew cut. "I wouldn't mind just staying in the booth. I'm not into this whole science scene. I just want to make money—don't need to know what the nerds are doing to sell to them." He shrugged.

Priya rolled her eyes and sighed dramatically. "I think they are trying to help us learn to serve the client. In order to sell to them, you've got to understand them."

"Sales are sales. You don't need to know the ins and outs of the industry, you just have to know the high-points." Noah responded before taking a sip of his pop.

Priya looked like she was about to give a rebuttal, but Sadie's phone beeped—loud and obnoxious—cutting the conversation short. All eyes turned to her as she hurriedly retrieved it from the table. She looked up at the other interns. "Our lunch break is over," she said, her tone more questioning than statement.

Chloe glanced at her watch. "Our break doesn't end for another ten minutes."

"I factored in time for walking back to the expo hall," Sadie answered weakly.

The others exchanged looks.

Sadie knew those looks. She had been getting them her entire life. The looks that said, "brown-noser" and "over-achiever." Sometimes the looks also meant that she was uptight or too straight-laced ... that she just needed to relax and chill. Go with the flow.

The look she hated the most was the one that said "rule-follower."

Partly because it was true. Mostly because no one meant it as a compliment.

The urge to wrap up her remaining burger and start heading back to the expo hall poked at the nerves in Sadie's body, but she fought to ignore it and instead said, "I suppose it'll be okay to take the full thirty minutes."

"Well, yeah, you haven't even finished your burger!"

Sadie wished Priya hadn't waved a hand at her plate. The gesture pulled her gaze downward, and the itch to leave ballooned into a suffocating pressure. "Oh, I was going to save that part. It was so big." Once again, Sadie willed her voice to sound nonchalant.

"Yeah, they were pretty big," replied Chloe, suddenly wrapping up half of her burger.

Priya glanced down at her salad. "Yeah, the portions here are huge. I think I'm done with this salad." She speared the remaining few pieces of chicken with her fork and popped them in her mouth.

There it was, the permission Sadie needed to wrap up her burger. When she finished carefully folding the wrapper over the food, she looked up to see Noah watching her.

He dropped his eyes.

He must think I'm so weird.

If he did, Noah gave no further indication as he stood and offered the clear trays to everyone.

As the group made their way back to the expo hall, the conversation naturally drifted back to the topic of the party on Thursday. Dress code was discussed and plans for a rideshare to the event—they'd play things by ear for getting home—were made. Listening to them talk, Sadie realized how nice it would be to have Adriana and Mackenzie there with her. Friendly faces would make things less awkward.

You don't have to always be the odd man out.

Sadie shook her head. Where were all these random thoughts coming from? She didn't mind being the odd man out. It was who she was.

Oh really ...

Really, it was who she was. A little quirky. Goal-driven. Focused. She had standards.

Legalistic.

The thought stopped her in her tracks just shy of InnovGene's booth.

Was it true? Was she getting carried away with doing things *right*? Maybe, like with the alarm earlier, she had gotten a little too uptight with things. She thought she had loosened up a bit over the last couple of years at college. Maybe she needed to loosen up a bit more? She was an adult, after all. She would have to figure out how to navigate this world of business ... this world of coworkers going out for drinks ... this world of casual relationships. Not that she should get rid of everything, but maybe it was time for her to reevaluate where she could let go a bit more.

Hazel-green eyes, dark hair, tall, strong shoulders ... the image of Derek not only filled her mind's eye but shocked her heart into a fluttered beat.

He'll be here tomorrow. When he notices you, you want it to be for the right reasons.

The heat jumped to her cheeks.

Even if she wanted him to notice her ... and notice her not because she was weird or odd ... she wouldn't know the first thing about how to do that.

Mackenzie does.

Right. She'd ask Mackenzie for help tomorrow.

———— · ————

Spreading her arms wide, Katie allowed herself to fall face first onto the king-sized bed covered with a pin-tucked white comforter and more pillows than she felt the need to count. The momentum against the mattress resulted in Katie's petite frame bouncing away from the bed and then meeting its plush top again with force. The pillows near the edge of the bed plummeted to the floor.

Stress-induced knots in the pit of Katie's stomach untangled themselves and escaped her body as peals of laughter, albeit muffled by the comforter. She rolled onto her back, flinging her arms out to the sides, and sighed.

It had been a long day, starting with the TV spot and followed by three in-person podcast interviews, a quick lunch with her publicist, then a radio spot, and three more podcast interviews via video conferencing. Although she had seen Andrew take video calls, the experience was a new one for Katie. She was glad she had gone through the in-person interviews before doing the ones online; she hadn't realized how much she depended on a person's body language to navigate a conversation until today.

The day wasn't over, though. Katie had about an hour to regroup before heading to her book launch party. Her publisher rented a private room at a nearby restaurant for the event. There would be fancy hors d'oeuvres and fancy decorations. Katie had even bought a fancy dress for the occasion. It wasn't a large event, but there would be a number of people in attendance, including fellow authors who had become dear friends over the years and fans who had won tickets.

A chirp from her phone caught Katie's attention. She rolled over to the edge of the bed and reached down toward the floor where she had dropped her purse. Leaving the purse on the floor, she unzipped it, fished out her phone, then zipped it back up.

She rolled over until she was on her back once more, pushing her hair out of her face and raising the phone so she could read the text.

How goes it out their in the big apple?

Katie sighed. You'd think for someone who was in a field that relied on communication, Derek would have figured out the differences between their, there, and they're by now. Sometimes she wondered if he did it on purpose to annoy her?

Ignoring the grammatical error, she responded.

Pretty good, actually.

Nice.

How's it going there?

Would he notice she spelled it correctly?

It's going.

Stressed out?

Is there any other way to be here?

Um, yes, and you know that.

It feels different this time.

She reread the text and sighed.

Carr?

Carr.

The dread started in her toes, then slowly dug its claws into her skin as it crawled its way up into her chest.

How bad is it?

It's not good.

The dread reached Katie's head, stuck a finger into her mind, and stirred up thoughts. She stared at the phone screen. Did she really want to do this right now? Miles away from home? When she was finally focusing on something that brought her joy? Something that didn't involve the genius of her husband? Something that let her be in the spotlight for once?

"Whoa." The word sounded loud in the quiet room. "I am proud of Andrew," she assured herself before letting her hand holding the phone drop to the bed. It chirped almost immediately. Katie brought it up again to read Derek's text.

Except, it wasn't from Derek; it was from Summer.

I need your help with something.

Katie sat up quickly. Summer had never reached out to her like this in all the years they had known each other. *What do I say, Lord?* She prayed.

Start simple, came the answer.

She swiped her finger across the keyboard on the touchscreen.

what's up?

Can I call you?

of course

Her phone rang almost as soon as she hit send. Katie answered it. "Hey."

"Hi." Summer's voice was clear.

"Hi. How are you?"

"Good. How's New York?"

"Good."

"Good."

Silence.

Just as Katie was about to ask how she could help, Summer spoke up. "Listen," she said bluntly, "when you get back into town, I need you to do something for us. For the company."

"Okay ..."

"I need you to not ask any questions."

"What?"

"When you get back, there's going to be a lot going on at the conference. A lot of it won't make sense to you. A lot of it won't sit right with you either. I know you, Katie; you'll want to ask Andrew all these questions, want to press him for information. Carr will be there too, and I know you don't trust Carr—I promise you, none of us do. I'm telling you this now so that you have time to process it. This week, especially at the conference, it won't be the time to confront Andrew or Carr. We need to get through the conference. After that, you can ask all the questions you want. But you're going to have to trust me that the best thing for Andrew, and for the company, this week, is for you to stay out of it."

"Of course," Katie responded calmly. Then, with a bite in her tone: "Since you know what's best for *my husband*."

A beat passed, then Summer replied, "It's my job, Katie."

"Right."

"Truly." It almost sounded apologetic.

No, *it's my job*, is what Katie really wanted to say. Instead, she said, "I'll behave, I promise."

"Just until after the conference, then you can ask him anything."

"Anything?" Katie pressed.

Another pause. "Thank you for understanding, Katie. Good night."

So, Summer was refusing to go there. "Good night, Summer." Katie responded, then hung up.

She let herself fall back against the bed once more. Her fingers found the nearest pillow and tugged it over. The pillowcase felt cool against her flushed skin as she muffled her scream of frustration.

"Wanna grab dinner?"

Derek looked up from his computer to see Summer leaning against the frame of his office door, her white coat draped over her arm.

"Hello to you too," he replied, reaching for the mouse. With a few quick clicks, the documents and project timelines he had spent the entire day poring over disappeared from the screen.

"Sorry." Summer smirked as she clasped her hands together, her coat now draped over both. "Hey, Derek," she greeted him with mock cheer. "How's your day been?"

His fingers guided the laptop closed. "Oh, hey, Summer." He feigned cheeriness, then let his face drop into annoyance as he leaned back in his chair. "It's been a shit show. How about yours?"

"Same. Wanna grab dinner?"

"Is my brother coming?" Derek asked, trying to sound casual.

"No, why?" Her voice matched his tone.

Derek hesitated, then said, "I'm avoiding him." He picked up his phone as he stood from the desk and slid it into his pocket. "Family issue."

When he reached her at the door, Summer raised her deep brown eyes to his and said, "Anything I can help with?" She searched his face. "Since I'm practically family, you know."

The question hit him like a punch to the head, knocking loose tightly stored memories and tilting his world into their history.

First: Their shoulders merging into one another as they both attempted to exit the Econ 101 class door.

He said, "Ope!"

She said, "Oh, you guys really say that here."

Her voice wrapped itself around his heart and he walked her to her next class.

Once she was inside, he hustled back across the college campus to his class. It wouldn't be the last time Summer made him late for something.

Next: Summer leading him down a row of cubicles, introducing him to her coworkers.

A light floral scent clung to her—sweet and delicate. That Christmas, he bought her a gift basket filled with soap, lotion, and bath salts, all in that unforgettable Sweet Pea fragrance.

She asked, "How did you know?"

He answered, "I sniffed every bottle in that store until I figured it out. Had a headache for a week."

Then: An open pizza box sitting between them on a conference table.

Summer held a slice in one hand and a piece of paper with the Veridian Solutions logo in the other. She took a bite absentmindedly, then paused, realizing he was watching her. She met his gaze.

Her eyes asked, *What do you want?*

It was both a question and an invitation. Derek didn't hesitate. He closed the distance and cupped her chin, lifting her face slightly to his.

His lips answered, *You.*

Finally: The bright red of Brenda's nails against the white of the platter she held over the sink.

Hours before, it had held slices of Thanksgiving turkey. She deftly moved a sponge over the platter, applying more pressure to the stubborn spots.

She asked, "When are you going to marry her?"

He said, "Slow down, Mom. We just got through Andrew's wedding."

The sponge froze mid swipe.

Her eyes spoke for her: *You're playing house, Derek. Man up.*

It was true; Summer was practically family.

But not fully. Not anymore.

Derek slipped on his coat and willed the memories back to where they belonged. He smiled to reassure Summer—and himself, if he was being honest—and said, "You can help by taking me out to dinner!" He waved her out the door. "I'm thinking Gibson's."

She put a hand on his arm to stop him. "Excuse me, it's your turn. I paid last Tuesday."

Derek pretended to think deeply. "No, I'm pretty sure that I paid last week."

"Oh, you did, huh?"

"Yep, it was at Uno's."

"That was two weeks ago. We went to Silver Spoon last week."

"You must have me confused with someone else—I never eat Thai," Derek joked, but the humor faded as he caught a flicker of fear in Summer's eyes.

She recovered quickly, however, and nodded. "You're right. I had a meeting last week with some vendors. They took me there. Sorry about that. You're right, it's my turn to pay."

Follow the lie.

No. He didn't want to deal with it last night, and he definitely didn't want to deal with it this evening. "Hey," he said, his tone reassuring, "I was just messing around. We went to Fredrick's last Thursday. It's totally my turn to pay."

Summer let a smirk play at the corner of her lips. "That's right." She playfully poked him. "It is your turn." She led the way over to the elevator at a quick pace. "Steak sounds fabulous," she tossed over her shoulder.

Once more, a memory escaped the mental barrier and assaulted Derek:

Summer in front of those same elevators a few years prior ... the day she had joined InnovGene as chief operating officer.

Carr had suggested the hire.

Her hair was shorter back then ... up at her chin and with bangs. The haircut framed her face and highlighted her eyes. She stood with a coat draped over her arm then too, a more generic coat, of course—definitely not the designer one she held right now. Back then, they stood waiting for the elevator with both Andrew and Carr. Andrew suggested they get lunch at a new restaurant down the street to celebrate her first day. She answered his suggestion with, "Steak sounds fabulous."

It was supposed to be you.

The thought rammed into his skull just as it had that day all those years ago.

"Hey, where did you go?" Summer's voice pulled him back into the present. She pushed the elevator button.

"I was thinking about the day you joined the company."

Summer laughed.

"What's so funny?"

"I can't believe you actually remembered that today is my work anniversary. You never remembered important dates when we were together."

"Wait, that's today?"

Summer crossed her arms. "See, I knew you didn't have it in you to remember a date."

"You know me well." Derek responded. "That makes ..."

"Four years." Summer filled in. She paused. Derek could see her considering walking down memory lane, which he desperately hoped she would decide against. As if hearing his silent plea to avoid the subject, she simply asked, "What made you think of it?"

He shrugged. "Something about the way you were standing by the elevator and said that steak sounded good. You did the same thing that day."

"Oh, really? You must have been paying close attention to remember something like that," she said coyly, taking a step toward their past.

"Well ..." He shrugged, letting the rest hang in the air and refusing to revisit a love story they'd both abandoned—it was the only way he could handle being here with her each day.

Summer followed his lead and let the conversation drop. She changed to the safer topic of the Cubs game last night and the devastating loss. She asked Derek if he thought they had a chance against the Brewers to win the division.

"Maybe."

It was supposed to be you.

The elevator doors opened.

Summer stepped inside, fishing her phone out of her pocket. "I probably should call ahead and see if I can get us on the waitlist."

Follow the lie.

Derek put a hand on the door to stop it from closing.

"Hey, Summer—"

She looked up from the phone.

It was supposed to be me.

Derek took a deep breath. "Summer, where did you watch the game last night?" He paused. "Who did you watch the game with last night?"

She didn't move.

He didn't move.

The elevator chimed an open door alert.

Summer shook her head slowly. "No, Derek. You really aren't ready to ask those questions."

"What? How can you know—" He stopped suddenly as Summer pressed her lips into a thin, resolute line.

She said, "Not tonight." But her eyes said, *What do you want?*

What did he want?

He wanted to take her to dinner.

He wanted to avoid the conversation for one more night.

He just wanted to sit across from her, eat, laugh, and enjoy her company.

You want to pretend nothing is wrong.

Summer was right. He wasn't ready to ask those questions.

Derek took his hand off the door and stepped into the elevator next to her.

Neither one of them spoke as the metal panels closed on the office.

Summer had thought to warn Katie not to go there with the questions; she didn't think she had to do the same with Derek. Why did he suddenly get the gumption to confront her? This wasn't something he needed to confront right now.

Just like Katie doesn't need to confront Andrew, right? The question assaulted her as they turned the corner to hail a cab.

No, this was different.

Katie had every right to confront Andrew. She was his wife. Which is why Summer told her she could ask the questions—*after* the conference. For now, Katie needed to play the role of supportive wife, not the one of inquisitor and judge.

She had asked Katie to wait for the sake of the company. They had bigger fish to fry. Bigger issues to take care of. Bigger things—things that affected all of them and all of their employees.

But her and Derek? Well, they weren't married. Who she was sleeping with wasn't his business. And it really didn't matter when their kingdom was being threatened.

Doesn't it though? You should tell him.

"Like that's ever going to happen." Summer muttered under her breath as she exited the building.

"Huh?" Derek asked.

"Oh, nothing. Just realizing it got cold." She fished a pair of leather gloves out of her coat pocket and put them on as they walked up the sidewalk a bit to where cabs were more likely to stop.

Just yards ahead of them, the street musician from that morning knelt on the sidewalk near the corner, packing his violin into its case. The care with which he attended to the task captured Summer's attention. She noticed how his hands, weathered by age and the elements, cradled the instrument both with confidence and tenderness as he laid it to rest on the velvety, royal-blue lining. With the violin safe in its bed, the hands pushed the bow into its designated spot, turning a little lever to secure it in place. He closed the case, engaged the snaps, and hoisted it on his back with practiced ease. There was a simplicity in it all—from the setup and breakdown to his purpose: play. If the simplicity was the violin case, peace would be the velvety blue liner. A ping of jealousy shot through Summer's body like a pinball through its machine.

"Do you think he plays here purposely?" Derek asked as he tried to hail the cab driving toward them.

Summer watched the musician reposition the straps of the case on his shoulders before turning the corner and disappearing from her sight. She turned toward Derek. "What?"

"I don't know for sure." He shrugged as the cab pulled up to the curb. "I know he plays different spots, but sometimes I think he plays here on purpose. Like he's trying to make a statement or something." He opened the cab door and motioned for Summer to get in.

"Why would he do that?" Summer asked, confused.

"Like this morning—you were there, right?" Derek asked.

So he had noticed her standing there. Then he knew she had seen him put the money in the case. Did he do it because she was there?

"Yes, I was," she answered, climbing into the cab.

"Well, he's there almost every morning. Andrew, you, me ... we all have to walk right by him. Every day." Derek climbed in after her and gave their destination to the driver. He turned to Summer, waiting for her response. "Come on, Harlow, you're smarter than this."

Her amusement at his use of her last name overshadowed the insinuation that she was missing something blatantly in her face.

"Kingston Reed." Derek filled in the missing piece for her.

"No flipping way! That guy is Kingston?"

"I thought you recognized him!"

"Just from walking by him every morning, not from BioSphere!" She matched his volume and tone.

The cabbie swiftly maneuvered the vehicle in and out of building traffic, bringing up a wave of nausea for Summer. Not *now*.

She turned away from Derek, partly to hide the wave of nausea, but mostly to hide her embarrassment. She trained her eyes on the city lights shimmering against the evening darkness and willed her stomach to settle.

Once she regained her composure, she turned back to Derek and said, "I've watched him play a thousand times. I can't believe I didn't recognize him." *I feel like an idiot.*

"You really didn't recognize him?"

"I barely knew him back then ..." her voice trailed off.

"Back then." Derek repeated, a tone twisted around his words and suffocated the innocence out of the statement. It was this tone that drew her gaze back to his face, where she found his eyes waiting for her.

They asked the same question her own eyes had asked earlier of him: *What do you really want?*

What Summer really wanted was to go home, change into loose pjs, eat the cold pizza in her fridge, and binge watch a sitcom where everything wrong got tied up in a neat little comedic bow within 20 minutes.

What Summer wanted, however, didn't have any relevance to this moment. She asked Derek to dinner as a strategic move: get him into a public place before revealing the plan she and Andrew had developed that afternoon. A public place would ensure he wouldn't lose his shit. Derek had enough pride to resist acting out where others, especially complete strangers, could witness it.

Ultimately, that's what she wanted. She wanted the kingdom to be protected so it could flourish. She wanted to help the princes do their jobs well so that, one day, she could stake her claim as queen.

All other wants were just temporary distractions.

Summer didn't need to say it out loud; Derek knew how to read her.

What she wanted didn't include anyone else, not even him.

For a second, she wondered if he would push the issue, but then, in true Derek fashion, he looked away from her and said, "Ah, we're here. I'm looking forward to that steak."

Here we go.

Adriana's brain registered that her body was moving against her will and instructed it to stop. Her muscles immediately obeyed and jerked to attention, waking Adriana up in time to catch herself from falling forward in her seat. Slowly, the pieces fell into place.

The train had stopped.

Mackenzie and the other passengers were gathering their items.

The phone in her hand buzzed with a text from Mackenzie to their group thread letting Sadie know they had arrived at Union Station.

Her heart still beat at an anxiety-induced pace.

The phone in her hand buzzed again. This time it was from Sadie:

Awesome! I'm in the Great Hall. Meet me there.

Adriana took a breath and willed her heart to slow its rhythm.

Start with what you know to be true, came the instruction.

Good idea.

Yes, they were in Chicago.

Yes, they were at Union Station.

No they weren't at the Lincoln Park Zoo.

Yes, Mackenzie was with her. Yes, they were meeting Sadie.

Sadie was here. Sadie wasn't in danger.

Not yet.

Adriana shook her head to rid herself of the premonition.

Mackenzie's hand waving toward her, caught Adriana's attention. She pointed at Adriana and then formed an "O" and a "K" with her fingers. Her eyebrows furrowed downwards into the ASL equivalent of a question mark. She signed, "You okay? You look like you've seen a ghost."

Adriana shook her head. "I'm fine," she signed back. "Bad dream," she added, using her voice as she swiped away notifications on her phone. She turned the phone to Mackenzie. "Wish we were there."

"New York?" Mackenzie asked, shuffling into the aisle as the other passengers moved.

Adriana filed into the aisle after Mackenzie. "Yeah. It looks like such a fun event. Wish I had won the tickets."

Mackenzie turned her face toward Adriana so she could read her lips. "But then you'd miss out on the sheer joy of spending the next few days with me, learning everything you never wanted to know about gene therapy."

Adriana feigned shock. "What *was* I thinking?"

"You just woke up. You were momentarily confused." Mackenzie's eyes dropped to watch her footing as she stepped down from the train.

"True." Adriana followed Mackenzie's descent.

Mackenzie waited until Adriana was next to her to resume their conversation. "Plus"—the sarcasm dropped from Mackenzie's eyes, and adoration took its place—"you would have missed the brilliant Andrew Salvatore!"

"But," Adriana protested, "I would have gotten to see the brilliant Katie Ellison."

"Come on, you're not comparing a novelist to a genius scientist who has revolutionized his industry, and he's barely older than we are?"

"Um, isn't he like forty?"

"No! He's thirty-six."

"Um, barely older? I'd say a lot—"

"You're here!"

Adriana resisted the urge to reach up and turn down her hearing aid as Sadie and Mackenzie hugged and shrieked and excitedly jumped up and down.

Stay alert. The enemy is on the prowl.

The thought came and went quickly, taking with it the smile on Adriana's lips. This was going to be a long week.

Image Enticed

MY MORNING COMMUTE INTO the Loop, the downtown district of Chicago, is a simple one: I jump on the Red Line L two blocks away from my apartment and within a half an hour, I'm serenading employees on the way to their desk jobs in skyscrapers.

Once the morning commuters have entered their buildings, I serenade the tourists milling around taking in the sights.

In the evening, I travel on the L back toward my apartment, jumping off in the Lincoln Park neighborhood, with its million-dollar homes, to serenade the residents as they grab a bite to eat on weeknights and hit the bars on the weekends. My commute ends in Uptown when I walk in the door of my 400 square foot studio apartment.

I haven't always lived in the city. I grew up an hour and a half north in a little town called Waukegan. At least, it was little back in the 60s—and I couldn't wait to get out of it.

I was the first of my family to make it to college. First of my family to have a career, not just a job.

I fought my way past the competition, the racism, the incompetent bosses—clawed my way to the top. And when I got there, the adrenaline went straight to my head.

I thought I was untouchable. I was so wrong.

My business card was the first thing to go. Then the cars. Then the house. Then my wife and son.

The streets became my home until the mission gave me another. It was there that a violin was placed in my hands—a tool to scrape the rust from my joints and restore purpose to my soul. With purpose came a new home, and a predictable daily commute to and from it.

Except yesterday evening.

Yesterday, I had heard *linger* and obeyed.

It shouldn't have surprised me when Derek and Summer appeared shortly after; I'd been playing on that particular corner for the past two years and had seen them—and others from InnovGene—often.

The first time Andrew walked by me, it was unnerving. There he was, in the flesh—the man who had turned my world upside down. The only reason I kept playing that corner was because the Spirit told me to.

Over time, seeing them each morning became less and less jarring. Eventually, Andrew stopped walking past me altogether, opting for a car service instead of public transit.

Now, I don't think I could play anywhere else. Though, I do I find it easier to extend grace and forgiveness when the violin rests on my shoulder, gripped by my chin. I can lose myself in the notes that sing of the grace and forgiveness extended to me.

But last night felt different.

Last night, I felt seen.

Last night, I felt pitied.

And my bruised ego—once laid to rest—sprang to my defense, inviting bitterness to keep me company. Then anger pulled up a seat at the table for a moment, though I sent him away before he could flip it. Shame tapped in, switching places with bitterness. The commute home felt long, and my bed was a much-needed sanctuary.

Thank God for new mornings.

And new mercies.

Without them, I wouldn't be on the Red Line this morning, heading once more into the Loop and to my street corner.

The train doors open at the Grand Avenue stop, and I pull my violin case closer between my legs, hoping to make more room for those filing into the Red Line car around me—and to better secure the valuable instrument.

They barely make it onto the train before the doors slide shut, each young woman carrying a coffee in hand. Two of them sit on the seat opposite me, while the third stands, gripping the pole. Her silky black hair and deep brown eyes command attention, though her body language announces she would rather fade into the background.

I feel it start and wish it would stop.

Oh, Lord, not today.

The prayer is unanswered, and it begins.

First, the vibration: the heavy train door closing.

Then, the sound: the distorted announcement of the zoo closing.

Finally, an image: The brown-haired one no longer sits across from me. She stands in the lion's den, the keeper's door having slammed shut behind her.

Before her stretches a wall of steps, crafted to resemble a natural rock formation, beckoning her to descend further into the lion's domain. Just feet away, the lion lies poised, his head crowned with a lush mane and raised in sharp awareness of her presence. His tail sways in a slow, deliberate rhythm, marking the passage of each second as she hesitates, weighing her next move.

I have to stop her.

I grip the fence railing and heave myself over it, both relieved there is no one around to witness the bumbling effort and that I can actually get over the railing.

A slight tinge crawls up my legs as my feet hit the ground.

I ignore it. I have to get to her.

I have to stop her before she gets killed.

Before she gets maimed.

The clarification stops me in my tracks, and it's a good thing, too, because in the pause, I realize there is a deep moat that separates me from the lion and the girl.

As if mesmerized by the lion, she reaches out toward him but immediately retracts her hand. She slowly lowers herself down to the top step, hugging her knees to her chest. Her knees protrude from the distressed holes in her jeans.

"Get out of there!" I feel my vocal cords vibrate and my lips move, but no sound comes from my mouth, so I wave my arms back and forth—completely aware of how useless the act is. I look around frantically for a solution. I have to get to her before she reaches out again.

Out to the lion.

Out to the one ready to take advantage of her.

She lets one arm drop from her knees to the ground beside her. Her fingers run along the cracks in the concrete. She looks down and studies them for a moment, tracing the lines.

Noticing her gaze has moved off of him, the lion rises and begins pacing, his eyes never leaving her.

His prey.

She looks up, past the lion, out past the edge of the zoo to the city skyline, lit up against the night sky. A small smile finds its way to her lips. Hooking a strand of hair behind her ear, she stands and takes a step toward the keeper's door.

She's leaving the den. Relief washes over me.

A low rumbling growl stops her.

She turns back to the lion, more intrigued than terrified.

Why isn't she scared?

As if hearing my silent question, the young woman's eyes raise to meet mine. She shrugs just slightly, an answer that drives even more panic into my limbs.

And with the panic, an immense sense of helplessness;
I can't get to her. I can't stop her.

But she can. Look up.

There she is, the dark-haired one. The one that wants
to fade into the background.

The one created to make waves but refuses to do so.

She stands at the keeper's door, surveying the situation and wearing trepidation like a cloak.

The brown-haired one takes a step toward the lion,
who has not stopped pacing.

She pauses, glancing back at her friend.

Only for a second, though.

She's back to her descent before either of us can even
blink.

I start my own panicked pacing, matching the
prey-tracking pace of the lion.

The lion paces a few feet closer to the young woman.

She takes a step down, her eyes fixed on the ripple of
the lion's muscles as he paces.

The dark-haired one follows her. I can see her lips
move, but just like I struggled just moments to make a
sound, nothing comes from the friend's mouth.

The brown-haired one has reached the last keeper
step. She will have to jump down to be on the same level
as the lion. It's enough to make her question her choice,
and she hesitates. In response, the lion lies down, making himself look like a playful and gentle big cat.

Her friend has only made it halfway down the steps.

Neither of us will reach her in time.

She's lingering.

Staying longer than necessary. One lingers when
you're reluctant to leave because something, or someone, has your attention.

The lion and the young woman lock eyes. She smiles.

I suddenly understand; we don't have to reach her—we just have to break her attention.

I wave my hands in the air again, this time to get the friend's attention. "Hey!" I yell as loudly as I can as I jump up and down. This time, the sound comes out of my mouth. "Get her attention! Make her look at you."

But, the dark-haired one doesn't hear me. She doesn't do anything either. She just stands there, frozen in place.

With a decisive move, the brown-haired one uses her hands to push herself off the edge and down to the lion's level. Her feet hit the floor. Dirt flies up with the action.

"Get her attention!" I yell again.

She takes a step toward the lion.

"Stop!" I yell.

She reaches out her right hand to him, but turns away from him, as if she isn't completely sure she wants to do what she is about to do.

"Don't do it!" I want to yell again, but my voice has once again gone silent.

My hands, however, move. I hold my left hand flat, palm up, and bring my right hand, the palm of which faces me, sharply down on top of the left hand. The result is an X of sorts.

Instinctively, I know the meaning of the motion: Stop!

I make the movement again.

Then again.

The dark-haired one finally notices me.

She raises her own hands, understanding filling her eyes; she makes the movement as well. Timid at first, then again, stronger.

The movement captures the attention of the young woman on the lion's level. She looks up at me, the helplessness I feel echoed in her eyes. *Help me.*

The lion pounces.

She raises her hands in defense.

I raise my arms to shield my eyes, unable to watch the slaughter.

I take a second to realize the train has pulled to a stop, and the image has ended. Realizing it's my stop, I gather my belongings and stand from my seat.

The doors close just as I'm about to exit the train and, not wanting to tempt the reflex of the sensors, choose to wait until the next stop to get off. In the Loop, the stops are only a block or two from one another, and I can walk easily to my usual corner. Leaning against the back of a set of seats near the door, I stabilize myself as the train lurches back into action. I notice the dark-haired one is still standing. "Excuse me, do you want my seat?" I ask her.

She doesn't respond.

"She's deaf." The blonde-haired woman, who, I suddenly realize, wasn't in the image, answers me. She waves in the woman's direction, then uses a flurry of sign language to ask my question. The dark-haired one turns toward me and smiles. "Thank you." She says audibly while also signing it. She takes my offered seat.

It's not very long before the train pulls into the next station. I reposition my belongings, ready for my exit this time.

Tell her.

I sigh. *Really?*

Tell her.

She can't hear me.

She can read lips.

I know it's true.

Before I can change my mind, I move my hands the same way I did in the image. It works—she looks at me with a quizzical look on her face.

"Watch out for the lion." I say quietly so no one can hear me, but she can see my lips move.

Her eyes widen with surprise.

"Pardon?" she asks instinctively.

She got it.

The doors open. "I said, have a blessed day." I answer with a big smile, loudly this time.

The other two women smile. "Thanks!" they both chime in response.

But the dark-haired one remains silent. Her gaze fixed on me as I exit the train and head toward the stairs leading to the street. At the base of the steps, I pause and glance back at the train, catching a glimpse of her still watching me—her expression intent, as if trying to unravel a puzzle.

Day Three

O. M. G.

Mackenzie gripped Adriana's arm—and her attention—while signing the letters with an emphasized pause between each. Her face joined in the exaggeration, lips forming each letter and eyes widening with an expression that announced she had locked eyes on the infamous Andrew Salvatore.

Following Mackenzie's slight head nod, Adriana discovered they were indeed mere feet from the man who, according to Mackenzie, had the most brilliant mind to exist in this decade. Mackenzie continued, now turning her back to Andrew Salvatore and keeping her hand movements smaller and closer to her body, as to confide in only Adriana. "Dang ... look how gorgeous he is. How did he get so lucky? Smart and stunning?"

Adriana rolled her eyes at Mackenzie's swooning and put a hand on each of her shoulders. Using her voice, Adriana admonished Mackenzie to "get a hold of yourself, woman," before stepping around her to resume her journey toward the front row, where an interpreter was already conversing with other Deaf and hard-of-hearing individuals.

With a few quick steps, Mackenzie caught up to Adriana and signed, "We're going to walk right by him! Do you think he'll notice us? Should I introduce myself to him? I probably should introduce myself. I mean, when will I have this chance again? I should do it. How do I look?"

Adriana stopped, forcing Mackenzie to do the same. Letting the sharpness of her movements and facial expression underscore her annoyance with Mackenzie's rambling, she signed, "Seriously, knock it off. You're causing a scene."

Mackenzie crossed her arms. "Jeez. No need to get salty about it. What's the deal?" She didn't bother signing.

Adriana had turned on her hearing aids that morning, but they simply blended the many voices in the room together into one steady hum, mixed it with the upbeat music emitting from the overhead speakers, and crashed it into sounds of chairs' edges hitting one another as individuals shuffled into seats, forcing Adriana to rely on reading lips. Not her favorite thing, since Mackenzie was prone to using slang that wasn't always the easiest to catch. She managed the gist of her roommate's response, however.

The truth? Adriana was only here because it was mandatory for one of her classes, an ethics in scientific advancements class Mackenzie had talked her into taking together to fulfill a credit requirement. Being a liberal arts college, even though Adriana's major was in business, she had to take classes in different disciplines for a "well-rounded education." Mackenzie had insisted that it would be fun to take a class together and Mackenzie was a hard one to say no to. Neither of them expected the class to include a conference, but their professor was friends with one of the conference committee members and had gotten the class comped tickets. "You don't get it," Mackenzie had explained to Adriana, "This is like the *it* conference in gene therapy and biotech advancements. Anyone who is anyone in this industry will be there. We're so lucky to attend!"

It didn't really matter how "lucky" they were; events like this were hard for Adriana to navigate, even with the help of an interpreter. Actually, it was the fact that she had to rely on the interpreter during events like these (no matter how grateful she was for said interpreter) that generated such an uneasiness for Adriana; using an interpreter meant she stuck out even more in the crowd than she already did. Being the center of attention was the last thing in the world Adriana wanted, while the limelight for Mackenzie was her zone of genius. On top of all this, sat the pressure to collect enough fodder for the required reflective paper due on Tuesday.

If Adriana was being honest with herself, though, it wasn't college expectations or hearing impairment that had her on edge this morning. No, that honor belonged to the hours-long conversation in Sadie's living room the night before, where Sadie quizzed Mackenzie relentlessly for tips on the art of flirtation, and Mackenzie rambled on about Andrew Salvatore's many theories and philosophies on life—many of which she had adopted as her own. It was a toss-up between which bugged her more, Sadie acting so out of character or Mackenzie being so in the groove of hers.

Freshman year brought Sadie into her life during an on-campus Bible study. They quickly connected over shared values and started attending church together. Sophomore year introduced Mackenzie to her during a meet-up for deaf and hard-of-hearing students on campus. Mackenzie showed up to get extra credit for an advanced ASL class she was taking. Even though she still signed with a hearing accent, her fluency with the language stood out. As their friendship grew, Adriana would realize that everything Mackenzie did stood out.

It was Mackenzie who had suggested they room together junior year. Despite a rocky start learning to navigate vastly different worldviews and living wildly different lifestyles, they fell into a good rhythm as roommates.

"I'm sorry," Adriana voiced to Mackenzie, then added in ASL, "I'm just having a hard time with all the commotion."

Immediately, Mackenzie's body language changed from irritation to full-blown apologetic as her hands hurriedly signed, "Oh, girl, of course! Yeah, this place's a vibe, for sure. We're definitely not in Kansas, Toto. Just turn your hearing aids off until they start. I'll interpret, if you need it. Come on." Mackenzie finished leading the way to the front, allowing herself one more covert glance Andrew Salvatore's way as they rounded the end of the row just feet away from him and headed toward their designated seating. Noticing them approaching, the interpreter introduced herself and explained that besides the main sessions, there would be an interpreter available at each breakout session. Adriana thanked her and took her seat next to Mackenzie.

Adriana's eyes scanned the room, processing more information in the quick glance than anyone else would have, even if they had studied it for a full ten minutes. Her position at the front of the room coupled with the lack of hearing brought into sharp focus the visual for Adriana. She took in the slump of shoulders and narrowing in of eyes on phone screens, for some a shield against conversation and for others a necessity as work to-dos refused to stay at the office. She also noted necks craning for familiar faces and hands waving wildly in the air to catch their attention. Wide smiles, friendly yet professional, and outstretched hands were offered to new contacts. Jackets were shrugged off and tucked under seats, along with purses and swag bags. Seat partners swapped stories, jokes, and chuckles. Conference staff conversed with venue staff, verifying checklists on clipboards and adjusting expectations with hand flourishes. Coffee cups (most from the cart outside the room, with a smattering of thermoses) in one hand and programs in the other. The energy in the room was palatable: a mix of optimism, excitement, curiosity, nervousness, and possibility.

And then there was Andrew Salvatore.

Now seated with one leg crossed over the other and the program open in her lap, she let her curiosity get the best of her and glanced the way of the man Mackenzie swore was the greatest thing since sliced bread.

Her roommate wasn't lying when she said he was stunning. From head to toe, the man had constructed his look with intentionality and care. His dark hair, styled in a voluminous quiff, swept upward with effortless precision, the thick strands tapering toward the back. It boasted just enough texture to make the style feel relaxed, a sharp contrast to the neatly trimmed sides. He was clean-shaven and the slim-cut jacket of his charcoal gray suit fit him perfectly, its sharp lines emphasizing his broad shoulders. Paired with a crisp white shirt and a dark tie, his polished yet understated look exuded confidence.

Expensive too. Adriana thought.

There was no trace of tension or nervousness in Andrew Salvatore's posture as he raised a coffee cup—fresh from the cart, not a thermos—to his lips with smooth, unhurried ease. It was obvious; Andrew Salvatore belonged here. Not just here at the conference, but here ready to take the stage. Lowering the cup, Andrew rested it casually in the palm of his hand, his gaze drifting across the room. Adriana quickly dropped her eyes to her program.

Mackenzie leaned over and gave a small, quick wave to catch Adriana's attention. "I think I'm going to go up and introduce myself." She signed.

Adriana pulled her hands down quickly, using the sign for "right now?" She glanced over at Andrew Salvatore, now holding his phone in one hand, his thumb moving briskly across the screen. A smirk crossed his face before he tapped the screen and slipped the device back into his pocket. Where calm confidence had previously defined his posture, a hint of forced nonchalance now took its place. I *wonder what that's about.* Thought Adriana. To Mackenzie, however, she signed a quick "You, do you."

Mackenzie nodded, then signed, "Yeah, I think I'm going to go." She didn't move from her spot, however, rather simply uncrossed her legs, then crossed the opposite one over. Her roommate's hesitation brought a smile to Adriana's face. *Maybe she's not as invincible as she likes people to think.*

Come now, that's not so kind, is it?

Eh, probably not.

Probably?

Okay, yeah, it wasn't. Adriana resisted huffing at the conviction. *She's human, like the rest of us.*

Suddenly finding her missing bravado, Mackenzie rose from her seat but froze mid-motion as a woman approached Andrew. The woman, clad in a crisp white blouse tucked into a camel-toned, high-waisted midi skirt paired with brown leather ankle boots, exuded effortless style. Together, the couple looked like a scene from a magazine spread, their polished appearance showcasing the kind of wardrobe Adriana could only dream of affording once she became a big-time executive years from now.

"Wife?" Adriana included a quizzical expression with the sign.

Mackenzie leaned in close, as if disclosing a salacious piece of gossip, and signed, "Oh, god, no. That's Summer Harlow. She's the one Sadie thinks is so cool. Sadie said one of the interns told her that Summer and Andrew's brother Derek—that's the one Sadie's got a crush on—dated way back in the day. Those two do look cozy, though, don't they?"

Adriana let her surprise show on her face and asked, "How do you know that?"

"I checked out InnovGene's website. She's one of the top dogs there. Her picture is on it."

The house lights dimmed.

"Guess it's too late now." Mackenzie signed, resigned to the fact she'd have to wait to make an introduction.

He's on the prowl. Be alert.

The command poured over Adriana like ice water and shocked every nerve in her body to attention. *Wait,* she prayed as her brain tried to process what had just happened. *I thought that was about Sadie.*

No response came.

The MC took the stage, and the interpreter jumped into action.

Mackenzie pursed her lips together and signed casually, "We're here for three days. There's time." She nodded her head slightly, as if she'd adequately convinced herself.

"Yeah, you'll get your chance," Adriana agreed while fighting against the unrest in her own soul at the thought.

———— · ————

While Mackenzie swooned over one Salvatore brother in the main conference room, Sadie tried to be helpful at the InnovGene booth in the expo hall while keeping an eye out for the other.

Blair knew she should just tell the girl that Derek wasn't planning on dropping by the booth until the expo hour later that afternoon and put a stop to the craning neck and darting eyes, but the expo hall was empty, the booth ready to go, and Blair was bored. She started counting how many times she caught Sadie stealing a glance toward the entrance. The count was up to sixteen when her cell vibrated in her jacket pocket. Blair flipped it open to a new text notification. She opened the message and read:

hey babe. when do you get done today?

She typed back:

5pm. But it's Wednesday.

The response was quick:

wanna grab dinner before?

Blair considered the suggestion for a moment, trying to figure out if the timing would work. Sounds good, she finally typed, then exited the application and flipped her phone closed. Just as she replaced her phone in her pocket, Sadie's once again wandering eyes caught her attention and Blair smirked. That made seventeen.

———·———

Katie watched Andrew take the stage via the conference livestream on her phone as she waited for Laura to pick her up from the hotel lobby. As usual, he looked right at home on the stage, a trait they did not share but in him she appreciated.

She wondered when Andrew became comfortable elevated in front of a vast crowd. He had been that way as long as she knew him. *It was probably Brenda's doing.*

The morning light streamed through the windows with a softness that begged to be noticed, laying across the tile and illuminating a pathway from the glass to the middle of the lobby. For even the most cynical of writers, light like that would elicit from their dark soul a desire to wax eloquent about how light breaks through even the most challenging of times. But Katie's eyes were glued to the tiny screen in her hand, missing the fodder for poetry.

Instead, she studied the video of her husband, as if she could deduce from the five minutes he spent welcoming the attendees and offering them three points for making the most out of the conference before sending them on their way, if he missed her.

Because he should be missing her by now, right? She had been gone for more than 24 hours, and they hadn't talked or texted.

Just like you wanted.

Right. She let him off the hook while she was gone. She didn't think he would actually take her up on it.

He has a lot on his mind. Lots of stress.

The livestream of the main stage paused as conference goers shuffled from their seats to new ones in their chosen workshop sessions.

Yes, there was a lot on Andrew's mind ... she just wasn't one of those things.

You know that's not true.

Do I?

She shook her head to rid herself of the conflicted self-talk.

You are not alone.

She sighed. That was not self-talk. That was a reminder from the Spirit.

I just wish he was here with me. I just wish things were different, she prayed. On second thought added, *Not different, better. No ... deeper? More ...*

Honest.

There it was. The answer. Somewhere along the way, something had gotten into Andrew's mind and convinced him she wasn't for him. That she didn't support him fully. But that was the furthest thing from the truth.

Closing out the conference app, Katie swiped up on her social media apps, first checking Andrew's accounts, then Summer's and Derek's. None of them had posted updates, so she switched over to InnovGene's profile. The social media team was hard at work, capturing scenes of the conference from all the different perspectives. In a picture of the InnovGene booth in the Expo Hall, Blair stood at a high-top reviewing a clipboard, the boredom on her face clear to Katie. "You got roped into that, huh?" She muttered, swiping to the next picture.

It was a picture of Andrew studying a note card while waiting to take the stage.

He looked good.

Katie looked up from the screen, a sudden desire to share the photo with someone else taking over her. An empty chair met her glance, its pleated fabric seat, high back, and plush arms looking eerily like a laughing face. She frowned and looked back down at her phone.

With a few taps, the photo was shared to her own account with the added caption "proud of this brainiac."

She switched back over to Andrew's profile. The guy wasn't into the whole social media scene; he was too busy creating solutions for brokenness in people's bodies. Occasionally, when big things happened for the company or major life events occurred, he shared a glimpse of his life with the public.

Swiping up on the screen a handful of times brought the photo she sought into focus. The one from the beginning: Andrew and Derek standing in front of the set of windows that overlooked Lake Michigan. Between them, they held the brand-new InnovGene sign—a wild, optimistic excitement plastered on their faces.

Summer wasn't there either, and he trusts her with his secrets.

"Katie?"

Saved from drowning in speculation and self-pity by Laura's approach, Katie quickly closed the application before looking up at her publicist. The smile she forced onto her face was a shield, guarding her from Laura's uncanny ability to read trouble in a person's body language.

"Ready to go?" Laura asked, taking in the bags at Katie's feet.

"Yep." Katie nodded.

Following the carpeted flooring of the conference hallway like the yellow brick road leading to OZ, Andrew made his way to the first breakout session and the industry insights it promised to divulge. Blair made him swear on the grave of Dolly the Sheep that he would actually attend a few breakout sessions instead of just getting wrapped up in making deals and scratching backs. "You are a scientist first. Business guy after that." She reminded him with a shake of her finger.

"Hey, Salvatore!" A cheerful voice fell on Andrew's ear.

"Frenchie!" Moving his coffee to his left hand, he reached out and clasped the man's hand.

Frenchie's already wide smile grew. "I haven't heard anyone call me that in a couple of years."

Andrew shrugged, "Sorry, old habit."

"No, no. I like it. Reminds me of the old days when we were bright eyed and bushy tailed."

"As opposed to?"

"Stress lines around our eyes and gray in our hair, what's left of it."

Andrew ran his hand over his thick hair. "Speak for yourself."

"You may not be balding like me, but the stress lines around your eyes are as deep as the potholes on I-94."

Andrew let a groan escape his lips in mock hurt before asking Frenchie what he was doing at the conference.

"Teaching one of the breakout sessions.

"How'd you end up with that gig?"

"I missed a meeting."

"Oof. I feel that. Jensen wouldn't let you out of it?"

Surprise flashed across Frenchie's face. "I thought you knew."

"Knew what?"

"That I'm with GenTech."

"Well, I won't hold that against you."

"I appreciate it."

Frenchie glanced around the room. "Is Katie here with you?"

It wouldn't be the last time he'd heard that question over the next few days. Over the years, Katie endured workshop topics she didn't understand and conversations that often turned technical or work-related while being ever her charming self. He raised his coffee cup and took a sip to hide any red that might have made its way to his face. "Not yet." He took a sip before answering. "She's out of town, but will be here on Friday."

Frenchie smiled, "Find me on Friday then, so I can say hi. It feels like ages since the last time I saw her. Oh, I can have her sign my copy of her new book."

Andrew's countenance tensed, but he kept his voice relaxed. "Will do."

He pointed at Andrew's coffee cup. "I should have gotten myself a cup."

"There's a coffee bar across from the main session room."

"That's right." Frenchie glanced at his watch. "I think I can do it. Save me a seat?"

"Sure."

———— . ————

Summer had to hand it to the conference center—they had mastered the art of catering to attendees' two biggest needs: caffeine and connections. The strategically placed coffee bar served as both a refueling station and an informal networking hub, ensuring a steady stream of traffic—and revenue. It was a smart business move, and Summer had to admit she was impressed.

But the space served another purpose—one that mattered only to her. From her vantage point, she had a clear line of sight to her target, seated four tables away, shooting the breeze with a group of attendees. Raising the paper cup to her lips, Summer coaxed the last drop of coffee past her lips, eyeing her prey over the plastic lid.

Now empty, the cup sat in her hands, reduced to a fidget toy. If she timed it right, she could make this seem natural, taking any suspicion out of the situation. She had overheard one of them mention the time and knew it was just a matter of minutes before the group would stand and make their way to the first breakout session. When they did, she would be ready.

Summer played with the side of the coffee cup, pressing into it with the tips of her acrylic nails. What if they didn't plan to attend the first session? What if they were those attendees who skipped lectures to network? She glanced at her watch. There was still time.

What if you can't cut it?

Choosing to ignore the doubt-filled thought, Summer pretended to take another sip of coffee and check her phone to keep up the innocent act. They couldn't know she was staking them out. To be found out would be to reek of desperation and any bargaining upper-hand lost.

There it was! Another mention of heading to the session. This time it seemed to make a difference, and the group stood from the table, throwing away wrappers and gathering belongings.

Summer stood as well, bypassing the bin nearest her and, instead, walking to the can near the group—intentionally catching the eye of her target and offering a friendly smile. She tossed her empty cup with a nothing-but-net flourish.

Fully expecting all eyes to be on her when she turned around, Summer managed a slight hair flip as she executed the action, employing all her feminine charms to reel in her big fish. She smirked at the ease of it all.

The smile dropped from her lips as her own eyes took in the sight of Larson Carr grasping the hand of her prospect, his free hand patting the man's shoulder. Their handshake was firm and their smiles wide. Continuing their conversation, the group moved like a blob down the hallway toward the breakout rooms. And just like that, the window of opportunity closed.

You're losing your touch.

Well, if the Universe would toss a bone in my way ...

Summer shouldered her purse and turned, this time forgoing the dramatic hair flip, only to walk straight into the chest of another conference attendee.

"Ope," he muttered, steadying her by gently grabbing her shoulders after the collision.

"Michael?"

"Summer?"

She tossed a mental *Nicely played* to the Universe. To Michael she said, "Wow, it's been forever!"

"It has. I actually just ran into Andrew."

"Oh, really? Good. I'm sure he was glad to see you. Congrats, by the way, on your move to GenTech. I hear you landed yourself a pretty cushy position there."

He nodded. "It's pretty sweet, if I do say so myself."

Summer opened her purse and pulled out her wallet. "Hey, can I buy you a coffee? I would love to pick your ear about something."

Sensing a shift in the conversation, Michael hesitated. His eyes followed her wave toward the coffee bar, then landing squarely back on her, searching for the intention behind the question. "I'm supposed to meet Andrew in a session. He's saving me a seat."

"Oh, he won't mind." She smiled sweetly. "I'm sure of it."

———— ▪ ————

Andrew ducked into the breakout room and settled into a seat in a corner in the back of the room, attempting to cut off an approach by a peer or novice. True to his word, he reserved the seat to his left with his program for Frenchie. As a last defense, he retrieved his phone from the inner pocket of his jacket and assumed a posture of focus. To those in the room, he looked engrossed in email and business decisions, but in actuality, Andrew was scrolling social media. He hardly felt the need to post, but because of her work as a writer, Katie had a vibrant, daily presence. So, while he didn't go looking for her profile, she popped up in his feed almost immediately.

"She looked good, didn't she?" Derek's question jolted Andrew's gaze away from the picture of his wife at the book launch party. He looked up to find his brother standing in front of him.

"When did you get here?"

"To the conference? About 10 minutes ago." Derek motioned over his shoulder toward the sea of people. "I saw Summer in the lobby talking to Michael Dunning."

"Oh? I'm saving a seat for him." Andrew returned his phone to his pocket. "But this one is open."

Derek unbuttoned his suit jacket and sat on Andrew's right. "She filled me in last night."

"Summer?"

"Took me to a restaurant to tell me."

"Smart."

"Yep."

A tiredness hung around the corners of Derek's eyes, even more than usual for his brother.

If he can't stand the heat ... Andrew mentally shooed the doubt away and replaced it with concern. "You okay with this?" He asked Derek, a protective tone tingeing his words. As soon as Derek's eyes narrowed in response, Andrew knew he had made the wrong move. "I mean, I'm not sure I'm okay with it, so I can only guess what you ..." His rambling slowed. "...think of it," he finished weakly.

Derek eyed him steadily, as if debating between two courses of action. Finally, he let out a long breath, his cheeks puffing as a quiet "well" slipped past his lips. "Um, I'm not sure how to take it."

"We've got everything under control." It was surprisingly uttered with convincing confidence.

"You know—"

"Welcome!" the session's moderator commanded the room before introducing the speaker for the hour.

Derek leaned over and whispered, "Do you need me there tonight?"

The thought of the pending interaction with Carr later brought a hollowness to the pit of Andrew's stomach. "I don't think so."

"Will Summer be there?"

The question behind the question lingered between them as Andrew contemplated how to answer his brother. Wasn't Derek past this? It had been four years since Summer took the role of COO. Besides, it had been Summer who came to his office yesterday and helped him make a plan. Derek could have done the same, but he didn't. *That's why he doesn't have the job.*

Deciding simplicity was the best course of action, Andrew answered, "Yes."

Derek smiled, tapping the top of his knee as he crossed his leg. "Great." The smile was fake, of course. *Just like his influence over InnovGene.* Andrew brushed a piece of lint from his jacket and flicked it away. His phone vibrated.

Meeting set up for 12:30. Pinnacle Bistro.

Andrew tipped the phone toward Derek and whispered, "She did it."

Derek viewed the message, his lips pressing into a thin line. "Of course she did," he answered, keeping his eyes on the speaker. "She's Summer."

———·———

"There she is." Mackenzie pointed to Sadie standing at the InnovGene booth. The booth was massive, occupying the entire corner where two aisles converged at the front of the Expo Hall. Sadie seemed small as the towering display boards loomed over her.

Almost lost. Adriana thought as they made their way toward the girl.

Not quite, but getting there.

Adriana tucked the correction in the back pocket of her mind, having learned by now that if the Holy Spirit dropped a nugget of insight, there would be a reason for it later.

Sadie was the only employee in the booth not assisting an attendee, but she stood nearby, listening in on a conversation with a female coworker. When she noticed their approach, her face lit up with excitement as she eagerly made her way over. "You're here!"

"We're here to whisk you away to lunch. Ooh, candy." Mackenzie exclaimed, selecting a mini chocolate bar off the display table and immediately unwrapping it.

Sadie turned to Adriana. "How was this morning?"

"Not as bad as I thought it would be. I went to a session called *Building a Biotech Company*. That was pretty interesting."

"Yeah, she totally ditched me this last session." Mackenzie chimed in.

"Sorry, but I wasn't about to suffer through a presentation on the latest in CRISPR-Cas9 research."

"Your loss. It was fascinating. Can you leave?"

Sadie glanced around, looking for someone. Not seeing them, she turned to a nearby woman interacting with an attendee. Sadie waited for their conversation to end, then she asked, "Blair, do you know where Derek is? I am trying to figure out if I can go get lunch."

Blair repeated Sadie's action of glancing around before shrugging. "I have no idea where he is." She glanced down at her watch. "Go ahead. I'll hang back here with Amit and Ken. We can hold down the fort."

Sadie nodded. "Okay. Then, after lunch, I think I'm supposed to attend sessions. Should I check back in here, or just go, do you think?"

Blair contemplated the question, her eyes narrowing as she tapped a finger against her cheek. "I'm not really sure. How about this? You go to lunch, then go to the sessions. Then, check back in before you head home. I'll let Derek know that's the plan."

"Sounds good." She turned to Mackenzie and Adriana. "These are the friends I was telling you about this morning."

Blair smiled big. "Oh! Welcome!" She reached a hand out. "I'm Blair."

Mackenzie used her fingers to spell Blair's name to Adriana before taking the outstretched hand. "I'm Mackenzie. This is Adriana."

Blair swiped her right hand over her left palm. Next, she pointed both index fingers and brought them toward each other, like little people greeting each other. She finished by pointing to Adriana.

Adriana's face registered her surprise. "You know ASL?" she signed the question while voicing it.

Blair shook her head. "That's all I've got. Sadie taught me that this morning. It's been ridiculously slow in here until about an hour ago."

"Well," Adriana smiled, "It's nice to meet you too."

"Hey." Blair turned back to Sadie. "Don't forget about tonight. It'll be fun, I promise." She traced a cross over her heart and held up a hand as if swearing to the truth.

"Will do." Sadie answered as she collected her purse.

As they walked out of the Expo Hall, Adriana asked Sadie what Blair meant.

"Oh, she invited us to join her and her friends at a bar tonight."

"Wicked." Mackenzie said as she quickened her steps toward a directory map to locate the food court.

"It's all good," Sadie assured Adriana.

"What's all good?"

"It's not really a bar, more of a bar and grill. And it's with Blair's church small group. They get together for Bible study on Wednesdays, but tonight they are just hanging out."

"Okay," Adriana said slowly, not sure where Sadie was going with the conversation.

"I know it's not Mackenzie's scene, but this is someone from work." Sadie's cadence quickened and Adriana zeroed in on her lips to keep up. "She's really cool, and she's up there a bit on the corporate ladder at the company. This could be a really good connection for me later on in life. Plus, how often do we get to hang out in the city together?"

Adriana raised her hands both to slow Sadie's speech and calm her anxiety. "Hey, you don't have to convince me. I'm game."

Sadie winced. "Do you think Mackenzie will care?"

Adriana shook her head. "Nah."

"Oh good." The tension released from Sadie's shoulders. "Besides, she'll get that whole party vibe she likes at the event tomorrow night."

Before Adriana could respond, Mackenzie bounced back over and pointed off to their right. "That direction."

"Lead the way," Sadie instructed.

———— · ————

"Okay, we've done the catching-up part. Now, let's get to the part where you tell me what you want from me. Actually, first, I want you to explain why you went through Michael instead of just reaching out yourself? I mean, I saw you this morning. Thought you were coming over to say hi."

Fork and knife posed mid-slice into his steak, Steve Granger reminded Summer of a business tycoon dealing a sleazy deal in a movie. The resemblance ended there, however, as Granger had proven himself on more than one occasion to be a stand-up guy. Assertive but not cocky, smart but not full of himself.

Summer liked Granger. Summer respected Granger. Summer needed Granger to play ball.

She knew the only way to get him to do it was to lay their cards out on the table. On this point, she and Andrew had disagreed at length. Andrew didn't want to reveal too much too soon. Granger, though, valued efficiency, and Summer thought it best to play into that. In the end, Andrew deferred to her judgement and followed her lead. Even now, he turned to her to answer Granger's question.

"Carr."

"Ah." Granger resumed, slicing into his steak.

"I'm gonna level with you." Summer reached for her iced tea. "We want to end our ties with him. He's pushing for things that don't jibe with us. But ..." she trailed off, allowing Granger to come to his own conclusions.

He took a bite of his steak, then turned to Andrew. "He's been with you since the beginning, hasn't he?"

Andrew sliced into his own steak as he answered. "Yes, he has been. But, sometimes, business relationships need to adjust when those involved outgrow one another."

Granger raised an eyebrow. "You've outgrown him? Then what do you need me for? Which you do, right? Otherwise, we wouldn't be doing this right now."

Straight to the point. Efficient.

Summer took a sip. "He's outgrown us."

"But you can't continue without his investment?"

"We could for a bit, but money doesn't grow on trees." Summer shrugged, willing her body language to remain casual while internally fighting the nagging fear hanging out at the edges of her consciousness. "He's got a different agenda for InnovGene that doesn't jibe with the company's vision and mission." Jibe? *Why do I keep using that word?*

Granger sat back in his seat and eyed them both. Summer wondered if he too was judging her overuse of the word. Mirroring Granger, she sat back in her chair and rested on the arm.

He waved his hands as if juggling an invisible conundrum, then finally spoke. "I think I can guess what his agenda is. I've heard enough stories about the guy, but I'm struggling to see how GenTech fits into your vision."

Andrew's eyes fell on Summer, but she resisted looking at him. Doing so would undermine her position of authority on the matter. It was Andrew's company, but it was Summer's plan. A grenade that would blow up their dealings with Larson Carr once and for all.

Not all your dealings. The thought brought with it a wave of nausea. Summer suppressed both. *That's a problem for later,* she told herself.

Granger took her silence for a change of heart and tilted his head to the side. "Making a move like this—it's a tough call, I know. Believe it or not, I've been in your shoes before. I've been CEO of GenTech for fifteen years. Investors, board members, shareholders ... they all have grand plans for the company. Some, good." He shrugged before leaning back in his chair once again, this time crossing his arms. "Others, selfish."

Summer rolled her shoulders back and flashed a confident smile. "Carr's plan falls in the latter category. Which is why we're coming to you."

"Okay then." He unfolded his arms and retrieved his fork and knife. "Spill it."

"It has to do with our license for the regenerative gene therapy we're developing for accelerated healing." Andrew jumped in. This time, Summer let her gaze migrate toward him, letting him read her reproach in it. He responded with a slight nod of acknowledgement.

"We've been under review for a few months now," Summer explained. "You guys are about to go under review for your own regenerative gene therapy, right?"

Granger nodded, taking a sip of his soda as Summer continued, "Carr wants us to be a clear winner." A pause for emphasis. "We want our customers to be the winners."

"A laudable goal," Granger responded. "Still not seeing where we come into play."

Most men in business enjoy the cat-and-mouse dance that often finds its way into business dealings—it being the closest thing to scratching that primal itch to expand one's territory—but Andrew wasn't one of them. That's why he had Summer.

But, whether it was the ticking away of the clock that drew them closer to Carr's ultimatum or the cloud of marital conflict, something ate away at Andrew's typical tolerance for the game of business and brought forth annoyance, underscored by the clatter of fork against plate as he released it. "You're gonna make us spell it out, aren't you?" he asked.

Granger dragged his finger down the side of his glass, creating a condensation free path from top to bottom. "It's like he doesn't understand how this works." He looked up at Summer.

You're losing him.

Summer remained calm, her tone steady. "There would be fifteen percent profit-sharing for the first three years, a drop to five percent for the next two, with the share ending in the fifth year. Plus, we'll share any research and clinical trial data that could help you refine your product."

Granger leaned forward, eyes narrowing. "And all we have to do is?"

"Delay seeking licensing for a year," Summer responded smoothly.

Granger's jaw dropped in disbelief. "You've got to be kidding. I've got people to answer to, just like you."

Summer waved away his protest. "What's a year?"

"Two," Granger corrected. "A year to apply, then a year to get approved."

"2020. There's something about the turn of a decade. The press release practically writes itself." Noting too much patronizing in her tone, Summer backed off into a more genuine one. "Perfect timing to release a new product."

"Delaying licensing means delaying profit."

"Hence the offer of profit sharing."

"Fifteen percent is next to nothing."

"No," Summer tilted her head, "What's nothing is the profit you'll add to your bottom line while waiting for licensing. Which, even if you applied today, won't happen for at least a year. Maybe even longer."

"And gets pushed off even further if I agree to this."

"So, you get it then!" she said cheerfully. "You get to choose: delay and guarantee profit sharing now, and, in two years, collect on top of your own product's profit. Plus, your product will be stellar when you release because you'll benefit from our ground-breaking advances—and, let me assure you, there are several them. Or, apply now and wait to collect for two years, by which time we will have left you in our dust at the starting line." Summer picked up her fork, a first since the server delivered her salad, and brought a forkful of greens, fruit, and nuts to her mouth. "Mmm. This is delicious." She rested her fork on the plate and picked up a napkin. The dab was dainty at each corner of her mouth before she replaced the napkin in her lap and rested her hands on top.

Summer raised her eyes to Granger's. There she found the wheels of logistics, financials, and politics clearly turning.

Gotcha.

Blair rested her forearms on the high-top, letting it absorb her exhaustion and boredom as she cradled her phone and stretched her calves.

"They aren't half bad."

Cynthia's comment pulled Blair out of her reverie. She straightened on instinct but paused when Cynthia motioned for her to stay as she was, then joined her at the table.

Blair settled back into her previous posture and asked, "Who's not bad?"

"I said they're not *half* bad. The interns. It's been a long freaking day."

"It always is. I thought you weren't going to be here?"

Cynthia let her forehead drop against her arms. "I'm not supposed to be here, but I got a text saying I was needed, so here I am." She rolled her eyes. "Ends up, they didn't actually need me. The next two hours can't go by fast enough. Wait, are you looking at wedding stuff?"

Repositioning, Cynthia looked over Blair's arm at her screen. "No way! Is that your dress? Get out. It's gorgeous. You're going to be so pretty."

The gushing caught Blair off guard because it was the first time anyone outside of her bridesmaids had done so with her. Her engagement had been met by mixed responses. Some celebrated the announcement. Most tolerated it. No one had straight up opposed it, though she wondered if she should ask the pastor to skip the "does anyone object" part of the ceremony—just in case. She knew the pending wedding would test her relationships, and so she had kept planning close to heart. Cynthia's excitement felt like a salve on an open wound. *They don't want to celebrate with you. Their loss. She gets it. Pretty? Hell yeah.* The thought came out of left field, exposing a bitterness squatting in the corner of Blair's heart, grasping at any scraps tossed its way.

She repeated the thought out loud. "Hell yeah. I will be pretty."

Cynthia laughed at Blair's exclamation. "What is Sam going to wear?" She asked.

"This." Blair pulled up a gray suit.

"That's really nice."

"Yeah, with it being a spring wedding and all, I thought it would be a nice way to go."

"Yeah, and gray is so trendy right now. What about the Bridesmaids?"

Blair obliged with a picture of two women in a bridal shop, one in a soft pink and the other in a soft green.

Cynthia took the phone from Blair and used her index finger and thumb to zoom in on the photo. "So pretty. Are these your colors?"

Blair nodded as she reached over and swiped the screen to reveal a vision board.

"Oh look at you. I like it."

Blair's smile widened at the approval. "Thanks. It's coming together."

"When's the date again?"

"May 11."

"That's less than nine months. It's gonna fly by." Cynthia handed the phone back to Blair and let her forehead drop on her arms again, this time with a little dramatic flair. "I'm never gonna get married."

Blair rolled her eyes, though with her head down Cynthia missed it. "Come on. You're still young."

Cynthia sighed, rotating her head a fraction to peek out at Blair. "I'm older than you."

Blair's face registered her surprise. "You are?"

Cynthia straightened up. "We've been over this. Yes, my birthday is in December, yours in March."

"Right. Sorry."

Cynthia flopped a hand around, a pathetic attempt to wave away the apology, then propped her chin up on her hands, her elbows offering support as they leaned on the high-top.

Blair let a chuckle escape her lips. "What's your deal?"

Cynthia glanced around the quiet expo hall, a lull before the storm that was sure to come during the dedicated expo hour at four. She sighed. "It's being around these interns. With their naivety, optimism ... the world is their freaking oyster, and they know it." She grabbed Blair's shoulders. "But they don't value it." She let her hands drop.

For a second, Blair thought Cynthia would drop the theatrics and resume her typical steady outlook on life, but Cynthia continued counting on her hand exactly how the interns didn't value their youth. "First of all, they take for granted how effortless it is to get up in the morning. They don't realize the same people see you every day, which means you have to pay attention to your outfits. Rotation, baby, it's an art. But, they don't know that yet. They also don't get how much sleep they have right now. It's all going out the window soon. The late nights trying to have some sort of social interactions coupled with early mornings and stressful days … sleep is gone. We're surviving on coffee out here in the real world. That's another thing they don't know yet. Everything freaking costs an arm and a leg. I had to start making coffee at home."

"I think the *college* interns know a little bit about being broke," Blair interrupted.

"Yes, but they don't have the crushing responsibilities of a car payment—"

"Don't you ride the CTA?"

Cynthia ignored her and continued, "And monthly expenses like rent and utilities, and … oh, oh, repaying student loans! They know it's coming, but it's like this far-off thing for them right now, you know? They just don't get it. And the dating scene. Right now, they feel like they have all these options out there in the world. But we know better. The good ones are few and far between, and when you find a good one, you snatch them up and hold on tight. You know what I'm talking about—you've got Sam."

Blair did know. With the invention of dating apps, the romantic landscape had become a landmine of terrifying and damaging interactions. Meeting Sam was like stepping into a hot-air balloon and being whisked out of a land she never wanted to visit again.

Often during their lunches together, Cynthia had complained about dating, but she had never been this despondent. Blair softened her tone. "Hey, what's going on?"

Cynthia shrugged. "I just don't want to end up alone."

Blair nudged her with her shoulder. "Come on, aren't you seeing someone?"

A smile played at the edges of Cynthia's mouth. "Yeah."

"And, from what you told me he seems to be pretty nice."

The smile widened, confirming Blair's statement. She continued with as much an encouraging tone as possible. "See, there are plenty of good guys out there. Maybe this one will surprise you."

A faintest flicker of doubt ran across Cynthia's face, but she covered it quickly with a nod and a "yeah, maybe," making Blair question if she had imagined it.

"Thanks, Blair."

"No problem."

Cynthia checked her watch. "I'm gonna run to the restroom before the crowd comes."

Ask her. This came from a different field than the one before. Outside her heart and yet also within, offering to fill her both with compassion and courage.

Blair resisted the offer. *I always ask her, and she always says no.*

Ask her anyway.

I'll just bother her. She argued.

Ask her anyway.

She's gonna feel pressured. She reasoned.

Ask her anyway.

Annoyed. A last defense.

Ask.

"Hey Cynthia?"

Cynthia stopped in her tracks and turned back to Blair. "Yeah?"

"A group of us are heading out to Vertical tonight. Wanna come?"

Cynthia smirked. "That's right, it's Wednesday."

Blair nodded. "Yeah. We're just grabbing drinks." She almost added, "I promise," but something caught in her spirit, and she felt odd saying it. Instead, she said, "You seem like you could use the distraction."

Cynthia's lips pursed together at the statement, as if the words meant something more to her than she wanted to let on. In the end, she wrinkled her nose then sighed. "You know what? I really could. Text me the deets."

Blair picked up her phone, then looked up suddenly at Cynthia, "Oh, wait."

Cynthia turned back around again. "Come on, I really have to go now." She did a little potty dance to emphasize her words.

Blair raised her hands in mock defense, shielding her face as if bracing for an attack. "I just thought I should let you know I invited Sadie and her friends, so you'll have to deal with the youngsters if you come."

Cynthia turned on her heel, tossing over her shoulder as she headed in the direction of the restroom, "You're killing me, Smalls."

———— · ————

"All Hail the Queen of badass," Derek announced with a playful bow as he approached Andrew and Summer on the patio off the conference lobby. He noted Summer's gathered hair, twisted over her shoulder to protect it from the breeze off the lake.

The elaborate praise lassoed a grin onto Summer's lips. "Why thank you," she responded, her posture the most relaxed he had seen her in days. Her eyes followed him as he pulled a chair out from the table, the metal feet dragging against the cobblestone patio, and lowered himself into it.

The gaze lingered a moment longer than necessary, betraying her admiration of his physique. As he settled into his chair, lacing his fingers and resting his elbows on the arms, his look told her she was caught. Hers told him she didn't mind.

"It's not final," Andrew said in a somber tone, yanking Derek's focus from their flirtation back to the issue at hand.

"It's as good as final." Summer retorted, pulling her jacket closed around her torso and buttoning it.

Derek tossed a glance between the two, trying to judge who had a more accurate assessment of the situation. Andrew's far off stare over the lake concerned Derek, prompting him to press his brother for details.

Andrew didn't bother looking at Derek as he answered, "Granger's calling an emergency meeting with his board in the morning to vote on it."

Derek's brows furrowed as he glanced at Summer. "I thought your text said Granger was good with it?"

A strand of hair, having escaped the twist over the shoulder, danced in Summer's eye. She moved it back into place as she answered, "He is good with it. He made the phone calls. We were done with dessert by the time he returned. When he came back, he shook our hands. He said the meeting tomorrow is just a formality."

"Then what's the hesitation?"

In the lack of Andrew's response, Derek could hear the waves of the lake beating at the rocky shore.

His brother turned his gaze upon them. "Final enough I can text Carr to back off the bribe? Exactly." The staring off into the distance resumed. "If this doesn't work ... if it all backfires ..."

If it all backfires ... Derek let his mind wander back to the restaurant the night before sitting across from Summer as she laid out the plan, speaking of the dominos falling without addressing the initial topple. In order for this all to work, Granger's board had to vote in favor. No wonder his brother was stressed. The fate of their company rested with complete strangers who had GenTech's interest at the forefront of their minds, not InnovGene's.

A new thought alighted in Derek's mind: the fate of their own company wasn't the only thing at risk. Rapidly working out the "what ifs," Derek realized all paths were leading toward their destruction.

The most obvious being if GenTech pulled out of the deal, forcing them to rely on the bribe Carr would have already set into motion, making them accomplices to unethical practices—which, if found out, would have devastating consequences, including criminal charges, jail time, and sanctions by the FDA on past, current, and future work at InnovGene.

The less obvious, though more sinister, was if Carr found out their deal with Granger and either pulled funding and bankrupted them, or worse, brought the whole kingdom crashing down by revealing Andrew's eight-year-old secret.

Over the years, he had watched his brother approach multiple challenges, and every time, the man had walked into them with full steam and full arrogance that he could figure his way out. A fear tingled at the base of Derek's skull, then spread out over his arms and down his torso and legs, digging its talons into him and squeezing. His brother wasn't just stressed, he was ... s*cared.*

That's what it was. Derek couldn't remember a time where he had seen that emotion on his brother, but in this moment, he wore it like a cloak, making him almost unrecognizable. He didn't look like Andrew.

He looks like you.

The thought was not a reassuring one. Derek was fully aware of his weaknesses, but he didn't expect them in his big brother. To see them so vividly on display now unanchored Derek's world. He felt the sudden need to reach out for a brace against the looming capsize.

"Andrew?" The tone in the question mirrored the fear on his brother's face.

Andrew closed his eyes and sighed.

Softly landing a hand on his arm, Summer's brought Andrew attention to her. "Hey, hey, look at me."

Anchoring him. Derek thought, desperately wishing she would do the same for him. But Derek wasn't Summer's primary concern right now. *I never am.*

He mentally waved away the bitter thought. It wasn't the time.

"We will get everything tied up tomorrow." Although she talked to Andrew, her eyes had found their way back to him. Registering the fear in his face, her own changed. Contempt replaced compassion.

It'll never be the time. You're not him.

There it was—confirmation of the truth he had suspected for the past four years: Summer believed him to be incompetent. She had taken his job for a reason, and it wasn't the one they fed her long ago about him enjoying marketing more than operations. He was incompetent as a leader. He crumbled under pressure. She knew it.

More than that, she agreed with it.

Of course, he could lead his marketing team. There wasn't anything at risk with the ad campaigns they ran or the content they put out. But in this bigger arena, where everything could be lost with one wrong move? He was a coward.

Summer turned back to Andrew. "Don't text it. That puts things in writing. You can pull him off to the side during the advertisers' meet and greet tonight. Once everything is locked in with Granger, we'll send in a tip about Carr, and he'll be caught. It'll all be over."

Derek watched his brother close his eyes and nod his head, his face contorted but resigned to trusting that Summer had the kingdom under control. Andrew muttered something under his breath before retrieving his phone from his inner jacket pocket. Sensing the crisis was averted,

Summer removed her hands from Andrew, righting herself in her own chair.

Even as he watched the confidence return to Andrew like color to a person's face after an illness, Derek knew things had shifted.

Shifted between him and Andrew.

Shifted between him and Summer.

Shifted in the kingdom.

You have a rock. Put your feet back on it.

It was Derek's turn to stare out over the waves, watching as they first clawed at the shore in resistance to the ebb, then clawed for dominance with the flow.

———————— · ————————

Adriana was the first to spot Katie Ellison entering Vertical. It was in the brief seconds she had let her eyes wander the restaurant, taking in the exposed brick, black pipes, and long farmhouse tables with a glance around the rectangular space. When Adriana's gaze first identified Katie, she stood at the top of the short stairs that led from the carryout counter down into the dine-in space where Adriana and the others sat waiting for their food. The handle of a small carry-on provided rest for Katie's hand as she surveyed the room, obviously looking for someone.

Adriana swatted toward her roommate, then quickly fingerspelled Katie's name and pointed in her direction. Mackenzie and Sadie both turned to look.

Sadie whipped back around to Adriana, excitedly, "You're right! It's her."

The outburst interrupted the flow of conversation at the table, which had consisted so far of Blair answering questions from the other women—Sandy, Morgan, and Barb—about the conference, with Cynthia chiming in occasionally to supply missed details. Talk halted as they turned to see what had captured the girls' attention.

Morgan squealed with joy, pushing back her chair and rising from the table. "She's here!" She bounded over to welcome Katie with a hug.

The personal recognition of the novelist caught Adriana off guard. She debated with herself if she should retrieve *Lies that Became Us*way, from her backpack, which sat safely tucked out of the way at her feet. As she reached for it, she noticed Barb and Sandy exchanged quick glances, surprise etched in their faces as they asked each other with a simple look if the other was aware Katie would be joining them. The answer was an obvious "no" from both. They sent the question Blair's way who met the silent question with a shrug. Adriana decided against pulling out the book, at least for now.

Blair turned suddenly to the girls. "Wait, how do you know Katie?"

Mackenzie shook her head and jutted a thumb at Adriana and Sadie. "I don't. They do."

"We don't know her," Sadie hastened to clarify. "We're reading her book."

"Oh!" Sandy exclaimed. "She'll be excited to meet fans."

As if putting the equation together, Mackenzie rested an elbow on the table and swept a finger toward those seated at it. "Wait, how do you know her?" she asked.

"Church," answered Sandy.

Mackenzie leaned back in her chair. "Ah."

"Except," Barb offered, "Blair also knows her from work."

Mackenzie reached for her diet soda. "She works at InnovGene?" she asked before taking a sip.

Blair shook her head as if it was an absurd thought. "No, she's married to the owner."

Mackenzie choked on her drink. "That's Katie Salvatore?"

"I didn't take Andrew's last name when we got married." Katie rolled her small carry-on right up next to the table and retracted the handle. "So, no, it's Katie Ellison. Cynthia!" Katie hurriedly rounded the table and gave Cynthia a side hug in her seat. "It's been too long!"

"I just told Blair the same thing the other day." Though her tone was pleasant, Cynthia's face displayed discomfort as Katie's arms scrunched her into the awkward squeeze.

The novelist proceeded to give the obligatory hugs around the table to her friends before turning her attention back to the three girls. "Hi there. I don't think I've met you all yet."

"Sadie is a new intern, and these are her friends Mackenzie and Adriana. They are attending the conference." Cynthia explained.

Katie smiled sweetly as she took her seat. "Oh, really? Just an iced tea, please." She addressed the waitress who had conjured out of thin air at the sight of the newcomer.

"You're not going to order food?" Sandy asked, motherly concern etched in her voice.

"No, I ate at the airport before my flight."

"Did you come straight here?"

"Yeah." Katie looked sheepish as she answered, removing her beanie and flattening flyaways. "I got off the Blue Line and thought, I can either go home or come here first. I decided I wanted to see your lovely faces."

"Not ready to go home yet?" Sandy asked gently.

Katie's lips pressed together into a flat line, worry dancing at the corners of her eyes briefly. She confirmed Sandy's suspicion with a slight nod, then chased away the worry with a big smile that she bestowed on Adriana who sat across from her. "Are you enjoying the conference?

The smile, with all its warmth and welcome, compelled Adriana to give one of her own. "Yeah. Though, to be honest, a lot of it goes over my head. I'm not a scientist."

Katie gave her a quizzical look. "Then why go?"

"We're here with our college ethics course for extra credit."

Katie shrugged her coat off with a chuckle. "That's a pretty good reason."

"Mackenzie, though," Cynthia interjected, "is getting her degree in biochemistry. I think she's hoping for a chance to meet Andrew."

Something flickered across Katie's face, but she retained the smile as she turned to Mackenzie. "Ah, you're a fan of Andrew's work?"

"I've read all his books, his research papers ... I've been following his career since I learned about him in high school."

"Oh, wow." Katie looked around the table. "She really is a fan. Do you go to school in the city?"

"No, out in the west burbs. St. Vincent's University." Mackenzie explained.

Katie thanked the waitress as she took her iced tea. "Are you girls from Illinois?"

Adriana shook her head. "I'm from up near Kenosha and Mackenzie's from Kansas."

"Oh! I love Wichita."

"Wichita is in the southern part of the state. My town is a small, rinky-dink one more in the northern part."

"I think we could probably figure out a time to introduce you to Andrew, right?" Katie turned to Blair.

She nodded and responded, "I already sent him a text."

Mackenzie's eyes widened. "Thank you! You have no idea how much that means to me."

"I think Blair can imagine." Katie tossed a smirk Blair's way. "She once was as doe-eyed about Andrew-the-scientist as you are now."

Blair scoffed away the suggestion, raising her beer bottle to her lips and taking a sip with an air of mock innocence. Laughter rippled through the table.

Adriana watched the exchange closely, her eyes ping-ponging around the table to catch words formed on lips then tossed between individuals. The pure joy on Mackenzie's face at the prospect of meeting her idol prompted Adriana to wonder about the coincidence that the novelist was also the scientist's wife.

All things worked together.

Adriana smiled at the Biblical reminder and added mentally, *For our good and His glory.* That included Mackenzie's good—even if she didn't appreciate it.

A proud look resting on Barb's face caught Adriana's attention and pulled her out of her reflection and back into the conversation. She had missed something important. Something about her.

"Adriana, your book!" Sadie pointed down to the bag beneath the table.

Deducing that the conversation had shifted to her consumption of Katie's book, she fished it from her bag, moving her bread plate out of the way and setting the book on the table.

"May I?" asked Katie, reaching a hand out toward the book. The novelist took it from Adriana's extended hand tenderly, noting her bookmarked spot with a smile. "You're almost to my favorite part."

A pen appeared from someone's purse, allowing Katie to inscribe the book. Task complete, she recapped the pen, closed the book with a flourish, and looked at Adriana with gratitude. A facial expression replaced it—one Adriana, even with all her years of watching faces intently, couldn't identify. Whatever the emotion Katie felt, she felt deeply. She hesitated in returning the book and instead rested her hand on the cover.

"I've done a lot of interviews and events the past two days, but you're my first in-the-wild fan. This storytelling gig ... well, so much of it is done alone. When you release the book, well, it's like you are inviting the world into this private, sacred space. You don't really get to know who it is that comes into the space, unless they tell you. So, thank you for letting me sign your copy—it means a lot to me."

Adriana took the book from Katie's outstretched hand, stunned by the author's appreciation, and repacked it into her bag. It was a coincidence she even had the book with her; she had tossed it in that morning just before they left Sadie's apartment, thinking if things got too boring—or, more likely, too hard to follow—she could just read. She hadn't done anything special, and yet that tiny decision gave Katie something she obviously needed tonight.

For her good too.

———————·———————

"My place or yours?"

The familiar voice snaked into Summer's ear from behind, eliciting a chill that raced from the base of her neck down to the backs of her knees and increased the pace of her heart. She froze, her hands halting in the slipping on her gloves. The moment she had been actively trying to avoid all day had finally caught up to her.

After the day's sessions had ended, Summer and Andrew attended the evening event, a meet and greet of the conference sponsors. She managed to dodge the interaction, letting Andrew do the heavy lifting while she kept engaged in conversation with colleagues she strategically put between her and the voice that had crept up on her. In retrieving her coat from the check, she had let her guard down, and now here he was, enticing her into his arms.

Would that be so bad?

They were powerful arms.

She closed her eyes.

Inviting arms.

Enveloping arms.

Distracting arms.

Arms that belonged to hands well versed in how to caress her body in a way that felt ... so *damn good.*

Her eyes fluttered open, and she tugged her glove up around her wrist.

"Oh, come on now, you're not gonna make me beg, are you?" The voice asked, barely louder than a whisper, his warm breath tickling the side of her neck.

Tugging the other glove on, she responded, "I think you've gotten the wrong idea. I am a lady, and my momma always told me that a lady deserves dinner before dessert."

He chuckled, the sound of it bringing a smile to her lips. She had grown to like that reaction. It sounded like it came from deep from within his chest. Manly.

She retrieved a lip gloss from her purse, exuding a practiced air of nonchalance as she applied it, even though she applied it because she knew he liked the shade on her.

Derek does too.

She ignored the thought and recapped the lip gloss, tossing it into her purse, and snapping the accessory closed.

"Are you finished teasing me?" he asked, placing a hand on the small of her back.

Her head whipped toward him, surprise flashing across her face at the boldness of such a public display of intimacy. She stepped away, casting him a sharp, reproachful glance.

"Someone might see," she hissed under her breath.

He closed the distance between them once more, this time keeping his hands off her. "Ah, that's why you've been avoiding me all day." He shoved his hands into his pockets and offered a casual shrug. "Hey, we're just two colleagues grabbing dinner. There's nothing wrong with that."

He was wrong, of course. She hadn't avoided him out of fear of being seen together, rather to avoid him seeing her together with Granger. But, now confident the deal would go through, she allowed her gaze to rest fully on Larson Carr's athletic form and his choice of a traditional black suit. His hair was shorter than it was Monday when they watched the Cubs' game together on his hotel couch. She liked it and the way it drew attention to his strong jawline. Summer forced herself to look up from his lips and to his eyes. "Dinner, huh? You learn fast."

"Well, I've met your mom, and she is a force to be reckoned with."

Summer's eyes narrowed as she tried to place the event, eliciting another chuckle from him.

"Two summers ago. You were showing her around InnovGene. I was there for a meeting with Andrew."

"You barely met her. You said all of five words to each other."

"It was all in her look."

"She does have an uncanny ability to convey a lot with a look."

"You must get that from her."

Summer rolled her eyes.

"So, where are we going for dinner?" He turned toward her, taking her scarf from her hands and draping it around her neck. He lowered his voice. "Just to be clear, when I say where are we going for dinner, I'm asking if we are getting room service in yours or mine."

"I don't have a room here."

With the casual response, reality slammed an unexpected fist into Summer's chest. If she had been a character in an action film, they might have used special effects to visually represent the air knocked from her body—in slow motion, of course—emitting outward like sound waves then rapidly returning to her with impact, her eyes widening with the force.

She didn't need a hotel room at the conference center because she lived in Chicago. Her condo was located on the twelfth floor of a historic building in the Gold Coast neighborhood. She could see the Navy Pier Ferris wheel from her bedroom window.

She refused to order deep-dish pizza from the touristy traps, opting instead to get it from the little hole-in-the-wall four blocks down from her place.

Her favorite spot in all of Chicago was a little bench on North Ave beach, especially at night when the skyline was lit up down Michigan Ave.

Whenever her mom came to visit, she made Summer take her over to Humboldt Park to get authentic Puerto Rican food—not bothered at all that it took them almost twenty-five- minutes to drive the four miles.

Summer loved the zoo.

Hated the L and tolerated the CTA buses.

Had memberships to all the museums.

Ate ice cream at Sally Qs almost every Saturday night.

Bought her groceries at the corner of LaSalle and Division because they had a parking garage, and Summer refused to be one of those people who used a little rolling cart to tote their bags home.

That parking garage also served the clinic where she had an appointment in the morning.

He deserves to know.

"Okay then. 2034."

"2034?" Summer repeated, her brow furrowing.

"My room number. I figured we should head there separately since you are so worried about being seen by your princes."

At the insult, a sudden protectiveness surged through Summer. "They're your princes too," she shot back.

Carr scoffed, his laugh tinged with contempt. "Pawns, more like it."

Summer stumbled back a step, surprised by the admission. If that's what he thought of Andrew and Derek, what did he think of her?

That's a dangerous question.

She motioned toward the entrance doors. "Um, not tonight ... I ..." She pressed the back of her hand to her forehead. "I forgot, I have an appoin—" She caught herself. "I have a meeting scheduled at the office first thing."

"You can leave from here."

"I don't have clothes with me."

"Send Emma for them."

"She already went home for the night."

"So?"

"She's working late tomorrow because of the party. I can't ask her to do that."

"That never stopped you before."

Without sufficient excuses to rescue herself from the awkward situation, Summer smiled and shrugged. "For as smart as you are, Larson, you aren't picking up what I'm putting down." She said it playfully, though internally, she wrestled against a rising anger. He had backed her into a corner, so to speak, and Summer Harlow did not appreciate it.

You knew who you were getting into bed with.

She didn't appreciate that thought either.

"What exactly am I missing?" he asked, his tone still light but his face darkening.

She leaned in a bit, letting her hand land lightly on his arm. She softened her tone as much as possible. "I can't tonight, but I'll make it up to you, I promise."

Carr scanned their surroundings, then swiftly guided her down a hallway and around a corner. Once safe from prying eyes, he gathered her toward himself and met her lips with his own.

It was everything she dreaded and everything she longed for.

When Carr pulled back from the kiss, he smirked. "I miss you. You barely let me touch you the other night."

Continuing to use playfulness as a defensive tactic, Summer responded, "It's a good thing, too. I think it was a 24-hour bug or something. You should be thank—"

His kiss cut her off. He dropped his lips to just below her jaw. Then to her neck. The resulting sensations demanded every fraction of her focus.

Carr was the one to break the trance when he lifted his lips to her forehead, then leaned his own against it. "Can I get you to reconsider?" He played with a button on her coat, slipping it in and out of the hole.

She put a hand over his, stopping the motion. "Sorry. Not tonight," she repeated.

"Raincheck?"

"Of course."

"Tomorrow night?"

"The party's tomorrow."

"So?"

"Maybe."

He took a step back from her, sizing her up as he straightened his tie. "I hate sharing you."

Summer didn't miss a beat. "I didn't realize we were exclusive."

"We're not." He wrapped his arms around her waist, drawing her in close to kiss her again. "Doesn't mean I like it." Another kiss.

Surprised by the admission, she placed both hands on his chest and gently pushed him away so she could see his face, looking for the intention behind the information. "What are you trying to say?"

He shrugged. "Just making an observation."

"Do you want to be?"

"God no."

"You don't, you know."

"Don't what?"

"Share me."

"Yes, I do."

She untangled herself from his arms. "No, you don't. I share *you*." Her annoyance filled in around the words.

Carr slipped his hands in his pockets and rocked on his heels. "No, you don't." He replied with an air of smugness.

The revelation, apocalyptic in nature, rained down fire on the carefully constructed wall around this secret garden Summer gave herself permission to play within. Inside, she was allowed to take off the crown and mantle of responsibility and think only of herself. When it was time to go, she did so confidently, trusting the walls of casual non-commitment to protect her playground. If the walls were gone, it was no longer a secret garden. It was an open field of fertile soil with some seeds already sowed.

"Come on now." Carr pulled her back into his arms. "You're thinking about this too hard. Let's just go upstairs."

The conversation suddenly felt like a shark circling a shipwrecked survivor and an instinct to swim away as fast as possible washed over her. Instead, she said, "Why don't you fill me in? Because, I don't get it. Who do you share me with?"

He gave her a knowing look, one that tried to coax her to admit the truth they both already knew. When she didn't do so, Carr said it for her: "InnovGene."

She scoffed in protest.

He mocked it.

"You're the one in love with InnovGene." She attempted to untangle herself from his arms for a second time.

"No," Carr corrected, tightening his hold on her, "I am the one who owns InnovGene."

Surprised at both his resistance and assertion, she stopped struggling. "The Salvatores own InnovGene."

"You're smarter than that," he snapped, then softened as he added, "I know Andrew told you."

"Told me what?" she said, playing dumb.

Carr glanced aside, pondering her words, and sniffed dismissively. "See," he leaned in and whispered into her ear slowly, "I share you." Abruptly releasing her, he strode down the hallway toward the elevators, leaving her standing there with her mouth open, staring after him.

Did you really think you could wrestle with the snake and not get bit? The icy thought froze her in place.

Summoning her resolve, Summer walked in the opposite direction. The hallway brought her back to the lobby, like a path out of Wonderland, and deposited her into a cacophony of chattering couples, luggage rolling across the marble floor, and doormen offering to call for cabs.

She stopped just shy of exiting the hotel—hand on handle, ready to push—while pieces of the exchange played repeatedly in her head.

He didn't want to share her, so he forced her to pick a side.

Or did she force it?

Was that it then? Were they over?

Not unless you pick you.

With a decisive tug, she opened the door and exited the building, the cold autumn night meeting her flushed face.

———————·———————

I can't hang out tonight.

Andrew reread the text, analyzing it for more context as he rode the elevator up to his apartment. Even on the sixth reading, there wasn't any more explanation. He started to type the question, "Why not?" but stopped when the elevator doors slid open, interrupting and convincing him it was the wrong move.

Man, this day … he thought it was going to get better tonight, but now … he probably should just go to bed and bring it to a close.

No problem. See you tomorrow.

He sighed his disappointment, shoving the phone into his pocket.

Having already removed his jacket and tie during the car ride, he went to work on rolling up his sleeves, though he wasn't sure why he bothered now that he was home for the night instead of going out. He would probably just change into pajamas once inside.

The sound of instrumental jazz met him at the condo door.

The handle gave way. Unlocked.

He closed his eyes against the realization the condo was occupied. He sighed again, unsure if he was disappointed or relieved. His wife had made it home in time for his keynote address. Not only was she home in time, she was home early.

Andrew released the door handle and pushed it open with his shoulder. As he did, the sight of Katie sitting in the armchair by the bay of windows in the living room greeted him.

Her gaze pulled away from the city skyline and fell on him. "I have questions, and I want some answers." Her voice was calmer than he had expected it to be, catching him off guard. Covering his surprise, he guided the door closed, turning his back to her. "I thought Summer was going to call you," he responded.

"Summer isn't my husband. And she's not your wife. I am." Katie paused. "What the hell is going on, Andrew?"

Image Blurred

I DON'T KNOW HER name, and she doesn't know mine.

I do know that she works at InnovGene. Years of playing in my prime spot have given me a front-row seat to the employees of InnovGene grabbing lunch.

The crowds were particularly engaged with my music this afternoon and loose with their cash, delaying my usual migration to the north side of the city for the dinner and drinks portion of the city's evening. I deftly dodged tourists and commuters alike on the sidewalk before weaving in and around the rush-hour cars stalled in the intersection. Every moment mattered to circumvent another street musician getting the bright idea to take up residence on my usual profitable corner.

My knees had pleaded with me to slow, to go easy on them, but I ignored their creaking cries and hurried to the Red Line station.

The momentum of my hustle slowed my recognition of her exit from the InnovGene office building. She spun out of the rotating door right into my shoulder. Instinctively, I steadied her stumble.

Her expression shifted from surprise at the collision to gratitude for my help. "Thanks," she said, tossing her head slightly to clear the hair that had swept over her eyes. Opposite of the sweep, she wore her hair short to her scalp, giving me a clear view of the jewelry dangling from her ear: a cascade of rainbow-colored, glittery stars.

"You're welcome," I answered her, righting the violin on my back.

She made a bee-line to the curb, scanning the nearby cars, but the one she desired hadn't yet arrived. There she still stood, waiting, the hem of her red dress hugging her calves and her arms hugging a manilla envelope against her striped faux fur coat.

A black sedan pulls up.

The woman yanks the door open, tossing the packet on the dash of the car before climbing in.

First, the vibration: the bounce of a wheel over dirt, gravel, and stone.

I glance at my watch. 5:43 p.m. *Come on, I've got to go.* I plead.

Then, the sound: the laying of hand on horn.

Finally, the image: the woman holding up the oncoming traffic, headlights illuminating the trepidation in her face as she stands in the middle of the road, hands on the car hood. Behind her, street lamps overhead cast light on the split in the road and the two resulting paths which divert from it.

The differences between the two options are stark. First, a simple two-lane street, worn with use, extends out like a straight arrow toward a fortified city with living walls of greenery encircling it.

Second, a new multi-lane road snakes off from the first, ramping up and over it in a flourished twisting bridge, vines etched into the concrete parapet walls. It too seems to head the city's direction, but its bends make it difficult to identify the end destination.

The woman crumbles onto the hood of the car, folding her arms in to create a cradle for her forehead. Her earring rests against the satin fabric of her dress sleeve.

I realize the sound of the horn is not from the car under the woman, but from the ones behind it. The woman doesn't move.

A car emerges from behind and maneuvers to pass the woman and the car she leans on. It accelerates up the ramp. Like a dam breaking, vehicle after vehicle passes the woman, a flow of engine and metal onto the ramp.

A horse-drawn carriage replaces sedan as the next vehicle to maneuver around the woman. At the driver's urging, the animal pulls the carriage forward, proceeding down the two-lane street in a steady trot.

She has a decision to make.

The woman's back rises and falls in jagged rhythm, betraying the uneven breaths dragged in by her lungs.

With curiosity, I walk around the stalled vehicle and am met with hundreds—no, thousands, maybe even millions—of cars and carriages waiting their turn. Instead of an organized row, the vehicles have taken up every available space, creating a sea of metal, rubber, and wood, hardly distinguishable from one another. Each, I suddenly realize, carrying at least one individual in the driver's seat.

I don't understand the decision to be made.

That's because you've never had to make it.

A raindrop falls on the woman's hand.

She raises her face from her arms and examines the sudden wetness with surprise. She turns her hand over, as if she's seeing it for the first time. As she rotates her hand back, the lamplight catches the diamond of her engagement ring.

Another drop hits the hood of the car, creating an ever so slight plink upon impact.

She slips the ring off her finger and holds it pinched by both hands, elbows providing support as she evaluates the trinket.

Another drop hits her cheek.

She wipes it away.

Why am I seeing this? I pray. *I don't know her.*

But, I do.

I can't help her.

I didn't ask you to.

Then why?

The clouds open their arms, dropping their gift of hydration to the ground without reserve.

The woman blinks, clearing her eyes.

Wipers engage, swiping away moisture and startling the woman with the sound of rubber dragging against glass. She straightens quickly, her arms falling to her sides—the ring still pinched between her left thumb and index finger—and her gaze trained on the individual behind the wheel. I can't make them out from where I stand, but I can see intimacy in the gaze.

The longing.

The love.

The sound of wooden wheels catches both mine and the woman's attention and we turn to see another carriage maneuver around the stalled vehicle. Instead of pulling around and proceeding forward, it stops parallel to the car.

There is no driver.

Yes, there is.

Ah, the woman.

That's her decision. She can either take the reins and continue down the road, or climb into the car and be driven up the ramp with all its twists. *Lord, I still don't get it. Why are you showing me this?*

Compassion. Empathy. Kindness.

A heavy responsibility settles into my heart. Closing my eyes, I lift my face to the heavens. The rain feels cool against my flushed skin. When I lower my face, the image is gone, but the rain remains. I pull the hood of my jacket up over my head and continue my trek to the Red Line station.

Day Four

THE TANTALIZING SMELL OF tiny appetizers filled Katie's nostrils as soon as she entered the event space. Instinctively, her hand shot out and grabbed the passing morsel just in time. Scanning the room for other offerings as she popped the caramelized onion tartlet into her mouth, she zeroed in on a tray of meatballs. New mission acquired, Katie weaved in and around the crowd of conference attendees toward her target. They cleaned up sharply for a bunch of nerdy scientists, Katie thought with a smirk as she selected the largest meatball she could find. Years of attending these things had taught Katie one thing: make sure you eat enough before you drink. She pre-gamed with a protein bar during the car ride over.

Her gaze landed on a server offering Arancini to Derek and hurried her steps across the room. She sidled up to Derek just as he popped the crispy fried risotto ball stuffed with mozzarella cheese in his mouth. Her sudden appearance halted the server's retreat and Katie plucked an Arancini from the tray. "Thank you," she said, realizing she had failed to thank the last server. She vowed to do better the rest of the evening.

"Well, hello there, sister-in-law."

"Hello to you too, brother-in-law."

Katie popped the Arancini in her mouth before accepting his hug. Whiskey already hung on his breath.

"I didn't know you were going to be here tonight."

"I didn't tell anyone—just in case of delays or something."

"Makes sense."

Derek stepped back and evaluated her outfit. He let out a whistle. "Brenda Salvatore would be so proud."

She received the compliment with a coy shrug, placed a hand on her hip, and struck a few poses, modeling the midi dress.

While shopping for her New York trip, the dress caught Katie's eye as she hung her not-wanted items on the rack outside the dressing room. The dress waited patiently to be returned to its spot on the sales floor. The olive green satin begged to be touched; she ran her finger down the side before gathering the fabric between her fingers and extending the dress wide to evaluate its silhouette. The mock neckline, sleeveless design, blousy bodice, cinched waist, and a-line skirt pleased Katie, prompting her to check the size and, finding it to be hers, carried it back to her dressing room. A sophisticated and chic woman stared back at her in the mirror. He hadn't said it in so many words, but Katie was aware Andrew missed the woman in the mirror. She hadn't set out to make a physical statement of the drastic intangible changes in her life—first her faith, then her vocation—but, over time, she had swapped her corporate chic wardrobe for a hipster one.

Can't you just give this to him?

She could. The dress was added to her bag.

Not that it had mattered. After their interaction last night, Katie was convinced Andrew wouldn't care how she dressed tonight. Choosing to keep the disappointment in check, Katie gave Derek a pleased, modest smile and said, "Your mother did teach me everything there is to know about dressing to the nines."

He grinned at the praise bestowed upon his mom. "You were a good student. Well done."

"You don't look too shabby yourself. I see you guys kept up the tradition of serving her favorite appetizers."

Derek glanced around the room as if he could survey the offerings. His lips pressed into a line, sadness tugging at the corners of his eyes but forced to share the space with a pleasant memory of his mother. "Yeah. I'm guessing that's part of the SOP at this point. Hey, do you need a drink?"

"Do you even need to ask?"

"What do you want?"

"White wine."

"Coming right up."

Katie watched as the crowd swallowed him up. Placing her clutch on the high-top table next to Derek's empty whiskey glass, she took the moment alone to survey the room, looking for anyone she might know. She bobbed her head to the beat emanating from the band at the front of the room. Back in the day, she and Andrew would close down the dance floor, but the chance of that happening tonight was slim, at least for Andrew, as he would be busy schmoozing all night. Katie, however, had fulfilled her duty: show up. She supposed nothing was stopping her from swinging her hips a bit.

A scattered mix of high-top and low tables lined the perimeter of the dance floor, offering space for conversation. Many of the faces were longtime attendees of the conference. These were the colleagues that would keep Andrew in work mode over the next few hours.

Having emerged from the crowd, Derek stood at the bar counter at the back right corner of the room with a few others, waiting for the servers to pour, shake, and mix their drinks. His fingers tapped the countertop in time with the band. Maybe he would join her on the dance floor, Katie thought with a smile.

Floor-to-ceiling glass doors comprised one wall of the event space, leading to a patio that overlooked Lake Michigan. The lake remained hidden, obscured by the interior lighting and the darkness outside. Katie's gaze settled on Blair searching the room for a familiar face. Katie waved her over.

Blair's red dress swished and bounced as she made her way toward Katie. Knowing Blair, it was probably vintage 1940s, thrifted from her favorite boutique in the Wicker Park neighborhood.

"Love the dress," she let Blair know as soon as she was near enough to hear. "Did you come alone?"

"No, Sam has gone to get us drinks. How about you?" She set down a manilla envelope and placed her clutch on top of it.

"I came alone, but Andrew's already here. I haven't seen him yet," Katie answered, choosing to avoid the real conversation behind Blair's question. She wasn't ready to talk about what happened after she left the bar and went home.

"I just saw him talking to Cynthia." Blair placed her clutch next to Katie's.

"Ah. We'll probably run into each other soon enough."

"Are you ok—"

"Here you go. Oh, hey, Blair." Derek tossed a big smile her way as he handed Katie her wine glass. "Look who I found." He stepped aside, motioning to Cynthia, who emerged from behind him. Derek motioned to the empty table space in front of Blair. "Do you need a drink?"

"No, Sam went to get something for us," she answered. "Hey, have you seen Andrew? Or Summer?"

"Summer? No. Andrew's over there, though." Derek pointed toward a large group.

"Do you need him for something? I'm headed over there. I can relay a message if you want," Cynthia offered.

"Thanks, but I need to talk to him about something. I'll catch up with him in a bit."

"Sounds good. Hey, how did the interns do today?" Cynthia turned a judgmental expression toward Derek. "I should be asking you this question, since you were supposed to be in charge of them."

Derek smirked, obviously pleased with himself for figuring out how to skirt intern-sitting duty. "Something came up."

"You should at least introduce yourself to them," Cynthia scolded.

"I'll swing by the booth tomorrow."

"No need. They are all sitting at that table over there." She motioned toward a table by the glass doors. Sitting with the interns were Mackenzie and Adriana. "I'm sure you can find some time tonight to make your way over and say hi. The whole point of having this program is to help them learn skills and make connections." Cynthia poked Derek in the chest. "You're a connection, boss."

Amusement spread across Derek's face. He held up a hand. "Scout's honor. I promise to say hi to the interns."

Satisfied, Cynthia assured the table she would find them later, then left on her mission to track down Andrew.

"She doesn't know you weren't a scout, does she?" Katie asked with a smirk, taking a sip of her wine.

"Nope," Derek answered, his boyish grin wide.

Eyeing him sipping the glass of whiskey, Blair addressed Derek. "When you go over, remember to behave."

Derek shrugged. "Sure thing." He took another sip. "Can't promise about the rest of the night, though."

"Dude."

"You're too easy to ruffle, Blair."

"What's this about?" Katie interjected.

Blair eyed Derek. "One of the interns has a crush on Derek."

Katie laughed. "When have they not?"

Derek waved his hands between Katie and Blair. "See! I told you this is not my fault. I can't help my good looks. My parents had good genes."

Blair turned to Katie and lowered her voice. "It's Sadie."

Katie's eyebrows furrowed, not quite understanding why that mattered.

"She's a Christian." Blair offered as an explanation, leaving the rest unspoken.

"Hey, I'm a Christian," Derek protested. "Everyone at this table is. What does that have to do with anything?"

Blair played with the chain strap of her clutch. "When was the last time you went to church?"

As the last word rolled off Blair's tongue, Derek's body language shifted from casual confidence to exposed vulnerability. Like a tablecloth shaken out and draped over a table, an awkward silence fell between the trio. Neither of the Salvatore brothers had set foot in a church since the day they buried their mother three years ago, a fact both Blair and Katie were well aware of, yet Blair had forgotten in the moment.

Brenda dutifully dragged her boys to church every Sunday, and when Katie came on the scene, tried to drag her along as well. Having been raised by atheists herself, Katie found Brenda's propensity for the religious laughable, especially for such an intelligent woman. Although Brenda had spent her entire adulthood as a homemaker and didn't possess a stunning resume of accomplishments as did her husband and sons, one conversation with Brenda proved to anyone that she was just as astute and shrewd as the Salvatore men and very much the backbone of their success. Katie couldn't reconcile the fact that someone as smart as Brenda could believe in a fantasy.

Bit by bit, like a pickaxe chipping away at ice, Brenda's actions (and the words that matched) reshaped Katie's initial perception into a realization that Brenda's faith was the steady and enduring engine that drove her everyday life. Brenda defined success by what was true deep in her soul, and that definition weaved compassion, grace, and generosity in her interactions with family, friends, and neighbors alike. For Brenda, faith and logic were two sides of the same coin.

Despite this reframing, the first time Katie attended church with Brenda, her mother-in-law laid in a casket clothed in a gold and white herringbone tweed blazer, her make-up caked on thicker than Brenda would have tolerated in life.

"Sorry. I wasn't thinking ... I just ... what I meant ..."

Having upset the typically unflappable Derek, Blair struggled to get a coherent thought out, prompting Katie to come to her rescue. "We know you believe in God." She laid a hand softly on Derek's arm. "But the way you live your life is just ... different."

"Different, huh," Derek repeated the word with a noticeable irritation in his voice, slipping his arm out from under her hand and reaching for the wide tumbler once more.

"Right. Different."

"Like you are?" Derek asked Blair, tilting his glass to guide her gaze over her shoulder. He turned to Katie. "Mom would have had a conniption fit if she knew they were getting married at that church."

Katie bristled. "That was uncalled for," she reproached him, hoping that Blair's fiancé Samantha hadn't heard the comment.

The conversation had derailed fast. *Lord, make him keep his mouth shut*, she prayed fervently.

When Samantha reached them, she handed Blair a glass of red wine. Blair immediately raised the glass and took a long sip. Katie had to give her props; Blair maintained her composure as she lowered the glass, even while Derek's gaze remained steadily fixed on her. He played with his glass but didn't speak.

"Sam," Katie greeted her with a warm hug. "How are you? Wow, I love your hair," she added, admiring Sam's twist-out curls, which framed her face with their natural, springy spirals.

"That's right, you haven't seen it. I decided to switch things up. Hey, Derek." Sam gave him a little wave. He returned the greeting with a polite nod.

"The bangs are great," Katie went on. "They really draw attention to your eyes. Is it technically a mohawk?"

Sam got excited. "Yaass!" She slapped Blair on the shoulder playfully. "My boo here didn't even notice that. I was like, how could you not?"

Katie chuckled.

It fell quiet.

"How are things at the hospital?" Katie asked, feeling a compulsion to fill in the void while simultaneously feeling irritation toward Blair. She poked the bear, and he rose to defend himself, swiping a claw her way in the process. Both were hurt, and Katie didn't know how to help without it seeming like she was picking a side.

As Sam lamented the uptick in flu cases and the resulting staff shortage, Katie's mind wandered.

With Brenda's death came a pulling away from religion for the Salvatore brothers. For Andrew, her death was a release from obligation, allowing him to fully embrace the atheism he had toyed with since college. For Derek, her death was the thrust to push him over the edge of discontent, allowing him to fully embracing the perspective that, while God may exist, He didn't care about Derek.

For Katie, though, the life alternating loss of her young mother-in-law pushed her into an existential crisis. That first Sunday after the funeral, Katie attended church with a turbulent heart and thousands of questions. Now, three years later, the upheaval had been replaced by a supernatural peace and scrupulous research (her journalism professor would be so proud) gave most of her questions answers.

Not all though—a few pertaining to the bigger question of "What does it really mean to follow Jesus in the present day?" remained. Questions like: Did the fact that they lived in such a drastically different culture than ancient Israel change things? What commands of Jesus still held weight? What has the church gotten wrong over the centuries? What are they getting wrong now?

Did it matter that Blair was marrying a woman?

Blair loved Samantha deeply, and Samantha loved Blair. They supported one another, worked through conflict graciously, and both professed Jesus as Lord. That was more than Katie could say about her own marriage. Derek was right, however, that Brenda would have been upset if they married in the church—though Katie doubted she'd have a full-blown conniption, as he suggested.

When Blair first joined their small group, before Katie was involved, Sandy and Barb probably hoped they could disciple Blair out of homosexuality, showing her passage after passage of what they believed were pretty clear verses. But Blair disagreed. "If God made me, and He loves me, then I think He is okay with who I am and who I choose to love," she argued.

Shortly after, she met Sam. Soon, they were serious. Then, engaged. Sandy and Barb had remained consistently against the situation while remaining kind, open, and loving toward Blair—much like Katie imagined Brenda would have.

Samantha attended church with Blair but refused to attend the small group. "How can you call them friends if they are against us being together?" she protested.

Blair shared the question with Katie, asking for her thoughts.

Katie herself struggled to reconcile what seemed to her a fairly clear mandate in Scripture with the secular arguments against it, prompting her to read every book she could get her hands on—across multiple perspectives. While still confused, she was certain of one thing: it was her job to love Blair. Nothing more. She told Blair as much and suggested that maybe Sandy and Barb were also capable of both caring for Blair while still disagreeing with her choices.

Like she did with Derek. His lifestyle of excessive drinking on the weekends and hooking up with a new woman every few weeks was, in her opinion, an attempt to avoid dealing with deeper issues, not to mention destructive to his physical and emotional health. But that was his burden to surrender. Her job was to show up for him and keep pointing him back to the love of God that he doubted so passionately. Maybe one day, he would be able to see it.

Katie forced her thoughts back to Sam, who explained she had to take two nursing shifts the day before.

Derek tossed back the remaining contents of his glass. He set the glass down with a restrained force, the result of which was a dull thud, and turned to leave.

"It's really important you all get your flu shots—"

Blair raised a hand to interrupt Sam. "Your mom took me to that church," she stated, stopping Derek's retreat.

There was that bold spirit.

Derek turned back to her. "So?" He shrugged. "She took me too. And you apparently have a problem with me."

"Derek, come on. That's not true."

"But you have to protect the little innocent intern from me?"

Samantha shot a wide-eyed inquiring look at Katie. A slight lift of her hands from the table and a shake of her head let Sam know it was best to let things unfold.

"No." Blair's voice held steady. "I am asking you to help protect her from herself by not encouraging her infatuation."

"What do you think is going to happen?" he asked incredulously.

"I think you're gonna flirt with her and she's gonna follow your lead."

"Let's play this out—never mind the fact that I've never even talked to this girl once and I couldn't pick her out of a line-up if I had to—but say I did find her attractive and we started flirting. Isn't it up to her to decide how far she wants to take it? She's an adult."

With a huff, Blair crossed her arms. "You really don't get it, do you? She's one of the good ones. She's got a standard—a line in the sand. I don't want her to cross it just because you charmed your way into a one-night-stand."

At hearing the insult to his character, hurt flitted across Derek's face. It quickly changed into a defensive grimace. He pinched his index finger and thumb together, his other fingers curling into his palm, and used the fisted hand to punctuate his words. "See, that right there. Gah. It's so presumptuous to think you have the final say about what someone can or cannot do with their own lives."

"Not me! The Bible."

"Once again, how convenient you get to tell that girl what she has to do with her life while you get to cherry-pick what to do with yours."

"That's not fair."

"Hey," Derek raised his hands in defense. "I say you all can do whatever the hell you want. You're two consenting adults. But you dragged my mom into this, and she would tell you straight up you're living in sin."

Sam moved to interject, but Blair held out a hand to stop her. "I didn't bring her up, you did. And, dude, if she was here, she'd be the first one to tell you you're screwing up your life—literally."

"Ha! Jokes on you. She already did."

Derek's face fell as he registered his own words. The finger he had pointed at Blair at the start of the exclamation fell to his side as if every ounce of conviction had left him.

Side looks tossed their way from nearby attendees quickened Katie's pulse. A blow up between InnovGene employees was the last thing the company needed right now. She reached out to put a hand on Derek's shoulder, but he slinked away from her, tilting off balance slightly but righting himself quickly. He put a hand up between himself and Katie and shook his head. Without another word, he withdrew from them. They watched him as he exited onto the patio.

With the 180 in Derek's behavior, the fight had left Blair's face, and she leaned into Sam's embrace. Sam gave her a little squeeze. "Forget him. He's drunk. Let's go dance."

Watching the couple make their way hand-in-hand toward the dance floor, Katie didn't notice Andrew coming toward her until he was almost at the table. Her clutch provided the perfect distraction from his advance. She retrieved her lip gloss and pocket mirror to touch-up her lips.

"What was that about?" Andrew kept his voice low as he motioned toward the patio, a mixture of annoyance and concern crisscrossing his face.

Katie looked at him over her mirror. "Nothing important."

"Sure looked important."

She shrugged and returned the lip gloss and mirror, snapping her clutch closed. "Well, nothing important for Andrew Salvatore, CEO of InnovGene."

In the tense beat that followed, Katie regretted her words and the disdain that wrapped around them. Blair and Derek may have taken their hurt away from the table, but she obviously remained with hers.

Andrew sighed. The sound of which dragged against Katie's temperance, prompting her to cross her arms, the flames of annoyance flashing in her eyes and daring him to make a move in the direction of reconciliation.

Unheeding the challenge, Andrew opened his mouth and uttered, "Maybe we should—" before stopping abruptly, his attention drawn by something in his peripheral vision.

He took a step closer to the table and picked up the manilla envelope Blair had left behind when she left to tear up the dance floor. Now in Andrew's hands, Katie could see his name written in small uppercase letters in the top corner. He tilted his head, curious.

Of course he'd stop mid-sentence about their relationship to check something for work. It was Katie's turn to sigh. "Blair came with it," she informed him before leaving him there fumbling with the metal clasp.

Katie considered going out to the patio to see if Derek was okay, but decided against it, knowing his pride needed some space. Instead, she headed over to the bar to see about getting a bottle of water, snagging another meatball from a passing tray as she did.

What are you doing?

In the exhale of her breath, Katie ignored the question, choosing to pursue her hunt for water to avoid introspection.

"Katie!"

The familiar voice drew Katie's glance over her shoulder. "Michael!" She gave him a hug. When they pulled apart, Michael congratulated her on the new book.

"Aw, thanks," she said, reaching for the water the bartender held out to her.

"I didn't know you were going to be here, otherwise I would have brought my copy of your book for you to sign."

"Michael, really? That's so sweet of you to buy a copy. Find me tomorrow. I'll make sure to sign it."

"Really? Great. I saw you on TV, actually."

"No kidding!"

"Yeah, you did really well. Especially when they started grilling you about Andrew and InnovGene."

Katie played with the water bottle in her hands, running her fingers around the ridged cap, occasionally stopping to unscrew and screw it back on. "I appreciate that."

"I mean," Michael continued, "considering everything going on, I'm sure it was hard to—" He paused, searching for the right word. "Dodge it."

The pit of Katie's stomach dropped. She had pressed Andrew on the details of the company's situation last night, but he had, to use Michael's word, dodged her questioning, assuring her that he and Summer had everything under control. She needn't worry about a thing—everything was being settled that morning, and she'd find out the details on Friday.

Along with everyone else in the world. She thought bitterly. To Michael, she simply said, "Hmm, I'm not sure what you mean."

"Oh." He looked like a kid caught with his hand in the cookie jar. "I just assumed Andrew would have clued you in on the agreement between InnovGene and GenTech."

For the second time that night, an awkward silence filled the space between Katie and another individual.

Michael nervously filled the void. "It's wild how fast it went down. By the time I got all the details, contracts had already been drawn up. Speaking of, do you know where Summer is? I need to ask her a question about that."

Katie uncapped her bottle. "Sorry, I don't." She took a sip of water, letting the cool of the water calm the rising ire in her soul. "Would you excuse me?" she asked, barely allowing Michael to respond before heading toward the patio doors.

The sweet smell of the recent rain which had brought in cooler temps—a welcome respite from the warm room—hung in the air. Relief rushed over Katie when Derek was not to be found among the handful of individuals occupying the patio; she needed a break from the Salvatore brothers and their world. Drawing in a deep breath, face lifted toward the night sky, Katie paid attention to the way the brisk air pricked at the inside of her nose, commanding nerves to attention before descending into her lungs where it did the same.

"Needed some fresh air?"

Katie lowered her gaze to see Sadie sitting a few feet away on a low stone wall that extended protectively from the side of the building, enclosing the patio. Where Sadie perched, the ledge was dry, shielded from the rain by an overhanging tree branch. With her back to the lake, Sadie could easily see the well-lit interior and its occupants.

Katie joined her on the wall. "Yeah, these things are overwhelming."

Sadie nodded her agreement. "It's so loud in there," she said, as if having a sudden realization.

Katie laughed. "It really is, isn't it?"

"It wasn't too bad at first, but once more people arrived, it just really ramped up."

"Yeah." Katie kicked her legs, playing like a little kid with too much energy but relegated to staying in one place. "Hey, did Derek come by your table and introduce himself yet?"

A blush crawled up Sadie's neck. She looked down at her hands. "No, he didn't."

The poor girl's discomfort at the mention of her crush amused Katie, reminding her of her own similar experiences. "How did your friends like the second day of the conference?" Katie changed the topic to the girl's noticeable relief.

Sadie picked up a leaf that had fallen from the tree and twirled it between her fingers. "Mackenzie is in heaven right now. Science, drinking, and dancing. It doesn't get much better than that for her. She's on the dance floor right now with Noah and Chloe."

"And you're out here?"

"Well, Adriana and Priya went down some deep fandom rabbit hole. I just got bored listening to them."

"You didn't want to dance?"

The corners of Sadie's lips tugged downward into a frown, but she fought against it with a weak smile. "Um, I don't mind dancing. It's just—Noah and Mackenzie coupled up, and Chloe was flirting with this other guy she met while dancing. I just felt like ..." Her voice trailed off.

"The odd man out?" Katie filled in.

The phrase brought a distressed look to Sadie's face, cultivating a maternal instinct in Katie. "You okay?" she asked with concern.

"Yeah, I'm fine. It's nothing," Sadie said, trying to cover her unrest.

"Doesn't sound like nothing."

Sadie pushed back her cuticle with a fingernail. "It's silly, really. I should just let it go and get back inside."

Playfully bumping the young woman's shoulder with her own, Katie coaxed her to share. "Come on. Seems like you need a friendly ear."

Sadie protested, "I'm sure you've got better things to do."

"Nope. I'm hiding from my husband right now," Katie responded lightheartedly.

The offhanded remark seemed to crack Sadie's reservation. "Well," Sadie began. "That saying you used, 'odd one out,' hit the nail on the head. I never really felt like I fit in anywhere. My parents were both missionary kids. They didn't become missionaries, but our family was still heavily involved in our church. And conservative. You know? Not like jean-skirt-long-braided-hair conservative, but I wasn't allowed to watch certain movies or listen to certain music. I wasn't allowed to go to certain places or do certain activities that my friends could. Most times, it didn't bug me, but sometimes it put me at odds with the other kids and I hated that. I was weird to them, you know?"

Katie laughed. "I had a few kids like that in my school and yeah, I totally thought they were weird."

"See!"

"It sounds like your parents were just trying to shield you from the brokenness of this world."

"Mmm hmm."

"That didn't sound very convincing."

"Well ..." Sadie drew the word out and scrunched up her face. "They were just so ... legalistic. It was kinda toxic."

"How so?"

"Well, my first college roommate thought I was a freak of nature because I hadn't had beer or gone to a party. She couldn't fathom that I never went behind my parents' back. Called me a goody two shoes."

"What is this, the fifties?" Katie joked, smiling when Sadie responded with a chuckle.

"She was kinda right, though. I never broke the rules and there were a lot of them! When I finally started drinking alcohol—just a drink or two, nothing excessive, and l made sure to wait until I was twenty-one so I didn't break the law—the idea of telling my parents ... yikes, I just couldn't do it. I knew they'd be disappointed."

"Look, I'm in my mid-thirties and there are many things I don't tell my parents about."

Katie's light-heartedness brought another smile to Sadie's face. It dimmed a bit, though, as she glanced toward the glass doors. "I didn't pop the bubble I was raised in, but I've definitely moved the boundaries of it."

"That sounds like growing up."

Sadie turned to face Katie. "That whole odd-man out sneaks up on me. Like tonight, Adriana and Priya are talking about a movie series I wasn't allowed to watch growing up. It's like this whole world with its own language that I'm still not a part of."

"Why don't you just watch the movies now?" Katie suggested.

Sadie shrugged. "I don't think about it until moments like this. Like I said, it's silly. I shouldn't be upset about it, but it just makes me feel like I missed out on things."

"Hmm."

They fell silent, watching a couple head inside the building. The opened door let a mix of music and conversation spill out as the pair walked past the bar, where another young couple stood—the young woman leaning on the young man's shoulder, laughing at something he said, both speaking loudly to be heard over the music and standing tantalizingly close.

"That's Noah. And that's my roommate, Mackenzie. She's not coming back to my apartment tonight." Sadie predicted with a roll of her eyes.

Katie uncapped her water and took a drink to cover her uncertainty in knowing how to answer. She wondered if she should take the silence that had fallen between them as an opportunity to head back inside and join Blair and Sam on the dance floor.

"I wasn't allowed to date either. That's another thing that made me different." Sadie confided, bringing the conversation back around and hindering any return inside. "They stressed the purity culture stuff."

"Purity culture?"

"Yeah, the whole save-yourself-for-marriage thing."

Sadie's use of air quotes and a sarcastic tone elicited a laugh from Katie. "You say it like it's a bad thing."

"Eh. Sure, pre-marital sex is frowned upon in the Bible, but the whole emphasis on your virginity as being some kind of gift for your spouse ... it's kinda extreme, especially for girls. In high school, it felt like the whole burden was on me, you know, to not only keep myself pure, but every guy I interacted with, too."

"Oof. As if high school isn't already hard enough."

"Exactly! In college, though, I let some of that anxiety go. Realized you can't really be responsible for what someone else does or doesn't do."

Katie thought of Blair's fight with Derek earlier and sighed. "Ain't that the truth?" she muttered, then realized the irony that she was sitting with the cause of their argument.

Sadie watched the attendees through the glass thoughtfully. Suddenly, she turned to Katie. "Where do you land with the whole sex-before-marriage thing?"

Katie let out a "whew," at the directness of the question. Sadie double-backed on her question, a red creeping in her cheeks. "No, no. It's fine," Katie assured her. "Um, well, until three years ago, I was an atheist, so this wasn't even a question. Andrew and I lived together for a year before we got married and we definitely were sleeping together the entire year before while we were dating. But, I'm pretty sure there's a verse or two in the Bible against it," she quipped.

"But, you two are married. In the end, it all worked out."

Katie thought about Sadie's assertion for a minute. "He's not the only guy I slept with, though, and I definitely am not the only one he slept with." *Is sleeping with.* The thought snuck up on her, blowing on the embers of anxiety, coaxing it into a full blow flame.

"Would you do it differently? If you could go back?" Sadie's question brought Katie's focus back to the moment and quelled the storm brewing within her. Katie's facial expression turned quizzical. "You mean, if I was a Christian back then, would I have done it differently?"

"No. Just knowing now what you know about relationships and marriage, would you do it differently? Not slept with anyone?"

Katie tried to puzzle out where Sadie was going with this line of questioning but came up empty. The question was one she hadn't ever contemplated. "Hmm," she vocalized to give herself more time to think.

"I just wonder sometimes," Sadie continued, not waiting for Katie's answer. "If maybe the church is being too legalistic about all this stuff? I mean, we are physical creatures with needs, you know? There's science behind it. Lots of happy marriages happen, despite people sleeping together before—or even with others before they met their spouse, like you guys. It doesn't seem like the destructive thing I was taught it was, you know? And, I just wonder if maybe we've made a bigger deal out of it than necessary. Maybe a ramification of the patriarchy, you know? A way to keep women in check while men got to do whatever they wanted? And maybe, maybe, we've made an idol out of purity?" Sadie's questions tumbled out of her, one on top of the other, giving voice to the knotted up internal deliberation.

She's not asking the right question.

What should she be asking? Katie prayed.

Does it matter?

A rightness about the question landed in Katie's gut. She repeated it out loud. "Does it matter?"

The question stunned Sadie, prompting her to raise her hands in disbelief. She said, "Whaaat? Huh? Um, I don't understand," while her body turned, as if seeking someone to explain. Turning back to Katie, she exclaimed, "Of course it matters! It changes everything."

"Why? Why does it matter what the science or our culture says, or how the patriarchy took advantage of women, or even the idolization of purity by the church? Or, even how strict your parents were. Why do these things carry weight for you now?"

Sadie's hands dropped to her lap where she studied them, quiet.

A sudden compassion hit Katie as she observed Sadie looking so young and so lost. "Sadie, I don't really know you. But you seem like you have a good head on your shoulders, and these questions are valid ones. I think this is what the Bible means when it talks about working out our salvation."

"I just envy them sometimes." Sadie flapped her hand despondently at the event space.

"How so?"

"It just seems so easy, the way they move through life. They aren't conflicted about things. They know what they want, and they just go for it. No standing on the outside debating if they should go in."

Katie started to disagree with her, but thought better of it as she recalled Blair's request for Derek to help protect Sadie from herself. Maybe Blair was onto something? She halted, choosing her next words carefully. "What are you standing on the outside of?"

The fingers of one hand played absentmindedly with her thumb on the opposite. "Life." Sadie raised her hands and gave a half-hearted shrug.

"No."

Confusion clouded Sadie's face. "No?"

"No, I wouldn't do things differently if I were to go back in time," Katie answered honestly.

Sadie nodded with resignation, as if Katie confirmed something she already knew.

"Following Jesus changes everything," Katie emphasized the point. "The funny thing is, this isn't the first time tonight I've had this conversation."

"Really?" Sadie stressed the word, marking her surprise at the revelation.

"Really."

"Look, this whole sex conversation is complex. People, even Christians, disagree about where the boundaries lie. Some people think sex is fine outside of marriage for committed couples. Others believe it's just a tool to satisfy a primal need and doesn't need commitment as long as both participants are consenting adults. I have a friend who believes teenage sex is not only a normal coming-of-age activity but necessary to have healthy adult relationships. I've heard people defend polyamorous and open relationships. I've been told unhappiness in a marriage justifies adultery. Then there's the straight vs gay debate. Or, even the debate that gay sex is okay as long as it's within a marriage." Katie's mind jumped back to the question Derek had posed to Blair. "It all boils down to the same question: shouldn't someone be able to choose what they want to do with their own life? With their own body?"

Katie stood from the wall and turned toward the lake. "Stand up. Here." She maneuvered Sadie to face the lake. "What do you see?"

"Black."

Katie ignored the sarcasm. "Look up."

Sadie did as instructed. "Stars."

"We aren't the ones on the outside looking in. You aren't the odd man out. This," Katie waved up at the sky and then around her, "this is His kingdom, and we live in it." She rotated Sadie again, so she once more faced the attendees. "Many of these people were enticed into a shadow kingdom, a kingdom where they mistakenly believe they make the rules, rules designed to satisfy their wants and needs. But you don't live in that shadow kingdom. You live in a kingdom of surrender. We don't just believe in Jesus, we follow Jesus and His wisdom. That wisdom challenges the self-focused wisdom of the shadow kingdom."

A kingdom of surrender ...

Wisdom that challenges ...

Derek was right; Blair was cherry-picking what commands of Jesus to fit her own self-focused wisdom. What she would do with this new revelation, Katie wasn't sure. Maybe she should have a conversation with Blair?

Pray.

Right, she was jumping to confrontation when she should first ask for direction.

Noise from the party spilled onto the patio again as a group emerged through the doors and congregated around a designated smoking area. The commotion pulled Katie's attention from the moment and reminded her of the conflict she had left inside. It was time for her to stop hiding from Andrew. "I probably should get back in there."

"Yeah, me too." A wrestling remained behind Sadie's eyes, though she tried to hide it by adding a lightness to her voice.

Caught off guard that her words had not brought Sadie to a place of peace about her moral standards, Katie moved to say more to encourage the young woman, but Sadie cut her off. "Thanks again for this. It was really helpful. I appreciate it."

Taking the cue, Katie motioned for Sadie to lead the way back inside. As she followed the young woman toward the set of doors, she couldn't help but feel she had somehow failed a test. She rubbed her hands over her cheekbones, careful not to smear her eye make-up.

"Katie Ellison?"

She dropped her hands from her face and found a young man wearing a press lanyard. "Yes?" she asked cautiously.

Encouraged by her response, the young man extended his hand toward her. "Hi Katie, my name is Christopher Miller. I work for the Chicago Tribune."

Katie eyed him suspiciously as she shook his hand. "Can I help you?"

He took her question as an invitation and pulled out a notepad and pen from his back pocket. "I was wondering if you would be willing to answer a few questions about your book."

"Oh, sure," she said, gesturing to Sadie to indicate it was okay for her to go inside without Katie.

"Great. Okay, so, first, congrats on the book."

"Thanks."

"What prompted you to write it?"

Katie's mind rapidly searched through her mental files for the approved story she had shared numerous times in the past few days. Shuffling through the bullet points, she provided an abbreviated version for Christopher. "I saw a couple on a bus, in love, but the woman asked the guy how his meeting had gone. He said it had gone well, but then his eyes darted away from her. I remember thinking, he's hiding something. That made me think about all the little lies that we sometimes can excuse away in the name of loving the other person. The question plagued me: What was he hiding? They got off at the next stop and took their answer with them. So, I made up one."

"Yes, that's what you said on the morning show the other day."

The statement set off a warning signal in Katie's head. She stood up. "I'm sorry, I really do need to go back inside. My husband is waiting for me."

The reporter stood as well. "Oh, no worries," he said kindly. "I just have one more question for you: is the real reason you wrote the book to expose your husband's lies without blowing up your marriage?"

Katie's jaw dropped. "What? That's absurd."

The man scribbled something on his notepad, irking Katie in the process. "What are you writing down? Stop writing things. I didn't answer your stupid accusations."

Christopher Miller jotted down another note before saying, "I didn't make any accusations, I asked you a question. You're the one who got defensive. Which, in my experience, means a person is hiding something."

His analysis of her reaction made Katie regret it, and she pulled back quickly. "Sorry, you just caught me off guard, ambushing me here and all. You made me think you weren't just going to ask me about my book when really you are looking for a scandal to sell your paper."

"To me, they are one and the same," he responded. He considered her for a moment, then fished a business card out of his wallet and handed it to her. "Here, if you decide to go on the offense, here's my number. I'll also be around all day tomorrow. Just find me."

Her hand reflexively accepted the extended card.

As the reporter stuck his notepad and pen into the pocket of his jacket, he told Katie, "I actually read your novel. I enjoyed it. Have a good night." He left her standing on the patio staring at the card.

Katie looked up dumbly at the spot the reporter vacated, then toward the building where he had rejoined the party. With a decisive move, she opened her clutch and shoved the card into it.

She needed to find Andrew. He would know what to do with a reporter poking around where he shouldn't. If he was asking her questions, someone without any real access to pertinent information, then he wouldn't be beyond asking questions to actual employees. The last thing they needed was a reporter stirring up doubt among their company. Especially since the insinuation of wrong doing in the company was unfounded.

You sure about that?

The question halted her tug on the door handle. It was unfounded, wasn't it? There may be some secret, sensitive situation that she wasn't privy to, but it couldn't possibly be more than that, could it? And it must not be that sensitive if Michael had mentioned the agreement so casually to her. She needed to find Andrew. The thought of having to talk to him when they were still mid-fight was displeasing, but Katie would have to get over it for the time being in order to protect InnovGene from slander.

Summer! She could tell Summer about the reporter and still avoid Andrew. Summer would know what to do. Probably even more than Andrew, to be honest.

She pulled the door open and advanced through the crowd, her eyes scanning the room. The reporter was nowhere to be seen. Perhaps he had come only to question her? She decided it was still best to inform someone of his presence, just in case he came back. She resumed her scanning, this time looking for a familiar face.

The first one she identified was Cynthia standing at the bar, waiting on an order. Flagging her down, Katie approached the woman and asked if she knew where to find Summer.

Cynthia shook her head. "I haven't seen Summer at all tonight."

There goes that plan. Swallowing her pride, she asked, "What about Andrew?"

Cynthia took two drinks from the barkeeper. "That I can help you with. He sent me to get him a drink. Follow me."

Cynthia navigated through the crowd, with Katie trailing behind her. They paused at a high-top table where Andrew was engaged in conversation with two other men. At first glance, he appeared relaxed and enjoying himself, but his hand playing with the clasp of the manilla envelope—a nervous tick she had learned to recognize over the years—caught her attention and told her otherwise. Something worried him. Katie wondered if the reporter had already got to him? Or, maybe something else was bothering him? Something to do with the envelope?

Why should you care? He's got it under control, right?

Cynthia set his drink down in front of him, drawing his attention from the conversation. His face registered surprise at seeing Katie as well. He acknowledged them both with a curt nod before turning his attention back to the conversation.

It was his left hand that played with the clasp. With each small fidget, his wedding band caught the light and reflected it back.

For better or for worse.

Her heart won out against her pride, populating an image in Katie's mind of her taking his hand in hers. She played out Andrew's surprised reaction in her mind. He would suspect her of an agenda, but she would reassure him with a smile and a soft caress of her thumb against the back of his hand. In her mind's eye, his eyes displayed his gratitude for the comfort.

"Did you need something?"

Andrew's question pulled her out of her imagination and squarely back into the reality of a struggling marriage. With the others having left the table, Andrew's face rested on her, waiting for a reply. He was still playing with the clasp. "What's that?" she asked, pointing.

"Nothing important," he answered dismissively, echoing Katie's words from earlier.

"Sure has you all in a tizzy," she pointed to his fidgeting hand.

He ceased playing with the clasp abruptly and reached in his pocket. Retrieving a hotel keycard, he slid it and the envelope across the table to Cynthia. "Can you take this upstairs to my room?"

Cynthia immediately protested the menial job and suggested one of the interns complete the task instead.

"I rather you do it. It's got some important documents in it. I don't want to get lost."

Cynthia took the key card and pointed it at him. "This better be the last work-related thing I do tonight. Remember, this night is supposed to be a reward for all of our hard work at InnovGene."

A softening touched Andrew's face. "I know. I promise."

Katie waited until Cynthia was out of earshot before she turned to him and huffed, "You have a room here?"

He casually took a drink, staring out over the room as he did. Slowly, he lowered the glass to the table. "I got the room for us when I was first asked to do the keynote. I thought it would be a fun little getaway to celebrate. When you chose to go to New York instead, I decided to just stay at home. The room was already paid for, but I didn't want to be here alone. After last night, though, I decided it was probably best for me to stay here tonight. That way I can work on my keynote without bothering you, and I don't have to rush to get here in the morning." He finally looked at her.

Don't ask questions.

That's what Summer had told her on the phone. Don't ask questions. Don't press for information. Don't rock the boat. She couldn't shake the feeling that this was punishment for disobeying that command last night. Was her husband's pride so fragile that he couldn't handle a few questions? She didn't want to find out. "I need to talk to you," she said.

"I thought you didn't want to talk."

"Not about last night, there's this reporter—Wait! I'm not the one who didn't want to talk. You were."

"I tried talking to you earlier."

Katie scoffed. "Here?" She motioned around her, then hissed, "Here? You want to talk about us—about our marriage—in the middle of a freaking party that you're hosting? Okay, fine. Let's talk about how you only came up to me earlier because you were afraid of Derek making a scene."

Katie felt the rage bubbling up inside her, as well as a warning in her soul to resist it. Ignoring the warning, she moved toward the edge of fury. "Then, when you realized I was mad about last night, you tried to smooth things over. Again, so there wouldn't be a scene. But you couldn't even manage that." Closer still. "You got distracted by work. That envelope. Ugh."

Katie gave into her frustration, bending her arms at the elbows and motioning toward him, shaking the air when it was clear it was him she wanted to shake. "You're always choosing work over me." She let her arms drop to her sides.

Andrew focused on his glass. "You're the one who went to New York."

"Are you really that mad about the book?"

He crossed his arms. "No, I'm mad I don't have a partner who supports me and instead puts her own ambition before us."

"For goodness' sake!" she exclaimed, then quickly lowered her voice. "You're talking about yourself. I do support you. I don't understand how to make you see that."

"Just admit it, Katie. You couldn't get away fast enough," he accused through gritted teeth.

Her eyes widened. "It's not like there was anything asking me to stay."

Andrew looked surprised. "Of course I wanted my wife here! I didn't think I had to spell it out for you."

"You never tell me anything anymore. Summer—"

"Not this again."

"Well, if the shoe fits."

"Katie, she's the COO of the company, of course I share those details with her. I also share them with Derek. We're the leadership team. I have to."

"You want me around, but you don't want to share anything with me. How's that fair?" she asked.

"If I'm not telling you something, it's for your own good. I need you to trust me."

"And I need you to start being honest."

"I am honest with you."

"Not with me, with yourself."

"What are you getting at?"

Katie opened her mouth to respond but paused. "We can't do this here," she said firmly, redirecting his attention to Blair and Mackenzie approaching from behind. She took the moment of distraction to retreat from the fight.

There was, if her memory served her right, a lounge area in the woman's bathroom, complete with comfy chairs tucked out of the way of prying eyes. It would be the perfect hiding place.

Katie grasped the ornate handle and pulled open the bathroom's heavy wooden door, revealing a mirror that stretched from the coffered ceiling down to the marble-tiled floor. She veered right and was greeted by the sight of Adriana standing over the sink patting her forehead with a paper hand towel. Her eyes registered Katie in the mirror and she greeted her with a smile and a quiet "hi."

"Here." Katie pulled a little packet from her clutch and offered Adriana a sheet from it.

"What's this?" the younger girl asked.

In the empty bathroom, Katie could more clearly hear the lack of inflection in her tone, reminding her that Adriana was deaf. At Vertical, the girl leaned over more than once to ask Mackenzie to clarify the conversation. The fluidity with which the two moved their hands had impressed Katie. She could almost see them painting the conversation on the air between them. Not knowing any sign language herself, Katie made sure to look at Adriana as she explained the sheet removed the oil and sweat from the forehead without messing up makeup.

Adriana smiled. "That's cool. Thanks." She used the sheet to dab away the sweat from her olive-toned skin. "It gets so hot out on the dance floor."

Katie nodded. She thumbed in the direction of the room. "Blair's introducing Mackenzie to Andrew. If you want to meet him, I can show you where she is."

Adriana shook her head with a polite smile. "Blair already asked me. Thank you though." She rinsed her hands and dried them.

Katie watched the simple action as if it would give her an answer that was just beyond her grasp. She snapped her fingers. "I get it! You don't like him."

The sudden movement surprised Adriana, causing her to jump. She put a hand to her chest in response and laughed, but she didn't deny the observation.

"You don't like my husband. No, no, I get it. Honestly, I don't like him much at this moment."

"It's not that I don't like him. I don't like how Mackenzie idolizes him. She parrots all his beliefs and theories."

"She's not the first and she won't be the last." Katie pulled her lip gloss out of her clutch and used the mirror to guide her in applying it. "It's a casualty of an industry that tries to play God. They replace him with one of their own." She twisted the cap back on and tossed it back in the clutch. "You can tell her he's human, just like everyone else. He screws up just like everyone else. And, for all the brainpower he has up in his head, he does a lot of dumb crap."

The commentary brought an amused look to Adriana's face. She tossed the used paper towel and the sheet Katie had given her in the garbage. "It wouldn't change her mind."

"Eh, probably not. Might be worth a shot though."

A silence fell as both women fell into their own contemplation. "Hey," Katie brought them out of their reverie,

"I talked to Sadie earlier today. She seems to be a bit off tonight."

The mirth left Adriana's face. "Yeah, I noticed that too."

"Good. So you're keeping an eye on her?"

Adriana nodded. "I'm trying to." She glanced down at her watch. "We'll be leaving soon anyway. She probably just needs a good night's sleep."

"Right," Katie agreed, aware that Adriana was downplaying her own concern. A thought crossed her mind, and she asked, "Did Derek swing by your table and introduce himself tonight?"

"Who?" Adriana asked.

"Derek Salvatore, Andrew's brother. He works at InnovGene and was supposed to introduce himself to the interns tonight," Katie explained.

"I don't think so."

"Oh. Thanks."

Adriana glanced toward the bathroom exit. "Well, thanks for the ... thingy." The young woman acted out the motion of mopping her forehead.

Katie laughed. "Any time."

Adriana gave her a slight wave and left Katie alone in the bathroom.

What are you doing?

The question once again landed with a check in her gut. What was she doing? She was avoiding Andrew. She was angry at him. Angry at him for not giving her a straight answer last night, for leaving before dawn this morning to avoid talking to her, for accusing her of not supporting him just now.

She fished around in her clutch until her fingers found the tube she was searching for. Watching her reflection in the mirror, she spritzed the perfume on her wrists and rubbed them together.

Katie was tired of being dismissed so easily out of his life and then expected to be involved only in the ways he wanted. They had agreed to a full life together, a full partnership—it was even in their vows. But here he was, hiding things from her and changing their agreement.

Like you changed it?

The accusation paused her hand midway through reapplying her mascara. How had she changed things?

You said you'd be by his side no matter what, but the first moment you could, you told him he was wrong.

Katie's hand dropped to the countertop. Where was this coming from? She never said Andrew was wrong. Except, she realized, to tell him she disagreed with him on the existence of the divine. *You changed and tried to force him to do the same.*

She studied herself in the mirror. She hadn't tried to change him, had she?

You doubted his intellect.

You doubted his work.

You doubted his decisions.

You made him feel small.

When had she done that? Katie searched the archives of her mind, looking for proof of her innocence. She came up short. Instead, memory after memory of their conversations assaulted her, bringing with them damning evidence of her skepticism.

You elevated your own needs above his own. You are selfish.

You don't do enough to show your support.

You don't respect him.

Katie used the countertop to steady herself.

You have never been on his side.

You chose your own ambition over him.

You cut your hair short and changed your clothes because you knew he would hate it.

You went to New York to hurt him.

No, that was a lie.

You drove him into the arms of another woman.

The flame of anxiety rekindled, quickening Katie's heart beat and shifting her nerves into overdrive.

Start with the truth.

Katie clung to the instruction like a life-preserver. *I am loved, forgiven, and redeemed.* She started. *I am not perfect, but I am also not selfish. I have changed. Not to hurt Andrew, but to heal my own hurt.*

She raised her eyes to her reflection.

I am not responsible for Andrew's behavior.

"I am one in whom Christ dwells and delights. I live in the strong and unshakable kingdom of God. The kingdom is not in trouble and neither am I." She straightened her shoulders as she uttered the quote from James Bryan Smith.

Whatever comes, I am cared for by a good and faithful God.

The sound of frantic movement pulled Katie's eyes from the sink to her left. The realization she wasn't alone in the bathroom made her jump out of her skin, an expletive escaping her lips of its own volition. Still reeling from the unexpected intrusion into her solitude, Katie caught the back of the individual as she threw herself into one of the toilet stalls. Retching met Katie's ears.

Unsure whether to check on the person or respect their privacy, Katie stood frozen. Then, deciding that if it were her, she'd want someone to ask, she called from the sink, "You okay?"

Silence met her question.

"Do you need water? I think there's some in the lounge area." Katie's voice trailed off as she realized the person had bolted from the lounge area. She had been in there the entire time, hiding like Katie had intended to do. "What about paper towels? Do you need those?"

The sound of the toilet paper dispenser rotating answered her. At the flush of the toilet, Katie decided it would probably be best if she left the bathroom to spare the individual embarrassment. She snapped her clutch closed and glanced around to make sure she wasn't forgetting anything. Noticing an extra paper towel that had fallen from the countertop basket, she picked it up and tossed it in the trash. Satisfied she had everything, she turned to leave, catching in the mirror the sight of Summer emerging from the toilet room. Shocked, Katie whirled around to face her.

Not saying a word, Summer returned to the lounge area. Katie followed her, watching as she flopped onto the couch, her black dress a sharp contrast to the white couch. Summer pulled her feet under her and Katie realized she was barefoot, her heels in a pile at the foot of the couch. Her despondent posture conflicted with the neatness of her slicked back bun and pristine designer dress.

Katie poured a glass of cucumber water. When Summer refused it, she took it back to the armchair opposite the couch. She sat and waited.

Finally, Summer sighed. "I'm—"

The sound of another woman entering the bathroom cut her off. She retrieved her clutch from the end table beside her, opened her wallet, and pulled out an ultrasound picture. Without a word, she tossed it onto the coffee table between them.

Katie couldn't bring herself to pick it up—not until she got the answer to the unrelenting question now pestering her.

"Your perfume ..." Summer's explanation trailed off, her hand subtly flicking through the air to imply the disaster that took place earlier. "Won't have to worry about that after Saturday."

Sensing Katie's confusion, Summer looked up at her and lowered her voice, "I have an appointment at the clinic on Saturday." Summer seemed to mull this information over as if it was the first time she was hearing it. "I've already let it go on too long." Her voice shifted from matter-of-fact to annoyance.

I am not responsible for Andrew's choices. Katie repeated to herself as she worked up the courage to ask what had to be asked. Swallowing hard, she whispered, "Is it Andrew's?"

Summer's shock surprised Katie, but not as much as her response. "God, no!" She grabbed her shoes from the floor and put them on, as if the suggested affair had, like jumper cables attached to a battery, jolted her into action. "I can't believe you think I would do that to you, Katie." She swiped the picture from the coffee table and put it back in her wallet. "No."

Summer tilted an ear toward the main section of the restroom, listening as the other woman washed her hands. When the sound of the restroom door closing confirmed they were alone once more, she announced, "It's Carr's."

Not sure she had heard correctly, Katie asked, "Carr's?"

Glancing at her watch, Summer stood from the couch. "Yes, that is what I said. I should make an appearance before the party ends. You coming?"

"I didn't know you two were together."

"It was—" Summer hesitated. "Casual." She picked a piece of lint from the hem of her dress and smoothed the fabric once the inspection was complete.

"Have you been in here the whole night?"

A breath escaped Summer's lips with a puff. "No, I actually just got here. I took a nap after I got home from the clinic and overslept." Embarrassment colored Summer's face.

It was the first time Katie had ever seen Summer embarrassed. Impulsively, she stood from the chair and reached out to embrace her. The woman dodged her arms and asked, "What are you doing?"

"Trying to hug you."

"Why?"

"You looked like you could use one."

"I've got to go."

Katie blocked her exit. "Summer, not even five minutes ago you were not okay."

"I told you, that was your perfume."

Summer tried to step around her, but Katie met the movement with her own. "I'm talking about before that."

Summer crossed her arms. "I have to go, Katie. You know things fall apart if I'm not around."

"I think you can take some time to process—"

"What do you think I've been doing all day?"

By the look on her face, even Summer seemed surprised by her own aggressive response, prompting Katie to step out of her way.

She hesitated, as if about to say something, but thought better of it and instead uttered a simple, "Thank you." Summer's heels clacked hurriedly against the tile floor as she left the bathroom.

Katie took a deep breath and counted to twenty. Each clack of her own heels echoed softly, spaced by long pauses as she slowly made her way to the door.

Once she emerged from the restroom, she took in the room with a sigh. What was she to do now? She didn't want to follow Summer's path toward Andrew, and she didn't feel like dancing. That left one choice.

"A shot of tequila, please," Katie requested once she reached the bar.

"Sure thing. Let me just finish this drink first, and I'll get that right up for you."

"Of course, sorry."

What are you doing?

Again, that question. What was she doing? She was getting a drink.

Using the countertop to stabilize herself, she shifted her weight off her foot and rotated her ankle. She shifted her weight again and rotated the other ankle, stretching her leg out to the side to help stretch the calf muscle. What was she doing? Regretting wearing these shoes.

What are you doing?

Trying to get through this stupid party.

The bartender put her drink up on the countertop and pushed it toward her with two fingers. The question came again as she picked the drink up in her hand. *Katie, what are you doing?*

An honest answer finally found her: avoiding the pain.

She didn't want to talk to Andrew, but she had come to the party because she knew she would find friendly faces and fun distractions. That plan had backfired on so many levels, and now she was trying to fabricate distraction with tequila. Not much unlike what Derek attempted nearly every weekend.

A sudden desire to find Derek and apologize hit her. Blair might have started the argument, but Katie could have done more to cultivate peace between them. He didn't deserve Blair's insult to his character, and she should have said as much.

Leaving the drink, Katie weaved through the crowded room in search of her brother-in-law. Much to her surprise, instead she found Larson Carr and another man approaching her. At the sight of Carr, Katie almost wished she hadn't left the drink behind.

Carr greeted her enthusiastically, turning to introduce his companion, Kenji Kimura. Kirmura was on the board of a subcommittee for the conference that issued awards, Carr explained, and had a question for Katie.

She shook his hand and asked, "How can I help you Mr. Kimura?"

"Kenji, please. Katie, the committee has selected your husband to receive the Founders' Medal tomorrow for his work with NeuroGene-X. His work in 2013 laid the groundwork for many of the breakthroughs we're seeing today. We plan to give it to him after his keynote."

Katie's eyes registered her surprise. "Oh, wow. Does he know about this?"

"No. The nominations are even secret, so he doesn't even know he's in the running." Carr looked pleased.

"The committee likes to ask the winner's family if they would like to say a few words and present the award."

It took Katie a moment to process the information. When it clicked, she let out a little, "Oh, my."

"I'm sure," Carr stuck his hands in his pockets and rocked back on his heels, "that it would mean so much to Andrew to have his loving wife present him the most prestigious award he has ever received. It's such a fantastic way to show your *support*."

A chill ran down Katie's back as Carr emphasized the word "support." They locked eyes and Katie was certain he had done it purposefully. He was aware of Andrew's doubts. The fact that Andrew had been discussing their marriage with this man of all people was the salt rubbed in a wound.

Lord help me not lose it, she prayed before putting a smile on her face and informing Kimura that she would be "delighted" to present the award to Andrew. Kimura thanked her and the men took their leave.

It wasn't until Carr turned back around and, with an air of innocence, asked, "Hey, did you meet that reporter I sent your way?" that she realized he had played her right into the position he wanted.

"A reporter did approach me earlier. He didn't mention you, though," she answered, trying to keep her tone steady.

"Ah. Maybe a different one."

"Maybe."

"Enjoy the rest of the party, Mrs. Salvatore," Carr said, lifting his hand in a farewell gesture.

Katie bristled. Carr was the one who had suggested she keep her last name Ellison when she married Andrew. He hadn't forgotten; he was reminding her his golden pony was the most important thing right now.

Tension gripped her neck and crawled north where it pounded into her skull. That interaction was, Katie decided, the final straw. She was done with this night—nothing could redeem it. The coat check was her new target.

Katie headed toward the designated area for ride shares, cabs, and limos as soon as she traded in the little blue ticket for her coat. The rain had resumed, its drops pinging against the metal awning overhead. As she walked, she dialed the number to their driver. She informed him she was ready to be picked up.

"I'm sorry, Katie, Andrew gave me the rest of the night off," he informed her, his voice apologetic. "I'm already at home."

"Oh."

"Want me to call the company and have them send another driver to you?"

"Don't worry about it. I'll just get a cab."

The taxi stand was on the far end of the designated area, and Katie quickened her steps in its direction. She pulled up short, however, when she realized Derek stood at the stand with the interns and Sadie's friends.

Katie watched two of the girls climb into a cab, Noah holding the door open for them. Mackenzie gave Sadie and Adriana a quick hug and climbed in after them with Noah closing the door behind them. He took the passenger seat, and the cab pulled away.

Sadie's prediction was right. Katie thought with amusement as she resumed her progress toward the stand.

Derek placed a hand on Sadie's back and encouraged her to scoot over to avoid something on the sidewalk. She followed his lead, taking a step toward Derek. He slid his hand from her back up around her shoulders.

Katie quickened her steps, a queasiness finding its way to her stomach.

Derek opened the door of the next cab that pulled up and held it open. Adriana gave Sadie a quick hug goodbye and climbed in. Derek closed the door behind Adriana, then stepped back up on the curb next to Sadie, returning his arm to her shoulders. He pointed to the black Audi that had pulled up behind Adriana's cab.

Katie wondered if she should call out to Derek. Or, maybe Sadie? Should she even get involved?

In the end, it was Adriana who poked her head out of the cab window, reaching out a hand and yelling, "Sadie, stop!"

The couple halted their progress, and Sadie turned back to Adriana. "Huh?"

"Stop. I said stop," Adriana said. A beat passed, then she added, "You forgot to give me the key to your apartment."

Sadie stared at the outstretched hand.

Adriana waved it to remind Sadie she had still yet to give her the key.

Katie hurried her steps, but the Spirit prompted her to *Wait, watch.* Katie obeyed, stopping a little way off from the unfolding scene.

"Sadie," Adriana repeated.

The young woman stirred and turned back to Derek. "I ..." she faltered, as her eyes locked with Derek's once more.

"Sadie!" Adriana called again, her hand still outstretched toward her friend.

Sadie closed her eyes, took a deep breath, and rolled her shoulders back. Her eyes opened with determination. "I can't go with you."

Derek straightened and assumed a posture of white-flag surrender. "Hey, it's totally up to you. No pressure."

"I appreciate that. I'm still ..." She pointed to the cab. "I'm gonna go. Yeah."

Derek nodded and opened the door of the cab. Sadie paused and turned back to Derek. Only the cab door separated them.

"I'm not going to pretend," she said, picking at the rubber lining on the inside of the door frame, "that you'll have any kind of interest in me after I get in this cab. I get it—it's a this-night-only kind of offer. No, no, I'm not mad about it. I just wanted you to know that I know that. Just so there isn't any awkwardness when we see each other around InnovGene."

Derek regarded her for a moment, then stepped out from behind the door and opened his arms, gesturing to coax her into a hug. "Thanks for that." He gave her a friendly squeeze, then released Sadie. He shut the door once she was inside, then tapped the roof of the cab.

Katie sided up to him. "Thank you."

Derek did a double-take then shrugged. "For what?" He made his way over to the Audi, motioning for Katie to follow him. "I take it you're heading home?"

"Yes, I am." Katie tucked her clutch under her arm and buttoned her coat as she followed him. "For not turning on the Salvatore charm and making it even harder for that girl to say no to you."

Derek opened the door for Katie, climbed in after her, and shut the door. "I don't know what you are talking about," he answered, playing dumb.

Derek gave Katie's address to the driver, then gave another address that she knew was not his condo. She decided not to question him about his destination and instead said, "I supposed I should still be annoyed with you for even stirring up things to start with."

Derek shrugged again. "I introduced myself to the interns because Cynthia made me. They asked if I wanted to dance.

Somehow, Sadie and I ended up on the dance floor together and hit it off."

"Somehow," Katie repeated, her skepticism apparent.

"Yes, somehow," Derek answered, defending his innocence in the matter. "That Noah kid suggested heading over to that new bar 20/20 Social. Everyone seemed game except Adriana. I suggested Sadie give her the apartment key so Adriana could let herself in. Then, I told Sadie my apartment was near the bar Noah suggested."

"How convenient."

"I thought so."

"Blair see you together?"

"Yep."

Katie rolled her eyes. "So, you were trying to stick it to her."

Derek looked out the window, tapping a finger against his lips thoughtfully. "Maybe a little. But, mostly," he confided in Katie, the boyish grin from earlier in the night reemerging, "I was just enjoying myself."

Katie studied him for a moment. "I believe you."

"In the end she stayed true to her morals."

The finger returned to his lips, but instead of tapping, he rested it as if a deep thought wrapped itself around his mind. Finally, he turned to Katie and said, "Brenda Salvatore would be proud of her." There was a forced lightness in his voice, betraying the fact that the revelation was more painful than humorous.

They both fell quiet as the cab maneuvered through the city's streets. Soon enough, the vehicle pulled up to the curb of Barrel & Brine.

"Scott will come back for me after he drops you off," Derek explained, noticing Katie's confusion. "It keeps me from getting into too much trouble, you know? Will you be at the keynote?" Derek put a hand on the handle and gave a little tug. Handle engaged but not opening the door, he waited for her reply.

Katie nodded. "Yeah. And get this, I just found out they are giving Andrew an award and want me to present it to him."

"Really? Okay then ..." Derek leaned over and gave her a peck on the cheek before stepping out of the car. "See you tomorrow, Katie."

Image Replaced

THIS TIME, THERE IS no vibration.

No sound.

Only an image invading my dreams as I sleep: a red sun hanging low in the sky, painting everything around me, including the white farmhouse I stand before, in a rose-tinted hue.

A ceramic frog holds the screen door open, inviting entrance into the house. I place my boot on the bottom porch step but hesitate as a sound finds me: a series of sharp, tearing noises mixed with the rustling of leaves and stems.

They are coming from behind the house.

Go.

I walk through the overgrowth, pausing at the corner of the house to bend under a low-hanging oak branch. Its canopy plays with the red sun to cast eerie shadows over the yard. The sound grows more distinct the closer I get to the back of the house, a gritty uprooting, with the occasional snap of a tough steam.

The man's back is the first to greet me.

Next, his hands ripping ivy from an old stone well.

Finally, the sword at his hip.

My presence goes unnoticed as he continues his work, removing stems and leaves, and clawing at the well with vigor.

Having completed the task, the man rises from the ground and surveys his work, hands on his hips. Satisfied with his effort, he claps his hands together and rubs them eagerly.

There is nothing particularly remarkable about the well; uniformed gray granite bricks form the base. There is no wellhead or bucket. Despite its simplicity, the man approaches it with expectation. Placing his hands, one at a time, on the edge of the well, he gazes into it.

The plunge of face into the surface of water is quick, startling me into a scramble toward the well. Within a few strides, I sidle up to the man and reach for him, trying to pull him away from the well, but my hands refuse to find a solid grip. Frustrated, I move around the well to get a better view of the situation.

Where water should fill the well, a swirl of pink, purple, and blue turn round and round, splashing over the man's semi-submerged head, playing with the strands of his hair as it does. Upon closer inspection, I see a thin sliver of gold weaving throughout the swirl. This feels familiar.

Impulsively, I reach out to touch it but stop when a warning goes off in my head. The thud of hand hitting well draws my attention back to the man. I realize he's been under too long and needs to come up for air. He struggles to free himself. "Come on, man." I encourage him. "Come on. You can do it."

His hand goes limp. It's too late. I stumble back from the well, my hand covering my gasp.

It's *never too late.*

The removal of his face from the surface is forceful, bringing with it the sound of water displacement and an arching water spray from the whipping of his hair. The momentum of the action propels him away from the stone and onto his back, limbs sprawled awkwardly. Panting for breath, the man rests a hand over his heart, half-covering the lion crest on his chest.

I recognize him: Derek.

With some effort, he stands up, repositioning the sword at his side. His long, quick stride takes him back to the well. He doesn't waste time grabbing the edge with both hands. However, he takes his time, lowering his face into the depths of the well. I position myself opposite Derek, surprised to find water there instead of the colorful swirl.

This time, as his nose meets his reflection's nose, I feel the warmth of the water penetrate the pores of his face as his flesh breaks the surface. The water laps at his hairline and I feel it at mine.

He opens his eyes.

At first, it stings; then, with the passing seconds, it becomes bearable. A comforting bearable. Blanketing calm infiltrates my joints and massages the hurt out of them. Like a mother's warm embrace.

Just as Derek's body relaxes, the pounding in my chest doubles. My lungs communicate their painful lack of oxygen. That's when the swirl of color begins once more, beckoning me to plunge deeper into the well.

Pain replaces comfort and, with a quick movement, Derek pushes himself out of the well and away from its pull. Falling back onto the grass once more, he grasps for breath.

Every limb in my body feels weak—no, dead. Dropping to my knees, I notice Derek grimace as he tries to move. He falls back, his chest rising and falling in a jagged rhythm. The fresh air presses in on all sides of us.

I crawl over to him, placing a hand on his chest to feel for a heartbeat. It's there, but it's weak. His hazel-green eyes stare beyond me. I follow his gaze up into the rose-tinted sky and see little white particles falling from it. Snowflakes. I catch one in my hand, studying it closer when it doesn't melt upon contact. To my horror, I realize it's a piece of ash. I glance around the property, looking for the culprit.

The house is on fire.

I push myself up onto my feet, ignoring the throbbing in my body, and take a few steps toward the building.

Movement from Derek stops me, and I watch as he rolls onto his stomach and pushes himself up on all fours. Thinking he too is headed for the house, I hurry my progress. At the porch step, I turn to see if he's caught up.

He's not by my side.

He's crawling back toward the well. Just shy of it, he collapses. A bit of hope leaps up inside my chest, only to be crushed by Derek's outreaching a hand and gripping the side of the well. He pulls himself up, his biceps flexing with the effort, then throws his other elbow over the side to hook his progress. He pulls his knees under him first, then gets a foot planted. With another strong heave, he stands himself upright over the well once more.

I realize he is going to do it all over again.

A cry for help emanates from within the house.

The moment of debate between burning house or crumbling man feels like a lifetime.

Decisively, I take a step toward Derek.

He plunges his face into the water.

Lights.

Pressing.

Suffocation.

I put a hand on my chest, trying to push the feeling away. Just when I think I'm going to die from the pressure, Derek jerks and falls backwards out of the well.

He inhales, braces himself, then propels himself back onto his feet.

The ashes collect on his shoulders as he walks back to the well, agony etched into the lines of his face. Back at the well, relief fills his face.

He plunges his face beneath the water again. I want to scream as the pressure returns. He's not just hurting himself; he's hurting me.

He can't see the damage.
I close my eyes, but when I do, I see the swirl of color. I press on my eyes to stop it.
Another jerk, and he's back on the ground.
I feel the pressure release me long enough to run to his side. He's staring up into that red sun again, taking deep breaths. I kneel by his side and put my hand on his chest. I can't feel a heartbeat, but I can see his eyes searching for something. He sees me for the first time. I jerk back in surprise, but he catches my hand and repositions it.
He seems relieved. He closes his eyes and his breathing calms. I realize the heartbeat has returned.
One more time.
The voice startles both of us. It pricks the crown of my head, and I swat at the air—nothing meets my hand.
Just one more time.
I turn around to see who said it, but Derek grabs my hand tighter.
One.
I feel the voice at the base of my skull.
More.
It reaches back up to the top of my head. I look down at Derek and see his face scrunched up, as if he's trying to fight against the voice.
Time.
The voice cracks; it feels as if the word is dripping down the side of my head toward my ears. Derek's hand twitches in my own, causing me to look down. Tension washes over his whole body. Letting go of my hand, he rolls over, pushing himself up from all fours into a kneeling stance, then straightening to his full height.
His body moves forward, but his eyes plead: *help me.*
"Help me!" comes a cry from within the house.
Let it go. Let it wash over you.

That voice again. I spin around, trying to figure out where it is coming from.

Just one more time.

Forget your failures.

As Derek shakes his head to rid himself of the voice, I finally understand why the well feels familiar. It belongs to The Dragon, and I've been here before—long ago, when I believed his lies. I've thrown myself at it too, believing it would solve what I couldn't.

Forget your inadequacies.

Derek freezes.

Forget your lack.

Forget your brother.

Forget.

Derek's elbows bend, but he hesitates just at the surface, a piece of ash floating down on a slight breeze catching his eye. He follows its journey all the way down into the swirl of color. He looks up.

Then behind him. Identifying the source, he snaps into action and rushes toward the burning house.

I follow him up the porch stairs, past the open door, and into the house. The door shuts behind me with a bang, reminding me that this is how every horror movie begins, as well as the fact that the side character always dies. My nerves are on edge, and I've had enough. I turn to leave.

You are not alone.

I release a giant sigh. *You promise, Lord?*

To the ends of the Earth.

If ever there was a moment where that phrase felt true, it would be this one. The house feels alive. Oppressive. I realize, surveying my surroundings, that Derek and I stand in the middle of a small farmhouse kitchen someone has converted into a make-shift laboratory. Beakers sit among cast iron skillets. Bunsen burners alongside cooling bread. The light from the red sun outside casts the same rose-tinted illumination in here. There is no warmth in it.

Derek runs a hand over the wooden table before stepping over the threshold into the next room. The fire must be coming from deeper in the house, I realize, following him.

A series of lights flicker into action like dominos, casting light on a large empty room, except for the lone throne that occupies its center. In it, the other Salvatore brother sits. If he sees us, he gives no indication.

I've been here before as well, tantalized by the prospect of taking my place on the opulent throne, one richly adorned with intricate gold inlays and sparkling diamonds.

Lord, protect me.

Above Andrew's head, a golden eagle perches atop the throne, its wings unfurled to form a dramatic, fan-shaped crown to the throne, seeming to me more peacock than eagle. His hands rest atop two intricately carved lions positioned as guardians of the seat of power. Majestic etchings of eagles, sharks, snakes, and lions meticulously adorn the throne's base.

To the untrained eye, the overall effect is one of overwhelming luxury and authority, evoking a sense of awe and desire. My eyes are not untrained, however, and they cut through the distorted vision to the broken, ugly chair beneath the facade.

"Show yourself," I command.

There it is—the vibration that has been missing from this image: heavy boots over a wooden floor.

The Dragon emerges from behind the throne and rests an elbow on the arm, smug. "He looks good there, doesn't he? Just needs a crown." The Dragon vanishes, reappearing directly in front of me, plucking a crown from my head. "Remember this?" he asks before he vanishes once more and reappears next to Derek. "Pitiful," he murmurs before proceeding to Andrew.

The scent of smoke wafts to my nostrils, prompting me to scan the room for its source. I notice Derek has detected it, too. His gaze suddenly halts, fixed on something high above us. I follow his eyes to see two banners—one bearing the crest of a royal family and another bearing the mark of allegiance to a specific kingdom—both engulfed in flames, threatening to come crashing down on Andrew's head.

He needs to vacate the throne, comes the discernment.

"Oh, does he now?" The Dragon teases as he twirls the crown with his talon-like finger, the metal spinning smoothly as it circles, catching glints of light from the fire above with each turn. "Why? So you can take it again?" The Dragon snaps the fingers of his free hand.

The throne's seat collapses, sending Andrew into a sudden plummet. Instinctively, I lunge forward, desperately reaching out to halt his fall. My hand meets his, the weight of his body pulling me to the ground. "Derek, help!" I yell. Looking over my shoulder, I see The Dragon offer the crown to Derek. Something in the way Derek takes the crown in his hands and studies it reminds me of his interaction with the well outside.

"Come help!" I yell again, trying to get a better grip on Andrew's hand.

"He's busy," The Dragon sings.

For the first time, Andrew and I make eye contact. Shock replaces the fear on his face as he recognizes me. "Give me your other hand," I instruct him.

He raises his hand to obey but stops when he realizes he holds a stack of papers in it. In the upper right corner, in all uppercase, is my name: Kingston Reed.

"That's fine. Just let it go and grab my hand."

He slips slightly and hugs the papers close to his body in response.

"Take my hand," I repeat, glancing over at the distracted brother and back at the stubborn one.

Andrew slips again, so I reinforce my grip with my other hand. Still hugging the papers close to his heart, Andrew closes his eyes.

My grip is slipping rapidly. I attempt to pull him up, but lack the leverage, with Andrew's body acting as a counterweight to mine.

"Come on!" I yell.

Trying to grab his other arm, I lean further over the edge. Pieces of the ground give way under me and Andrew's weight pulls me over the edge and into the abyss.

My fall abates as suddenly as it began, leaving me suspended midair.

I am so aware.

Aware of each moment of blame that is mine.

Aware of every wrong.

Every mistake.

Every hateful word.

Every bitter thought.

Like a million little pins pricking me with guilt, eliciting a painful reminder of each failure. My inabilities. My shortcomings.

I try to swat away the pricks, but they double in number and intensity. Giving up, I hug myself tight and close my eyes against the darkness.

Against the emptiness.

Against the loneliness.

Hey now, to the ends of the earth, I said.

I open my eyes to a white, pure light burning the darkness away like fire does to the edges of a photo.

Released from suspension, I drop into the front pew of a beautiful chapel. Along each wall, stunning stained glass stands over the sanctuary in testimony to the witnesses who have come before.

Behind the pulpit, however, the stained glass tells the story of an empty cross. I drop to my knees, prostrating myself at the altar.

My name is spoken over me like a healing balm. I am asked to look up, and I obey.

My violin and bow lay at my fingertips.

For your king, play! For the kingdom, play!

I wake from the dream with a start.

It takes a moment, but I reorientate myself to my bed and my apartment. Checking my nightstand clock, I see I should have been up twenty minutes ago and throw back the covers, swinging my feet over the edge. As they touch the cold floor, I am met with one more promise whispered to my soul: Behold; I *am doing a new thing.*

Day Five

"What are you doing here?"

"Um, this is my apartment," Sadie responded as she stepped aside to open the door wider for Mackenzie to enter. The girl pushed past her, kicking her heels off onto the nearby floor mat and tugging the bright red UIC hoodie covering her blue strapless dress over her head. She tossed it across the back of the couch on her way to the bathroom.

Sadie picked it up, folded it over her arms twice, then put it next to her laptop bag. She had seen Noah change into it last Friday before leaving work and figured he'd want it back asap.

"I didn't expect you home yet!" Mackenzie called out before closing the door. She reappeared just as quickly. "Can you unzip me? He drove you home, didn't he? Lucky. I left early because Noah said the 47 bus doesn't come around often, so I should give myself extra time."

"There," Sadie announced as she finished unzipping Mackenzie's dress, then sat back down at the table where Adriana sipped her coffee, watching the whirlwind interaction.

"Thanks! I'm gonna jump in the shower."

Mackenzie shut the door behind her, and the sound of the shower starting met Sadie's ears. She turned to Adriana and asked, "Is she always that chipper in the morning?"

Adriana smirked, taking another sip of coffee. "Yep. Pretty much. Though I'm sure the brisk walk to and from bus stops probably amped things up a notch this morning." She pulled the open Bible on the table closer to her.

With her friends both occupied, Sadie headed into her galley kitchen to make herself a cup of coffee, putting a kettle of water on the stove and adding enough scoops of coffee grounds for both her and Mackenzie to the French press while she waited for the water to heat. Opting to wait in the kitchen for the kettle to whistle, Sadie set to emptying the dishwasher. The repetitive task allowed her mind to wander, first to the question of if she had a clean blouse to wear today considering she hadn't done laundry in a week, and then, after she remembered her red sweater was clean and would go great with her check-print trousers, onto recalling the series of events last night that landed her here this morning instead of the bed of Derek Salvatore.

Not a series of events, a series of choices.

Choices that unfolded after she left Katie on the patio. First, the choice to join the fun on the dance floor. Next, to consume two glasses of wine in the hour that followed. Then, the choice to ignore a call from her parents instead of answering and explaining she had forgotten to let them know she'd be at a work event tonight during their usual catch-up phone date. Instead, she texted:

sorry, work event all week. I'll call Saturday.

Staying at the table when Blair offered to introduce Mackenzie to Andrew? A choice.

Staying at the table when Adriana left in search of the restroom? Another choice.

Applying Mackenzie's lessons on the art of flirtation when Cynthia led a less-than-enthused Derek to their table? Definitely a choice.

Then, insisting Derek join them on the dance floor when Cynthia's phone dinged with a notification and she left in a hurry. Another choice.

Next came the choice to close the distance between herself and Derek and allow her hips to convey her choice to set aside rules and standards for the rest of the night.

Finally, a choice to say "sounds good" when Derek whispered in her ear that his condo was right around the corner from the bar Noah suggested, if she was interested in seeing it.

What happened next felt less like a series of choices and more like events, though, she supposed, she was always fully in control. Gathering their belongings, the group prepared to leave, Noah going off with everyone's coat check tickets in hand, and Mackenzie, Priya, and Chloe heading to the restroom. Derek left with the promise of being right back. Only Sadie and Adriana remained at their table.

"Here, let me give you the key before I forget," Sadie said. The zipper stuck on the fabric inside of the clutch.

"Stop."

Sadie looked up from the clutch at Adriana. "It's stuck. I need to get it unstuck."

Adriana didn't respond, simply crossed her arms and watched as Sadie continued her struggle with the little metal piece. The zipper gave way and Sadie looked up with relief. "Whew, I was worried there for a second."

"You can stop this."

Sadie looked at Adriana, confused. "Stop what?"

"At any time. You can stop this."

"Adriana, you're gonna have to give me more than that to work with. Did I offend you or something?"

"Other than sending me back to your apartment alone in a city I barely know?"

Sadie didn't want to read between the lines of the statement, so she instead whipped out her phone. "Here, I'll text you the address of the apartment and the security code. Everything will be written down, so you don't have to worry about communicating with the cab driver. You can just show the text."

"That's not what I'm worried about."

"What then?"

"Um, you. I'm worried about you. This isn't like you."

Sadie shrugged. "Maybe it is."

Adriana shook her head. "No, you don't go off with a guy you just met."

"He's not a stranger."

"You're right, he's your boss. That's worse."

"He's not my boss."

"That's just semantics, and you know it."

Sadie shrugged. "So what if it is? I'm an adult, I can make my own decisions. And I just don't see what the big deal is. Don't be a such a killjoy." The sound of immaturity in her words caused her to wince, though she quickly hid it by looking back down at the phone. It perturbed her, especially since her words were supposed to convince of the opposite.

Adriana sighed, uncrossed her arms, and picked up her phone. "Send me the text."

Sadie typed up the information and hit send. "There." She looked up at the phone to see Adriana's face had softened toward her. "What?" she asked.

"You're really gonna do this?"

Sadie didn't answer her.

Noticing Noah returning from the coat check, Adriana stood from the table. "Fine. But I just want you to know that you can always stop this thing you put into motion. It's never too late to stop."

The rest of their party returned to the table at that moment, cutting Sadie off from responding—not that she had any genuine desire to do so. Derek soon rejoined them, taking Sadie's hand in his own, and leading the group out of the event space, down a few hallways to the elevators, through the hotel lobby, and out the doors to the taxi stand.

She was barely aware of the navigation. But the way his fingers interlaced through hers, the smell of his cologne, and the quickened beat of her own heart? She was acutely aware of those.

She went through the motions of saying goodbye to Mackenzie.

Again, when she said goodbye to Adriana.

The moment her hand slipped into Derek's, a daze had fallen over her, Sadie realized as she put the last dirty dish into the machine. She followed automatically the course of actions set into motion with that intimate contact. Adriana's frantic reminder about the apartment key engaged the brakes and put the choice back in her court once more.

"I want to hear all about it."

Sadie finished pushing the start button on the dishwasher before turning to answer Mackenzie, who stood in the kitchen doorway, dressed in tan slacks, a white blouse, and a navy blue blazer with the sleeves rolled mid-way up her forearm.

"Hmm?" She knew what Mackenzie was referring to but chose to ignore it, moving over to the counter where the French press waited to be used.

"Your night! I was so proud of you for going after that snack."

"Wow, crass much?" Adriana commented from the table.

"How did you even catch that?" Mackenzie whipped around, incredulous.

"Great hearing aids." Adriana shrugged. "Plus, you talk loud. And," she revealed with a grin, "I could see you in the mirror over there."

Mackenzie rolled her eyes, then addressed Sadie once more, this time positioning herself so Adriana could be part of the conversation. "So, tell me. Come on. Oh, wow, this coffee is good."

"It's the French press. I don't make it any other way now."

Mackenzie momentarily set her mug down so she could push herself up onto the countertop. From her new perch, she eyed Sadie over her mug, took another sip of coffee, and waited.

Sadie shrugged. "There's nothing to tell; I didn't go home with him."

"Whaaat? Is this your fault?" She pointed to Adriana.

Adriana narrowed her eyes in thought. "Kinda?"

Sadie shook her head. "No, it was my choice." She offered a bagel to Mackenzie, then took one over to Adriana at the table. Returning to the counter, she stuck another bagel in the toaster and pushed it down. Sadie turned back to Mackenzie, resting against the countertop. "I decided it wasn't something I wanted to do."

"Why?" Mackenzie's face scrunched up as she asked the question, betraying the fact that she thought the decision was completely ludicrous.

"I didn't want to."

"I don't believe you. You definitely wanted to slap that. It was so obvious." Mackenzie circled her hand in front of her face. "Thirsty ... all over it."

Sadie ignored the insinuation that her feelings the night before had been on full display for all to see. Thankfully, the toaster disengaged, popping up the bagel and giving her a reason to turn her reddening cheeks away from Mackenzie. "I changed my mind."

A seriousness fell over Mackenzie's countenance suddenly. "Was he a dick to you? Gosh, you think you get a good read on someone and then they go and prove you wrong. And guys with money are the worst. Thinking they can just say or do whatever just because they have money."

Sadie held up a hand to stop her rant. "He was fine. Perfect gentleman all night."

"Oh good. I was worried that I was losing my ability to judge for douchiness. I don't get it then. What changed your mind?"

Why won't you answer her? It was a gentle reproach from the Holy Spirit. The answer was simple: she was worried about what Mackenzie would think about her. She didn't want Mackenzie to think she was one of *those* Christians. Prudish, naïve, out of touch with the real world ...

What does it matter?

Right.

Sadie put the butter knife down on the plate next to the bagel. "Well, it was too ... fluid."

"Huh?"

"Here was this gorgeous guy wanting to spend the evening with me. This man that I've been thinking about non-stop since I first noticed him in the hallway at Innov-Gene. I just kept thinking, finally! He noticed me. Someone noticed me." Sadie picked up the bagel and took a bite. "And from there, I just went with it, went with the flow of things. It was like this fluid stream carrying me along, not rigid or legalistic." Sadie tossed a look at Adriana, knowing she would understand that word better than Mackenzie. "That's why I couldn't go through with it."

"I don't get it."

"I don't expect you to." Sadie shrugged. "We believe in God, you don't. You move through life without a higher authority to answer to."

The statement put Mackenzie on the defense. She shifted on the counter. "I have morals. I'm a good person."

"That's not what I'm talking about. The Bible is pretty clear: keeping sex within marriage is part of God's standard. I'm a Christ follower. That means I need to live by that standard, too."

Mackenzie shook her head. "It's so repressive. Sex is part of human nature. It's a good thing. Not something to kill with marriage."

Adriana laughed. "I don't think marriage kills sex."

Mackenzie raised her eyebrows and shrugged. "Just ask any married couple."

"It doesn't really matter," Sadie interjected. "It doesn't matter what anyone else thinks. Jesus has made it clear He doesn't think sex belongs anywhere other than marriage."

"Let me see if I've got this right. You didn't sleep with Derek last night because thousands of years ago, a guy said not to? Even though our ancestors fought hard against the patriarchy so that we didn't have to be trapped, barefoot and pregnant in a kitchen, our lives completely controlled by the whims of some man."

Sadie sighed. "I don't think Jesus wants women trapped barefoot and pregnant in the kitchen."

"She's right." Adriana stood up from the table and came into the kitchen with her Bible. She flipped to Genesis. "I know you don't believe in a Creator."

Mackenzie rolled her eyes.

"Yeah, I know, I know. But, let's put that aside for a second. Sadie and I believe there is a Creator, and He made humanity in His own image to reflect Himself. He made two genders: male and female. Hang with me for a second—" Adriana held up a hand to stop Mackenzie from launching into a gender theory argument. "He made the two because humanity needed both to do the tasks God had for them: be fruitful, multiply, fill the earth and subdue it."

"So, you're telling me the only reason for sex is to have babies? What kind of backwards *Hand Maid's Tale* shit is this?" Mackenzie jumped off the counter. "If that's what you all believe, see you in twenty years when your body is wrecked by having babies and you're depressed because you've lost yourself while your life's only purpose was to make your husband and kids happy."

The intensity of the outburst was surprising, especially coming from Mackenzie, whose usually sunny disposition could, at times, be downright annoying. There was obviously something behind it, but before Sadie could question her on it, Adriana continued.

"That's not quite it. Yes, the first part is about having children, but the second part is about creating and cultivating the world around them. It's about creating a beautiful life together. Adam couldn't do this by himself, he needed Eve. I know scripture doesn't straight out say this, but it's kinda implied that Eve couldn't do it by herself either. So, God created them for each other, to do together what each other couldn't do on their own."

"So, I can't have a fulfilling life without a man? Or kids?"

"No, no. Just let me finish the thought."

Mackenzie crossed her arms. "Okay, but hurry up. We've got to get going."

Adriana flipped to the first chapter in Romans. "This is a letter the Apostle Paul wrote."

"I know who Paul is."

"Okay, good. Can I read it to you?" Adriana waited until Mackenzie gave her a resigned shrug, then she read:

> ... since what can be known about God is evident among them, because God has shown it to them. For his invisible attributes, that is, his eternal power and divine nature, have been clearly seen since the creation of the world, being understood through what he has made. As a result, people are without excuse. For though they knew God, they did not glorify him as God or show gratitude.

"Paul is referencing Genesis where it talks about how God had a plan for humanity to be his representatives on earth, His image-bearers, co-ruling it with God in His wisdom. That's what Paul is talking about when he says 'the invisible attributes of God are known' through what He's made. That's the world, but, mostly, it's us. We were supposed to partner with God, learning from his wisdom. But humanity wasn't content with being created in God's image, they wanted to *be* God. Genesis talks about this too."

Mackenzie rolled her eyes. "Right ... the whole apple eating fiasco."

Adriana hesitated and glanced at Sadie, her eyes asking if it was worth continuing if Mackenzie would just continue to be annoyed. Sadie jumped in. "Hey, do you want a bagel?"

Mackenzie nodded, and Sadie popped the bagel into the toaster. She turned around to see Adriana wrestling with the decision to continue. "Mackenzie," Sadie asked gently, "What do you know about that apple eating fiasco?"

Mackenzie shrugged. "Eve thought it would make her wise, so she ate it. I don't get why God wouldn't want her to be wise. It feels low-key mean to stick that tree in the garden and then be like 'don't touch.'"

Sadie nodded. "That always bothered me, too."

This response seemed to surprise Mackenzie, so Sadie continued. "Someone pointed out to me that God wasn't trying to keep them in the dark; He was being a good father to them. Protecting them from too much too soon. He asked them to trust and obey His wisdom for their good."

The bagel popped up, and Mackenzie crossed the kitchen.

Adriana studied Mackenzie as she smeared the cream cheese on her bagel, as if looking for an answer to a question. Finding it, she closed the Bible. "I know it seems outrageous that something that is pleasurable should have strict rules around it. A rigidity to it." Adriana glanced at Sadie.

"Especially when you think of it as something to be consumed, not something to contribute to. But sex is a small part of the big picture. In God's wisdom, it's a tool—not a prize—enjoyable and beautiful, yes, but ultimately meant to bring about life."

"Hold up there, Preacher." Mackenzie took a bite of her bagel. "What about those who can't have kids? What then? They don't get to be part of the big cosmic plan?" she asked as she chewed the mouthful.

Adriana shook her head. "God cares just as much about how humanity watches over and takes care of the world as He does about filling it with people. To all the animals, He says 'multiply' but to the humans, He says 'multiply and rule,' meaning, take ownership and responsibility for creation. Humans are supposed to reflect God's character when they do—that's a large part of this big cosmic plan and something we all, regardless of kids and marriage, play a part in. And we're supposed to do it by trusting and obeying the wisdom of God. According to God's wisdom, sex is still a tool to be used by a married man and woman. We often try to rule this world with our wisdom instead of God's. That's why Jesus died, so He could bring us back into a right-relationship with God and help us live according to His wisdom ..." Adriana's words trailed off as she noticed Mackenzie glance at the clock.

Mackenzie cracked her neck in both directions before saying, "Yeah, so, I love you girls, but, like we established at the beginning of all this, I don't believe in God, and I definitely don't believe he created the universe in seven days." She put her dishes in the sink. "Jesus was probably a real person, but was he God? Yeah, no. I kinda feel bad for you. I mean, you missed out on having an amazing night with a guy you've been pining over, all because you believe this grandiose idea about sex instead of realizing it's just a primal response." She cracked her knuckles on both hands.

"Now, I've got to take care of this hair. We're leaving at 8:15, right?"

Sadie nodded. They watched Mackenzie disappear into the bathroom before Sadie turned to Adriana and said, "Hey, don't be discouraged. That was probably the most helpful explanation of why not to have sex outside of marriage that I've ever heard. She may not have gotten something out of that, but I did. Last night Katie told me that following Jesus changes everything, and I think I see that now more than ever. At the end of the day, we have to surrender the throne back to Him, trusting His wisdom more than our own."

"Lean not on your own understanding ..." Adriana quipped with the quote from Proverbs.

Sadie chuckled, "Yeah, exactly."

It got quiet as they both brought their dishes to the sink and Adriana gathered her belongings from the table. Books in hand, Adriana turned to go, but Sadie waved a hand to catch her attention before she got far.

"Hey," she said once Adriana had turned back to her. "How did you know what to say to me? That thing about the fact that I could stop at any time?"

Adriana became very self-conscious. "You wouldn't believe me if I told you."

"Try me."

"I had a dream while we were on the train coming into the city the other day. In it, you were in a lion's den, and I couldn't get your attention. I started signing the word stop," she demonstrated the sign, "and that finally broke your attention from the lion."

"Whoa. That's crazy."

"Yeah." Adriana gave a little shrug. "But, mostly, I just said what I thought I would want someone to tell me back when I was in your shoes."

The questioning look on Sadie's face prompted Adriana to expand on the statement. "During holiday break freshman year, I flew home from college and met up with my boyfriend at the time Chris. We had been together since senior year in high school, and were doing the long-distance thing. He was going to a college about an hour outside our hometown. During that break, he was telling me all about these friends he had made at college. He kept mentioning this one girl. Fast forward to New Year's Eve, we join up with his friends and she's there." Adriana shrugged. "I got jealous and worried. Even though we both had decided to wait until marriage to have sex, we ended up sleeping together that night. I was ..." Adriana searched for the words, "I don't remember thinking about losing him, but there was this whispered fear at the back of my mind. It seemed logical that I needed to show him physically how much I loved him in order to keep him. Which is wild because he never made me feel that way, and if you had asked me any other day, I would have said that was a ridiculous train of thought."

Adriana looked down at the pile in her arms. "He kept saying things like 'we shouldn't' and 'are you sure about this?' He was asking me, but I think he was also asking himself. I remember thinking, 'will he ask again?' but he never did. That's when it felt like things were too far gone to stop." Her face scrunched up as if rejecting a thought. "He would have stopped if I had asked. Not that kind of situation. Chris is a good guy. It was just like this perfect storm of fear, desire, and waiting for each other to call it."

"What happened after that night?"

"We slept together a few more times before going back to school. At that point, I think we figured the train had left the station—so why not?" Adriana threw up her free hand. "But then I went to back to campus for the spring semester. I joined that Bible study group where I met you. And we gradually drifted apart over the next few months."

Sadie looked thoughtful. "I kinda remembered you mentioning something about needing prayer about if you and your boyfriend should stay together. Do you think you broke up because you slept together?"

Adriana shook her head. "Not really. I think we broke up more because of the distance. It was hard to nurture our relationship over texting and video chats."

"Do you regret doing it?"

"Regret it? A bit, yeah."

A quiet reflection fell between the women, broken only when Sadie's eyes landed on the clock sitting on the end table and she exclaimed, "Oh, crap! We have ten minutes before we have to leave."

Adriana's eyes darted to the clock as well. "Oh, goodness." She turned on her heel, then spun back around almost immediately. "Hey, Sadie, I just want you to know. While I'm really proud of you for coming home last night, if you had gone home with him, if you had made that choice, there would have been grace and forgiveness. God would not have held it against you. You wouldn't have been damaged goods," she used air quotes around the phrase, "or something stupid like that. I had to work through that shame myself. Jessica," Adriana paused to make sure that Sadie recollected their Bible study leader, "was the one who pointed out that my virginity wasn't my identity. Purity isn't something that can be lost, it's something to be pursued."

The statement washed over Sadie like a wave of kindness, and she pulled Adriana into a hug in response. "Thank you."

———— · ————

Derek stared at the manilla envelope on the table in front of him with his name in the upper right corner in all uppercase letters. Next to it sat the pistachio latte he had ordered from the conference center's coffee shop upon arrival. It had long since gone cold.

He discovered the envelope laying on the floor on his way out the door this morning. It had been slid under the door the night before, the shoe print on its face a damning testimony to his alcohol-induced stupor. On the car ride over, he opened the packet, then immediately texted Summer telling her to meet him at the conference center before she talked to Andrew.

She had texted back that she was on her way out the door and would be there in twenty-ish minutes. That had been twenty-eight minutes ago. Derek sent a few texts asking if she was almost there, but she hadn't responded. His concern wasn't so much for her safety as it was for the ticking time bomb that was the packet's contents, and whether Summer would arrive in time to advise him on how to handle it before everything blew up in his face.

———·———

The bus accelerated from the stop and pulled into the flow of traffic, forcing Blair to grab an empty seat before she lost her footing—a common challenge during the morning commute. She plopped into one and scooted in toward the window, positioning her laptop bag between her legs, pinning it with the inside of her calves and knees.

Last night, as they rode the bus home from the party, Sam had asked her, "Why *do* you care so much?"

Sam had sat next to her, leaning her head against Blair's shoulder, their fingers intertwined. Sam's dark complexion sharply contrasting with the pale white of Blair's. It hadn't taken long for Blair to circle back to how irate she was with Derek for leaving with Sadie. She ranted for a bit about how he had made a promise to her and said he was a man of his word and here he was, breaking the promise. She thought he was better than that. After letting Blair carry on for a bit, Sam sat up and looked Blair squarely in the face. "Boo, why *do* you care so much? Do I need to be worried?" She lowered her voice. "Do you have feelings for him?"

"What?! No. No, it's nothing like that."

"Okay, okay. I believe you. But, if it's not jealousy, what is it?" When Blair didn't respond right away, Sam added, "Seems like maybe you're projecting something onto the situation? I just can't quite figure out what."

"I don't know." Blair answered truthfully.

"Well, maybe that's something to mull over, Boo?" Sam suggested as the bus pulled up to their stop. She changed the conversation. "So, where did we land about last names? Come on, you have to say that Blair Bennett has a ring to it." Sam bumped Blair's shoulder playfully.

"I thought we were talking about merging our names together?"

"Yeah, but Dolton-Bennett, or even Bennett-Dolton, is such a mouthful."

Blair smirked. "Okay, but why does your last name win?"

"Boo, come on. Bennett. Dolton." Samantha weighed the choices with her hands. "Bennett is clearly better."

The morning bus pulled up to the next stop and halted, the motion jolting Blair out of the memory of the night before and back into her confusion of the morning.

Mulling over why she was so upset over the Derek-Sadie issue was all she had done since Sam posed the question. The more she mulled it over, the more confused she got. She too grew up in a Christian home like Sadie, but, unlike Sadie, Blair's family attended a much more progressive church. She had been raised to accept people from all different backgrounds and lifestyles. It made coming out to her parents as bi easy-peasy—half the kids in her youth group were gay.

She had plenty of relationships in college, with both genders, and she had nothing against having sex before marriage, straight or gay, even though her small group ladies—including Brenda when she was alive—had done their fair share in trying to show her the errors of her ways. But God and her had always been tight. She couldn't fathom how the God who loved her so much wouldn't be pleased with her relationship—especially this one with Sam, which was full of love and happiness. She reasoned He had to be.

Where Sadie landed on same-sex relationships, Blair wasn't sure, but she could tell she wasn't the type to just casually sleep around—maybe even the type who didn't sleep around at all. Something deep inside of Blair wanted to help Sadie stay true to her convictions. Something unrelenting, almost desperate. Why did it feel like Sadie staying on the straight and narrow had some kind of ramification on Blair's life? That's what she couldn't figure out.

It didn't matter anymore. Blair had seen Sadie leave with Derek—it was too late.

———·———

"I got one too." Summer tossed a manilla envelope, identical to Derek's, other than that it was her name in the top right corner, onto the table next to his.

"What are we going to do?" Derek asked.

Summer took a seat across from him. "Well, first, we should figure out if what's in mine is the same thing that's in yours."

Dropping his eyes to the table, Derek answered, "It was an offer."

"You mean a bribe."

He rapped his knuckles against the table, then looked back up at Summer. "Yep."

"Same." In one smooth move, Summer leaned back in her chair and crossed one leg over the other, lacing her hands together and resting them on her stomach, her thumbs playing with each other.

To an acquaintance, the move would seem casual, even nonchalant, but Derek wasn't an acquaintance; in their years together, he had learned to read her body language, and it was all but declaring that Summer was rattled. He slid his envelope out from under Summer's and tossed it toward her.

Summer's thumbs stopped fiddling, her eyes falling to the envelope and her lips pressing into a thin line of contemplation, eyeing the packet as if it was a wild animal that might bite if she outstretched her hand. After a beat, she snatched it from the table, apparently deciding it was worth the risk.

———— · ————

Sitting on the edge of the hotel bed, Andrew rested his forearms on his bare knees, hands clasped, as he blinked the sleep away from his eye, regaining his composure after being startled by the wake-up call.

First task: take a shower.

Then: get dressed.

Andrew glanced toward the wardrobe where today's suit hung. He had picked it, thinking it made him look distinguished, something he thought would work in his favor as he gave his keynote this morning.

His eyes turned upon the table across the hotel room where his computer and tablet rested. He needed to remember to grab the tablet to review his speech.

Next to the tablet sat two manilla envelopes. *Time's a-ticking.* The thought dug itself into his mind like a pickax into a block of ice, chipping away any remaining pretenses that ignoring the envelopes' contents would make them go away.

Andrew stole a glance at the sleeping form in the bed next to him. Certain he would go undetected, Andrew strode over to the table and quietly grabbed both envelopes. He wondered for a moment if he should hug them tight to his body or let them dangle in his hand nonchalantly, should sleeping beauty wake up and see him. Opting for the more casual look, Andrew made his way toward the shower.

The chirp of a notification on his phone caught his ear on the way to the bathroom and pulled his attention to the pile of shoes and clothes at the foot of the bed. His phone was still in the pocket of his pants.

The notification was for a text from Summer telling him all the paperwork with GenTech was signed. The time-stamp read 6:18 a.m. He checked the time on the phone. 7:48 a.m. He needed to get his ass in gear. Closing the messaging app, he caught sight of another unread text sent the night before at 10:45 p.m.: Is she gone yet?

A ruffling of sheet and comforter came from the bed, reminding him of the task at hand—and the threat of being caught. Andrew quickened his steps to the bathroom and pulled the door closed behind him, careful to minimize the sound.

He rotated the shower knob, and a burst of cold water hit his forearm, bringing with it the thought that she might try joining him. Andrew locked the bathroom door. Then he turned his attention to the envelopes.

The clasps on the first envelope—the one Blair had brought to the party—no longer lay flat. Andrew bent them upward and slipped the flap open, adjusting the metal prongs slightly to free it.

The contents slid out onto the vanity in one fluid motion: a photograph, a paper with a single typed paragraph, a press release with a sticky note stuck to it that said 11 a.m., a pile of business cards, a stack of stapled papers, and a card from the hotel with the number seventeen written on it.

As it had each time before, the sight of the envelope's contents tightened Andrew's chest with panic. He leaned both hands on the counter, letting his head drop as he drew in a breath, willing it to fill his lungs with oxygen-carried comfort.

A knock on the bathroom door brought a fresh wave of panic. He shoved the contents back into the manilla envelope.

"Hey, I need to use the bathroom, wondering if I can jump in there real quick?" The voice was so soft he almost couldn't hear it through the door and over the running water.

"Yeah, give me a second." Andrew slid both envelopes between a stack of towels on the linen shelf. As he pulled open the door, a wave of déjà vu washed over him; just as she had done last night, Katie stood before him.

They stumbled through an awkward shuffle, each starting and stopping, unintentionally blocking the other while trying to be considerate. They both chuckled at the little dance.

"Here." Andrew stepped aside, allowing Katie entry before trying to exit once more. He shut the door behind him and sighed.

When he was a kid, Andrew's mom would have said that he had gotten himself into a pickle jar, meaning that the situation was a spicy mix of tough circumstances. The silly phrase did the trick to relieve stress from a challenging situation. Andrew rubbed his hands over his eyes and mouth. There was no relief from the stress this time.

Carr knew about the agreement with GenTech. The included photograph of their meeting with Granger left no doubt. Andrew's goose was cooked—another one of his mom's favorite phrases.

Katie thanked him as she exited the bathroom, crawling back into the bed and pulling the comforter up to her chin.

Andrew hurried back into the bathroom, the transition from carpet to tile now more obvious to his fully awake body. He would need to shower quickly; Cynthia told him last night that he needed to meet the A/V team by 9 a.m. to have the lapel mic attached.

That wasn't the only thing they talked about last night.

As he climbed into the shower, the memory of Cynthia holding out his keycard to him last night resurfaced. Her question "should I hang onto this?" filled his mind as Andrew stood under the streaming water, allowing it to cascade through his hair and down his face, washing away the haziness of the morning and bringing with it a startling clarity.

Cynthia had made it sound like a question, but it was, in reality, an invitation to take their relationship from flirty fun to physical, something Cynthia had been hinting at for quite some time. Andrew had pretended to not notice the hints; ignoring them meant he could ignore the fact that he was dangerously close to stepping over a line that he had vowed to never cross.

Retrieving the manilla envelope and fighting with Katie last night at the party had weakened his resolve. If he was being honest, his resolve had started weakening on Monday when Carr brought up the bribe and Katie had left him to go to New York. He hadn't wanted to eat dinner alone and Cynthia made sure he didn't. When he walked her to her condo door that night, she asked if he still planned to stay in the hotel room (an idea Cynthia had suggested) even though Katie was out of town? He had known then she had an ulterior motive behind the question, but, just like the other hints, he had ignored it and simply answered, "I'm not sure."

Andrew wiped the water from his eyes and picked up the shampoo bottle. He hadn't flat out lied to Katie about the hotel room, but it was only a half-truth.

When Cynthia held the keycard between them, Andrew looked down at it in her hand, then let his eyes wander over her figure, taking in the low-cut blouse and the elegant layered black tulle skirt. He raised his eyes back up to her face, appreciating the way she had styled her long hair black hair in loose waves. She smiled under his admiring gaze. Doing so emphasized her high cheekbones and expressive almond-shaped eyes. His eyes dropped again, this time to her lips, a bold red color.

She supports you. Sees you. Sees your genius. Values it.

It was the truth—Cynthia had been by his side day in and day out since joining the company a few years ago. At first, it was simply because that was her job as chief of staff, a role that made her Andrew's right hand, streamlining strategic initiatives, overseeing projects, and acting as Andrew's liaison with other departments. While Summer's focus was on guiding the company's overall direction, Cynthia's priority was ensuring Andrew could do his job as effectively as possible, including taking on projects that lacked a dedicated owner and would have otherwise landed in his lap. That's how she ended up overseeing the interns. Slowly, their professional relationship turned to a friendship outside of the office. In the past few months, their friendship turned flirty.

She wants you as you are. She doesn't want to change you. She makes you happy.

The thoughts tumbled one on top of the other, assaulting him with reasons for nullifying the vows he made five years ago to Katie.

Even now the next morning, standing in a shower while his wife laid in his bed, the reasons felt weighty—valid—and demanding his attention.

He shook his head to rid himself of them, just like he had done last night. Last night, however, when he had started to tell Cynthia no, she stopped him with a knowing smile and a soft, "Andrew, it's me; you don't have to put on a show."

"I'm not—" The sight of Katie over Cynthia's shoulder conversing with Larson Carr and Kenji Kimura sparked concern in Andrew for a split second, but Cynthia pulled his attention back to her by reaching up and fixing his tie. She locked eyes with him. "Look, tomorrow is a big deal. You have your keynote and then the announcement about GenTech. We'll go up to the room and you can practice your speech on me. We can get a pizza delivered. God knows these apps don't hit the spot."

At the memory of her words, Andrew scrubbed the shampoo into his hair with a little more vigor. How had he missed the slight against his mom's favorite appetizers last night? It hadn't even registered. Had he really been that distracted?

The answer was an obvious yes. As she talked, Cynthia's eyes had traveled down to his lips, revealing she intended to do much more than just help him practice his speech and eat pizza.

You want her.

"No, I don't." He denied the thought through gritted teeth as he ran the bar of soap over his body. The water washed away suds, but the accusation remained. *You wanted her last night, and you want her still.*

He had told her to keep the card, promising to text when he headed up to the room. They had parted ways, each to finish out the party doing their respective roles. Andrew had completed the remaining rounds of greeting colleagues, sneaking glances of Cynthia here and there, letting the anticipation build. He watched Derek leave with the interns. Shortly after that, he saw Katie leave as well. Eventually, the party died down, with attendees heading to their rooms for some shut-eye before the early sessions the next morning. He, too, took his leave when the clock struck 10 p.m., texting Cynthia on his way up to the room.

He hadn't been in his room long before the knock came. It surprised him since Cynthia had a keycard. He wondered if she felt weird just coming right into his room. When he opened the door, however, only a manilla envelope, just like the one from Blair, greeted him.

It contained five photographs of him and Cynthia, all cozy moments throughout the week, including the moment from that night where she had asked about the keycard. He may not have slept with Cynthia, but these photographs made a compelling case he was having a full-fledged affair. A second knock made the pit of his stomach drop; what would be waiting for him on the other side of the door this time?

Nothing could have prepared him to find Katie standing before him.

Climbing out of the shower and grabbing a towel to dry off—wrapping it around his waist once he was done—Andrew reviewed that moment in his mind's eye.

Katie's curled hair was still pinned into the updo she had been sporting earlier at the party, but she had traded her olive-green dress for a pair of skinny distressed jeans and an oversized gray knit sweater—the same sweater she'd worn the night they met. Just as it had during that first meeting, the sweater accentuated her blue eyes. Back then, her hair was a light brown, not the deep chocolate she kept it dyed these days. Tonight, red puffiness framed those blue eyes.

Get rid of her. The thought came.

That's not who you need to get rid of. The correction came just as quickly as the first.

"Can I come in?" she had asked.

"You going somewhere?" He jutted his chin toward the small carry-on bag in her hand while discreetly slipping the photos, which he had been using the door to hide, back into the envelope.

She looked down at her hand, then back up at him. "Depends on how the next few minutes go. Can I come in?" she repeated.

Don't do it, came the warning.

She's your wife, came the reminder.

"How did you know which one was my room?"

"I asked Gloria."

Of course, Katie had asked his executive assistant; she had gotten used to getting details from Gloria over the years. She obviously wanted to talk to him if she had tracked him down.

She went to New York. An argument for refusing her entry.

You should have gone too.

The reprimand came as a surprise to Andrew. In the months leading up to Katie's travel to New York, he had focused so much on the fact that she was choosing to go that he never thought about going with her. He could have gone there and been back in time for the party, he realized. Why had that thought never occurred to him before that moment?

InnovGene needed you. An excuse.

Your wife needed you. A revelation.

"I wasn't planning on coming over, but when I got home, there was an envelope waiting for me like the one Blair gave you."

Another revelation. This one quickened his heart rate and prompted him to open the door to her. As he followed her into the room, he had texted Cynthia to wait and that he'd let her know when Katie left.

Spitting toothpaste from his mouth, Andrew reached to turn off the sounding reminder on his phone that he needed to get down to the A/V team. He hurriedly ran gel through his hair. Satisfied that every strand of hair was in its proper place, he grabbed the two manilla envelopes from their hiding spot between the stack of towels and carried them to his suitcase. Before hiding them among his clothes, Andrew removed the paper with the typed paragraph and folded it up. He grabbed fresh underwear and socks, using them to conceal the folded paper.

He had briefly considered bringing the packets along to share with Summer and Andrew so they could strategize, but he dismissed the idea. This was a message meant for him alone—a warning with consequences that fell solely on his shoulders.

Tip-toeing around the room so as to not wake Katie, he dressed and collected his tablet, wallet, and keys from the table. He placed the folded press release into the inner pocket of his suit coat. Tossing one last glance at the sleeping woman in his bed, he headed toward the door but paused before he reached it.

A sudden desire to wake her and tell her everything washed over Andrew. When he left the party last night, Katie was not the woman he expected to have in his room, much less his bed, but this morning, there she was.

If Brenda Salvatore was here, she'd tell him that there "ain't nothin' fallin' apart that God can't duct tape back together." And if she was here to tell him that, he would have to set his scientific explanations that denied the existence of God aside and let her have this one.

He and Katie were out-of-step. Getting back in sync felt audacious, maybe even impossible. But, last night she had shown up, concerned about his reputation and the future of InnovGene and, suddenly, it seemed plausible.

Her envelope contained an article that hinted that she was trying to expose shady dealings at InnovGene through her novel, citing anonymous sources that claimed she had proof that Andrew had been part of some unethical dealings. The article had a sticky note with 11 a.m. written on it. Before he could respond, she assured him she had already written a press release stating there was no connection between her novel and InnovGene. She had already sent the release to the reporter. She had also emailed the press release to her agent for release first-thing Friday morning, cc'ing Summer, Derek, and Cynthia so that they would have access to the press release as well, should they need it.

As she stood there, apologizing for the level of scrutiny her novel had brought to the company that she never intended it to, Andrew couldn't see any sign of the heartless, non-supportive wife he had somehow come to believe her to be.

Instead, he saw her with a startling clarity—beautiful, kind, and smart—as if faulty wipers had been smearing the view for years, and now, with one clean sweep, she stood before him, vivid and undeniable.

She wasn't just beautiful, kind, and smart; she was a talented storyteller. Even as a journalist, she had managed to make the facts of a situation sound intriguing and exciting. As a novelist, she had made the story sing off the page. He read the first draft of the novel way before she had pursued publication. It was good—really good. Publishing it was the obvious next step. Why had he seen a threat in her doing so?

He surprised both of them when he cut her off by saying, "I should have gone with you to New York."

It was the first time he had been fully honest with both himself and with Katie in months. With the truthful revelation came a familiar feeling of belonging. He didn't want her to leave. He mentioned pizza was coming and suggested she stay.

While they ate, he asked her questions about New York, and she asked him about the keynote. They talked long past midnight, reminding him of their early dating days when they were just getting to know one another.

When Katie suggested she should get going so he'd be well-rested for the morning, Andrew suggested she stay. Her glance at the king-sized bed asked the question her lips did not: *Am I welcome?*

He answered the question by gently taking her into his arms and kissing her tenderly.

Yes, last night felt like a chance to begin again—a chance he didn't realize he desperately wanted until it was held out to him. How could he have been so close to shattering it?

Andrew crossed the room quickly and rounded the bed to the side Katie slept on, the morning light seeping in around the curtains and falling on her face like a spotlight. As his lips met the skin of her cheek, her eyes flew open, surprised. Her look melted into a smile. "Good morning."

"Morning. I've got to meet the A/V team. See you down there?"

"You bet," she said, raising her head off the pillow so she could give him a proper kiss goodbye.

As the hotel door shut, closing the sweet retreat from the stress of this world behind it, Andrew became very aware of the fact that the next few hours were either going to make him or break him.

——— · ———

A hand shot out and stopped the elevator doors from closing. Quickly, Adriana hit the open-door button to help. She was surprised to find out the arm belonged to Andrew, but was less surprised at Mackenzie's obvious excitement at seeing him, greeting him with a wide smile and a very chipper "good morning."

He acknowledged the trio as he entered the elevator with a nod, a smile, and a mumbled "morning" before looking back down to the phone in his hand, his thumbs quickly tapping against the screen. It wasn't until Sadie shifted her bag up on her arm that he looked up and did a double-take. He pointed to the book in Sadie's hand.

"Is that Katie's book?"

Sadie turned the cover toward him. "Yep. I'm hoping she'll sign it."

He held out his hand to her. "May I?"

Sadie handed it to Andrew before giving Adriana a curious look. Adriana shrugged in response.

"It looks good. I haven't seen it yet." Andrew turned the book over and read the back.

The elevator slowed to a stop a few floors above the lobby. The doors opened to a man waiting, tall and brooding. At the sight of Andrew, his lips stretched into what might be called a grin. To Adriana, however, it seemed more like the smug expression of a player who realizes they've just gained a significant advantage over their opponent. Catching sight of the man, the corners of Andrew's mouth turned down. He handed the book back to Sadie.

"Good morning," the man offered as he took a spot right next to Andrew. "Salvatore."

Andrew acknowledged the man with a curt nod.

The doors closed. Two more floors passed before the man turned toward Andrew and asked, "Did you get my little present last night?"

"Hmm?" Andrew kept his eyes trained on the door.

There was that smirk again. "Good. I hope you put it to good use." The doors opened to the hotel lobby. The man fixed the cuff of his sleeve inside his jacket as he stepped out of the elevator. "Good luck today, Salvatore." He strode off toward the main session room.

Andrew hung back with the girls, turning to them with a forced smile, and declaring, "You know what? You should come to the panel event after my keynote."

"We don't have VIP tickets," Mackenzie explained.

"I'll text Cynthia right now to make sure you get in."

"That would be awesome. Thank you!" Mackenzie made a note in her phone of the time and room details Andrew gave them.

Andrew glanced toward the main session room, then looked at his watch. "I'll see you in there," he announced, then headed toward the men's restroom.

"Who was that guy?" Mackenzie asked as they walked toward the main session.

Sadie shrugged.

"That seemed weird, didn't it?"

"Who knows?" Adriana answered, glad to be out of that man's looming presence.

Once Andrew left the hotel room, Katie kicked back the comforter and hurried across the room to his suitcase. Originally, she had turned to ask him about the plan for the day, but the sight of him hiding the envelopes in his suitcase stopped her. It suddenly dawned on Katie that they had discussed the envelope that had showed up for Katie last night, but the conversation had never turned to the one addressed to Andrew. After such a lovely evening of reconciliation, Andrew hiding something from her unsettled Katie. She pretended to be asleep until Andrew kissed her cheek goodbye.

She hadn't expected things to go where they did when she showed up at his door. The carry-on in her hands was packed in expectation that he would tell her he wanted a divorce and Katie heading to her parents' house to mourn the loss of her marriage.

Instead, as she shared with Andrew how the manilla envelope showed up at her door and how she had combated the claims of the article, she noticed Andrew's body language and his face soften toward her.

She was very intentional about not apologizing for publishing the book—she believed she was supposed to release it into the world—but she could see the can of worms it had opened for Andrew and InnovGene, and for that she was truly sorry. In bringing empathy and compassion to the hotel room, the door to reconciliation opened.

Now, however, as she scurried across the room to the suitcase, Katie felt duped by the night. She dug the manilla envelopes out from under Andrew's clothes and quickly opened the clasp of the first one. Turning it upside down over the table, a pile of papers and business cards, a photograph, and a card with the hotel's logo on it tumbled out of the packet. She lifted each item and inspected it, unsure what to make of what looked like a business deal in the photograph, a press release with a sticky note attached, incorrect business cards, and a stapled together stack of papers with so many numbers and big words, her eyes crossed while trying to read it. She dropped it to the table and reached for the second envelope, noticing it was significantly lighter than the first.

The photo evidence of the affair she had long suspected was both shocking and validating. The last shred of hope that Andrew wasn't truly cheating on her raised its soft voice and suggested that, yes, while they were quite close and cozy in the pictures, there was no kiss or other intimate pose. It argued that, while suggestive, these photos did not present a shut and closed case.

Katie ignored the shred of hope and welcomed anger, despair, and indignation to take a seat at the council of what-to-do-next. They repeated the question that had found her in Millennium Park on Monday: *Would it be so bad to have it all crumble?*

That question tumbled around in her mind as her eyes caught sight of the card with the hotel logo on it and the number seventeen.

Seventeen.

She hurried to her purse, unzipping an inside pocket and fishing out a mailbox key. While she had told Andrew about the article in her manila envelope, she had, for reasons she couldn't quite explain, kept the information about the key to herself. Holding it up, she inspected it. Sure enough, the attached label bore the number seventeen.

Skipping the shower, Katie threw on the nicer of the two pairs of jeans she packed in the carry-on and buttoned up the loose-fitting, silky purple blouse. She slipped on the heels she had packed, grabbed the keycard Andrew had left on the table for her, and hurried out of the room with the mailbox key in hand.

Finding the business center felt like it took an eternity—Katie had to ask for directions from two separate employees before successfully locating it—but, soon enough, she stood in front of the mailbox that matched the number on the key in her hand.

You can turn around.

It was true and infuriating all at the same time. She could walk away. She could pretend she wasn't being dismissed, lied to, strung along ...

Laughed at.

Yes. That too. Andrew and Cynthia must be falling off their chairs in hysterics about how she hadn't the slightest clue about their infidelity. The woman had the audacity to sit across the table from Katie the other night and act like they were friends. It made Katie want to throw up and punch something all at the same time.

Instead of doing either, she stuck the key into the mailbox. With the turn, a click met her ears.

The door released.

A stapled stack of papers full of dates and data, identical to the one in Andrew's envelope, sat waiting for discovery. A pang of disappointment hit Katie as she pulled it from the mailbox—until she flipped through the pages and realized they weren't identical. The pages up in the room had Andrew listed as the author while these papers gave credit to another: Kingston Reed.

Although she had never met him, Katie recognized the name of Andrew's mentor from BioSphere, the company Andrew worked at before starting InnovGene. She had always wondered why the two had lost touch with one another when Andrew had left BioSphere to start his company. Chalking it up to just the busyness of life, Katie had never pushed for information—not even when Kingston seemed to disappear from the industry's community overnight.

The pieces began to fall into place for Katie: Andrew had stolen Kingston's work and passed it off as his own.

"The secrets and lies continue to pile up with this man," she muttered as she pulled out her phone and dialed Blair. Barely allowing the woman to greet her, Katie asked when she would arrive at the conference center.

"I'm already here."

"I need you to meet me somewhere."

"Well, I was trying to grab a cup of coffee before the keynote. Want to meet me at the coffee bar across from the main room?" Blair asked.

"Sure, but first I need to run back to my room."

"Your room? Katie, is everything okay?" The concern in Blair's voice was audible.

"I'll tell you when I see you," Katie responded.

On the elevator ride back up to her room, another thought wormed its way into her mind and took the liberty of somersaulting around: *Tell them who he really is. Tell the truth.*

Make it crumble.

Be free.

———·———

Summer let the photograph of herself and Andrew meeting with Granger drop to the table. "Carr wants you to know he knows we went behind his back."

"No. That's not it."

"Hmm?" Summer looked up at Derek in confusion. "What then?"

"He wants me to remember Andrew did it without me. So this," Derek searched the stack and pulled out a contract and a business card, "becomes more tantalizing." Summer took the items from his outstretched hand. The contract, similar to the one in her own envelope, would give Derek majority shares in the company. The business card read: Derek Salvatore, COO.

"Flip it over."

Summer did as instructed and found "11 a.m." written there. She reached for her own packet, retrieved a typed press release with 11 a.m. written on a sticky note and passed it along to him.

Derek's eyes scanned the press release, his jaw clenching slightly as his eyes read. Having read the press release at least a dozen times since receiving it last night, Summer knew the contents almost by heart.

It has come to the attention of the leadership at InnovGene that Andrew Salvatore utilized proprietary information, obtained during his tenure at a previous company, in the development of NeuroGene-X, the initial product brought to market by InnovGene. As a result, Salvatore has been removed from his role as CEO, and the company will initiate a comprehensive investigation into the circumstances surrounding the founding of InnovGene. We want to assure our stakeholders that our current product line remains unaffected by these issues, reflecting our ongoing commitment to ethical scientific practices. We will continue to introduce our latest innovations to the market as planned. The role of CEO will be assumed by Summer Harlow, who has served capably as our COO for the past four years. We are confident in Harlow's ability to guide our company through this transition.

When he finally lowered the paper, Summer was prepared to soothe his panic. However, the expression on his face was not one of distress. Instead, a resolve creased the lines around his eyes, surprising Summer.

"You finally have the keys to the kingdom," he said.

Much like the feeling of falling in between awake and dreaming that causes a body to jump back to reality, Summer's body reacted to the statement with a jerk and pulled her back into a state of fight. "So do you," she responded.

"Never wanted them."

"We both know that's not true."

"Not like this."

"Of course not. Me neither."

"11 a.m., what is that?"

Summer shrugged. "The end of the keynote?"

"You know what? Andrew got one of these packets, too."

"He did?"

"Yeah, Blair brought it with her to the party last night."

"Why did she have it?"

Andrew shrugged, contemplating the pile of papers on the table. "I thought this was a bribe. But maybe not."

Understanding dawned on Summer and she sat up in her chair, picking up the pieces before her one by one, glancing over the contents again, this time with fresh eyes. "It's a threat." She fell back in her chair once more, the fight gone from her. "This is Carr's kingdom. It always has been. Andrew crosses him, he's out."

"I don't get it." Derek's eyebrows furrowed. "Why does he think we would go along with it?"

"Because he knows we always choose ourselves," Summer answered matter-of-fact. "You out of a need to protect your insecure ego. Me out of a need to advance my ruthless ambition. He's putting us on notice, reminding us he controls our destiny, so we fall in line."

"Suppose, maybe, this time, we choose someone else?"

"Why would this time be any different?

There was no argument raised in response to Summer's question, just a quiet resignation. Derek took the moment to bring his latte to his lips, but a sudden thought sent him in a different direction. "Wait," he said, setting the coffee cup down abruptly on the table, "Andrew already crossed Carr."

"What do you mean?"

"The contract with GenTech. It's all signed, right?"

Summer nodded.

"Then what's Carr's play here? The contract takes care of the competition issue. I don't get it."

A fear crawled up the back of Summer's neck. "That contract does more than just get rid of the competition. It gave us a footing so we could turn Carr in for bribing the committee without worrying about losing his funding."

"Do we even have proof that he bribed the committee?"

"I'm still waiting on that. But I should have it any time now. You said Blair brought Andrew's envelope?"

Derek nodded.

"Why would she have it? Something's still not adding up." Summer whipped out her phone and pulled up Blair's contact.

———— · ————

Cynthia was waiting for Andrew as he exited the restroom, fire in her eyes. She held up her phone and pointed to it. "Seriously? I don't hear from you all night and then I get this." She read from the phone: "Please make sure Sadie and her two friends can get into the panel event after the keynote." She looked up from the phone. "Are you shitting me right now?"

Andrew hushed her and quickly led her into an empty room, shutting the door behind them. "I was just about to come find you," he started while reaching for her shoulders.

She shrugged away from him. Holding up a finger, she said firmly, "No, you don't get to do that."

Dropping his arms to his side, Andrew mustered up the most apologetic look he could. "I'm really sorry, Cynthia. Katie came by last night to talk. I couldn't just turn her away."

Cynthia crossed her arms. "So, when she left, you just what? Forgot to text me?"

Andrew didn't respond.

Cynthia's eyes grew wide, and she took a step back, creating distance between them. "Oh. I see. She didn't leave."

"No, she didn't," he admitted.

"Did you sleep with her?"

Andrew winced at the bluntness of the question but was more struck by the anger in Cynthia's tone, as if she was the betrayed spouse and not the potential mistress. The topsy-turviness of the situation became even more clear to Andrew. By giving Katie the cold shoulder these past few months while stroking the warmth of passion in Cynthia, he replaced one with the other, switching their roles in his life.

Until last night.

Last night, he welcomed Katie back into the role of wife, back into his arms, and back into his bed. She had fallen into all three with relief.

Cynthia crossed her arms, letting him know she still waited for his answer. The corners of her full lips tugged down into a frown.

You still want her.

No, Andrew wanted Katie.

You still need her.

That was actually true. He had not welcomed Katie back into the role of confidant. That role Cynthia still fully occupied for him.

"Cynthia," he said softly, looking deeply into her eyes. This time, when Andrew reached for her hand, she allowed him to take it. "I need you to do something for me."

"Answer my question first."

Andrew swallowed hard, his gaze shifting away from her as he answered, "Yes, I did."

Cynthia rolled her eyes with a disgruntled huff, pulling her hand out of his once again and recrossing her arms. When she returned her gaze to him, he could see a growing resentment.

You lose her, you lose everything.

Andrew needed Cynthia tightly in his corner for the next two hours. There were so many facets to Carr's demand for the end of his keynote; he needed Cynthia to orchestrate everything to perfection, like she always did. He needed her support. He needed her unwavering acceptance of Andrew. He needed her.

You want her.

Andrew expected her to step away from him again, but she surprised him by standing still as he closed the distance between them and wrapped his arm around her waist, pulling her in close to him and tipping her chin up so he could lock eyes with her. "Cynthia, I really need you right now." It was barely a whisper.

She eyed him, searching out the sincerity in his words and, in finding some, smirked. "Get it right, Salvatore. You always need me." She brushed a piece of hair away from his eyebrow.

Andrew rested his forehead against hers. "I need you." He said, but they both heard it as "I want you."

He heard her sharp intake of breath as he drew near, felt her lips press into his neck before trailing up to his jaw. But when her lips reached his cheek, the memory of his goodbye kiss to Katie cut through the haze, jolting him back to reality. "Not now," he murmured. Loosening his grip, he stepped back from the embrace, his movements deliberate as he reached into the inner pocket of his suit—an attempt to mask the awkwardness of pulling away. He retrieved the folded paper and handed it to her.

Cynthia tugged at the hem of her shirt and hooked her hair behind her ears before taking the paper from him. "What's this?"

"Just read it."

Andrew watched her as her eyes scanned each line, registering surprise then understanding. She looked up from the paper and refolded it. This time, putting it in the pocket of her slacks. She glanced at the watch on her wrist. "You're late to meet with the A/V team."

Knowing that was Cynthia's way of telling him she would take care of everything, Andrew simply nodded as he buttoned his suit jacket before turning to leave. Her hand on his upper arm stopped him.

"Andrew."

"Hmm?"

"Don't ever leave me hanging like that again."

———.———

It was Derek seated at the table in the coffee bar lounge with Summer and Blair, Sadie realized as she and the other interns passed from the expo hall to the main session. His elbow rested on the table, his fist propping up his chin while his other hand gripped the arm of his chair. Something about his posture—the tension in his shoulders, the way he seemed anchored in place—made it look like he was bracing himself for something. Concern bubbled up in Sadie, but she dismissed it with the reminder he was a high-level executive. Of course he looked concerned; there was always something to be worried about in business.

When he turned slightly to look at the passing group, Sadie dropped her eyes to the floor. Even though she had told him last night that they were all good, she really had no desire to test that theory so soon.

When they entered the main session room, the conference MC was already welcoming the attendees to the last day, recapping the amazing speakers on the main stage and praising the numerous breakout session presenters. He reminded everyone to check out the awesome vendors in the expo hall, then asked how much they enjoyed the InnovGene party the night before. A roar of cheers and applause erupted.

"I know I enjoyed it," Noah confided in Sadie with a grin as they walked to empty seats in the back of the room. Sadie was about to tell him she'd bring his hoodie Mackenzie wore home to work on Monday after she washed it, when Cynthia suddenly appeared at her side. "Good, you're here. Come with me," she said, her voice barely above a whisper.

"Me?" Sadie whispered back, pointing at herself.

"Yes, you."

"Do you need me too?" Noah asked.

Cynthia considered the question for a moment, then shook her head. "Maybe. Have your phone on you. Tell Priya and Chloe to do the same."

She didn't give him time to respond. With a wave to indicate Sadie was to follow her, Cynthia turned and headed toward the exit, making it necessary for Sadie to hurry her initial steps to catch up. Keeping pace with Cynthia, however, wasn't difficult—Sadie's longer legs and strides made it easy to stay a few feet behind her as they crossed the room. From this vantage point, she caught the moment Andrew's gaze shifted, his attention locking onto Cynthia as she passed him at the A/V booth where he was getting mic'd up. Sadie's focus honed in on their boss, the MC's voice growing quieter and the bodies around her blurring indistinctly.

Andrew's posture mirrored his brother's, looking as if he too was bracing against what was to come next. It was such a deviation from the fluid way he took the stage on Wednesday and the relaxed way he navigated last night's party, that the concern Sadie had dismissed just moments before resurfaced. It was Cynthia's glance in response to Andrew's—serious, unwavering, her expression etched with resolve—that sent a wave of apprehension tightening in Sadie's chest.

The whole exchange had taken just seconds, yet, when Sadie would recall the moment later, it would replay in her mind like a slow-motion scene from a movie—ending with Cynthia pausing at the door to make sure Sadie was behind her, then slipping through it as discreetly as possible.

Sadie's hand stopped the door from fully closing, but before she stepped through it, she glanced back at Andrew. His eyes, having followed them, met hers but dropped quickly.

They live in a shadow kingdom. The reminder was more than just a recall of the comment Katie had made during their conversation on the patio last night; it was a prompting from the Holy Spirit to be on guard.

As she pushed the door open wider and slipped through, Sadie prayed under her breath, "Jesus, take the wheel."

To Blair, Sadie's reaction in passing Derek looked like embarrassment rather than shame or regret. It was not the reaction of a girl smitten, nor of someone recovering from a heartbreak, but simply the desire to avoid an awkward situation.

When Derek all but ignored Sadie's passing, Blair felt compelled to ask what happened last night—the two had been so cozy, and now nothing? But Summer cut her off by asking how Blair had ended up with Andrew's envelope before the party.

"Huh?" Blair asked, confused.

"The envelope you brought to the party for Andrew."

"Oh, Carr gave it to me."

It was obviously not the answer the others expected from her, but Blair was still distracted by the situation with Sadie, so instead of elaborating on the origin of the envelope, she looked quizzically at Derek and asked, "Did she go home with you last night?"

"What?" Derek replied, confused. Understanding came quickly, however, and his face scrunched up as he said, "Oh. No. Not that it's any of your business." Annoyance sat at the edge of his tone.

"Blair," Summer chastised her, "Focus. Carr gave you the envelope?"

Blair tossed her head slightly to clear her curiosity, and her hair, from her face. She crossed one leg over the other and bounced it gently as she answered. "Yeah. I worked all day at the office trying to catch up from being in the expo hall on Wednesday. I even brought my dress with me so I could work right up until the party. As I was leaving, Carr came out of the elevator. Oh, hi, Katie."

Blair moved her purse off the seat next to her so Katie could sit in it. Before she took the offered chair, Katie gave Derek a hug and Summer a slight wave of acknowledgement. Blair continued as Katie placed the envelope Blair had brought to the party last night on the table next to the two already there.

"Is that when Carr gave you the envelope?" Katie asked, prompting Blair to continue her story.

"Not exactly. He said that Andrew was up for the Founders' Medal and that the committee needed some additional information before they made their final decision. They asked to see the research for NeuroGene-X, the product Andrew started the company with. He asked me to pull it."

"That didn't make you suspicious?" asked Derek.

"Of course it did," Blair answered, uncrossing her bouncing leg and setting her foot down flat next to her other one. "Because Summer had already told me to send it to the committee three months ago."

The table turned to Summer who confirmed the information with a nod.

"I told him I already sent it their way months ago, and he put this fake smile on and said 'Oh, good. Well, I also need you to pull it because we have a potential investor. They'll be there at the party tonight, and I want Andrew to have it for reference.' He and Andrew have asked me to pull research for investors before, so I really didn't have a reason not to do it. It only took me a few moments to pull it up and send it to the printer. He waited for the print-out while I ran to the bathroom. When I came back out, he was on a call. He covered the receiver and said, 'see you at the party' before heading out the door. When I picked up my stuff, I saw the envelope on my desk. He had forgotten it, so I brought it with me since he said Andrew needed it at the party."

"He didn't forget it." Summer gathered her hair away from her face, twisted it, and laid it over her shoulder.

"Hmm?"

Summer sat up in her chair, surveying the envelopes on the table. "Larson Carr is a calculating, strategic individual. He's made it this far in life because he's always three steps ahead in the game while everyone around him barely knows they are playing it." Summer pointed to the envelope. "This is the one? What's in it?" She asked Katie. In response, Katie dumped the contents on the table for everyone to view. The pieces fell right next to the content from Derek's and Summer's envelopes.

Summer gathered the business cards together, then put the three photograph copies of their meeting with Granger together. Next, she gathered both copies of the press releases with the notes stuck to them and the contracts giving Derek and Summer majority shares in the company. Finally, she straightened the stack of research and picked up the hotel card with the number seventeen on it. "What's this for?"

"This." Katie held up a mailbox key and another stack of stapled papers. She placed the stack on the table, placing the key on top, and slid it into position next to Andrew's research. She indicated with a wave that Blair should review both. "What do you notice?"

The different names on the identical research stood out to Blair immediately, a knot forming in the pit of her stomach as she continued to review the two documents, checking for any details that would explain the discrepancy.

"What is it?" Derek asked Blair.

"It looks like Andrew stole Kingston Reed's research and passed it off as his own," she answered in disbelief. "See the timestamps at the bottom of the files? This one with Kingston's name on it is from back in 2008, while the one from Andrew is from 2009. They are identical ... the data, the wording, the references, the typos ... the only difference is the timestamps and names." The shock was evident in her voice but, surprisingly, was missing from Derek and Summer's faces—a fact that Katie noticed as well.

"Derek, your brother *stole* research from his mentor." Katie stated, as if he had missed the point the first time.

Derek and Summer exchanged a look, then, methodically, Summer began gathering the pieces and putting them back in their respective envelopes.

Panic washed over Katie. "Wait, what are you doing?"

Summer stopped suddenly, looking purposefully at Katie and said steadily, "Remember how I told you to not ask questions until after the conference?"

Blair's eyes ping-ponged from Summer's face to Katie's, then to Derek's, and back to Katie's. A sadness had replaced the panic in her face as she simply nodded in response to Summer's question.

Summer reacted with her own slight nod, as if trying to convince herself as well that they would all be okay. She resumed putting the pieces back into the envelopes, all but the research with Kingston's name, which she left on the table in front of her. She worked quietly while the others watched her actions, waiting for her to give further explanation or instruction.

When she had completed the task, she looked up at each of them, pointedly, and said, "Carr has given Andrew the deadline of 11 a.m. to do something. I can't figure out what it is from the pieces we have here. Something must be missing, something that let Andrew know what it was that Carr wanted him to do. These," she motioned to their own envelopes, "were never meant to give us a clue to that information, it was meant to warn us not to interfere, and," she paused to give Derek a knowing look, "tempt us to side with Carr should Andrew put up a fight." Summer closed the flaps on each of the envelopes, slipping the metal clasps into place. Once done with each one, she gathered the envelopes into one pile.

"So, there's nothing to do?" Katie asked.

Summer shook her head slowly, but definitively.

"And you guys knew about this?" Katie pointed to the research in front of Summer.

Both Derek and Summer nodded their heads.

A fire ignited in Blair—a mix of anger at the deception and frustration at her own powerlessness to stop it and the resignation of those who might have. Her mentor, the man who she had worked so closely with over the years, had stolen the research of his own mentor! The brilliant mind she had learned so much from was a fraud. Not only had he stolen the research and passed it off as his own, he had lied to her again and again. Telling her stories of working on the research late into the night, they had commiserated about the difficulties of waiting for that moment of scientific breakthrough when all your sacrifice and stress becomes worth it. They suffered challenges together and rejoiced together. Many of the advances NeuroGene-X brought laid the foundation for the work they were doing now.

When she couldn't go home for the holidays, Andrew and Katie invited her to the Salvatore's. Meeting Brenda led to attending church with her, which led to having a small community of women who, even if they disagreed with her, loved her. She had spent many more holidays and events with the Salvatore family. Andrew and Blair were more than just teammates; they were friends.

On impulse, she reached for the file, but Summer stopped her by placing her own hand on it. "What are you going to do with it?" Blair asked.

"Shred it."

"We have to report it."

"The data in here," Summer tapped the research, "is part of your work with RegenX, right? You whistle-blow, we're talking about a regulatory freeze and investigation into everything we've ever made here. It would be the end of InnovGene and the good work we're doing. Think of the patients who need this therapy. Think of future therapies that will be developed because of the ground-breaking work you're doing now. Stop being so short-sighted."

Blair crossed her arms. "What he did was wrong. Unethical."

Derek sat up in his chair, placing both forearms on the table, and used his hands to emphasize his next point. "There's more to the story than just Andrew taking the—"

"Stealing."

"Shhh." Derek lowered his own voice. "Stealing the research. Andrew can explain it to you later, but right now, we just need to get through the next hour."

Unsatisfied, Blair turned to Katie to get her take on the situation. Katie just shrugged and shook her head, resigned to let it go for now, but obviously not happy about it.

"How can you be okay with not reporting this?" Blair asked.

Fingers tapping against the arms of her chair, Katie looked thoughtful as she mulled Blair's question over. The tapping stopped.

"Trust me, I'm not okay with any of this. More than you know. But, I'm trying to put my emotions aside for right now, for the sake of all those involved, the patients, the employees ... waiting a couple hours isn't going to make that much of a difference. After the conference, we'll sit down with Andrew and get answers to all our questions. Right, Summer?"

Katie waited for Summer to confirm with a nod, then slapped the arms of her chair and stood up. "Okay, we have a plan."

The others followed her lead and stood from the table, each gathering their items and tossing away empty coffee cups. When Blair turned from the garbage can, she saw Katie lean in toward Summer and ask, "How are you feeling?"

Summer's body tensed at the question, but she tried to cover by running a hand over her hair near her temples. It was a silly motion as her hair was slicked back into a high and tight ponytail. "I'm fine," she answered Katie. Without waiting for the others, she took off toward the main room, tossing over her shoulder, "Let's go. It's time for his keynote."

Blair caught Katie's gaze and gave her a questioning look, but Katie waved away her concern and indicated that they should follow Summer.

———————

Taking his place center-stage after being introduced, Andrew could see Katie leading Summer, Derek, and Blair to seats toward the front. As she reached the row, Katie hesitated, leaned in close to Summer and said something, then stepped out of the way so Summer could file into the row first and take the empty seat next to Cynthia. Derek and Blair followed suit, with Katie taking the seat at the end of the row. At the sight of Katie, a calm settled in Andrew's body, quieting the nervousness that rattled him and restoring the charism and ease that typically defined his posture when he spoke.

She made it.

For some strange reason, he still, despite their evening together, doubted she would show up—especially as the minutes passed, drawing Andrew closer to the time for him to take the stage. But it had been a silly worry; here she was.

The applause died down, and the room quieted with anticipation. Andrew let the quiet continue for another beat, teasing the audience's expectation. They were like a dog sitting with a cookie on its nose being told to "wait."

Now.

"It's an honor to stand here today and reflect on how far we've come in the field of genetic medicine. In the last decade, science has advanced through the art of asking good questions. Questions like, What if we could repair nerve damage at the genetic level? What if we could rewrite the body's own healing process? What if patients with no options suddenly had hope?

"Those questions have led to breakthroughs that have reshaped medicine—advancements our scientific forefathers could never have imagined, bringing unprecedented healing and renewed hope to millions worldwide. It has taken years of dedication, brilliant minds," Andrew waved a hand over the audience, "and unwavering belief to make it possible. And now, the impact is undeniable."

Andrew paused as the applause swelled, then faded.

"But innovation doesn't stop. It can't stop. Humanity depends on us to keep asking the hard questions, to push boundaries, to imagine the impossible ... to explore what we do not yet understand, refine what we do, and reimagine what could be. Science isn't just about what we've accomplished—it's about what comes next."

"I have heard others accuse the scientific community, particularly in biotechnology and gene therapy, of 'playing God.' Well, I say—if not us, who will? We have a moral obligation to take these minds of ours and serve our fellow humans with them. Our work is life-giving. It's life-creating. If saving our neighbor from illness and giving them a new lease on life is 'playing God,' then may we all be guilty of that sin."

Andrew allowed the weight of the words to settle, pausing just long enough for them to land.

"Because advancing this industry is imperative for those who suffer, I want to focus today on three key areas where we, as a community, can have the greatest impact. The responsibility we carry isn't just to push boundaries, but to do so with integrity, ensuring that the advancements we make today stand the test of time tomorrow."

———— · ————

Playing God ...

Adriana felt every hair on the back of her neck with Andrew's statement. She snuck a glance to her right where Mackenzie sat on the edge of her seat, pen scribbling over a notebook page in a futile attempt to capture each word rolling off Andrew's tongue.

Andrew didn't really think he was god-like, right? It was just a figure of speech to emphasize the gravity of the work this industry accomplished, right?

The blatant lack of humility and the overtly immense ego was almost more than Adriana could truly comprehend. She had never sat in the presence of such self-importance. It was both astonishing to Adriana and off-putting.

Mackenzie was eating it up.

She wants to belong.

Adriana tried to focus on the interpreter's hand movements and facial expressions as he conveyed Andrew's keynote, but her mind insisted on turning the phrase over and over again, inspecting it from every angle.

She wants to belong.

Belong to what?

Something bigger.

Bigger than what? Then a normal life? Bigger than a regular career? Bigger than the American dream?

Bigger than what?

Kansas.

It was so simple—Adriana couldn't believe she had missed it all this time. Mackenzie was always tearing down her home state, especially her small town. And that outburst this morning? The one about a woman resenting life because she had spent it serving her husband and kids? She wasn't talking about some abstract idea. She was talking about her own parents.

This career wasn't just a job for Mackenzie—it was her way out. A chance to become everything she believed her mother wasn't: strong, smart, self-sufficient, impactful ...

And Andrew was the spokesperson for that escape. No wonder she hung onto his every word, as if they were the lamp lighting the path out of Elkwood, guiding her into a world where she didn't have to sacrifice her own happiness.

Adriana shifted in her seat, trying to regain a comfortable position. Was it really that wrong? Wanting a different life than the one your parents lived? Was she not doing exactly the same thing? She was certain that Mackenzie would see it that way.

Lord, I don't know how to point her to you, she prayed as she shifted in her seat once more.

Mackenzie's fingers discreetly spelled out the word "ok" while her face displayed a quizzical expression.

Adriana signed she was fine, just couldn't find a comfy spot, then brushed Mackenzie's concern away with a wave of her hand and a facial expression that emphasized that she was good.

The pen scribbled down another gem from Andrew.

Adriana forced herself to focus once more on the interpreter's face and hands.

———·———

With each task she completed for Cynthia, the tightening in Sadie's chest grew into a full-blown crushing coupled with an overwhelming nausea. The tasks themselves were nothing significant or nefarious, yet a prevailing sense of wrong accompanied them. While she worked, Sadie's mind tried to unravel why her gut screamed "something's wrong" although there was no evidence to support the claim. If anything, their tasks were in response to a wrongdoing. A surprising one at that. Sadie still couldn't believe the information she had learned. It seemed preposterous, but she reasoned she hadn't been at InnovGene long enough to understand the work or the employees that went on there.

They had worked quickly and independently, each with their own list of to-dos, Cynthia on the phone most of the time while Sadie's work consisted mostly of sending emails, filling out forms, and writing up a formal statement. When she ran the copy past Cynthia, the woman gave her approval, then slid a list of media outlets ranging from mainstream to scientific-niche. "If any of these reach out to us, you can respond with that statement."

"How will I know they've reached out to us?"

"Here's the login and password for the media request email. Sign into it from your phone. Your one job is to be glued to this for the next few days. Yes, even over the weekend. The news probably won't make it to the mainstream outlets, but the small scientific news outlets will be all over this. Don't respond with anything other than the statement. If they press for more info, you send those over to me."

"Isn't this what the communications or PR team does?"

"Not when it's this sensitive," Cynthia answered. She glanced at the wall clock and said, "We need to get back in there."

As they entered the space, Cynthia had turned to Sadie and said, "When Andrew gets to his last point, that's when I need you to do it, okay? No sooner, no later."

The need to time things just so only added to Sadie's sense of dread as she sat a few rows back from the stage, waiting for Andrew to make his last point so she could complete her final task for Cynthia.

Jesus, why does this feel wrong? she prayed. *It's not like I can say no. I don't have any real reason to. Ugh. This feels so wrong, and I can't tell why.*

Sadie pressed a hand to her stomach, as if the action would get rid of the hollow feeling there.

"Which brings me to the final key area I wanted to discuss with you all this morning."

Sadie's ears peaked up at Andrew's statement.

It was go-time.

Cynthia's intern stood from her seat and walked toward the row where Cynthia sat with the others, signaling to Andrew that the wheels were in motion.

He decided to look at the other side of the room while she did what needed to be done. It would make what he had to do next easier.

You don't have to go through with it.

What choice did he really have?

There's always a choice.

The thoughts felt foreign.

"At the heart of every breakthrough is a decision—how far are we willing to go? How much are we willing to risk in the name of progress? Biotechnology has always been about pushing boundaries, but pushing boundaries without ethical grounding isn't innovation—it's recklessness."

The words flowed effortlessly from Andrew, having practiced them over and over in the days leading up to the conference.

"The responsibility we carry as scientists, as innovators, as leaders in this field, is to ensure that what we create serves humanity—not just ambition."

This was it.

Andrew's heart pounded against his ribs, his pulse a relentless drumbeat in his ears.

When sharing the keynote with Katie last night, he had left out this next part. He crafted it with Summer on Tuesday night after they figured out their plan to partner with GenTech and expose Carr. This was the moment in his speech where he would lay out the dirty details of Larson Carr's dealings, freeing the company from his grip—and finally allowing Andrew to stop looking over his shoulder.

Why had they thought they would get away with it? Carr was a master manipulator; he knew that from his decade-worth of dealings with the man. It had only gotten worse over the years as the man amassed wealth and power.

Let go and he lets go.

A silly thought. There was no letting go. Doing so would lead to his ruin.

"That means holding ourselves accountable, ensuring that our work stands on integrity, not shortcuts. Because in the end, it's not just our reputations at stake—it's the lives of those who trust us to get it right." He adjusted the speed of delivery to emphasize his last point. The room erupted into applause and cheers. Andrew forced himself to breathe evenly, to keep his expression calm. "And speaking of accountability ..."

The energy shift in the room was palpable. The applause faded.

Choose better. Choose honest.

The thought felt familiar ... recent.

Katie.

She said she wanted him to be honest.

She doesn't understand you. Doesn't get you. Doesn't understand the sacrifice.

Andrew steadied himself. He really had no choice.

Carr had decided for him.

He could do this right now and hold on to everything he'd worked so hard for over the years—hold on to all the breakthroughs, the people he'd helped, the employees whose livelihoods depended on him, the recognition, the impact ...

Or he could turn on Carr, and this world would come crashing down on him. He would lose everything. His reputation. His prestigious standing in this industry. His success.

He'd lose his kingdom.

His throne.

"Last night, InnovGene was made aware of a serious breach of ethics. An individual within our senior research team took it upon themselves to engage in actions that do not reflect the values of this company. Specifically, they approached a member of the licensing committee in an attempt to influence the regulatory process for our upcoming product approval."

A ripple of shock moved through the audience. Murmurs spread across the room, heads turning toward one another. Andrew pressed forward, refusing to look toward the seat where Blair sat just moments before. Not that she would be there if he looked; by this point she should be on her way back to the office where security waited to escort her to her desk to clear it out. Andrew suddenly wished he had a podium to steady himself against the wave of guilt that threatened to take him down.

She's young. She'll recover. You did the right thing. It was an icy truth that froze the growth of guilt, but did nothing to eradicate it.

"While this does not change the legitimacy of our work, it is unacceptable. Integrity is the foundation of everything we do, and we will not allow individual misjudgments to undermine the trust we have built. Effective immediately, we are launching a full internal review, and the individual responsible has been removed from their position."

The words landed like a hammer. Andrew's throat felt tight, but his expression remained composed. It was done, and there was no taking it back now.

"Accountability to ethical standards is a must if we are to continue to do good for the world around us. I implore you, each of you, to ask where we can do better in this area. We stand on the edge of possibility. Every discovery, every advance, every step forward we take is a step toward a future where the impossible becomes reality. Where disease is no longer a life sentence. Where the limitations of today become the stepping stones of tomorrow. And that future isn't waiting for someone else to create it—it's waiting for us. The visionaries. The relentless minds in this room who refuse to accept 'good enough.' Who will keep asking 'What if?' Who will push forward when the rest of the world says stop. Because that's what we do. We challenge. We innovate. We lead. This is our time. This is our responsibility. Let's move forward together—ethically, boldly, and without fear of what's ahead."

Andrew stretched out both hands toward the audience and said, "Thank you." Bringing his palms together in front of his chest, he gave a bow of acknowledgement as the crowd rose to its feet, accompanied by a roar of approval.

He started walking off the stage but stopped at the sight of Larson Carr, accompanied by Kenji Kimura, who was holding a small box in his hands. Kimura motioned for him to walk back to center stage.

Confused, Andrew obeyed, his eyes dropping to the row where Cynthia sat, both Blair and Katie now absent from their seats. Derek and Summer remained in their seats, Summer's expression unreadable, but Derek's full of shock.

Cynthia caught his eye and mouthed "You did great." Her expression turned sour as her eyes fell on the person next to him, causing Andrew to turn to find the source of her displeasure.

Katie stood there, Kimura's box now in her hands.

Kimura stepped forward, mic in hand, and thanked the crowd once more as they settled back in their seats and quieted.

"This year's Biotech Frontiers Conference has been one for the books, and I sincerely hope you've enjoyed your time with us. As many of you know, this conference is organized by The Global Institute for Genetic Advancement. Over the years, GIGA has used this conference to present our prestigious awards. This year, when considering which award to give and to whom, we knew it was time to formally acknowledge Andrew Salvatore for the pioneering work he has done over the past decade. Here to present Andrew with The Founders' Medal in Genetic Medicine for his work on NeuroGene-X, is Andrew's wife, Katie Ellison." Kimura handed the mic to Katie, indicating she should take his place.

Andrew watched Katie take the mic and spot from Kimura in pure shock, as if watching a dream unfold.

It was a dream, Andrew realized. A longing for recognition had resided for so long in his heart, he feared it would never happen. Yet, here he stood, about to receive one of the top awards in his industry in front of all his peers. It was a dream come true.

"It's not often that we get to witness history being written in real time." Katie began, a nervous tinge to her voice, "Today, we celebrate not just innovation, but perseverance—the relentless pursuit of discovery that turns impossibility into reality. The work being honored here has changed lives. NeuroGene-X isn't just a scientific breakthrough—it's a testament to what happens when bold ideas meet unwavering determination. At its core, this moment represents years of dedication, sacrifice, and belief in something greater than ourselves."

Katie's voice caught, and she finally looked up at Andrew.

There in her eyes, Andrew saw the most heart-breaking thing he could: disappointment. The realization that pride did not accompany Katie's words slammed into him with brutal force. It took everything in him not to stumble back under her gaze. Instead, he tugged at the sleeve of his jacket before clasping his hands together in front of him.

"I have had the privilege of seeing firsthand the passion that drives today's honoree. While the world knows him as a scientist, a researcher, and an innovator," Katie gave him a small smile, "I know him simply as Andrew, son of Peter and Brenda Salvatore, brother to Derek Salvatore, and my husband."

Katie turned to the audience, obviously going off script. "Unfortunately, my mother-in-law passed away three years ago, and my father-in-law could not be here today because he recently had surgery and couldn't travel. I asked my father-in-law if he had any words for his son on this special day. He had many."

She paused and allowed the audience to chuckle.

"But I wanted to share just a few with you now." Katie pulled her phone from her pocket and set it atop the small box. Holding the mic to the speaker, she pressed play—Peter's voice, strong and resonant, filled the room.

"For as long as I can remember, Andrew has been someone who refuses to accept limits—someone who has always been willing to chase what matters most. While other guys were worrying about cars and women, Andrew was worried about solving the suffering of those around him. He hated seeing anything hurt—a bird, a mouse, a snake...it didn't matter, he wanted to fix them all, much to his mother's chagrin."

The crowd chuckled but quieted quickly in order to hear Peter's next words.

"When his mother was diagnosed with MS in the early 2000s, I saw Andrew's passion become a crusade. In the end, he couldn't quite help her; the disease progressed too quickly, leading to her passing away from complications just a decade later. I know not being able to help his mom was devastating to Andrew, but his mom would be so proud of Andrew and the way his work has gone on to impact millions of lives globally. I know I am."

Hearing his father's pronouncement of pride brought tears to Andrew's eyes. No one but Andrew knew they were tears of grief, guilt, and shame. If his father and mother knew what he had done, not just back in the day, but today, firing an innocent worker—a friend—to protect his own skin ... they would be appalled. Ashamed.

Katie removed the phone from its perch on the box and put it back in her pocket. She took a deep breath and looked out over the crowd. "I don't pretend to really understand what you all do—I just write novels—but I know for a fact that without the support of this community, and the partnerships Andrew has formed over the years, he would not be standing here today to accept this award. His success is in large part because of those who mentored and guided him when he needed it most."

She locked eyes with him as she said "mentored." The weight of her gaze was digging into his already raw conscience—silent confirmation that his worst fear had come true. Katie knew about Kingston Reed.

Suddenly, the disappointment in her eyes made sense. If she knew about Kingston, she probably knew that Blair was blameless as well. Andrew's eyes snapped to Carr, who met his gaze with a smug look that slowly stretched into a wild, Cheshire Cat grin.

Carr had made sure she knew. Probably another attempt to remove her from Andrew's life. It might just have worked, Andrew realized with panic; the Katie he married would have a hard time reconciling the fact he had acted in such unethical ways, but the Katie she now was, this Katie who had faith in God, that Katie would want to walk away from him.

"So, it is with great honor that I introduce the recipient of this year's Founders' Medal in Genetic Medicine—Dr. Andrew Salvatore." Katie managed to keep her voice level as she made the final announcement. Opening the box with a flourish to reveal the medal, Katie presented the award to Andrew, drawing up on her tippy-toes to give him a kiss on his cheek after he took the box from her. She handed him the mic.

He wanted to whisk her off the stage, to explain how Carr had backed him into a corner and he was just fighting his way out. To make her understand that he did this for them, for their company. To help her see that, while it looked bad, he wasn't the bad guy here. But now was not the time; the audience expected him to say something.

Andrew wiped the sweat from his forehead with the back of his hand and said, "Whew."

The audience chuckled.

"I don't know what to say." Finally, some honesty. "So, I am just going to say thank you to the GIGA committee for the recognition, to this community for your support, and to my wife for putting up with all the ups and downs over the years as we navigated to this point. Finally, I want to thank my team at InnovGene, specifically Summer Harlow and Derek Salvatore. You both have walked by my side through the biggest challenges, and I will say this award belongs to you as much as it does me. Thank you."

A cursory glance over at Summer and Derek revealed his expressed gratitude during his acceptance speech did nothing to cover the magnitude of going solo in the decision to attribute Carr's infraction to Blair.

Andrew walked back over to Katie and waited there with her while Kimura wrapped up and dismissed the audience to the final breakout session of the conference. Once the crowd shifted into a shuffle to the breakout rooms, Katie took off down the stage stairs, forcing Andrew to hurry after her.

Summer, Derek, and Cynthia, having already exited the row, watched Katie and Andrew's approach.

"Wait! Katie!" he called after her.

She spun around quickly, forcing him to halt his progress, her dark hair whipping around and smacking her cheeks with momentum. "I can't believe you threw Blair under the

bus—after all she's done for you—because of that man."
Her last words, whispered, dripped with hatred.

"I had no choice."

"There's always a choice." She spun back to the row of
chairs, gathering up her purse and slinging it over her
shoulder.

"No, no, there wasn't." He reached toward her, but she
slapped his hand away.

"Let her go, Andrew." Derek instructed, grabbing Andrew's forearm and pushing it away from Katie.

The authoritative action from his brother surprised
Andrew, and he took a step back, raising his hands to
show he had no intention of trying to reach for her again.

Belongings now in hand, Katie gave their little group
a once over, her eyes lingering on Cynthia. She turned
a searing look on Andrew. "The worst thing about this,"
her voice took on a mocking quality to it, "is that you,
this uniquely brilliant man, turned into a freaking cliche
by sleeping with your admin."

"I didn't sleep with her." Andrew quickly corrected her.

"I'm not his admin." Cynthia protested.

Katie rolled her eyes at Cynthia. "You keep telling
yourself that." She took off.

Derek sprang into action to follow her, tossing Andrew
a disgusted look as he did.

"I didn't—" Andrew began his defense, but Derek ignored him, continuing to hurry after Katie.

Andrew turned to Summer.

She handed him a pile of manilla envelopes. "Guess we
don't need these anymore, do we?" Her hands free, she
smoothed her blazer. "Katie's right, there is always a choice,
and your choice to not come to us with this was your
biggest mistake. I got an email with proof just as you took
the stage. We could have taken Carr down. Instead, you

chose you. Since you obviously don't need my help, my resignation letter will be on your desk on Monday morning."

Her retreat was slower, more collected, but no less dramatic than that of Katie's and Derek's.

"Don't worry about them. They'll realize you did the right thing. Things will cool off over the weekend." Cynthia's hand on his arm startled Andrew and drew his attention from Summer back to his chief of staff.

As if in a daze, his eyes traveled from her hand up her arm to her smiling face. It was a sincere smile, meant to bring him comfort, he was sure, but the room had tilted, and his world was turning upside down, so what was meant to bring him peace only stirred up a renewed panic.

He dropped the envelopes on a nearby chair, then clawed at his tie, attempting to loosen its grip around his neck.

"Hey, let me help you."

He swatted Cynthia's hand away. "No, no. I got it." Having finally worked the knot out, he yanked the tie off, dropping it on the envelopes.

Both hands on his hips, he tried to take a deeper breath, but his lungs wouldn't cooperate. He pulled his jacket off and dropped it on the chair as well.

"Hey, hey, settle down. You're drawing attention to yourself."

The room was nearly empty now—the crowd having moved on to the breakout session—but several attendees remained chatting with one another while the conference staff worked to set the room for the closing session. He noticed a few stealing glances his way.

"Um, excuse me."

Andrew spun around to find the intern Cynthia had asked to escort Blair out of the room. The young woman fidgeted with her phone.

"Yes, Sadie?" Cynthia asked.

"I was sent to get Andrew for the expert panel. They are waiting on him."

"He'll be right—"

"No, tell them I had to leave."

Sadie looked confused, unsure what message to take back to the panel.

Andrew picked up the pile of envelopes, jacket, and tie and extended them toward Sadie. "Tell them I had to leave, then take these up to my room." He turned to Cynthia. "Give her your room key."

She hesitated, obviously surprised by the instruction. "But, I ..."

"Give it to her."

Cynthia eyed him for a moment, trying to figure out if he was serious. Realizing he was, she retrieved the card from her purse and handed it to Sadie.

"Okay, take this up to my room. Wait. Here." Andrew removed the Founders' Medal from the box, sticking it in his pocket before placing the box on top of the pile in Sadie's arms. "The room number is 4112. You can leave the keycard in the room."

Sadie's eyes betrayed the fact that she had many questions, but she knew better to ask any of them.

As she left, Andrew sat down in a chair and cradled his head in his hands. He tried taking in another deep breath, but it was a jagged inhale, hindered by the tension in his body.

He still had his reputation.

His success.

His kingdom.

His throne.

But he was alone.

He made a choice to protect everything they had worked so hard for. To protect everyone, and now they were all gone.

To protect them? Or yourself?

An honest question. Was he willing to answer honestly?

"Andrew?" Cynthia asked, her voice full of trepidation.

No, he wasn't alone. He rubbed his hands across his face, then looked up at her, deep regret having taken up residence in his expression.

It told her everything she needed to know. She sucked in her lips, then rolled them out, allowing a little puff of air to escape as she did. "Of course. I should have known better. I don't know what I was thinking." She removed her phone from her purse.

"Cynthia, I'm so—"

She held up a hand to stop his apology. As she typed on her phone, she said, "Sadie has a list of approved media outlets and a statement ready to give. Gloria said security is walking Blair out as we speak. All board members and execs have been informed of the situation. Sadie filled out the IT forms. I gave HR all they needed. Blair's email will forward to Jim Daughtry. You have a meeting first thing Monday with the research team." She looked up from her phone. "I just emailed Amit Patel and asked him to take care of the interns today. You can figure out what to do with them on Monday because I will not be there."

"Cynthia, please." He ran his hand through his hair, stopping halfway to tug on the strands.

"Expect my resignation via email."

"You don't have to do that ..."

The protest was weak, and Cynthia rolled her eyes in response. She pressed the power button on the side of her phone and stuck it in her purse. "Go to hell, Andrew."

His eyes dropped from her face to the diamond design on the carpet just inches from his feet, and they stayed fixed there. Seconds slipped into minutes, then into an hour, until attendees began reemerging through the doors for the closing session.

It was then that Andrew finally stood from his chair, checking his pocket for the Founders' Medal, and walked out of the room. He continued past the registration tables, navigated around the long line at the coffee bar, made his way down the hallway, and headed toward the hotel lobby.

Once there, he walked straight to the doors.

Then, straight out of them.

———·———

Sadie followed Andrew's instructions, first informing the panel moderator of his unexpected absence, then taking his belongings up to his hotel room. On her way back to the main conference room, she noticed Andrew slipping out the hotel lobby doors into the autumn sunshine and wondered briefly where he was headed.

The two tasks took so long that by the time she headed back to the main session room, the closing session was nearly over, so she hung by the doors until the MC gave the last farewell before approaching the other interns.

None of them had seen Cynthia or Derek since the end of Andrew's keynote, which meant they had no idea what to do with themselves. There was no reason to return to the Expo Hall—they'd already helped pack up that morning—so the question on the table was whether they were expected to go back to InnovGene to finish out the remaining work hours.

The argument against returning was that by the time they got there, they'd only have about two hours left in the day. The argument for it? No one wanted to get written up.

Amit showed up just in time with the official answer that they should take off for the rest of the weekend. He informed them that they should check in with him on Monday morning.

"Why not Cynthia?" Noah asked the question on all their minds. "Does it have to do with that announcement Salvatore made?"

Amit pulled a tissue from his pocket and wiped his nose. "Probably. Look, Cynthia emailed me and said that I needed to take over your supervision for the time being." He folded up the tissue and glanced around the room for a garbage can. "I'm not exactly sure why me. Not like I really have the time to babysit you guys." Locating the can, he said, "See you Monday," then walked over to toss in his trash.

All eyes turned to Sadie.

She raised her hands defensively. "Don't look at me. I don't know why."

"But you were helping Cynthia. What happened? We saw you walk Blair out. Was she who Andrew was talking about?" Chloe asked. "Give it. Spill the tea."

Sadie crossed her arms. "Yes, I had to ask her to leave and go clear out her desk at InnovGene."

"Oh my God. I wouldn't have expected her to do anything so ... *bad.*"

"You just never know what a person is willing to do, or even why." Priya shrugged.

The group fell quiet as they gathered their belongings and checked notifications on their phones, bringing a halt to the questions that nagged at Sadie's conscience. Why would Blair risk the success of Regen-X by bribing the committee? Besides, it just seemed so outside her character, especially as a Christian. Though, Sadie supposed, being a Christian didn't automatically guarantee that you would act in a way that was Christ-like.

Even so, something wasn't sitting right for Sadie. Mackenzie and Adriana's approach cut off any additional mulling over of the situation. Sending a goodbye the way of the interns, Sadie turned to welcome her friends with a smile, explaining she was free the rest of the day and suggesting they grab a deep-dish pizza across the street for a late lunch.

On the way to the restaurant, Mackenzie pressed for details, clearly unsatisfied when Sadie repeated the same explanation she'd given the other interns.

"Come on, you've got to know something—you were asked to walk her out!"

"That is seriously all I've got." Sadie yanked the restaurant door open, met by the warm, savory aroma of baking dough, melted cheese, and spiced tomato sauce.

Mackenzie didn't bring it up again until they were seated at the table, pulling pieces of the pie off the hot pan, melted cheese stringing in stubborn refusal to let go of its fellow slices. With her hands paused mid-motion, holding a slice of pizza halfway to her lips, she said, "Isn't that Derek sitting at that table over there?"

Sadie turned in her seat to see Derek Salvatore sitting at a table all by himself, jacket off and tie loosened, an untouched pizza slice on a plate in front of him and an empty beer stein next to it. Unlike his rigid posture earlier that morning, Derek now seemed to have melted into the chair. He wasn't exactly relaxed; instead, he appeared as if he had lost the spine to hold himself upright.

Go to him.

No, she wasn't going to do anything of the sort. Turning back around in her chair, she picked up her pizza and took a bite.

Mackenzie and Adriana trained their eyes on her as she put the slice back down on her plate. "What?" she asked, wishing they would stop looking at her so intently. "Yeah, it's him."

"He looks rough." Adriana stated the obvious.

Sadie nodded her agreement, then took a sip of her root beer to hide her discomfort.

Go to him.

No. She wasn't going to embarrass herself. Especially after last night; she would come off as clingy—and she specifically told him she didn't expect any further interaction. To walk over to him now, outside of work, would directly violate that statement.

Besides, what exactly would she say when she got over there?

"For the Holy Spirit will teach you at that very hour what must be said."

Sadie wasn't convinced that Jesus' words to the disciples about speaking when questioned by authorities applied to this situation, but she couldn't deny the peace that settled over her body upon recalling it.

She wiped her hands on her napkin, then pushed her chair back from the table.

"Are you going to go over there?" Mackenzie asked, excitement at the prospect evident in her voice.

"I'm just going to say hi."

"Yeah, you are." Her smirk told Sadie that she saw this as a reviving of the missed opportunity from the night before.

Adriana's facial expression, on the other hand, was simply open curiosity—unsure of Sadie's end-goal in approaching Derek, but not completely closed off to the idea.

Standing from the table and taking a few steps toward Derek felt far more difficult than it should have; Sadie's limbs felt uncooperative and heavy with dread.

Somehow, she managed to make it over to Derek's table, drawing his attention with her approach. Before his face relaxed into a friendly smile, Sadie caught a fleeting glimpse of the despair that lingered beneath.

"Hey, Sadie," Derek greeted her.

"Hi," she responded.

An awkward silence settled between them as Sadie remained standing, towering over him, offering nothing more than the brief greeting. Derek made it even more awkward by motioning for her to step aside as the server approached with a fresh beer in her hands. Sadie hurried to move out of the way, only to bump into the back of a seated patron at the table behind her.

Derek's expression changed from friendly to amused at Sadie's clumsiness. As the server retreated from the table, he asked Sadie, "What can I do for you?"

"Um ..."

What could he do for her? Why didn't she think this through a bit more before she walked over to the table?

"We noticed you, and I felt weird not saying hi," she managed weakly.

He smirked. "Okay. Well, thanks for that."

She didn't move. Her limbs no longer felt heavy, but buzzed with nervous energy. A sudden desire to curb it by sitting hit Sadie, and she dropped into the open seat at Derek's table. His eyes registered his surprise at the action, but Sadie ignored it, focusing instead on getting the words out. "Something's wrong," she eked out.

Derek sat up straight in his chair. "Are you talking about earlier? I know that probably was rough to be part of. Cynthia should have never asked you to do that. Unfortunately, these things sometimes happen. Hiring and firing is part of business."

Sadie shook her head vehemently. "No, there's something else about this. I can't quite put my finger on it. Something ... Blair, she looked like she was blindsided when I told her she had to go clear out her desk. Not caught, but caught off guard. She mumbled something about being the scapegoat. Derek, I don't think she did it. And, your brother, when he was leaving, he was a mess. I think the guilt got to him."

Derek tugged at his pants around his knees before lacing his hands together and leaning on the side of his chair, giving Sadie the sense he was avoiding confirming her statement and, in turn, doing just that. The revelation brought a pressure to Sadie's chest. She massaged the spot at the top of her sternum with her fingertips in an attempt to relieve it.

"Didn't Amit give you the rest of the day off?"

Sadie nodded.

"Then, I suggest you stop worrying about work. I'll see you on Monday." He raised the stein to his lips.

Sadie watched him closely as he did, fully aware he was using the glass to hide his discomfort from her, a move she had just done herself moments before. He knew Blair was innocent, and he didn't like what happened anymore than Sadie did. The difference between them was that Sadie was simply a powerless intern, while Derek had the position to put a stop to the wrongdoing. Instead of stepping up, he sat here fueling his avoidance with alcohol. With this new awareness, courage bubbled up in Sadie from her toes to the top of her head. She rose from the table, resting a hand on the top of her chair and fixing Derek with an intense gaze.

He moved from leaning on the chair's arm to sitting upright, crossing his ankles and tucking them neatly beneath his seat.

"You're right. I'm just an intern. Worrying about this is way above my non-existent paygrade. Here's the thing, though, you own half of the freaking company—"

"That's not quite how it—"

"Whatever, you know what I mean. Now, I get the sense that you didn't choose to do this to Blair, but, Derek, you can stop it."

"It's not quite that simple."

"Why not?"

"You're young, Sadie. Life is still black and white for you."

"Wrong is black and white."

"No, no, it's not." He dismissed her words with a shake of his head while pulling his phone out of his pocket and checking it. He replaced it in his pocket and pulled out his wallet.

"I disagree."

"Well, like I said, you're young." He fished out two twenties and tossed them on the table next to his still uneaten slice of pizza. "I've got to go. I'll see you Monday." He rose from his seat.

Just as she could recognize his discomfort before because it so closely mirrored her own, in that moment it became very clear to Sadie that Derek, like herself, had not only entertained different ideologies to support his desired outcome, but had mulled them over until they dominated his reasoning. He had embraced the unsettling argument that knowing a true course of action might be impossible. The irony of the full-circle moment was not lost on her: here was the object of her pining, lamenting the nuances of choosing to do the right thing.

No other gods before Me.

No other gods. It was an odd statement, but a fitting one. To give credence to other worldviews that contradicted God's commands was to allow them to have a place of authority in one's life. It may not look like the ancient practice of bowing before a golden calf, but it sure shared the same nature.

God, I'm so sorry, she prayerfully confessed. She knew God's grace and mercy had protected her from herself last night, and, even more impactful, that she was deeply loved and forgiven.

Just as she had a choice to walk away from the situation last night, Derek had a choice to walk toward the situation today. She couldn't leave until she told him so.

"I'm not being naïve." She pushed her chair in. "It's not the concept of right and wrong itself that's complex, but our unwillingness to choose what's right that complicates things. We consider a situation, imagine all the possible choices and their consequences, and talk circles around ourselves to the point we believe these possibilities outweigh the actual moral truth. We tell ourselves what we want to hear to avoid having to be obedient to God."

Derek removed his jacket from the back of his chair and proceeded to put it on, refusing to meet Sadie's eyes. "Goodbye, Sadie." He pulled his phone out and focused on it.

The conversation was over.

As Sadie returned to her table and took her seat once more, Adriana asked her if she was okay.

With surprise, Sadie realized the answer was "yes." She had moved through the day, doing the best she could with the information presented to her from a powerless position on the lowest rung on the corporate ladder. At the end of the day, even though she had been a pawn in whatever shady dealings had gone down this morning, when it came to speaking up for what was good and right, she was obedient. Now it was up to Derek to do the same.

She smiled at Adriana and Mackenzie. "It's been a weird day. But, yeah, I'm good."

Just as Derek expected, Andrew sat on a bench facing Lake Michigan, one foot resting on the opposite knee, an arm casually draped over the back of the bench. In his free hand, he twirled the Founders' Medal, letting it run through his fingers.

His brother hadn't seen him; Derek still had time to back out. He could walk back through the tunnel under Lake Shore Drive to the other side, where his driver waited at the cul-de-sac at the end of North Avenue. Andrew wouldn't have even known Derek had been there.

No one would.

He could go home and write his resignation letter. Maybe even sell his stocks in the company and move to Cabo. He liked the resort town, and it would mean avoiding the winter weather that would hit Chicago in a little over a month.

Derek turned his back to Andrew.

The wind that met his face took his breath away, bringing with it a recall of Sadie's words: "We tell ourselves what we want to hear to avoid having to be obedient to God."

Where did she even get off talking to him about being obedient to God? His mom had been obedient and look what it got her.

Peace?

Derek shook his head to rid himself of the suggestion, but it held on persistently. It was an apt word to describe his mom's final days as the MS worsened and complications stole her final bit of health.

It was a word Derek wished for his own life, though he had a hard time admitting the fact. But, as Sadie stood up to him—the conviction she spoke of anchoring her right before his eyes—Derek felt enormously jealous of her.

Jealousy ultimately persuaded Derek to instruct his driver to head to North Avenue Beach, where he was certain to find Andrew if he was as distraught as Sadie described. The beach had always been a place of retreat for Andrew in times of trouble.

In recent years, Derek had experienced many moments of jealousy of others. Of their success, their income, their possessions, their relationships, their accolades, their promotions ... the list was long. As his heart coveted what others had, it had grown more distraught and unsettled. But, in this moment of jealousy, he didn't experience the same unnerving feeling. Instead, the turbulence in his heart lessened a bit, as if confirming he was right to desire what she apparently had. What Katie had too, he suddenly realized.

The peace that anchored Sadie was the same peace that prevailed in Brenda Salvatore's life up until her very last moment with them. A peace Derek knew in his youth, but exchanged at some point for a promise of something better. In the end it was all a lie, leaving him discontent and alone.

A predicament Andrew had gotten himself in as well.

Derek turned back toward his brother, taking the necessary steps to close the distance between them, and sat down on the other side of the bench. "We're quite the pair, aren't we?" he announced.

His sudden appearance startled Andrew, causing the man to tighten up his relaxed posture, pulling his arm down from the back of the bench, dropping his foot from his knee, and straightening up. "What are you doing here?"

Derek ignored the question. "Our parents tried so hard to pass along their faith, didn't they? Taking us to church twice a week. Having us memorize verses. Making us volunteer. And yet, here we find ourselves, you an atheist and me an agnostic, neither of us giving any consideration to what they lived out so dutifully."

Andrew gave Derek the side-eye. "What?"

"We've been acting like we're so smart, you know? You this brilliant scientist and me, this marketing genius."

"Why do you get the genius title? I think that's more my thing."

"Hush now."

"I'm just saying, I've actually been called a genius. I'm not sure you've ever been called that."

"Seriously? You're going to fight me on this when I'm trying to tell you something important."

Andrew smiled and raised his hands defensively. "Sorry, proceed."

"We thought we were so smart. But, Andrew, we're dumb asses." This brought a slight chuckle from his brother, so Derek continued. "You screwed up, big time."

"You don't have to tell me that. I know."

"But I did too."

Andrew gave Derek a confused look. "What do you mean?"

"I could have spoken up over the years, suggested a different course of action. I almost did too, but then Carr convinced you to move Summer into my position. Instead of having the hard conversations, I took the easy road, allowing myself to become bitter and jealous. It consumed me."

Andrew sighed. "Don't be so hard on yourself. Carr didn't make it easy. Neither did I."

"Don't let me off the hook. It is my company too, my responsibility, but I didn't act like it. Instead of being a strong leader, I came up with excuses to avoid conflict. Then I found ways to avoid the guilt. I let the jealousy fester. Mom and Dad called me out on it over the years. They could see that I was jealous of Summer's position in the company, bitter about the fact that you replaced me with her. I was letting that jealousy and bitterness keep me from committing to her as a husband, but I just avoided that hard conversation, letting my discontent grow and drive a wedge between us. In fact, during one of our last conversations, Mom told me I was playing house with Summer and needed to man up. She told me my behavior was going against the good life God had for me."

"Sounds like Mom." Andrew relaxed back into his former position.

"I told her God wasn't in the business of giving me a good life, so I wasn't in the business of paying attention to him."

"Sounds like you." Andrew smirked.

"Sounds like both of us. Andrew, we've messed up. It's time to own up to that."

Andrew let his foot fall off his knee once again, this time leaning his elbows on his knees and dropping his head into his hands. "I don't know if that's possible."

"It is. You know it. I know it."

"I'll lose ev..." Andrew couldn't finish the word.

Derek put a hand on his brother's shoulder. "Dude, we're both living a lie. Integrity flew out the window a long time ago. Summer and Katie despise us. We lost an awesome employee. Our company is under scrutiny now. Carr proved he owns us. Even the intern that was all googly eyed about me has lost respect for me."

"Huh?" Andrew lifted his head from his hands and gave Derek a questioning look.

"I'll tell you another time." Derek let his hand drop to his lap and sighed. "Andrew, it's time for us to be honest. Mom was right all along. We were selfish, doing things our way, and it cost us the good life God had for us."

"I don't believe in God." Andrew mumbled into his hands.

Derek slapped his brother's back. "How's that working out for you?" He stood from the bench, buttoned his suit jacket, then jerked his head toward the tunnel. "Let's go."

Katie sat on her condo's balcony, holding her phone in one hand and Christopher Miller's business card in the other. The *Chicago Tribune*'s logo took up most of the card, but in small, yet readable, print the man's phone number and email took up the remaining space.

Tell the truth. Make it crumble. Be free.

She swallowed, attempting to clear the lump in her throat.

One call, that's all it would take to bring the walls tumbling down. It would mean Blair wouldn't have a job to come back to, but at least her name would be cleared. She deserved that much.

Andrew, on the other hand, deserved everything coming to him.

For stealing.

For lying.

For cheating.

One call and she would be free of the pain.

Is that really true?

Katie sighed.

No, it wasn't. It would just be more pain on top of what already was there. But Katie was a truth-teller. It's what had led her into the field of journalism. She couldn't just sit back and let this injustice go by without saying something, without exposing the truth. Her innermost being would never let it go.

This is not what I created you to do. It was such a gentle reproach spoken to her soul, Katie almost missed it.

The sound of the waves of Lake Michigan crashed along the shoreline and mixed with the noise from the traffic traveling Lake Shore Drive. She marveled for a moment at how she accepted the conflict between natural rhythm and the man-made route as normal. What other things had she just accepted as normal?

Ignoring the Spirit's conviction, she punched the numbers from the card into the phone and raised it to her ear. It rang a few times before clicking over to voicemail. At the sound of Christopher's voice encouraging the caller to leave a message, she hit end and then tossed the phone away from herself like it was a hot coal about to burn her. It landed a few cushions away on the patio sofa.

She could share the information and make it all crumble, but what would that gain her? In the end, all she would accomplish was making Andrew feel the pain, like he had caused her, but she would also destroy the lives of more people than just Andrew's.

This wasn't testifying to the truth—it was using information as a weapon for revenge.

"Ugh!" She tipped her head back and released her frustration with a guttural sigh. "So, am I just supposed to be okay with this?"

Her phone rang.

Katie's eyes snapped to it. She pursed her lips together and tilted her head. "Any chance that's you, God, answering me?" She chuckled at her own little joke before picking up the phone and looking at the caller ID.

It was Derek.

She answered it with an irritated "Yes?"

"Hey there. Andrew's gonna stay with me tonight to give you some space."

She hugged her body with her free hand. "I was going to go to the suburbs ... to my parents' house."

"Sis, you're gonna want to stay in the city."

"Why's that?"

"Because you're gonna want to be there tomorrow when we make things right."

Image Swayed

FIRST, THE VIBRATION: THE string against my finger as I draw my bow.

Next, the sound: the notes of my violin mixing with the horns of traffic and conversations splitting into a flow around me.

Finally, the image: Summer standing before me, her hair pulled up into a high ponytail. A pair of dark skinny jeans and leopard-print slingbacks peaking out from under her coat.

Lord, do my eyes and ears deceive me? This is reality, not a vision?

I am surprised to see her here midday on a Friday.

She seems surprised herself.

I finish my last note and thank the gathered crowd before packing up my violin. She hangs back until the last tip is tossed into the jar at my feet, then, she takes a step closer, hands in the pockets of her coat, and says, "Hi Kingston. I'm not sure you remember me."

"I remember you. Summer, right?"

She smiles. "Yes."

I put a lid on the tip jar and tuck it in the side pocket of my violin case. Looking up from my crouch, I see she's watching me curiously.

"Have you been doing this since you left BioSphere?" she asks.

My hands stop mid-routine, and I chuckle. "You mean since I was forced out of BioSphere? Not the whole time. For a few years now."

I continue to put the tools of my trade away while she stands there, silent. Perhaps I got excited for nothing; she doesn't seem intent on talking to me. My task complete, I stand from my crouch and send a smile her way.

"It was nice seeing you." Tipping my hat toward her, I begin my trek back to the Red Line station.

"I can help you take him down," she says before I can get even four steps down the sidewalk.

I know who she is referring to, but I stop and, without turning around, say, "Beg your pardon?"

"I believe this belongs to you."

The rustle of papers being pulled from a purse meets my ears, and I close my eyes against the possibility that Summer holds the evidence I needed a decade earlier to clear my name. An image from last night's dream pops onto the canvas of my mind's eye: Andrew clutching the paper in his hand.

There is a fight in my soul. To turn around would be to face a ghost. To walk away would be to invite a "what-if" to take up residence in my life.

Remember, I'm doing a new thing.

"Kington, I can help you get it all back."

I grimace. "I don't want it all back," I answer, still not turning around.

"I don't believe that."

She states it so matter-of-fact that I'm compelled to turn back to her with a small smile.

"I know, but it's the truth. Andrew may have stolen my research, but that job stole my perspective—my sense of what really mattered—long before he took my name off that," I point to the paper in her hand, "and replaced it with his. I don't ever want to go back to the man who conducted that research. He was arrogant, proud, and too fond of drinking to avoid conflict."

She mutters something unintelligible under her breath as she shoves the papers back into her purse. Her eyes return to my face and take up studying me, as if she can figure out what to say in order to persuade me to help her. Finally, she asks, "Can I buy you a coffee?"

Repositioning my violin on my shoulders, I respond in a jovial tone. "Now, that I do want!"

Summer leads the way to a cafe two doors down from my performance spot. Once inside, she drapes her coat over the back of a chair at a table for two overlooking the street. "Sit. I'll grab us coffee. What do you want to drink?"

I prop my violin up against the window, using my chair to keep it wedged there. "Vanilla latte, please—life's too short to drink sad coffee."

She laughs at my answer—at first a small chuckle, but then a full-blown laugh. It occurs to me that perhaps she hasn't had a genuine reason to laugh in a while. Carrying her laughter away with her, Summer approaches the counter and places our orders, leaving me to sit silently at the table, contemplating this sudden turn of events.

Shortly, Summer returns with our lattes. "Here." She hands me mine and sits across the table, taking a sip from hers.

I follow suit.

As she lowers her cup, Summer eyes me, the curiosity from earlier still turning wheels behind them. With a quick motion, she retrieves my research from her purse and places it on the table between us. She taps the stack of papers. "Carr is using this information to blackmail Andrew."

I take another sip, allowing the warm liquid to comfort the tightening in my throat at the mention of Carr's name.

"He stuck his claws into InnovGene, threatening all the good it has done ... the good it could do."

"He has a tendency to do that."

"I want to pry them loose." She raises her cup to her lips, looking at me over the rim. "I need to pry them loose."

The statement feels personal, more than just a concerned employee (or even a concerned friend) looking out for the greater good.

"Why you?" I ask. "Why not Andrew?"

She scoffed. "Have you not been listening? He's got Andrew on the ropes."

"What about Derek?"

Summer rolls her eyes. "Derek couldn't do conflict if it laid down, rolled over, and asked him to scratch its belly."

"Jeez, tell me how you really feel."

Leaning back in her chair, Summer interlaces her fingers and places them in her lap. "He's changed since you knew him."

I shrug. "I'm sure you all have. I know I have."

Her gaze drifts to the window. "I have solid evidence that would put Carr behind bars—today."

"Well, that's good." I tip the cup slightly and rotate it in a circle on its base. "Why the hesitation?"

"I kinda quit this morning."

I'm confused, and I let my face show it. "Then, why this?" I wave toward the research, then the space between Summer and me.

She tilts her head and purses her lips, taking time to contemplate my question. If there was a clock nearby, I'd probably hear it ticking. Finally, her shoulders shrug. "I want the kingdom."

I take another sip to hide my shock at the honest admission.

She wants stability. She wants a home.

Okay, maybe not as honest as I thought.

I wrestle to reconcile the discernment given to me by the Spirit with the strong, independent woman sitting before me, who just admitted her ambition for power.

She thinks control equals risk mitigation.

"And getting rid of both Carr and Andrew opens the door to the castle?" I ask, hoping she doesn't notice the quiver in my hand as I lower my cup to the table.

Summer nods. "Help me get rid of them, and I will get your job back. I'll get Blair back too. You'll like her. She's smart and loyal."

"Summer, it's been too long. I'm too old."

She doesn't look convinced. "You're what? Early 50s?"

I release a laugh from deep in my gut, slapping my thigh for good measure. "Girl, I'm almost 58."

"That's hardly old." She smirks. "Besides, that just means you have even more wisdom to share with the newbies."

A quiet settles between us.

Dismissing her suggestion with a shake of my head, I repeat my earlier argument that I don't want to go back to the way things were. "I don't need that kingdom, Summer. God took me out of it and placed me in a far superior one."

Summer sighs. "You are talking some Bible crap, aren't you?"

"Well, I don't label it as crap, but yes, ma'am."

Summer pops the lid off her cup, surveying the level of the contents. As she replaces it, she says, "I grew up Catholic."

"So, then you know all about King Jesus."

"Sure."

"Do you still serve him?"

Summer lets out a yelp of a laugh. "Um. Can't say I've thought of that in a hot minute."

"Do you?"

She doesn't answer me, letting her gaze drift outside once more.

"You see, I do." I slide the research toward me. "The only room for a throne in my life is the one He sits on. Didn't use to be that way. I used to think I deserved the throne, told God that too. I kicked him out of the chair, took matters into my own hands. Made decisions I thought were right and good. It took being brought to rock bottom for me to realize I was gripping the arms of a chair that didn't belong to me."

I pick the papers up and thumbed through them for the first time in a decade, allowing myself to enjoy seeing the data just a little. I did good work back then.

The stack of papers threaten to open the wound, but a scripture from Ecclesiastes pops into my mind and covers it like a balm:

> I know that there is nothing better for them than to rejoice and enjoy the good life. It is also the gift of God whenever anyone eats, drinks, and enjoys all his efforts.

Enjoy your efforts, Kingston, the Spirit encourages.

I let the stack drop to the table with a dramatic thud. "This work, it was good. I did good. We did good. But, it wasn't the good life. There was no peace in it."

Summer points to the violin case. "And there is in this?"

I nod.

Her brows furrow.

I clarify: "Don't get me wrong, researching could have been the good life, if I had lived with God's wisdom instead of my own. You look at me now and see just some old street performer and you pity me. But you should know, while my wages may fluctuate, there is nothing unstable about my life because it's anchored by trust in God, my provider."

"I'm happy for you." Summer puts her folded hands on the table. "But I'm done with everyone else's selfish choices dictating my life. I have to choose me for once. I just wanted to give you the opportunity to get justice."

"I wonder if maybe that's what you told yourself to convince yourself to come here, but it's not really what you want to talk about?" I say, introducing a fork in the conversation while wishing my cup wasn't already empty.

The wheels turn again as she contemplates the invitation to go deeper. "What happened? After Andrew left BioSphere?" she asks.

"What do you really want to ask, Summer?" I scratch my cheek, the scruff of my beard pricking at my fingertips.

She doesn't hesitate at my green light to get to the heart of what she really wanted to know. Leaning her forearms on the table, she reaches toward me with open hands and a posture of pure curiosity. "How do you not hate him for screwing you over?"

"Ah, now we're getting somewhere honest."

"I wasn't there when he did what he did to you. I was there, however, this morning when he screwed all of us over, and I just don't think I can show up to work and act like nothing's wrong."

"Hence, wanting to push him out?"

"Exactly."

"How did he screw you over?"

"We could have taken down Carr. Instead, Andrew turned on our senior researcher, who is completely innocent in all of this, to protect himself. History repeating itself, I tell you." Summer motions toward me.

Smiling sadly, I confess, "I wasn't as innocent as you want to make me out to be, but that's a story for another time. Why is it so important you take down Carr?"

Summer opens her mouth to answer, but quickly closes it and places a hand over her lips.

A fear inserts itself in my chest. "Summer, are you in trouble? Did Carr threaten you?"

She shakes her head. "No, nothing like that. The opposite, actually."

"He bribed you?"

She let out a quick chuckle. "Well, kind of. He orchestrated this whole complicated situation, and there were these envelopes that were part of it. Inside mine was a check and a waiver of parental rights."

Her expression falters, as if she can't quite believe the words coming out of her own mouth—or that she is admitting them to me at all. "I'm pregnant. It's Carr's. The check is the exact amount for an abortion." She exhales sharply. "I never told him I was pregnant, yet somehow he knew anyway." Her eyes narrow. "The guy's a snake."

I'm immediately reminded of the image I saw earlier in the week while Summer listened to me play my violin. *Let there be life.*

Multiple questions pop into my head—some helpful, and some just plain nosy. I shift through them quickly, trying to figure out which would move the conversation forward instead of simply prying into Summer's personal life. I finally land on one: "Did you need the money?"

Her amused facial expression betrays the fact that she did not, in fact—not even remotely—need Carr's money. "No. Besides, he knows I would never take the money from him."

"Then why give it to you?"

"Same reason he gave me the waiver. He's just making it clear—whatever I do, abort, place for adoption, or keep, it's not his problem. The money, the waiver—it's all just a way to wash his hands of it. So he can be absolved of the matter."

I take in what she says, feeling my eyebrows pull closer together and the skin around my eyes tighten. I blink hard and will my face to relax. "He gave you an out, Summer. You quit the company. Just walk away, dear." Surely she hears the fatherly tone in my voice and will heed it.

Summer pulls the stack of research toward her, tapping the edges against the table to align them into a neat pile. "Can't do that."

"Why not? You're gonna have to connect the dots for me, Summer. Not as sharp as I used to be."

"Highly doubt that." She puts the papers back in her purse. When done with the task, she folds her hands, placing them on the table and leaning in toward me. "Blair." She says simply. "I can't leave without fixing things for her. She's innocent in all this."

"Just like that baby you carry?"

Summer visibly jerks in response to my bluntness.

I motion to her purse. "Do you have it on you?"

"Have what?" she asks, guarded.

"The ultrasound picture."

"Why would you ask me that?"

"I get the sense you have it in your purse. You've probably looked at it at least a hundred times, even though you've tried to convince yourself it's not really a baby yet."

Summer crosses her arms.

"How far along are you?"

"I'm not answering that."

I lean forward, as if confiding a secret. "I never liked how ultrasound pictures are in black and white. The baby looks all gray, lifeless, you know?"

My mind recalls the image of the man lying lifeless in the grass before God breathed life into him, bringing color into his limbs.

"But babies," I continue, "aren't gray and lifeless; they have skin with blood pumping under it. Even this early." I motion to Summer's stomach.

"That's enough." She says calmly. "I'm not here to discuss this with you. I came to give you a chance at justice, but you clearly don't care."

I'm not quite sure how she manages to rise from her chair in both a huff and with elegant poise. I'm impressed.

Folding my hands together, I rest them on my stomach. "I don't need justice."

"Yes, you said that already." Summer pulls a business card from her purse and tosses it on the table. "If you finally come to your senses, that's my cell." She turns her attention to buttoning her coat.

"Summer." I say softly. She looks up at me, and I point to the man walking up behind her. "I think he might have the same idea as you." I stand from my chair, putting on my own coat as I address Derek. "If you've come to convince me to take down Andrew, Summer here has already tried and failed."

Derek puts up his hands to stop us both. "Can we talk?"

Summer shoves her hands into her coat pockets. "I'm done here."

"Please, Summer, just give me a few minutes. I promise you'll want to hear this." The plea in his tone breaks through her defenses, and Summer retakes her seat.

I follow suit, praying, *Lord, lead me in the paths of righteousness for your name's sake.* As I watch Derek pull a chair up to the table, I ask, "What is this about?"

Derek contemplates my question for a moment, then answers me with sincerity. "I suppose it's about choosing what's right instead of what's easy."

I smile wide. "I'm listening."

Day Six

"I DON'T GET IT. Why go? That man cost you your career. You don't owe him anything."

Blair's hand froze mid-air, the spoonful of cereal hovering over her bowl. She glanced to her right, where Samantha had sidled up to her at the breakfast bar. She swallowed the cereal already in her mouth before answering. "Because, Derek asked me."

"Aren't we mad at Derek?"

Blair rolled her eyes. "That was before I realized he kept his promise."

It was Sam's turn to roll her eyes. "Hardly. He totally would have slept with that girl if she hadn't walked away."

"He didn't push it, though."

Sam's mouth dropped open. "I should hope not! Why are you defending him? He told you we were living in sin."

Blair set her spoon back down in the bowl. "No. He said his mom would say that." Blair shrugged. "And she would have."

Throwing her hands up in the air, Sam exclaimed, "That makes it all okay? Why are you all calm all of a sudden? Last night, you were breaking plates right here in this kitchen."

"At your encouragement." Blair pointed her spoon in Sam's direction.

"Yes! Because you were livid and needed to let it out." Sam crossed her arms and shrugged. "A few broken plates don't seem like enough processing, if you ask me."

Blair took a second to formulate her response, dragging her spoon through the mixture of milk and corn puffs as she did.

"This morning I woke up calm and with this sense that God has things under control. So, I'm trying to trust God has a reason for all of this."

She looked up at Sam, whose look showed her doubt.

"Yes, I am angry at Andrew. I am! And I'm terrified I'll never be able to work in this industry ever again. I'm so, so scared. But these people have been like family, which made it hurt even worse. So, if there is a chance that, somehow, they will make things right like Derek promised on the phone last night, then I want to see it for myself."

A beat passed between them, then Sam threw her arms around Blair, pulling her into a tight hug. "Fine. You go. But you better be strong because they ain't family, boo. They are your bosses. You bring a lot to the table and they just threw that away yesterday. Stupid move. So, you better not let them screw you over again. You're a powerful woman, you don't need them. And, I swear, if they hurt you again..." she let the threat hang as she pulled back out of the hug. She smoothed Blair's hair and then kissed the top of her head. "I've got to get to the hospital. Call me after the meeting."

"Will do." Blair watched as her fiancée left the apartment. She turned back to her cereal.

She had neglected to mention to Sam one last reason she was willing to attend the meeting later that morning. Since Thursday night, she hadn't been able to stop Derek's words from reverberating around her mind: "You're cherry picking."

Likewise, she couldn't silence the question "Am I?" rolling around in there too.

Comments and questions aside, she wanted to apologize to Derek. She had been so rude to him, assuming the worst and not giving him a chance to prove her otherwise. Besides, Derek and Sadie were both consenting adults. Blair still held onto her resolve that there was an imbalance of power and a possible HR nightmare, but the way she had come down so hard on Derek about it? Her actions embarrassed her. She had overstepped, treating Sadie's choices as if they directly affected herself. Which was weird, considering Blair and Sadie lived their lives by different standards.

Not her standards. Not yours. Mine.

Suddenly feeling lightheaded, Blair gripped the edge of the breakfast bar to steady herself, closing her eyes against the epiphany and its implications.

She and God were tight, she reminded herself. He had made her the way he did. He loved her just as she was. They were good.

Right?

———·———

"The procedure is only 10 minutes, correct?" Summer asked the clinic nurse, taking the pen and clipboard the woman held out to her.

"Yes, but remember, you'll have to spend about an hour in recovery." The nurse put a thermometer in her mouth.

Summer glanced at the clock on the opposite wall and did the calculations. Noticing Summer's agitation, the nurse gently asked her if she had somewhere she needed to be as she removed the thermometer.

Summer nodded. "Work meeting."

"On a Saturday?"

"Yes, unfortunately."

"You're supposed to be taking it easy today. No stress. Skip the meeting."

Summer gave a half smile. "Can't do that. Besides, if it's not today's issue, it'll just be another issue in the future."

"You really should be resting. It is a surgical procedure. There'll be cramping and bleeding afterwards."

"I'll just be sitting and listening. No different from sitting at home." Seeing the doubt on the nurse's face, she added, "I promise, after the meeting, I'll go straight home, lay in bed, and binge-watch a show."

The nurse seemed satisfied with the answer and continued her prep as Summer looked over the paperwork. It explained the abortion procedure and the risks associated with it. The procedure sounded simple enough; since she was only eleven weeks, they would dilate her cervix and use a small device to remove the pregnancy tissue.

Her hand hesitated when she came to the designated field for signing her consent, her mind going to the spot in her purse where the ultrasound picture was tucked safely away.

Do what you need to do. Only you are looking out for your interests.

The encouragement landed true for Summer. She had worked so hard to get to this point in her life without help from anyone else, working hard to put herself through college and gaining one promotion after another once she entered the workforce. Her success was a direct result of the energy she gave to her career. A baby would divide her attention.

She wanted kids. Someday. When she was in a committed relationship. Then, she would have someone to help shoulder the burden of a kid. Right now, however, that wasn't her situation. Once upon a time, she thought it was in the cards for her and Derek, but her job at InnovGene had become a source of contention between them, leading to their split and her dashed dreams of having a family with him.

Insight filled in the gaps in her contemplation. With the loss of that dream, Summer had clung to a new one—becoming CEO of InnovGene.

If what Derek told her and Kingston at the coffee shop yesterday was true, her dream was about to come true.

Summer glanced toward her purse perched on top of her clothes in a pile on a chair in the corner.

Blood pumps through their veins.

Summer shook her head to rid herself of the internal voice of resistance. Like she had told Kingston, she had grown up in the Catholic church and heard that life began at conception. But the thing in the ultrasound picture wasn't viable outside the womb—it needed her body. It had already taken so much from her—her energy, her appetite, her focus—and it would only get worse as the months advanced. Then, after the birth? The impact on her life would be significant. Nothing would ever be the same.

It was her life that was affected.

Her body.

She was so close to having what she wanted.

Choose you.

The instruction was forceful, refusing to be ignored.

Summer raised her arm, surprised to see goosebumps. She ran a hand down one and then the other, bringing warmth to the chilled skin. She turned her attention back to the paperwork in her hands and signed her consent.

Handing the nurse the clipboard, she asked, "Can you give me my purse?"

The nurse fetched it from the chair and handed it to Summer.

"Here." Summer unzipped the inner pocket of the bag, fished out the ultrasound picture, and held it out to the woman. "Do me a favor? Toss this for me."

———————— · ————————

"It feels like we're doing something wrong. It being the weekend, you know?" Adriana leaned against the back of the elevator as they quickly ascended floors in the office building.

Sadie shrugged, pulling Adriana's attention away from the changing number above the door. "People work on the weekends all the time. We might even see someone in their office. We won't be long, just so I can show you guys my cubicle."

"And the lab," Mackenzie reminded her.

"Yes, the lab too." Sadie turned to Adriana. "Who knows, maybe you will be working here next semester for your internship."

Adriana crossed her arms and smiled. "No offense, but I kinda hope not. Too much drama for me."

"It's too much drama for me," Sadie replied, laughing.

The elevator slowed to a stop, and the doors opened with a ding.

In the lobby of InnovGene, stood the Salvatore brothers and—Adriana realized with a jolt of surprise—the elderly man from the Red Line.

Focusing so much attention on people's lips to catch their words often meant Adriana could recall faces with ease, allowing her to recognize individuals when most would not. She was certain that this was the same man who sat across from them with his violin. The same one who warned her to watch out for the lions.

He seemed to recognize her too, giving her a warm, friendly smile.

Andrew and Derek, however, greeted them with less friendly looks. Derek asked Sadie if Blair or Katie had told her about the meeting.

She shrunk back under his questioning. "What meeting? I just wanted to show my friends where I work. We can go."

"Wait," the older man said. "We met the other day on the L, didn't we?"

Adriana confirmed his question with a nod.

"I thought I recognized you three. What are your names?"

The girls exchanged glances before Sadie introduced each of them, starting with herself.

"It's nice to meet you. My name is Kingston." He gave each of the girls a little bow of acknowledgement, then addressed Sadie. "You work here?"

"I'm just an intern."

"Ah. Were you at the conference yesterday when Andrew made his announcement?"

She shook her head. "No, I was walking Blair—I had to do something during that time."

"It's okay." Kingston smoothed her anxiety with another warm smile. "Andrew filled me in on all the details of yesterday. I'm sorry you had to be part of that."

The apology drew tears to Sadie's eyes. She turned away from Kingston as she mumbled, "Thanks." Using the end of her sleeve, she dried her eyes. When she turned back to face Kingston, Adriana reached an arm around her shoulders and gave her a supportive hug. Sadie smiled her gratitude.

Kingston looked thoughtful for a moment, then turned to Andrew. "I think they should sit in this meeting."

Andrew didn't hide his surprise, nor his disagreement with the assessment.

"This is a private business meeting. She's just an intern who won't be working here in a few months, and these two don't even work here!" he protested.

Kingston shrugged. "You pulled Sadie into the situation, and she should get to see you unravel it. Plus, it'll be a good lesson in leadership. Consider it your way to give back to the next generation of world changers." There was a small twinkle in Kingston's eye.

Andrew protested once more before Derek finally held up a hand. "Come on, he's right."

"Fine. Follow me."

Andrew led the group into the conference room and motioned for the girls to take the chairs positioned against the wall. Adriana took a seat that would give her a good line of sight.

Andrew took the seat at the head of the table and indicated that Kingston should sit down in the seat to his right. As the man obliged, he asked Andrew, "Who are we waiting on?"

"Katie, Blair, and Summer, of course. The chairman of our board, our legal representatives, a few key investors, Kimura from the awards committee, and Carr."

At the name, Kingston repositioned himself in his chair before interlacing his hands and resting them on his potbelly, trying to mask his discomfort with a casual posture.

Adriana leaned over to Sadie and whispered, "Who is Carr?"

Sadie shrugged.

Turning to Mackenzie on her other side, she signed so the conversation would stay private between them, keeping her movements small so she didn't attract too much attention from the other side of the room. She asked Mackenzie if she would interpret the meeting.

"I don't know if I will be able to keep up." She admitted, her hands conveying her worry.

Mackenzie nodded her understanding and signed back, "Of course! Can you believe we are here for this? Once in a lifetime opportunity." She let her eyes go big to emphasize her signed words.

Adriana closed her hand into a fist and moved it up and down, like a head nodding. "Yep."

Movement in the doorway interrupted their conversation, both turning to see who had arrived. It was Blair.

Glancing around the room, the woman found an empty seat at the table, then pulled out her phone, giving herself a reason to avoid looking or talking to anyone else.

Adriana turned to Mackenzie and signed, "This is going to be interesting."

It was Mackenzie's turn to sign, "Yep."

——— · ———

The elevator doors opened, but Katie stood frozen in place, unable to move her limbs into action.

Derek had promised that this meeting was going to make things right, and she believed him. But what happened after that? After the meeting was done and all business errors corrected? Who would fix the personal ones? The ones that cut into her marriage and wounded her deeply?

No one would fault her if she didn't show up.

The elevator doors closed.

They didn't need her to make things right.

She pushed the button for the ground floor.

He wants you there.

"I really don't care what he wants anymore." She let a big sigh escape her lips.

The doors opened once more into the lobby of the office building. Katie hurried her steps across the marble floors and entered the rotating door.

Let no man separate what I have brought together.

No man. Not even Andrew?

"He doesn't even believe in you," she muttered as she exited the door onto the sidewalk.

"...they may be won over without a word by the way their wives live ..." The verse stirred in her heart as Katie exited the building.

A nearby car laid on its horn to motivate the car in front of it to move. When nothing happened, the horn sounded again. This time, the car jerked forward into action. The traffic sped up, attempting to get through the light before it changed to red once more.

Katie tipped her face up toward the sunshine.

You are not alone, no matter how lonely you feel. I am with you.

She sighed again and whispered, "I know, Lord."

For the past week, she had been asking for answers. For the truth. This was her chance to hear it. She may not owe Andrew the chance to explain himself, but she could be gracious toward him and give it to him.

Turning back around, Katie willed herself to cross the lobby.

She willed herself to step into the elevator and ride it up to the InnovGene offices.

When the doors opened this time, she stepped out.

Then she took steps toward the conference room.

She willed herself to open the door.

To acknowledge those in the room.

To take a seat at the table where Blair and a few others already sat.

The number of people in the room surprised Katie; she hadn't realized the meeting would be so public—or that all the key stakeholders would be involved.

When she settled into her chair, Andrew directed her attention to the man sitting across the table. He looked familiar, but Katie couldn't place him.

"Katie, I'd like you to meet someone. This is Kingston Reed. He was my mentor at BioSphere."

Katie's mouth dropped open slightly as the man rose from his chair and extended his hand toward her across the table. She stood from her own chair, as if in a daze, and took his hand in hers. He gave it a firm shake.

"It's so nice to meet you." Kingston said with a wide smile.

"Same here." Katie responded before taking her seat once more.

"We're just waiting for Summer and Carr before we begin." Derek informed her.

Katie nodded, placing her hands in her lap and positioning her feet on either side of the chair's base, gently swaying her chair from side to side. A thought occurred to her, and she clarified, "Summer is coming?"

Derek nodded. "Yeah, she had something to do this morning, though, so she said she would be here a little after one."

A disappointed look flittered across Kingston's face.

Katie briefly pondered the cause of Kingston's disappointment, all while fully aware of her own. Perhaps she should have made more effort with Summer—talking to her about the situation, ensuring she understood her options. Though, most likely, she wouldn't have made much progress. Summer was both intensely private and determined.

Andrew interrupted her thoughts by taking the empty seat next to her. She stopped swaying her chair as he leaned in close and whispered. "I know it's a lot to ask, but after this is over, can we talk?"

She nodded.

He smiled with relief. "Thanks." Andrew stood from the chair and returned to the head of the table.

Katie resumed swaying the chair from side to side.

———— · ————

Derek was about to call Summer when she arrived at the conference room with Carr right on her heels. Flushed with pieces of hair falling out of a loose ponytail, Summer took the seat to Katie's left. She slid her purse off her shoulder and placed it on the table in front of her. Rethinking that decision, she swiped it and placed it on the floor at her feet. Placing her hands on the arms of her chair at first, then moving them to her lap momentarily, Summer landed them back on the arms of her chair. She asked, "What did I miss?"

"We haven't started." Derek assured her, trying to catch her eye across the table, but failing to do so when she refused to look at him.

Larson Carr had entered the room in a much more composed manner than Summer, taking the seat to Andrew's left, directly across from Kingston. If Carr was unnerved by the presence of the man he had worked hard to destroy a decade earlier, he didn't show it. Instead of addressing the elephant in the room, he twirled his chair toward Katie, speaking to her over the empty chair between them. "Good afternoon, Katie."

Katie ignored him.

Carr turned his chair back toward Andrew with an amused expression. "The missus is a little testy today, Salvatore. What did you do?"

Andrew met Carr's insinuating gaze with a steady one of his own. He turned toward Derek. "Everyone is here. We can start."

Putting his growing concern for Summer aside for the time being, Derek acknowledged his brother's words with a nod, then opened the folder on the table in front of him.

———— · ————

Katie was willing to talk.

Andrew felt a hopefulness return to his heart for the first time since the keynote.

He needed to focus on the task at hand, though. Afterward, he could focus on repairing his marriage.

Andrew straightened up in his chair, arching his back slightly to bring about a relieving pop, then took the paper from Derek. He glanced around the room. Besides the empty seat between Katie and Carr, the room was full. The reporter he had invited had taken a seat against the back wall next to the intern and her friends.

A hollowness had taken root in his stomach, threatening to release whatever contents remained from yesterday's breakfast (he hadn't been able to eat since). A sip from his bottle of water brought a little relief, but Andrew knew the feeling resulted from his nerves and wouldn't go away until after the meeting was done—and only if everything went the way it was supposed to.

It's not too late. Walk away.

Andrew silenced the temptation to run.

Today, he was choosing to be the leader of this kingdom he should have been all along. He cleared his throat and began.

"Yesterday, I made an incorrect statement during my keynote at the Biotech Frontiers Conference that a senior research staff member had inappropriately approached a committee member about pushing our licensing through. You were told that the employee was Blair Dolton, and that we had taken measures to remove her from our company. In full transparency, and in order to clear Blair's name, I want to make it clear that I made that statement in response to blackmail. Blair Dolton did not undertake the actions I accused her of while onstage yesterday."

Blair's eyes snapped up from her phone to Andrew.

He continued, "I am deeply remorseful for the hurt that I caused Blair in making these false accusations. Over her time at InnovGene, Blair has been a crucial part of our research and development. Her loyalty and commitment to our mission here has moved us along more times than I can count. While we completely understand should she choose to reject the offer, InnovGene would like to reinstate Blair immediately. If she should choose to move on, once again we fully support whatever decision she makes. We will do whatever is in our power to help her obtain employment."

Andrew glanced down to double-check his next bullet point. "You may all be wondering what was so bad that someone could blackmail me into accusing Blair of wrong-doing. I will take this opportunity now to clear the air regarding this blackmail."

He wiped the sweat from his palm on the leg of his pants. Carr's expression had shifted from haughty to threatening, and Andrew immediately regretted looking his way. A glance out the window toward the lake acted like a palate cleanser for his eyes. When he returned his gaze to the room, he made eye contact with the various faces around the table before continuing.

"About a decade ago, I worked with this man, Kingston Reed. He was my mentor. Together, we came up with the basis for what would eventually become NeuroGene-X. We knew we were onto something really special." Andrew gave Kingston a little smile, and Kingston returned it with one of his own.

"However, our employer didn't agree. The company pulled funding and instructed us to go a different route. Larson Carr approached us both about striking out on our own, promising to provide his deep pockets toward further development. Kingston did not like Carr at all and refused to go into business with him. Carr continued to encourage me to strike out on my own, finally convincing me that my genius would be better served working for myself. Carr was certain we could negotiate a deal with BioSphere for the rights to use the research, since they saw no value in it. We just had one problem: Kingston was listed as an author on the research, and he didn't want to deal with Carr."

Andrew steadied his voice, which had grown increasingly shaky as he neared the moment of revealing the secret that had enslaved him for years. "Although we both had developed the research together, I began making statements that insinuated that Kingston was showing up to work drunk and that I had been carrying his workload for years."

A murmur went around the room, which prompted Kingston to interject with his side of the story. "It wasn't that far from the truth. Which is why everyone was so quick to believe him. I was full of myself. Proud and boastful. Felt undervalued by the company. Undervalued at home too. Started drinking to avoid going home in the evenings. Then started drinking at lunch too. It wasn't too large a jump to make, which is how he got me fired." The older man let a chuckle escape at the memory.

The sound of it made Andrew jump—it was so unexpected. But that's how it had been since Derek brought Kingston back to his condo last night to work out the details. They had gone over together what they would say, Kingston insisting that Andrew tell this side of things as well.

"I won't let you do this unless you tell them the truth about me. I wasn't so innocent in all of this. I needed to be humbled. God used you to do it."

Andrew had reluctantly agreed to Kingston's terms.

Carr shifted in his seat, but Andrew refused to look at him. Instead, he caught Katie's gaze.

"Under the impression that he hadn't really contributed to the research," Andrew explained, "Kingston's name was removed. Carr and I negotiated with the company for the right to use the research. Then, I started InnovGene, asking my brother to come on board. I didn't outright lie about Kingston, but I made sure people thought the worst about him, and that knowledge has eaten at me for the past ten years."

He could see in Katie's face that she believed him. He wondered if that would be enough to make things right between them. Would it give them a starting point at least?

Kingston folded his hands and leaned forward against the table. "I want to make this clear in case you all didn't just hear it. The kid didn't lie, but he did bend the truth in his favor. That's the part that got me in trouble. The truth. The truth was, I was too fond of my own genius and too fond of drinking. While Andrew might have tipped things against me, I set the wheels in motion long before that. I deserved to have my name taken off that research."

Andrew let Kingston's words sit in the room for a moment as he gathered courage for the next action item on his sheet. He turned his gaze upon Carr. The man's lips were pressed into a thin line, his eyes narrowed, and his expression one big warning to Andrew against continuing with this story. Andrew did not heed it.

"Larson Carr was privy to this information and used it to keep me in check and to gain more and more control over our company. When he suggested we bribe the licensing committee to push our newest development to market, I, along with my senior staff, decided it was time to remove his influence in this company. We struck a deal with GenTech and gathered proof that Carr had gone to the committee with a bribe. But Carr found out and blackmailed me into accusing Blair instead." Andrew turned to look at Blair. "I am immensely sorry that I chose to crumble under the blackmail instead of doing the right thing."

Tears spilled over and down her cheeks under his gaze.

"I am sorry, Blair," he repeated.

Carr pushed his chair back from the table and calmly buttoned his jacket. "This is slander!" he declared, scanning the room before fixing his gaze back on Andrew. "I'm going to sue you."

Andrew gestured to a man seated a few chairs away. "You remember our lawyer, Graham Petrović, don't you, Larson?" he asked.

Turning to Graham, he said, "Graham, would you mind escorting Mr. Carr out and explaining the evidence we've already submitted to the FBI, the SEC, and the health and safety regulatory authorities regarding his criminal activities?"

"Sure! In fact, our friends at the FBI are downstairs and eager to meet him." Graham replied, standing from the table.

Carr stiffened, his initial calm demeanor cracking. He straightened his jacket, a forced smile appearing as he put his hands into the pocket of his pants. "Very well, Mr. Petrović, lead the way," he said, his voice steady but his eyes betraying him with a flicker of worry.

At the doorway, Carr paused, turning back to Andrew.

"We'll see how well your evidence holds up in court," he said, trying to regain an upper hand. He tilted his head in such a way that it reminded Andrew of the way a snake bent when rising into a strike position. Then, his gaze shifted to Katie, a thin menacing smile forming. "And Katie," he added, his tone a blend of mock concern and veiled threat, "make sure Andrew here answers for all his choices this week. You deserve that much."

Andrew's concern about repairing the damage done to his marriage deepened with Carr's statement and Katie's reaction to it—she was visibly disconcerted.

Derek slid a paper Andrew's way, effectively refocusing him on the remaining tasks. Andrew picked it up, ignoring Carr's exit from the room, and held it up for the others to see.

"This press release will go out first thing Monday morning. The board has already been informed of its contents, as have other key people involved. Essentially, it outlines my immediate resignation as CEO of InnovGene with the appointment of Summer Harlow to replace me. Derek Salvatore will take her place as COO. While we are certain that my actions that led to the removal of Kingston's name from the research had no negative impact on the development of our products, we expect there will be a desire from our industry to execute an investigation. We commit to full cooperation with any such investigations. Additionally, we will be adding Kingston's name back on the research we conducted together, and we have extended a job offer to him." Andrew tossed a smile Kingston's way. "He hasn't answered one way or the other yet, though I sincerely hope he will consider joining InnovGene."

Andrew caught Kimura's eye and nodded. "I asked GIGA to remove my name from the list of recipients of the Founders' Medal."

A gasp rippled around the room. Andrew waited a second for it to settle before he continued.

"While the work completed here at InnovGene has made great strides for this industry, I did not accomplish it in a vacuum. I conducted this research with Kingston. After that, I had a team of immensely talented and dedicated scientists working with me to create products that have positively impacted patients around the world." Andrew stood from his chair and walked around the table to where Kimura sat, continuing to talk as he did. "I explained to GIGA that I do not want to be considered for any awards in the future, although awards recognizing our company as a whole would always be welcome. Kimura, I want to return this to you."

He held out the Founders' Medal, safely tucked into its presentation box, to Kimura. They had talked through the returning of the medal over the phone last night, but Kimura's face registered his surprise that Andrew had actually gone through with it.

"Thank you for your honesty, Salvatore." Kimura took the box from him.

As Andrew returned to his chair, he wrapped up the meeting. "I want to thank you all for coming here today, giving up a Saturday to hear this very long explanation and apology. If you have questions or concerns, please feel free to set up meetings with me next week. I know this is just the beginning of repairing the damage I have done, but I am committed to making things right so that InnovGene can continue to do good in our industry and in the world. Thank you all again for coming."

With that final statement, the plaster of deception that encased Andrew Salvatore and threatened to suffocate the life out of him cracked and fell away, leaving him exposed but able to breathe once again.

———————

"The LORD will fight for you; you need only to be still."

It was the promise given by God to Moses as Pharoah's soldiers trapped the Israelites against the sea of reeds, but it rang just as deep and true for Blair as she exited the conference room. She had been vindicated and her name cleared ... without any effort on her part. It was mind-blowing. A miracle. Totally a God thing.

She couldn't wait to tell Samantha all about it.

Blair pushed her chair away from the table and stood. The motion caught Andrew's eye, and he paused his conversation with Derek to stop her from leaving.

"Hey, you good?"

This close to him, Blair noticed the dark circles and puffiness beneath Andrew's eyes. A bit of compassion met her words as she answered him with a simple, "Yeah, I'm okay."

"I really am so sorry, Blair. I hope you will forgive me and come back to InnovGene."

Blair tensed up. How was she supposed to come back here after what had gone down?

Her hesitation must have been visible on her face because Andrew held up a hand and said, "You don't have to give an answer right now. Whenever you're ready ... just let

Derek know what you decide." He motioned to his brother, who stood nearby, waiting.

Hearing his name, Derek responded by walking over to the pair and asking, "Hmm?"

"I just told Blair to take whatever time she needs to decide about coming back to InnovGene and to get in touch with you."

Derek nodded his understanding.

"Thanks for coming, Blair." Andrew stretched out his arms to hug her.

Blair shifted her purse higher on her shoulder. She held out her hand.

He eyed it, then shook it. "Goodbye."

"Bye, Andrew." The steadiness of her voice surprised her, but it had a calming effect on her body and the tension released from her shoulders.

He stuck his hands into his pockets and gave her a curt nod before turning back to the others in the room.

Derek watched his brother's retreat, then said, "I know it couldn't have been easy for you to come, but thank you."

Blair acknowledged his gratitude with a small nod of her own, words failing her but an uncomfortableness finding a home in her stomach. "I've got to level with you."

Derek's eyes squinted in confusion.

"I owe you an apology for the other night at the party."

Derek dismissed her admission with a wave of his hand. "Pfft. What? No, come on. We both said things ... I was being an immature ass."

Blair chuckled. "That you were."

Derek sobered. "No, seriously, Blair. I know I haven't been the leader I should have been. You were trying to get me to see that."

It was the truth, and yet it wasn't. Yes, Blair had asked him to act with a proper respect for workplace dynamics, but that wasn't the whole truth and Blair knew it—she just couldn't articulate why not.

"Yeah, but I could have been less of a jerk about it," she offered.

"Don't. Where things landed the other night? That was me working through my shit. You don't need to own that."

His eyes shifted off of Blair and she followed his gaze to where Summer still sat at the table, her eyes focused intently on the windows across the room.

"How about we call it even?" Blair said, drawing his attention back to her.

Derek smirked, then held out his hand. "I'm game."

They shook on it as the chairman of the board approached and asked Derek to speak with him. Blair took the moment to make her exit.

As she neared the elevators, she called out, "Hold the door, please!"

When she stepped inside the elevator car, she found Kingston already there. She politely moved to the opposite side to give space between them.

Blair let herself sneak a glance toward Kingston. The older man wasn't what she expected. The way he carried himself seemed light, like he didn't take himself too seriously. Though, she realized, others had accused her of the same thing with her bold hair and clothing choices.

But this felt different.

It was like he knew exactly who he was, and that sense of security was liberating. Blair wondered how he had gotten to that point. Obviously, it wasn't because of his accomplishments or even his work—Derek had told her Kingston was a street musician these days—so it had to be something else.

Kingston clasped his hands together and rocked back on his heels while clicking his tongue. "I just don't know what I'm gonna do. It's a big decision, you know?"

"What's that?" She asked.

"Taking the job working here, it's a big decision."

She nodded as she fidgeted with the case on her phone, popping it off and putting it back on again.

"Andrew made a big decision today." He said, continuing the conversation.

Blair nodded again, glancing up at the changing numbers on the display above the door.

"A brave decision."

"Yes, I suppose," she answered. She ran a finger along the edge of her phone, now exposed without the case on it. She removed dust and dirt before popping the case back on.

"We all have brave decisions to make, you know. Especially when a decision goes against the norm. Against what the world celebrates. I mean, look at me. I'm almost 58 years old. Been out of this world for the past ten years ... contemplating going back into it. Do you think it's like riding a bike?"

Blair shrugged. "I don't know."

"We'd be working together, right? That is, if you come back to InnovGene. Are you coming back?"

She shrugged again. "I don't know."

"I hope you do. I've heard you are a stellar scientist. It would be nice to work together."

Blair looked at him and saw a twinkle in his eye. "So, you're gonna take the job?" she asked.

"Well," he put his hands behind his back. "God told me in a dream a couple nights ago that He was doing a new thing in my life. I think this might just be it."

Blair smiled. "That must be nice—to hear from God like that."

He studied her as the elevator slowed. When the doors opened, he held an arm across it so she could walk through. Matching her pace as they crossed the lobby, Kingston said, "The thing is, He talks to all of us through the Holy Spirit.

We just have to shut up long enough to hear Him." He indicated she should go into the revolving door first.

Once they were both on the other side, he tipped his head toward her and said, "Goodbye, Blair. See you Monday."

"See you Monday." she answered without a second thought. At the sound of her own words, she knew there was a rightness in the decision.

———·———

Summer didn't move from her spot when everyone else pushed their chairs away from the table.

She didn't move when the others gave handshakes and goodbyes.

She didn't move as the intern and her friends debated in hushed tones whether she was okay.

Or even when they left.

When someone congratulated her on her new position, she managed a slight nod of her head, but the rest of her body remained in place, hands on her knees, eyes locked on the sight of the lake out of the window.

The room emptied as the sunlight shifted from one side of it to the other, but Summer still didn't move.

"Did she know you were going to make her CEO?" Katie asked Andrew, her tone hushed like that of the intern.

"Yes, we told her last night."

"What's wrong with her?"

"I don't know."

She could hear their concerned conversation, but still she didn't move.

"Summer?"

She didn't move.

A hand touched her arm. A warm hand.

322   IMAGE OF THE INVISIBLE

She looked at the hand as if shocked to find it there, then up at the face that belonged to it.

Derek.

Her eyes followed him as he crouched down next to her chair. His voice soft and his expression full of loving care, he asked, "Summer, what's wrong?"

A haunting and devastating sob met her ears, but it wasn't until her body shook that she realized it was from her own lips.

Derek caught her as she crumbled from the chair, her momentum pushing him backward. He braced himself, preventing them both from falling. Now sitting on the conference room floor, he drew her into his lap, his tight embrace soothing her convulsing body.

"It wasn't lifeless!" she wailed, her words sounding like they came from someone else—outside of herself.

"What wasn't?" Derek asked her, smoothing her hair and rocking her gently.

The lament came from deep within, as if her very core had been dug into with a claw that gripped a portion of her and ripped it away.

They talked over her head.

Someone said the word "abortion." Another said the word "home."

Multiple sets of arms lifted her from Derek's lap, but the moment he rose from the floor, he gathered her back into his arms.

Her weight slumped against him, his body bearing most of it.

Together, they moved out of the room.

"Who would have thought we would get a front-row seat to something as dramatic as that?" Mackenzie asked Adriana.

They sat in facing seats on the train, riding back to the suburbs and their lives as college students.

"Not me." Adriana pulled her backpack up on the seat next to her and unzipped it. She retrieved her copy of Katie's book. "Think we should put any of this in our response papers?"

Mackenzie laughed at the thought, then fell thoughtful. "Maybe we should? What would you say about it?"

Adriana leaned against the headrest as she considered Mackenzie's question.

"Hmm. Maybe I would talk about how we sat in session after session listening to people talking about the great scientific advancements and the people pioneering them, but no one talked about the cost of making those gains."

"Cost?"

"Yeah, you know, the sacrifices. The late nights, the stress of perfectionism, the pressure to produce the next breakthrough, the balancing act of wanting to make a difference and personal ambition ... no one talked about that, but today we got to see firsthand the impact."

"I suppose." Mackenzie removed her Bluetooth earbuds from the front pocket of her backpack and stuck them in her ears.

"What about you?" Adriana asked.

Mackenzie shrugged. "Don't trust anyone. They always let you down."

"That's what you took away from this week?" Adriana flipped her book open to the spot held by her bookmark.

"Yep." Mackenzie sighed and pressed a button on her phone. She leaned her elbow on the seat, propped her chin in her hand, and stared out the train window.

Adriana closed her book and waved to get Mackenzie's attention. Signing, she said, "I know someone who won't disappoint you."

Mackenzie pushed the button on her phone again and took out an earbud. "I know you won't. But my heroes always do." She used her voice to answer.

"They are people, and people are flawed, you know? No one is perfect."

"Trust me, I know." Mackenzie rolled her eyes. "It was kinda like a roller coaster between yesterday and today. I was so happy for Andrew. Proud of him, even. But then today, I was like embarrassed for him."

"I can see that."

"He has nothing now. He's not running InnovGene, he's not doing research, he gave back the award. His reputation's tainted now."

"Yeah, he accepted responsibility for his poor choices."

"It cost him."

"No." Adriana set the book aside and switched to ASL to give herself the ability to be more expressive. "The deception cost him. It was just delayed. Today, we watched a man stop running and allow the consequences to catch up to him so that others didn't have to suffer on his behalf." Adriana paused, then signed, "If there's something to be proud of, it's that." She lowered her hands to her lap.

Mackenzie's eyes widened at a new thought. She pointed at herself with her eyebrows raised. Then, she turned her palms up, forming her hands into claws, and drawing them toward herself. She fingerspelled Andrew's name. Her right hand moved in a short arc from her left hand out, as if handing over money. She switched to voicing. "I don't get why Kingston didn't want him to pay, too ..."

Adriana followed Mackenzie's lead in switching to her voice. "Because he forgave Andrew a long time ago. Plus, I think he looks back on that time as God rescuing him from his own destructive behaviors."

The train slowed to a stop at one of the suburban stations. As Adriana watched passengers descend onto the platform, she added, "Maybe he felt like Andrew had suffered enough? Like you said, he lost a lot today."

"Maybe. I just don't understand how he could forgive him so easily."

Mackenzie replaced her earbud, but before she resumed playing her music Adriana stopped her by saying, "Mackenzie, it wasn't me I was talking about earlier. I probably will end up disappointing you." She hesitated. "Just like your parents did."

Mackenzie's eyes lifted from her phone to Adriana's face. "What?"

"You aren't exactly good at hiding it."

She crossed her arms. "Yeah. So?"

"I know how you feel."

Mackenzie scoffed in response, bracing herself against the sudden jerk as the train resumed its journey. "Really? With your parents? They are both so nice."

"I'm adopted, remember?"

Her posture softened at Adriana's reminder. "Right."

Adriana painted a picture for Mackenzie in the air with her hands:

"I don't have many memories of my childhood. I think I've blocked most of them out. But I have these little images, little snippets of moments. They are always without sound, and I think that's because I lost my hearing early on in my life. But there's this one that's pretty vivid in my memory. I was outside, chasing a butterfly. The sky is a brilliant blue, and the air is warm with a breeze. I think I am four or five, scrambling over junk in the yard and climbing up our playset, following this butterfly, totally believing I can catch it. As I go down the slide, the butterfly lands on the patio table and I think, this is it! I move so slowly—not wanting to scare it, of course. The way it opened and closed its beautiful blue-green wings was fascinating. I stopped. Suddenly, it seemed really mean to capture it, so I decided to just sit and watch it. I sat down in the grass slowly. I don't know how long I watched that butterfly, but something startled it and up it flew away from the table, and from me."

Adriana used one hand to wipe away a tear and the other to sign, "That was the day my mom took her life. Sometimes I wonder if it was the gunshot that startled the butterfly away."

Mackenzie moved from her seat to the spot beside Adriana and gave her a hug.

"I'm fine. Really." Adriana voiced as she wiped her face with both hands. "I don't tell many people that story because that beautiful day with that beautiful butterfly was the start of a dark time in my life. I'm one of the lucky ones; my adoptive parents welcomed me into their home when I was ten, and they have been nothing but loving, kind, and patient with me, even when I made it tough for them. But it took a long time before I could learn to trust again. And it took even longer to forgive my bio parents, especially my mom."

Mackenzie nodded. "I can imagine."

"You wonder how Kingston could forgive Andrew? It's probably for the same reason I can forgive my biological parents. Because I've experienced God's love and forgiveness for me."

Mackenzie removed her arm from Adriana's shoulders. "I don't believe—"

Adriana held up a hand. "I know you don't. I'm not trying to get you to. I'm just sharing my story with you. You look at your parents and all you see are weak, sad people who you have no respect for, and I'm telling you that for the longest time, I felt the same way toward my mom. Then I discovered the faithfulness of God's love toward me, and He helped me see my parents with compassion."

Mackenzie moved back to her own seat, picking her phone up. "I get that you've found some sort of comfort in religion, but that's just not who I am."

Adriana nodded. "I understand. If you ever change your mind and want to talk, I'm here."

Mackenzie bit her bottom lip as she nodded. "Thanks," she said, but gratitude was missing from both her tone and her facial expression. Pushing the play button, Mackenzie leaned against the window and closed her eyes.

Feeling like she had failed to convince Mackenzie of truth, joy, and hope, disappointment hit Adriana hard. She allowed herself to sway with the movements of the train for a moment before picking up Katie's book for a distraction.

As she removed the bookmark, her eyes landed on a paragraph on the page opposite of the one she had stopped reading the other night. Halfway down, a conversation between the main character and another individual filled the page, but it was just one line of dialogue that caught Adriana's eye: "Don't give up! These seeds you're planting, one day they will spring up into beautiful, life-giving plants."

Okay, Katie. Look at you sneaking a Bible verse in there. Adriana thought with a smirk. She pulled up a Bible app on her phone and typed the phrase into the search bar. Galatians 6:9 populated. She silently read: "Let us not get tired of doing good, for we will reap at the proper time if we don't give up."

Lord, I won't give up. Help me not give up. She snuck a glance toward Mackenzie who still leaned against the glass with her eyes closed. *So, one day, she'll know what it is like to be loved by someone who will never let her down.*

Adriana pulled her feet up under her and settled in to read for the remaining journey back to the campus and their everyday lives.

"Hey there. Can I come in?" Katie asked, standing in the doorway of Summer's bedroom.

Summer lifted her head off her pillow and glanced toward Katie. "Sure," she said, energy lacking from her tone, and let her head drop back to the pillow.

Katie moved across the room and sat gently at the end of Summer's bed. "How are you feeling?"

Summer flipped the pillow. "Embarrassed."

"Oh, hon. Don't be." Katie wanted to put a hand on Summer's leg, but she wasn't sure Summer would respond well to the attempt to comfort. Instead, she kept her hands in her lap and assured Summer that only Andrew, Derek, and she had been in the room. She gauged Summer's reaction to the information, then decided it was okay to continue. "I talked to a friend from church who has worked with many women who have had abortions."

She readied herself for a negative reaction from Summer for discussing something so personal, but it didn't come. Katie proceeded. "She thinks you might be experiencing Post-Abortion Syndrome. It's a type of PTSD. She gave me the names of a couple of counselors who have a lot of experience with this, as well as organizations that help women heal emotionally from the experience."

Katie paused again to see if Summer would respond, but once more she didn't. "You don't have to answer now," she added, "but if you want, I can make some calls for you, set up an appointment."

Summer finally looked at Katie. "Thank you," she whispered.

"Derek is going to stay here with you tonight, just in case you need anything."

Summer nodded. "Thanks," she repeated.

"Okay, you try to get some sleep. I'll stop by tomorrow."

Summer snuggled into her pillow in response.

Katie pulled the door shut behind her, Derek scarcely allowing her to finish before asking if Summer needed anything.

"She's going to sleep," she answered him.

Derek followed Katie into the kitchen, where Andrew stood loading Summer's dishwasher.

Andrew looked up at them and joked, "Who would have thought that woman let her sink pile up? I would have pegged her to be a clean freak."

Katie set to work, clearing away signs of the pizza they ordered after bringing Summer home. "Everyone has that one area of their lives they let fall to the wayside when they are stressed. For me, it's the bathroom."

"Folding laundry." Derek admitted.

"I forget to dust. Katie always has to remind me." Andrew added to the conversation, pointing a fork in Katie's direction and drawing a chuckle from the other two.

As Andrew worked on the kitchen and Katie the dining area, Derek set to making up a bed for himself on the couch. Once finished, he lowered himself into a nearby armchair and placed his face in his hands, the stress of the day finally hitting him. Katie gave Andrew a pointed glance, but her husband tilted his head toward Derek, indicating she should go over to him.

Katie kneeled next to Derek, placing a hand on his arm, similar to how he had comforted Summer earlier in the day. He raised his face to meet hers.

"She's going to be okay." Katie assured him. "My friend told me that, with help, Summer will learn how to move toward a place of healing. But she just suffered something horrific and traumatic and she's processing that. The best thing for us right now is to be there for her as she grieves for her baby."

330 IMAGE OF THE INVISIBLE

He let his head drop back in his hands. "Her baby ..." he repeated, letting the words linger in the space between them. "I can't believe she went through with it."

"I can." Katie responded.

Derek's head snapped toward her. "You what?"

"I think the enemy can do an excellent job of convincing us that the wrong choice is the only one we have." She glanced toward the kitchen where Andrew had just shut the dishwasher and pushed the start button. "I think, if today has taught us anything, it was that when we feel desperate, we operate from a place of fear instead of God's wisdom. You know?"

Katie took his hands in her own. "Summer is a strong, independent woman. But even strong, independent women need people to love them. That's your job now. Love her."

Derek nodded. "I hope she lets me."

Katie rose. "I get the feeling she will. It was your arms she felt safe enough to fall into. Remember, Derek, if you're not sure what to do, you've got the greatest comforter to lean on for direction."

He looked at her quizzically.

"The Holy Spirit," she reminded him.

His smile grew wide, and a light found its way into his eyes. "I'm getting reacquainted with Him. It's like seeing an old friend after a long time. Familiar, but a bit awkward, too."

Katie laughed, then gave him a hug. "I'll check in tomorrow after church. Love you."

"Thanks, Katie. For everything." He cast a glance toward Andrew, who just returned from taking the garbage down the hallway to the chute. "Don't forget, forgiveness is part of this whole Christian thing, too."

Katie rolled her eyes at him, but then sobered quickly. She took a deep breath and let it out slowly. "It's not easy."

"I know."

"Ready to go?" Andrew asked, walking up to them.

"Yeah, let me just grab my things."

Outside of Summer's apartment building, Andrew and Katie looked at each other, each hesitating to ask what would happen next. Andrew broke the silence by letting Katie know he still had the room at the hotel. "I can go there tonight, if you want me to."

What do I do, Lord? I'm not ready, she prayed.

Andrew looked down at this phone. "The car will be here in five minutes. How about you take it home? I'll grab a cab back to the hotel."

Katie crossed her arms against the chilly night. "If you're okay with that."

Andrew nodded. "I think it's for the best. But, Katie, if you're willing. I would appreciate it if we could talk tomorrow."

"Tomorrow's Sunday. I'll be at church in the morning."

"After that? Maybe we can grab lunch?"

Katie kicked a pebble on the sidewalk with the toe of her shoe. "Sure."

"Okay," Andrew said, his head giving a sharp, affirmative jerk as if clicking a mental switch into action mode. He turned to head toward the corner to catch a cab, but halted. Turning back to Katie, he offered a small, awkward wave accompanied by "See you tomorrow."

"See you tomorrow, Andrew."

Day Seven

BLAIR USED THE CHURCH bulletin to cool herself. It wasn't overly warm in the church, but her face still felt flushed as Pastor Craig recapped the verses in Exodus 20 that covered the first two commandments and launched into the third one: don't take the Lord's name in vain.

The pastor brought a chuckle from the church as he shared a personal anecdote about his adjustment of word choices as a ten-year-old to avoid disrespecting God's name while making exclamations.

"Now, I'm not saying there isn't value to the traditional view of this commandment relating to our use of the name of God. In the Bible, names carry significance. They are not merely identifiers, but they capture a person's very essence. We should treat the name of God with respect. However, I would like to suggest another view that I recently came across."

Blair's ears perked up. The prospect of hearing something new after growing up in the church was intriguing. Using her Bible as a hard writing surface, she placed her bulletin on it and flipped to the back page labeled "Sermon Notes."

"Our English renders the Hebrew word in this verse as 'take' or 'use,' but it could also be translated as 'take up' or 'carry.' It is very similar to the Greek word used by Jesus when he told his disciples that they must be willing to 'take up' their crosses to follow him. What if we were to look at this command in the light of carrying someone's name? I think the married women in the congregation can relate to this a bit more than the men, right?"

He allowed the laughter to settle before continuing, pinching the side of his glasses and repositioning them higher on his nose. "When a woman takes her husband's name, she aligns herself with his name, his identity, and his reputation." The pastor reached his hand out across the podium, emphasizing each point with it.

"When we take on the name of Christ, when we call ourselves Christians, we align ourselves with His identity, with His reputation. If our actions directly contradict Him, if the way we behave makes others think, 'If that's what a Christian is, I don't want any part of it.' then we have taken the Lord's name in vain!

"If we flippantly call ourselves Christians, but we do nothing to live in a way that reflects Christ and His commands, we take the Lord's name in vain! When we align our identity with labels that take precedence over our Christ-follower identity, we have taken the Lord's name in vain!"

With each statement, Pastor Craig's voice gained in intensity until he reached his ultimate point, dropping his volume to bring special attention to what he was about to say next.

"You are the image of God. That is your identity. Carrying his name, that is your purpose. Our goal as Christians is for the unbelieving world to look at our lives and see the grace, mercy, and love of our almighty God. But, more than that, seeing His character will bring them to bow down to worship Him.

"Look at Acts 9:15–16. God is speaking to Ananias about Paul. He says to Ananias, 'Go, for he is a chosen instrument of mine to *carry my name*,'" Pastor Craig said, adding a short pause after those three words to underscore them, "'before the Gentiles and kings and the children of Israel. For I will show him how much he must suffer for the sake of my name.'"

Looking out over his congregation with a sharp concern, Blair's pastor stepped out from behind the podium to address them. "I am afraid that the church in America has forgotten that taking up the cross is about aligning with King Jesus and carrying His name to the people around us. Choosing to be a representative of God's image, of His character, isn't easy and sometimes it brings a suffering to our lives that affects us. But, I pray we don't trade momentary comfort for everlasting impact for His kingdom."

Blair resumed fanning herself with her program. Samantha mouthed, "You okay?" Blair nodded her head and placed her hand in Samantha's, while continuing to use the makeshift fan.

She wasn't really okay, was she?

We're cool, right, God? she prayed.

I love you.

She looked down at the ring on her left hand.

"So God created man in his own image, in the image of God he created him; male and female, he created them. Then, God blessed them ..."

Yes, God had created her. To reflect Him. To align with Him.

To carry His name.

Mine. Not Samantha's.

But, I love her. She loves me. You made me this way!

Did I?

Samantha was good for her; she was a better person with her around. It wasn't a casual hook-up! They were committed to each other; the wedding was just a formality. They loved each other. God was all about love. He had to be okay with this.

Blair stood with the congregation for the closing hymn.

After turning it over obsessively in her mind, clarity hit Blair with sudden intensity, causing her voice to catch in her throat.

It had never been about Sadie; she had been fighting for herself.

Fighting for a firming footing. Something solid to point to. Something that proved she and God were good.

Every verse Sadie would quote to remind herself to save sex for marriage, Blair knew. And those same verses were adamantly opposed to this thing Blair called love.

Blair untangled her hand out from Samantha's. The woman's eyes were closed as she sang, and she raised her free hand in praise.

Derek and Sadie.

Blair and Samantha.

According to the Biblical authors, they all were in the wrong. That's why she got so rattled by Derek pursuing Sadie. Samantha had been right; Blair was projecting her situation onto Sadie's situation. She needed Sadie to choose right because somewhere deep within herself, she wondered if she was choosing wrong. Blair's chest tightened at the thought.

If she was choosing wrong, that stood to reason that she needed to repent and choose right.

It's time to make a brave choice.

A brave choice. That's what Kingston had said yesterday in the elevator. A choice that went against the norm. "Against what the world celebrates." He had said.

Blair let her eyes turn to take in her fiancée, singing with gusto, the lovely tones of her voice landing in Blair's ears. Samantha was a beautiful soul. Fun-loving, nurturing, kindhearted, thoughtful, and Jesus-loving. Everything she had ever hoped for in a relationship.

Feeling Blair's eyes on her, Samantha opened hers and looked back at Blair with a self-conscious smile. She leaned in and whispered, "Am I off-key?"

Blair shook her head, fighting back tears and hoping Samantha wouldn't notice. But, of course, she did. After being together for as long as they had, Samantha knew her well.

"What's up, boo?" she mouthed as the last song wrapped up.

Before Blair could respond, Pastor Craig began the benediction, and they both turned their attention to him. Once he dismissed the congregation, Samantha laced her arm in Blair's.

"Hey, let's go grab brunch. You obviously need to process the past couple of days. I told you, you can't be suppressing crap. You need to let it out."

Blair nodded and allowed Samantha to lead her out of the church. They turned at the end of the block onto a side street lined with trees whose leaves were at varying stages of taking on their fall colors.

Samantha suddenly stopped, the motion forcing Blair to stop as well. She leaned in and gave Blair a kiss.

"What was that for?" Blair asked with a chuckle.

Samantha shrugged. A silly smile found its way to her lips. "I don't know. I just know I love you."

When Blair didn't reciprocate the statement, her smile faded.

She dropped Blair's hand.

I have loved you with an everlasting love. I have continued to extend faithful love to you.

No, Blair and God weren't good—no matter how much she'd convinced herself they were.

But God had been patient with her. Gracious.

It was time, however, to make the brave choice.

The costly choice.

The hard choice.

The complicated choice.

Blair raised her hands to her mouth, her face contorting with an emotion that betrayed her distress.

Samantha crossed her arms. "Okay, boo, you're starting to scare me. What's going on?"

Blair dropped her hands and shook them out, then winced. "I can't take your last name."

Surprise crossed Samantha's face. "That's fine. I really don't care—"

Blair raised a hand to stop her. "No. I can't do this ..." She motioned between the two of them.

"Wait, are you breaking up with me?"

"Not really *with you*."

"What does that mean?"

"I think God doesn't want us together." Blair winced again. "I'm sorry, that didn't come out right. I've been thinking a lot about being bi or gay or whatever and if God is truly okay with it. I'm not so sure anymore. I know this is coming out of left field for you—"

"You got that right."

"But I've been turning this over in my brain for a while now. I just ... feel like I need to make a choice. Like I need to choose Him over us. I'm sorry, I don't want to hurt you! I love you!"

Samantha shook her head and threw her hands up in the air. "See, I knew if you stayed in that stupid small group, those women would convince you that God is judgmental like this."

"Isn't he though? He has a standard, which means there is judgement."

"No, I don't believe that God would be that cruel to create you one way and then condemn you for it."

"What if he didn't create us to be like this?" Blair closed the distance between them, her hands trembling slightly, the question escaping her like a prayer she wasn't sure she was allowed to speak.

"Like we can just turn it off?" Samantha scoffed. She threw up her hands, stopping Blair from saying anything else. "I can't do this right now." Sam turned away—then whipped back around just as fast. "I'm so mad right now! And just to be clear—you are breaking up with me, right?"

"Not you ... this life." Blair toyed with the engagement ring on her finger, suddenly aware of its weight. "I love you, Sam. I just ... I have to be honest about what's happening inside me." She slipped it off and held it out to Samantha.

"This life?" Samantha repeated, her hands emphasizing the words and highlighting her offense. "What you gonna do? 'Pray away the gay?' You've lost your mind. I told you they'd make you think there was something wrong with you."

"This has nothing to do with my small group." Blair insisted, her hand still outstretched, with the ring pinched between her fingers. "I can't explain it, but there's been this wrestling inside me. Not just this week ... though this week was ... intense. Like a spotlight. No, I don't think I'm gonna 'pray away the gay,' but I know deep down that this is what I need to do."

Eyeing the ring, Sam sucked in air through her teeth. She snatched it from Blair's fingers and shoved it into her pocket.

Blair could feel the tears gathering, but she fought them back. Swallowing hard, she tried again to assure Samantha it wasn't her, but rather a conviction that had led to this moment. Once again, Samantha stopped her with a raised hand.

"You don't get it, do you? They are the same thing to me. If you reject this life, you reject me, who I am. Me at my core."

"That's what I'm trying to say." Blair's voice took on an urgency. "Maybe it's not our core. We say we 'identify' this way or that, but what if we are wro—"

Samantha's glare dared Blair to finish the word. When Blair backed off, Samantha crossed her arms and looked down at the sidewalk where her toe played with a crack. "I want your stuff out of my apartment." Her voice was soft, but steady with conviction.

Even though Blair had been the one to set these wheels in motion, Samantha's declaration pierced the hypothetical and revealed reality. There was no coming back from this. Blair had decided, and it had cost her the love of her life.

That's what it seems like now, came the Spirit's comfort.

Samantha looked up from the ground and met Blair's eyes. She opened her mouth to say something, then thought better of it, turning and walking away toward the corner, where she raised a hand to hail a ride.

Blair let her gaze linger on Samantha until a red cab pulled up to the curb.

Turning away, she wiped at her eyes with one hand while reaching into her pocket with the other. She retrieved her phone and pulled up Sandy's number. When the woman answered, Blair asked, "Are you still at church?"

"Yeah, I am. I was just about to leave. Are you okay, honey?"

"No. Not really. I'm right outside the church. I need your help."

"Give me five minutes."

———·———

The smell of bacon woke Summer up, and she followed it into the kitchen, where Derek stood at the griddle flipping pancakes.

"Hey, sleepyhead. You hungry?"

His light tone was not lost on her. He was trying to treat her like he did any other Sunday morning they had spent together, including making their favorite Sunday breakfast.

She flopped into the nearest chair at the dining table. "Starving."

"Great." He busied himself with making her a plate and pouring her a glass of orange juice. He set both in front of her, then retrieved his own plate and glass and sat down across from her.

"You're wearing my apron?"

Derek glanced down at it and grinned. "The bacon grease was trying to attack my shirt."

"Your mom gave that to me," she said, remembering the fact with a smile.

"For Christmas, right?"

"Yep." Summer sighed. "She would hate me if she knew what I did yesterday."

Derek shook his head. "No, I don't believe that. She loved you. She would remind you that no matter what choices you've made in your life, God's forgiveness is always waiting to welcome you home."

Doubt clouded Summer's face. "I'm not sure."

"I am. Because she told me that my entire life, even as I made mistake after mistake."

Silence fell over the table as Summer cut the pancakes with the side of her fork and then speared them. She took a bite. Then another. The butter and maple syrup triggered a renewal of her appetite. Summer was joking when she said she was starving, but the truth was she hadn't eaten since Friday night.

They continued to eat in silence.

Taking her last bite, Summer let her fork drop to her plate and pushed it away from her slightly. "That was good."

"I'm glad you liked it."

"I think I'm going to lay down."

"Okay."

"Do you mind if I lay on the couch?"

Derek stood quickly from the table. "Here, let me move the sheet and blanket. I'll grab your pillow, too."

She watched him zip around the apartment, stripping the couch, retrieving her pillow, gathering unused blankets from the hallway closet, and setting her up in the living room to rest. "Here you go," He announced with a tap on her pillow.

As she settled in, he covered her with a blanket, then began clearing the table.

"Derek?" Summer called to him.

"Yes?"

"Can you just sit with me?"

Derek placed the plates he was holding in the sink, wiped his wet hands on his pants, and then walked over to the living room. He lowered himself into the armchair positioned opposite the couch.

Summer closed her eyes. "I think that maybe we have some things to talk about—"

"Summer, there's no rush." Derek interrupted her, causing her to open her eyes in response. What she saw in his expression was a gentle strength, deep love, protective leadership, and tender care.

He had stepped up for InnovGene.

Now, he was stepping up for her.

He rose from his chair and closed the distance to the couch, kneeling beside her and taking her hand. He kissed it softly. "I'll be here to talk whenever you're ready." Replacing her hand on the couch, he tucked the blanket in around her and assured her, "I'm not going anywhere."

She closed her eyes once more. "I'm gonna hold you to that."

"I'd expect nothing less."

Blair explained the situation briefly to Sandy as they navigated the streets of Chicago en route to the apartment.

She knew Sandy must be pleased—after all the years they had spent talking about God's design for sex and marriage—but the older woman was kind enough not to show it. Blair's heart was already hurting; Sandy wasn't about to trample on it with celebration.

When they arrived at the apartment, Sandy helped Blair pack up her belongings as quickly as possible, tossing items into empty tote bags and random empty boxes stashed in the guest bedroom closet. They managed to get it all to fit into Sandy's SUV. The process was chaotic, and Blair was sure she would need to go back later to grab things she had missed. It would have to do for now.

Sandy offered her couch until Blair could get into a new apartment.

"At least I still have a job, so I can afford to pay rent on my own again." Blair quipped as they pulled away from the apartment, working hard to make her voice sound lighter than she felt.

"True."

Silence fell between them.

"You know, it's okay to feel conflicted. It's not a simple situation," Sandy offered.

"I know." Blair shrugged, focusing her eyes on the road in front of them in an attempt to keep the tears at bay. She realized with a tinge of surprise that the vehicle in front of them was the same type of cab that had taken Samantha away from her earlier. There was no way it was the same cab, but Blair felt compelled to watch it as it took the next exit.

The exit split from the road and curved upward, twisting in an elaborate arc over the simple two-lane road they drove. Blair leaned her head against the window, watching the cab's ascent up the ramp. Just as Sandy drove beneath the exit's bridge, the cab disappeared over it—gone from Blair's sight, just like that.

"Don't get me wrong." Blair said, lifting her forehead from the window and looking at Sandy. "This freaking hurts. But at the same time ... this week was weird. Too many ups and downs for one week, for sure. Even though this breakup feels really shitty—sorry."

"Don't be," Sandy said with a smirk. "Seems like a good word for the situation."

Blair chuckled. "I don't know if I'll ever stop loving Samantha. But I do know God has never stopped loving me. The point is—"

She paused, searching for the words. Blair's gaze dropped to her left ring finger. The indentation was still there.

"I don't know. I just feel settled for the first time in days, and that's enough for now."

They had agreed to go out to lunch after church, but Katie had not expected to see Andrew on the church steps as she exited the building. "Have you been here long?" she asked.

He nodded, tapping the church bulletin against his palm. "Since it started."

Katie's face contorted in disbelief. "You stood out here for the entire service?"

"No, of course not. I sat inside and listened."

Katie put her hand on the railing and descended the stairs. "I can't believe you actually came to church this morning."

Andrew followed her. "To be honest, neither can I. But Derek suggested maybe it was time for me to revisit my thoughts about God."

"Any conclusions?"

"Only that I need to do more study before I can draw a proper one." He met her at the base of the stairs and clasped his hands behind his back. "So, where are we going to grab lunch?"

Raising her hands, Katie stopped him. "I need to ask you something."

Andrew crossed his arms, his shoulder tensing with the motion. "Yes?"

She tried her best to remove any hint of bitterness from her voice as she asked, "Did you sleep with her?"

Letting his arms drop to his sides, he shook his head.

"I need to hear you say it." Katie surprised herself with the admission.

Andrew's response was quick: "No, I didn't sleep with Cynthia."

Katie winced. "I saw the pictures."

Andrew glanced at the congregants flowing around them on the sidewalk like a river around a tree rooted in its bed. "Can we go somewhere quieter to talk?"

"Explain the pictures first."

"I ..." He bit his lip and stuck his hands in his pockets. He was in jeans and a polo, Katie suddenly realized. She couldn't remember the last time he wore something so casual. Relaxed.

Andrew took a moment to collect his thoughts, then answered. "I let things get inappropriate with Cynthia, but I never slept with her, I promise."

Katie threw her hands up in the air, turning away from him. Walking to the curb, she raised her hand to flag down a cab.

"Katie, please, wait. I didn't love her. I love you."

"That makes it better?" She kept her hand up.

"Look, look. I don't know why. It was like this lie had taken root in my mind and convinced me you despised me."

Katie's arm dropped. "What!" she exclaimed.

"I know! It was a lie, but I truly thought you wanted to leave me. That you couldn't stand me. I don't know where it came from, but it was there clouding my judgement." Andrew pulled his hands out of his pockets and reached out toward her, as if the movement would convince her of his sincerity. "I really don't know how it got so bad."

"You listened to Carr." Katie shrugged as if the answer was clear as crystal.

Andrew dropped his hands to his sides once more. "You're right." He dragged a hand down his face as if it would pull away all the regret and sighed. "Katie, I really do love you. There was nothing fake about the other night. I swear."

Katie's face betrayed the fact she wanted to ask him another question, but had thought better of it. She let out a puff of air. "I love you, too," she responded. "But," she searched for the words, "It's like we're standing face-to-face with thousands of shards hanging in the space surrounding us. As if our life together has been splintered by our choices into these tiny sharp pieces." It was her turn to cross her arms. "You betrayed my trust, Andrew. You hurt me in a way I never thought you would. You may not have slept with her, but you were heading there. You let her fill a place in your life that was mine and mine alone to fill."

"I know."

"Those shards, they have to be put back together, mended, repaired. But it'll take work to make that happen. And even after we put the pieces back together, the cracks will need to be filled with forgiveness, love, and grace." She shrugged. "I am hopeful, but I'm also being realistic. It's not going to happen overnight, and it'll take effort from both of us."

She tucked her hair behind her ear as she studied her feet. "Here's what I think we should do: I'm going to swing by and check on Summer. Then, I'm going to go home. While I'm gone, you can go home and pack a bag. I would like you to find another place to stay for the week."

"The week?"

"Yes, the week. I need that. I also need you to find a marriage therapist for us."

Andrew nodded. "I'll find someone."

"Good. We'll just take it step by step."

The noise from the traffic filled in for the silence that replaced their conversation. Katie could tell Andrew didn't want to move from the spot, almost as if he was afraid that in stepping away, he would lose her permanently. She took a deep breath and closed the gap between them. His cologne filled her nostrils. It was her favorite fragrance, and the smell of it relaxed the tension in her shoulder.

"Andrew, I promised for better or for worse. We're in a 'worse' season right now, for sure, but I'm not giving up on us. We just have to take some time and get some help to navigate this. We can work toward healing together. Like I said, I'm hopeful."

"I'm hopeful, too." His voice was hoarse with emotion and his eyes filled with tears.

Katie raised herself to her tippy-toes and kissed his cheek. "See you later."

Andrew quickly wiped away the tears as he asked, "Can I call you later?"

"Sure thing," Katie answered as she hurried to the curb to catch the attention of a cab rounding the corner. Her rush served its purpose, and the cab pulled up along the sidewalk. She climbed in, glancing one more time at her husband. He waved goodbye.

As the cab pulled away from the curb, a mix of emotions washed over Katie—hurt, relief, hope, and a faint resolve that this wasn't the end of their story.

They had brought truth into the light. Pried the talons of lies and deception from their marriage.

She was leaning on God's wisdom over her own. Embracing forgiveness. Trusting grace to fill in where bitterness threatened to take root.

Katie was not alone.

She finally felt free.

Image Restored

DO YOU SEE HIM? It's asked in the hush of my heart. *Look up.*

Not a tourist, and yet planted in front of me like one, stands Andrew listening to me use my bow to bring forth the notes of *Great is Thy Faithfulness* from my violin's strings. The coffee thermos in his hand reminds me of the one Katie carried with her last Monday. His jeans and puffer jacket are a sharp deviation from the designer suits he so particularly adorned.

Oh, what a difference seven days can make.

My violin sings the final note of the song, and the gathered crowd of tourists applauds.

I give a little bow to my spectators, then proceed to pack up my instrument. Andrew hangs back, letting me work unbothered. I stand and slip the case onto my back.

He steps forward and asks, "Can I walk you to your first day at InnovGene?"

"Don't see why not."

We walk down a block before I ask, "How did you know I'd be here this morning?"

He waved his thermos in the air. "Had a feeling that for you, playing that violin is about more than just a way to make a living."

I nod. "You're right. When I play, it reminds me of who I live for."

Andrew takes a sip from the thermos.

We navigate the next two city blocks in silence.

When we cross the final intersection before the office building, the same one I bumped into Katie at last week, Andrew abruptly stops.

"In the bustle of the past few days, I don't think I actually thanked you for how gracious you've been toward me. I don't know if I would have been so forgiving if I had been in your shoes."

I watch the commuters hustle down the sidewalk and cars dodge the frequent stops of the buses along Michigan Avenue.

Turning to Andrew, I say, "I used to call scientific research my playground, and I considered BioSphere my kingdom. Sure, I wasn't technically in charge, but I would say that without my work, there was nothing of value. Sometimes I can't even believe my level of arrogance! Then, God removed me from it. Humbled me. Reminded me that I'm not supposed to be amassing a kingdom for myself because I'm already a co-heir of His kingdom."

I motion to the city surrounding us. "This one. It's made up of people who He loves deeply and longs to be reconciled to. That's really my work, Andrew, pointing people to Him. For the past five years, He's had me do that with a violin. Now, He's asking me to do it in a lab once more. He forgave me and gave me a second chance. Who am I to not do the same when given the opportunity?"

Andrew's eyes drop to the thermos in his hands, and he plays with the plastic piece used to close the spout. "I can't shake the feeling that I'm no different from Carr."

I hold up a hand to stop him. "Don't go there. Carr gave his allegiance over to the god of money and power a long time ago. That dragon has his claws in him, deep. I am confident, however, that should he ever decide to repent, God will extend grace and compassion to him. That same grace and compassion you're getting a taste of now."

Andrew allows his eyes to travel to the busy street. "Well, I didn't deserve it, and I appreciate it."

"That's why it's called grace," I tease. "Now, don't waste it, man. Learn from this."

"I am trying to. I really am." He reaches his hand out toward me. "Thank you."

I clasp it with my own and give it a firm shake.

Andrew takes the lead as we resume our journey. He asks if I watched the baseball game last night, and we fall into a friendly debate about the city's rivalry between the North and South Side teams. The conversation continues as we enter the building and make our way up to InnovGene's suite.

The elevator vibrates beneath my feet as it speeds up quickly, then slows at each floor, depositing employees into their respective office spaces.

When we arrive at InnovGene's floor, the elevator sounds off with a sharp ding.

The doors slide open to the image of Blair waiting in the lobby of InnovGene, coffee cup in hand. She smiles as she hands me the hot beverage.

"Welcome back, Dr. Reed."

IMAGE
of the
INVISIBLE

He has rescued us from the domain of darkness
and transferred us into the **kingdom of the Son** he loves.

In him we have redemption, the forgiveness of sins.

He is the image of the invisible God,
the firstborn over all creation.

For everything was **created by him,**
in heaven and on earth,
the visible and the invisible,
whether thrones or dominions or rulers or authorities—
all things have been created through him and for him.

He is before all things,
and by him all things hold together.
He is also the **head of the body, the church**;
he is the beginning, the firstborn from the dead,
so that he might come to have first place in everything.

For God was pleased to have all his fullness dwell in him,
and through him to **reconcile** everything to himself,
whether things on earth or things in heaven,
by **making peace** through his blood, shed on the cross.

COLOSSIANS 1:13-20 (CSB)

The Verse Behind the Novel

These words from Colossians 1:13–20 shaped everything. Not just the title—but the soul of the story.

It reminded me:

He rescues.

He reigns.

He reconciles.

And even when we can't see it—He holds all things together.

Visit rachelfahrenbach.com/bookbonus or scan the QR code to download a full-color print of this Scripture—a reminder worth keeping close.

Download Your Free Discussion Guide

WANT TO GO DEEPER INTO THE STORY?

I've put together a set of journal prompts and discussion questions to help you reflect on the characters, the choices they made, and maybe even your own story.

Discussion questions like:
Throughout the novel, moments of "shattering" lead to deeper revelations. Where did you see brokenness becoming a doorway rather than a dead end?

And journal prompts like:
Is there a place in your life right now where something feels broken? What would it look like to trust that new growth could come from this place?

Interested? Download for free at:
rachelfahrenbach.com/bookbonus
Or scan the QR code:

BEYOND
the IMAGE

A COMPANION GUIDE TO
IMAGE OF THE INVISIBLE

What if the end of the novel isn't the end of the story?

Image of the Invisible invites readers to wrestle with identity, purpose, and faith through layered characters and soul-deep questions. If something stirred in you while reading, the companion guide is here to help you dig deeper.

Beyond the Image is a thoughtfully crafted resource designed for personal reflection. Through guided prompts, scripture connections, behind-the-scenes insights, and space to respond creatively, this companion guide helps you engage the spiritual threads running through the story—and your own life.

Learn more at rachelfahrenbach.com/beyondtheimage or scan the QR code below.

Author Note

Back when I was a young twenty-something, I commuted into the city of Chicago from the suburbs for my first job out of college. It was a two-hour commute from my home to my office, most of which was spent on the Metra train. While I was thankful for the pennies saved living with my folks, the four hours' worth of commuting to and from the office each day was significantly cramping my social life. Now that I'm an elder millennial, I realize what a special time that commute truly was.

Not only did it afford me the space to write uninterrupted for hours each day while not conflicting with my day-job (I wrote the first draft of this novel and another novel on that commute!), my daily journey into the city allowed me to practice the art of curiosity—an important skill for a novelist.

You have probably noticed that humans are creatures of habit, and there is no better example of this phenomenon than the train commuter. Every morning, I watched individuals park in the same spot, stand in the same location on the platform, board the same train car, and sit, not only on the same side of the train but also in the same seats.

When a newbie boarded the train, they inevitably disrupted patterns by sitting in someone else's seat. The resulting dance of confusion as the veteran commuter discovered their seat occupied and awkwardly sought a new one was amusing to me (at least until the day it happened to me). Because my ride started near the beginning of the line, I got to watch the domino effect of such a minor interruption. One person's choice, even made ever so innocently, had a ripple effect beyond what they knew.

Moments like these were about as exciting as it got each day. I treated this predictable, boring routine as most creatives would: I turned it into a game! Who is this person? What's their story? Why do they always wear that Miller Lite hat? When did they learn to crochet? Where do they work? I gave everyone nicknames and created backstories based on their clothes or uniforms, the items they carried with them, or the activities they used to pass the time (this was pre-smart phones, remember).

I had favorites. Like the middle-aged couple who always boarded the train together and sat together, but never talked to each other. Not a single word! He normally read the newspaper and she slept with her head against the window. Neither had a ring on. From what I could tell, they drove to the station separately. Every day they made the same choice to board without a word, to sit in the same seat, and to read and sleep. It was so robotic.

EXCEPT FOR THAT ONE DAY.

On that day, everything changed. They boarded talking to each other! The woman didn't stop smiling until they got off the train, and I'm certain she only stopped smiling because deboarding a train can be tricky if you don't watch your step. She found multiple excuses to put her hand on the man's arm as they walked onto the train and took their seat. Once they sat, the man put his arm around her shoulders and encouraged her to lean into him instead of the window. He didn't open the paper once that morning. And when he kissed the top of her head, I about fell out of my seat! For four months, I had watched them do the most non-friendly, non-romantic, non-affectionate same thing day after day. In twenty-four hours, an entire life-altering story took place—one that I was not privy to (nor probably anyone else), and only noticed because of body language. They didn't board the train the next day, or the day after that. After a few weeks, I realized I would probably never see them again. I felt both disappointment, and also a hope that their absence meant a beautiful beginning of something better for them.

Observation was not the only way I practiced the art of curiosity on my commute. For all the predictability of the morning train, the evening train was less so. Staying at work just fifteen minutes later could make all the difference in what seats were available when you boarded the train. If you had friends, they would be nice and save you seats. I eventually got myself some of those (one even set me up on a blind date with her nephew, and that date became fodder for another novel), but in the early days, I met a variety of people all because I sat in a new seat each afternoon.

Some needed to talk to distract themselves from a hard day in the office and some needed to distract themselves from the hard evening at home they were about to have. Others needed to share exciting news. Others, sad. Most were just bored or too tired from the workday to read, so they welcomed the chit chat. I often think about how open people were with me about their lives and the ups and downs they experienced in it. I was just a young stranger getting started in the world with such an optimistic (and somewhat naïve) worldview. Now, I realize just how much of a sacred privilege these conversations were.

My commute opened my eyes in a new way to the invisible struggles humanity faces each day, and how our interactions with each other, even the smallest of ones, have the potential to make a lasting impact, both positive and negative. That's when I first got the idea for Image of the Invisible.

But, it was my decision to exchange the commute for an apartment in Chicago that would allow this story idea to grow into the novel it is today. It was the city's lights against the beauty of Lake Michigan's shoreline that reminded me of both the Creator and those He created. Its street corners reminded me of the brokenness of this world. It was where I first saw a church community go to the hurting instead of simply waiting for them to show up on a Sunday morning. It's where I sat under a pastoral team who called out sin without shaming, held both scripture and the working of the Holy Spirit in high regard, and celebrated the witness within the creative arts. It is where I learned what a not-so-great relationship feels like, and what a healthy, Christ-centered one does.

Commuting to Chicago taught me everyone has a story and most of it is invisible to us.

Living in Chicago reminded me that those stories are never invisible to God, and that He often works in those stories through us—His image-bearers. Each day, we have the chance to reflect God's love, compassion, faithfulness, mercy, and forgiveness to the world—if we surrender our lives to His leading and live according to His wisdom.

While I will forever look back fondly on my time in Chicago, it was our move out the city to the suburbs that ushered in a time of celebrations, challenges, grief, and character refinement in my own invisible story that gave me the ability to add layers to this novel that wouldn't have been there twenty years ago.

Sometimes, I feel like I'm so far behind in my personal novel publishing goals, but then God reminds me of all the ways He has worked my life together for my good and His glory. My first job was as an editorial coordinator for a scientific journal for dentists. Before I landed that job, I had interviewed with a Christian fiction publisher in Michigan and a movie review magazine in Colorado. Both went with another candidate, and God brought me to a job that involved gross pictures of teeth and sentences where I only recognized about 60% of the words.

But, without my boring, non-fiction-editing job in downtown Chicago, that train commute and the people I met because of it, that city skyline pointing me to Creator and created, that beautiful church community living as image-bearers, that amazing man I ended up marrying who loves me fiercely and reminds me to keep my eyes on Jesus, none of it would have ever been part of my invisible story, and *Image of the Invisible* would not be in your hands today.

Now that it is, I pray this story reminds you of your own image-bearer identity and the deep love your Creator has for you. He knows the invisible parts of your story and He is working all things together for your good and His glory. May this story remind you to trust Him as He does.

Rachel Fahrenbach
Huntsville, AL

Acknowledgements

My desk is where I often complete administrative and business tasks, not where I deep dive into the creative. That mostly happens away from my desk, and so a special acknowledgment must be given to the spaces where I crafted (and re-crafted) this novel: the Metra train, Panera, Starbucks, the Huntsville library branches, and (my favorite) Honest Roasters in Madison.

I'm thankful to the staff at these places who opened the doors and put the pot on so I could sit my butt in a comfy chair, log onto their Wi-Fi, and sip good coffee while contemplating my characters' life choices.

These writing sessions would not have been possible without Team Fahrenbach: Steve, Payton, Carter, and Trevor. Besides sending me off to each session with "you've got this!" and gamifying my word count goals for the whole family, they have stepped up in various ways to keep our family on track while I have my fiction-writing blinders on.

Payton, Carter, and Trevor—authors will often call their book project their "baby," but I have never thought of this novel that way because I have the privilege of mothering you three beautiful souls each day. You blow me away with your creative and inquisitive minds and your tender and caring hearts! Thank you for understanding when I have to give extra hours to pulling a project together. But, mostly, thank you for being on this journey with me! Having you by my side makes it even more special.

Technically, these writing sessions would have never begun without my parents, Ed and Michele Holmes. My dad has always worked hard to provide for his family, especially with quality books he thrifted from Goodwill. His love of reading fiction fostered mine. My mom's love of reading non-fiction contributed to her thoughts on educational reform. She made sure my home education included lots of trips to the library and lots of time to consume a wide assortment of books and to write creatively. My parents made sure I learned how to learn (which has come in handy as an indie author) and that I could articulate my worldview. Mostly, they taught me how to ask good questions and make connections. They didn't blink an eye when I said I wanted to major in English with an emphasis in creative writing (though they suggested I double major in business management—which also has come in handy these days!).

Mom and Dad—Thank you for being the first people to cheer me on to pursue God's best for my life, especially in my relationships. I love you both so much!

Besides my family, God has surrounded me with so many amazing people who have encouraged me greatly on this novel-publishing journey.

Libby Conder, Pamela Henkelman, Julie Lefebure, and Natalie Ogbourne—Thank you for joining me in prayer every Monday for four years now to pray over the writing, speaking, podcasting, and coaching work we do. I am so grateful for each of you and the faithful examples you are of co-creating with God.

My writing accountability group—knowing I have to give a progress report each Monday has actually helped me stay on track. I appreciate your wisdom, insights, and feedback. Thank you!

When the final version of this novel took shape, I sent Erin Greneaux the beginning chapters and asked for honest feedback. I still remember getting her text message after she finished reading those pages. It was the first time someone else talked about the characters the way I saw them in my head, and it brought literal tears to my eyes. Most importantly, Erin, thank you for continuing to remind me to set down perfectionism, show up faithfully to the work, and let God take care of the rest.

I also want to thank my dad, my sister Ceilidh, and my friends Jenn, Jessica, and Nicole for reading the earliest drafts of this story and providing me with the feedback I needed to craft a better novel.

A thank you to Ben Torres, who called me a "true creative," then introduced me to Christopher Woods and Kathleen Egersheim—both of whom graciously read chapters from this story and asked the tough, necessary questions that helped uncover the story behind the story and go deeper with the characters.

Thank you to my Beta Readers: Ben Avery, Kathy Bell, Daisy Dronen, Sarah Frantz, Erin Greneaux, Heidi Lara, Brenda Lobbezoo, and Traci Stewart.

Thank you Loral Pepoon for lending your editorial eye to this project.

Emilie Haney—Girl, I knew you were talented, but I also knew it was going to be tough to create a cover because of the blended genre and ensemble cast—I was nervous for you! I didn't need to worry; you completely knocked it out of the park! Thank you for putting up with my long list of links to covers I didn't want mine to look like—and for somehow capturing this story so beautifully in your design.

A special thanks to Traci—you were the first friend I made when we moved to Huntsville, and our monthly coffee dates to talk all things writing (and everything else) are so life-giving! The honesty with which you approached the story in your novel inspired me to do the same in mine.

A special shout-out to my friends Jennifer and Courtney. Doing life together with you and our kids has been such a sweet blessing to come from this move to Huntsville.

Finally, circling back to my husband, Steve—because without him, I never would have finished revising this novel or published it. He reminds me to make space for the craft of writing, encourages me when I doubt my abilities, and celebrates my victories—even when he has no idea what I'm talking about. He believes me when I say that three hours spent staring off into space at the library was, in fact, me writing story scenes in my head. And he makes sure I have the time and space I need to write the story God's given me to tell.

Steve—you have shown me what it truly means to be an image-bearer of Jesus.

To bravely speak truth when necessary, always wrapped in love.

To wisely choose silence more often than is natural for me—because of love.

To show compassion and empathy that move beyond words into action.

To take steps of faithful obedience to God, even when it doesn't make worldly sense.

Most of all, thank you for keeping your eyes on Jesus—in the storm, the calm, and the celebration—and for reminding me to do the same.

About the Author

RACHEL FAHRENBACH WRITES LAYERED, character-driven fiction for readers drawn to stories that wrestle with questions of identity, purpose, and belonging. Her debut novel, *Image of the Invisible*, invites readers to consider how unseen truths shape the visible world around us—an echo of her belief that storytelling can be both a mirror and a compass.

Besides her fiction, Rachel is the author of *Rest & Reflect* and the *Dwell* Advent series, and hosts *The Business of Christian Fiction* podcast. She encourages Christian creatives to treat storytelling as both a calling and a craft, helping them build sustainable income and meaningful impact while honoring a rhythm of rest.

Rachel holds a background in both creative writing and business, and her winding path has included everything from editing scientific journals to co-founding a nonprofit food pantry. These days, she writes from her home in Huntsville, Alabama, where she and her husband homeschool their three children.

You can connect with Rachel and explore more of her work at rachelfahrenbach.com. She also loves connecting with readers on Instagram and Facebook—find her @rachelfahrenbach.

More From Rachel

Rest & Reflect: A 12-Week Sabbath Journal
Create a weekly rhythm of intentional rest and renewal. This interactive journal includes devotionals, guided questions, and journaling space to help you grow in your relationship with your Creator.

Gifted & Guided: A Prayer Journal for Entrepreneurs
Designed for Christian creatives and business owners, this journal helps you align your work with your faith through daily prayers, weekly reflections, and quarterly reviews.

Dwell: Advent Study & Liturgy
A fresh and creative approach to Advent, combining scripture study, short stories, and liturgy to explore the beauty of God dwelling with His creation.

Dwell: Advent Celebration Guide & Liturgy
A companion to the Dwell Advent Study, this guide equips groups and families to celebrate each Advent Sunday with intentionality—through meaningful meals, music, liturgy, and reflection.